Rock Chick Redemption

Kristen Ashley
Published by Kristen Ashley

Discover other titles by Kristen Ashley at:

www.kristenashley.net

Copyright © 2013 Kristen Ashley

ISBN: 1-4537-2069-3
ISBN-13: 9781453720691
Library of Congress Control Number: 2010911241
CreateSpace Independent Publishing Platform
North Charleston, South Carolina

Rock Chick Redemption

Kristen Ashley

Dedication

This book is dedicated to
Kathleen "Danae" Den Bachlet
My "Annette"
I thank the goddess for bringing to me a friend…
who lets me be just who I am.

Acknowledgements

When your dream is to write books and dreams are meant to be shared with the ones you love and your best friend for over twenty years lives half a world away (literally) but also edits your books, there is nothing better than to have the words "Kelly Brown edited" popping up all over your edited manuscript. Thanks for being with me, Kel, every word of the way.

And to my Rock Chicks and Ninja Queen Sisters, Lily-Flower and Lotus Blossom, I love you guys. Thanks for Sturgis, the time of my life. *JAKE!*

And to my Rock Guru, Will... you know how I feel.

And to my new Rock Queen, latest cheerleader and my friend since *forever*, Stephanie Redman Smith, thanks for reading, loving it and rooting me on. I love you, Steph, but you still can't have Luke. He's mine.

And to my sister, Erika "Rikki" Wynne and my brother, Gib Moutaw... we lost our anchor but our bond will never weaken. I would not be who I am if I didn't have you. You are so embedded in my heart, you have become my heart. I miss you every day.

And to my family, friends and readers... welcome back, thanks for coming and hang on tight, the ride is about to begin!

Rock on...

Part One

Chapter 1
Love at First Sight

It's happened to me twice, love at first sight.

The first time was Billy Flynn. The second was Hank Nightingale.

Billy didn't take and he broke my heart.

Hank, well Hank's a heartbreaker, to be certain, but I wasn't going to stick around long enough for him to do it to me. It wouldn't be my choice, not sticking around, but that was what was going to happen all the same and probably for the best. At least for Hank.

It's happened to me twice, love at first sight.

Billy and Hank are night and day, dark and light, bad and good.

Billy's the former of all those. Hank's the latter.

See, Billy's a criminal. Hank's a cop.

Billy looks like a young Robert Redford but instead of boy next-door charm, he has a bit (okay, a lot) of James Dean's *Rebel without a Cause* drifting through him.

I knew Billy well. I'd been with him for seven years, the last three of which I tried to break up with him and that didn't take either.

Hank looks like no one I'd ever seen before. To put it simply, he's beautiful. He's tall with thick dark hair, whisky-colored eyes and the lean, well-muscled body of a linebacker.

Hank has a cause. Hank's about justice.

And Hank has more cool in his pinkie finger at any given moment than Billy would have in a lifetime.

Don't ask me how I know this because I only knew Hank for a few days. Though it started when I learned he liked Springsteen. Anyone who likes Springsteen, well, enough said.

A little about me.

For some bizarre reason my Mom named me Roxanne Giselle Logan and everyone calls me Roxie. I have an older brother named Gilbert (we call him Gil because Gilbert is a shit name) and a younger sister named Esmerelda (we call her Mimi because Esmerelda is a shit name too). Needless to say, I lucked out in the sibling name stakes.

Dad let Mom name us. I think he did this so he could give her a hard time for the rest of her life. Dad and Mom love each other, a lot, and show it a lot (too much if you ask me). Growing up with your parents' constant public displays of affection was kind of embarrassing. Regardless of this, they were always ribbing each other and arguing... but in a nice way.

⌖

I didn't grow up thinking I was going to live essentially on the run (even though at first I didn't know that) with a criminal boyfriend, no matter how cute he was.

I grew up thinking I'd have a great job where I could wear designer clothes, I'd make a shitload of money and I'd have dozens of peons kowtowing to my every whim.

Before I met Billy, I was on my way.

Don't take that as me being screaming ambitious or anything. I partied through high school and college. I studied enough to make A's and B's (mostly B's) but it was really all about beer, the occasional bottle of tequila and rock 'n' roll. Dad said I was lucky I was a smart girl or I'd be fucked. Mom warned if I didn't get smarter, I'd end up fucked. Though Mom didn't use the f-word, I knew what she meant.

They were both right, in their own way, though Mom was more right.

Lucky for me, both my Mom and Dad—and Mom's father and her grand-father—all graduated from Purdue University. My great-granddad even had his name up on a plaque in the student union because he died in World War I. So I was grandfathered into Purdue. In other words, my family had such a history, and so many members in the Alumni Association, they couldn't say no. I got my degree no matter how much time I spent at Harry's Chocolate Shop, the bar at Purdue that I'm pretty sure my Mom, Dad, Gramps and great-granddad all spent a lot of time in as well.

⌖

I met Billy after I graduated from Purdue. I had a good job. I'd managed to get a couple of summer internships at website developing firms and one in Indianapolis hired me at graduation. I think this had more to do with the fact that I was office entertainment than anything else. I could be a little bit crazy (okay, maybe a lot crazy) and the two guys who owned the joint were hilarious, came to work in slogan t-shirts and ripped jeans and had to own stock in the local coffee chain, they drank so much coffee.

My colleague, Annette, also told me I got the job because of the way I looked. I knew I wasn't anything to sneeze at because I'd won the Teen Miss Hendricks County Pageant. I didn't go on to the State Finals because of a bout with mono and because beauty pageants kind of sucked.

I look like my Mom's side of the family; tall, built like what my Dad called a "brick shithouse" (I think this means all boobs and butt but I never really got the comparison) with dark blonde hair and dark blue eyes. In fact, all of us kids looked like the MacMillan side of the family, all tall, all dark blonde, all blue-eyed and my brother had a russet beard like Grizzly Adams and like my Mom's brother, Tex.

⊰⊱

I didn't know Uncle Tex. I'd never met him. He was in Vietnam and he checked out (seriously checked out) when he got back. None of the family ever talked to him again, except me. Though, I didn't really talk to him, just wrote to him and he wrote back.

I started writing letters when I was young. Don't ask me how I started, I just did. I wrote to anyone whose address I could get my hands on. I loved putting stamps on letters and I loved getting mail through the post. I wrote so many letters Mom started to buy me monogrammed stationery when I was twelve and she still buys me two boxes every birthday, deep lilac with an embossed RGL at the top and on the envelope flap.

Mom told me not to write Uncle Tex. She told me it was a waste of time, he'd never write back.

Talking about Uncle Tex made Mom's face get sad, which didn't happen very often. Usually only when she talked about Uncle Tex and sometimes when she saw me with Billy and thought I wasn't paying attention.

Mom and Uncle Tex were super close growing up, but he went into the army on his eighteenth birthday and went to Vietnam close to the end of the war and that was all she'd heard from him.

Uncle Tex wrote back to me though, surprising everyone. He wouldn't write back to Mom or Grams or Mom's two sisters, but he wrote back to me. Even when he was in prison for messing up a drug dealer, he wrote back to me.

Once, when I was fourteen, I caught Mom going through my stash, reading Uncle Tex's letters and crying. I didn't let her know I caught her and I had the feeling it wasn't the first time she did it either.

From his letters, I could tell Uncle Tex was a hilarious guy, crazy, like me (maybe a wee bit crazier). I'd never met him, but I knew why Mom loved him so much and, through our letters, I knew I loved him too.

I met Billy when I was twenty-four. I fell for him immediately and I fell for him hard.

He was good-looking. He had more energy than anyone I'd ever met. He made me laugh. He treated me like a princess. And he was really, really good with his mouth in a fast-talking kind of way *and* other kinds of ways besides.

Everyone hated him, Mom, Dad, Gil, Mimi and all my friends. I played them the Cowboy Junkies song, "Misguided Angel" and told them to get over it.

A year into it, Billy was living with me in my apartment and we were having the time of our lives; good sex, lots of laughs, tons of partying. I had no idea what Billy did to make his money and I was so lost in him, I didn't care.

Then one day, he said he had an opportunity in St. Louis that he couldn't pass up. He said, in six months, we'd retire and live in St. Tropez and I'd spend my days sunbathing topless and he'd pour me champagne before our gourmet dinners every night. He told me he'd give me the life I deserved, the life I was meant to have. Designer clothes, diamonds and pearls, champagne breakfasts, the lot.

I believed him (yes, I was twenty-five and yes, I was stupid). Even though everyone told me not to do it, even Uncle Tex. I quit my job, gave up my apartment and moved to St. Louis. I moved my shit there, got a job there and started over.

Six months later, Billy told me he had an even better opportunity and we moved to Pensacola.

Then to Charleston.

Then to Atlanta.

I should have seen this coming. Before he met me, Billy had gone from Boston (where he grew up), to Philly, to Cincinnati, to Louisville, to Indianapolis. I should have been pleased he spent a year in Indy with me.

By the time we made it to Chicago, three years into our travels, I was fed up. I had a blast in St. Louis, Pensacola, Charleston and Atlanta. I had good jobs in all those places and made friends. I hated leaving, I hated being on the road, packing, moving. Sometimes I had only a week to do it and in that week, Billy was long gone, telling me he was "scouting" our locations for the move. I was spending more and more time writing letters to all the people I left behind and was going to miss and I was done with being a nomad.

Furthermore, I was beginning to figure out why Billy was so cagey about how he spent his days and where he got his cash. It was always cash. He never brought home a paycheck. Sometimes it was a lot of cash; most of the time it was none.

At first, I believed in him, believed in his dreams and his fast-talk convinced me that the life I "deserved" was just around the corner. Then I *wanted* to believe, so I didn't ask too many questions. Then I couldn't believe how stupid I was for believing in the first place and set myself firmly in denial, which was a good place to be… for a while.

"To hell with him, darlin'," Uncle Tex wrote with his usual brutal honesty, "He sounds no good. Cut him loose and find yourself a real man."

Chicago would have lasted less time than all the rest if Billy had had his way. He was ready to roll after three months. I'd started my own web designing business. Annette had moved up from Indianapolis so I had a readymade friend base and I found a couple of good clients. We'd rented a loft that I loved. I was close to Wrigley Field (what can I say, I'm a Cubs fan) and I was only four hours away from family.

No way was I going anywhere.

So I told Billy he could go but I was staying.

We got in a big old fight that ended in tears. My tears. I was a crier. I cried all the time. I'd cry at a card with a picture of a cute, little kitty on it and I didn't even have to look at what the card said.

Whatever, we stayed.

This happened a lot. Billy would want to go. I'd want to stay. We'd have a rip roarin' fight, I'd cry, and then we'd stay.

Then Billy came home late one night and said we *had* to go. I could tell by the way he was acting that things I didn't understand, things I'd closed my eyes to all those years, were bad. As in really bad.

I didn't care. I dug in my heels. It hadn't been the same between us since the first time I refused to go. We'd been in a slow decline and I hated it. I wanted Billy to be a good guy and do right by me and himself but I was beginning to realize this wasn't going to happen. It broke my heart because we'd had good times; no, great times, and I'd miss him. But there was only so much a girl could take. I hated it that everyone was right about Billy but when you fuck up, you have to admit it, deal with it and move on.

I was ready to take Uncle Tex's advice and cut him loose.

When I told him this, Billy backed me up against a wall, his forearm against my throat, his pretty-boy face contorted and ugly with a rage I'd never seen before.

He'd hissed at me, "Where I go, you go. You belong to me. We're never going to be apart. You're fuckin' mine... *forever.*"

Needless to say, this scared me. Billy had never acted like this. I didn't like to be scared. I never watched horror movies, ever. I didn't *do* scared.

I knew at that point it was over. Any residual hope I had for Billy and me was gone in a blink. Firstly, I didn't like his arm at my throat. It hurt. Secondly, I didn't like the look on his face. It freaked me out. Lastly, I wasn't anyone's but my own.

In other words, fuck... *that.*

Somehow, we stayed in Chicago and whatever it was that had Billy in a panic calmed down.

I didn't. I packed his shit, put it in the hall and changed the locks.

This did not go over well. He broke down the door with a sledgehammer.

This did not go over well either. I had a conniption fit.

We had another rip roarin' fight and he talked me into taking him back.

Don't think I was stupid or weak. I had no intention of really taking him back. I had long since realized that Billy was exactly what Billy was and I didn't want any part of it. I'd loved him, yes, it was true, but he wasn't what I thought he was or what I tried to convince myself he was. I was beginning to fear the stink I sensed on him would start to transfer itself to me.

But a sledgehammer was serious business.

I was going to have to be smart, finally.

Therefore, I was building what I liked to call my *Sleeping with the Enemy* Plan.

I started to save money in a new account Billy didn't know about. I stashed newly purchased clothes Billy had never seen and would never miss at Annette's place and I left.

First, I went to my folks' house.

Billy came and brought me back.

I expected this. I was still stashing money and clothes at Annette's, biding my time.

Then I went to a girlfriend's in Atlanta.

Billy found me and brought me back.

Again, I waited.

Then I went to a hotel in Dallas.

Billy found me and brought me back.

This plan took a long time and this was unusual for me. I wasn't the most patient of people and I felt, acutely, that my life was ebbing away day-by-day, month-by-month, year-by-year. I had to see it through though, and I'm kind of stubborn so I kept at it.

It was the last time to leave Billy, a two-part end of the plan. I was going to go to the last place he thought I thought he wouldn't look, knowing, like all the others when I'd left breadcrumbs, he'd eventually look. Then, after he brought me back, I'd go there again, having set up the plan beforehand and getting help (I hoped) while I was at it.

Though things got kind of fucked up, mainly because Billy's stink had settled on me, just like I'd feared.

See, it was then that I went to Denver.

I went to Uncle Tex.

And, unfortunately, or fortunately, depending on how you looked at it (I looked at it both ways: fortunately, because I'd remember it with bittersweet

9

Kristen Ashley

clarity for the rest of my life, and unfortunately, because it would never last), it was then that I met Hank and my plan got totally fucked.

⋙⋘

Now I'm sitting on a stinking bathroom floor in a sleazy motel, cuffed to a sink and, if I can help it, Hank Nightingale will be a memory.

He deserves better than me.

I just hope I can figure out a way to make Hank agree.

Chapter 2
Whisky

This is how it began.

A few months ago Uncle Tex wrote to me about some folks he met, one of whom gave him his first job since Vietnam. He'd had it rough, readjusting when he got back from 'Nam. He spent some time doing time and was living meagerly off a small inheritance, including a house he got from a childless uncle who'd taken a liking to him, supplementing the inheritance by cat sitting. If you could believe it (I couldn't when I read it), Uncle Tex was now making espresso drinks at a used bookstore and coffee house called Fortnum's.

My Uncle Tex had been incarcerated for hunting down and then nearly beating a drug dealer to death. Now, several decades later, he was making fancy schmancy coffee.

How weird was *that?*

He seemed to like it, and his letters were filled with stories about all the people that worked there and the regulars who came in, especially the lady who owned it: India Savage. But, according to Uncle Tex, folks called her Indy.

In his letters, I could tell that Uncle Tex liked everyone, especially Indy, and lately, another girl named Jet. He said Indy had "spunk", and Uncle Tex liked spunk. He also liked mettle, which he told me Jet had, even though (he said) she didn't know it. Lastly, he liked sass, which he said another girl he worked with, Ally, had, apparently in abundance. In his letters, I could also tell that this Indy person had kind of adopted Uncle Tex and that it was changing him for the good.

So I worked Denver into my plan, thinking maybe this Indy had performed some magic and Uncle Tex wouldn't close the door in my face like he did with my Grams when she tried to visit all those times, and with my Mom, when she and my aunts went with Grams all those times. Therefore, I decided to add a second agenda item to my plan: getting Uncle Tex back to the family, and killing two birds with one stone.

⚜

It was a Sunday in early October when I arrived. I saw, for the first time, Denver's big, blue skies that went on forever, and the Front Range spreading across the west, making the words "purple mountain majesties" a reality to me. But even with the sun there was a nip in the air.

I arrived early in the morning, got a hotel room with cash. I didn't want Billy to find me just yet. I showered and did myself up. It was, to my thinking, a special occasion; meeting Uncle Tex for the first time. And furthermore, I loved clothes (well, I loved designer clothes). Mom said I wore my designer threads like armor. Dad said if they were armor, they weren't working because they acted more like a magnet.

Anyhoo.

I wore my hair to just above my shoulders and got it cut at a place that cost a fortune so it was all soft waves and little flippies at the ends. I did up my face and put on a charcoal-gray wool, to-the-knee skirt that fit like a second skin, cupped my ass, straight at the front and flicked out in kick-pleats at the backs of my knees. I wore this with a black, figure-skimming, wool turtleneck sweater and a pair of gorgeous, spike-heeled black boots that cost so much money I feared Billy was going to have a seizure when he saw the price on the side of the box. At my ears, I put in a pair of diamond studs that Billy bought me, likely with dirty money. But they *were* diamonds, and he didn't often help with the rent, so I kept them. On my wrist, I put on my silver Raymond Weil watch with its mother-of-pearl face, and finished the ensemble with my black, Lalique glass ring.

I couldn't afford all this, not with taking care of Billy and me. To feed my passion for labels, I saved and trolled for all my treasures, carefully hoarding money or trawling nearly new shops. Not to mention, I was addicted to online auction sites for other people's glamorous castoffs. I did it as a hobby. I did it because I loved nice things, and lately, I did it to remind myself of the life I'd left behind when I let myself fall in love with Billy. This also served as a reminder of why I had to find a way to get rid of him.

I spritzed with Boucheron, threw my little Fendi bag over my shoulder (bought for a third of its retail price, never used, from a soon-to-be divorcee at her pre-divorce yard sale), programmed the address in the sat nav and headed to Uncle Tex's house.

He wasn't home.

I was surprised. It was Sunday, and for years Uncle Tex had never left his block. Now he had a job, but I didn't reckon he was to the point of gallivanting around Denver.

Though, in his latest letters, it sounded like he was doing a fair amount of gallivanting.

I waited for a while and he didn't come home. So I went to a phone booth, looked up Fortnum's bookstore and programmed the address in my sat nav.

I found a parking spot on Broadway and walked up to the door, which opened at the corner of Bayaud and Broadway. It looked like a cool store; hip but not in a trendy way, in the way that only long-standing, cool-ass establishments could be hip. That was, to say, naturally.

I walked into the store.

And I loved it immediately. It smelled musty from what looked like acres of disorganized books shelved, from what I could see, willy-nilly at the back of the store.

I loved to read. I loved books, libraries and bookstores, and this, I could tell right away, was one of the best.

The front of the store was made up of the book counter to the left. On the right was a big espresso counter, and all through the middle were tables and chairs; armchairs and comfy couches, with low tables on which to set coffees.

I'd stopped when I'd entered and then my breath left me when I scanned the couches.

Sitting on the couches, all drinking coffee, were a bunch of men. Not just any men. It looked like *GQ* was having a convention and all the best looking guys had decided to have a coffee at Fortnum's before going to seminars on how to cope with being really, unbelievably, fucking gorgeous.

There were five of them. Two looked a lot alike; like they were brothers. But, of the lot, it was only the one with the whisky-colored eyes that got my attention. They were all looking at me, but the minute my eyes hit Whisky, I felt lightheaded and had to stand stock-still or I'd have fallen over in a dead faint.

13

I knew what it was. It had happened before when I saw Billy: that fatal attraction. But either it had been a long time, or I didn't remember how huge the feeling was, because it hit me like a freight train and I was thrown for a loop.

To cover this, I looked away and tried to walk calmly up to the espresso counter where a female version of Whisky was serving, and was her own feminine brand of gorgeous. She was watching the guys then she looked at me, grinning like something was deeply amusing.

"Can I help you?" she asked.

I'd forgotten why I was there, which was looking for my Uncle Tex, so I did what anyone would do when confronted with an espresso machine. I ordered a skinny latte with caramel syrup.

"Gotcha," she said, then went to work on my drink, and I realized I was holding onto the counter for dear life and utilizing all the powers I had not to look back toward the couches to see if Whisky was still checking me out.

Please, God, let Whisky still be checking me out, I thought.

Then I gave my head a firm shake to get rid of my idiot thoughts. I needed Whisky to be checking me out like I needed someone to drill a hole in my head. Which was, to say, not at all.

A fantastic redheaded woman, who I knew from Uncle Tex's descriptions had to be Indy, walked behind the counter.

She smiled at me.

I smiled back, and, as Whisky was no longer in my line of sight (although I could actually feel him in the room), I remembered why I was there. I opened my mouth to say something to her when the bell over the door went.

"I'm not speaking to you," a woman said in a voice that was both angry and obviously full of shit, and I turned to see who had come in.

It was like Fortnum's was For Gorgeous People Only. They needed a sign so normal people wouldn't wander in unwittingly and develop immediate inferiority complexes.

A tall and tremendously handsome Mexican man with a very pretty blonde woman was entering, obviously in the middle of a lighthearted tiff. I knew this because I'd watched my parents have millions of them.

"You're so full of shit." He said what I had thought and grinned at her like this was a lovable trait.

"What's shakin'?" the brunette behind the counter asked the couple.

"I'll tell you what's *not* shakin'. I'm *not* moving in with Eddie," the blonde replied, glaring at the man at her side.

Holy cow!

I stared.

Tex had told me about Jet, and how Jet had a crush on Eddie, and how Eddie was trying to capture Jet's attention, but even though she had a crush on him, Jet was having none of it. That was in one of my last letters. I'd received it only a few weeks ago.

Now they were talking about moving in together.

Boy, Eddie was a fast one.

"You are," Eddie retorted, still looking down at Jet.

"Eddie won't let me work at Smithie's. Or I should say, Eddie *thinks* he won't let me work at Smithie's," Jet told the brunette.

"I think you should let her work at Smithie's."

This came from the couches. I braved a look at them, wondering what Smithie's was. The comment came from a Native American guy with shiny black hair pulled into a ponytail at the base of his neck. cheekbones and eyelashes to die for and a shit-eating grin on his face.

I also noticed Whisky was no longer looking at me, but smiling and winking at Jet.

I felt my heart contract.

I tore my eyes away and saw Eddie was raising his brows to Jet like some point had been made.

It was a weird feeling, knowing these people and not knowing them at the same time.

"I thought you were moved in with Eddie?" Indy asked, and I turned around to look at her.

"It was temporary," Jet answered. She caught my gaze swinging back to her and she gave me a small smile before she stomped behind the counter. The stomping was obviously all show. Still, I could appreciate that she was good at it. My Mom would have given her a high five for form *and* execution.

This left me looking at Eddie. He noticed me and his black gaze shifted the length of me. I immediately got the strange sense that he did not like what he saw. Not that every guy who looked at me, especially guys who were obviously *very with* pretty girls, had the instant hots for me, but still, it was strange. It made me feel wrong, like I was invading, not wanted and not welcome.

I got this sense because his eyes, which were liquid with warmth and tenderness when he looked at Jet, turned completely blank when they locked on me, and Eddie didn't strike me as a blank kind of guy.

Then he turned, completely dismissing me and walked to the couches.

I also turned, feeling funny about his reaction. I shook it off, put my back to the couches (because I needed to focus, and another glance at Whisky would make me lose that focus; I knew this like I knew my favorite designer was Armani) and I faced the espresso counter.

The redhead, brunette and blonde were all talking behind the big coffee machine, looking like the *Witches of Eastwick*, but prettier and scarier. Since the redhead was Indy and the blonde was Jet, that left the brunette as Ally, and she was most definitely related to the brothers at the couches. Which meant (from what I knew from Uncle Tex's letters) Whisky was either Lee (which would be bad as I knew he was with Indy) or Hank (which would be bad, because Tex told me Hank was a cop, and thus not likely ever to be interested in the likes of me: a gangster moll, or whatever I was).

"I think you should move in with Eddie," Ally was saying, finishing up my drink.

"I'm trying to break up with him," Jet returned.

I gasped, because even if he dismissed me, who in their right minds would break up with Eddie? He was gorgeous.

They all looked to me.

"Don't worry," Jet assured me with another smile. She was pretty normally, but her smile made her spectacular. "I already tried to break up with him, but it didn't take."

I nodded.

"I know the feeling," I said, and I did, but I hoped this Eddie guy was nothing like Billy because I could tell I'd like Jet. She might have mettle, but she also had spunk.

All their faces got curious at my comment.

"Here's your coffee," Ally told me, handing me a paper cup.

I took it and set it on the counter. "What do I owe you?"

Ally gave me the damage, I gave her the money and then she leaned forward and asked, "What did you mean, you know the feeling? Do you have a boyfriend you can't get rid of? I know it's nosy, but I'm asking 'cause my brother's sitting over there and he's been staring at you since the moment you walked in the door like he wants to rip your fancy-ass clothes off."

I bit my lip and just stopped myself from looking over my shoulder toward the couches.

I was right. This was Ally, and since Indy was standing there, and Ally wasn't likely to point out that Indy's boyfriend Lee wanted to rip my clothes off, then we were talking about Hank.

Unattached, as far as I knew, but still a cop.

I didn't question the fact that Ally would say something like this about her brother to me. She seemed the kind of girl who called them like she saw them.

I leaned forward and made my first mistake of many that were to come. "Are we talking about Whisky?" I whispered, mainly because I couldn't help myself.

"Whisky?" Indy leaned in.

"The one with the whisky-colored eyes," I answered.

Indy smiled at the other two, then all three smiled at me.

"That's him," Indy confirmed.

"Are you Indy?" I asked, just to be sure.

She blinked, her face registering surprise.

"Yes," she answered. "Do I know you?"

"I'm looking for Tex MacMillan. He says he works here."

Her face changed, and I could see she was shifting straight into mother hen mode.

Yep, I was right. This had to be Indy.

But it was Jet who responded to me. "Who wants to know?" she asked, also, I noted, in mother hen mode.

I looked at Whisky's sister. She was not in mother hen mode. She'd rocketed straight to lioness mode, ready to tear me limb from limb if I gave even a hint that I was there for anything but a happy purpose.

I decided it was best to tell them quickly that it was a happy purpose, sort of. They didn't need to know about Billy.

"I'm Roxanne Logan. Tex is my uncle."

The two hens and the lioness disappeared instantly as three mouths dropped open and they stared in frank astonishment at me.

Then Whisky's sister shouted so loud I could actually feel all the male eyes at the couch area swiveling to look, "You have got to be *fuckin' shittin'* me!"

After that, for some bizarre reason, she threw her head back and laughed. Both Indy and Jet were laughing too, Indy so much she wrapped her hands around her middle and leaned over a bit.

"I don't believe it!" Jet yelled.

What in *the* fuck?

I stared at them like they'd lost their minds, which I feared they had, when Ally turned to the couches and shouted, "You are *not* going to believe who this is!"

"No, don't... " I said to her, and I looked out the corner of my eyes to the couches and saw they were all watching me, most especially Whisky, or Hank, his eyes somehow managing to look both alert and lazy. I felt the dizziness hit me again and I quickly looked away.

The bell over the door went just as Ally announced, "This is Roxanne, Tex's fucking *niece!*"

I closed my eyes, took in a deep breath and put my hand on the counter.

"Roxie?"

It was said in a soft boom. I'd never heard a soft boom, but that was the only way to describe it.

I opened my eyes, turned and stared at an older version of my brother Gil; an older version with a wild-ass beard. He was nearly as tall as he was wide, which made him humongous. Barrel-chested, blond-headed with dark blue eyes and a russet beard. He was wearing a flannel shirt and a pair of jeans, and there was a very pretty older woman at his side, leaning heavily into him, holding onto him with one arm while the other arm dangled strangely.

"Uncle Tex?" I asked quietly, but knew it was him and I felt tears come up my throat. As usual, I couldn't control them. Even though I tried to swallow them, they filled my eyes and started sliding down my cheeks.

"Jesus Jones! Roxie!" Tex gently disengaged from the woman, who stood somewhat unsteadily on her two feet with a nod to him and a smile at me, and then he took two gigantic strides towards me.

I put my hands up to give him a hug, but they glanced off his massive chest. To my shock, he bent low, grabbing me around my thighs, just above my knees, and he lifted me up and swung me around in a full circle.

"Roxanne Giselle Logan, the most beautiful fuckin' girl in the whole fuckin' world!" he boomed, full-on this time.

My nose started stinging and I sucked both my lips in to control the tears, but it was too late. I was crying flat out.

"Uncle Tex," I laughed through my tears, holding on to his shoulders. "Put me down."

He did and I landed hard on my high-heeled boots. He put his big hands on either side of my head, yanked me forward and planted a kiss on top of my hair. Then he shoved me back, keeping his hands where they were and he stared at me for a long time.

Then his eyes grew soft, and even a little misty, and his voice went back to the low boom when he said, "Fuckin' A, girl, you look exactly like your mother."

I held onto his arms.

"That's what Dad says," I told him.

Uncle Tex kept staring.

"Fuckin' A," he whispered and, to my total and complete mortification, I made one of those loud, crying hiccoughs.

He let go of my head and engulfed me in a hug. I put my arms around him, closed my eyes and pressed my cheek to his chest.

It would seem Uncle Tex wasn't going to close the door on me and I felt like I'd been blessed. I let out a deep breath and allowed myself a private smile through my tears.

He held me for a long time and I held him right back.

"I'd look forward to your letters every month. I would never have made it through prison if it wasn't for you, Roxie darlin'. Never," he said softly to me, but his voice was still loud.

I just nodded my head against his chest, tears flowing freely now. I was incapable of controlling it and no longer wanted to. What he said meant the world to me, and that he had the courage to say it meant even more.

"Been waitin' a long time, Roxie, to give you a hug. A long, fuckin' time."

My arms spasmed around him and I held on tight.

"Me too," I whispered.

His arms pulled me deeper into him and he squeezed the breath out of my lungs.

I opened my eyes and looked straight into Whisky's. I couldn't think of him as Hank, not yet. Right then, he had to be just Whisky to me. He was still watching me, leaned back in the couch, the sole of one of his booted feet resting on the edge of a table. But now his expression was different, the laziness was long gone and his eyes were totally alert.

"Uncle Tex," I started, still looking at Whisky, in fact, entirely unable to tear my eyes from his. "I... can't... breathe."

That was when Whisky smiled.

If I thought I couldn't breathe before, I was wrong. Whisky's smile was so damn good it made me forget how to breathe entirely.

"Sorry, Darlin'." Tex let me go, grabbed onto my arms and shook me so hard my head bobbed back and forth. "Yee ha!" he boomed, looked around the room and slung an arm around my shoulders. "This is my niece, Roxie!" he announced to all and sundry (like they didn't already know).

He jerked me around and my head snapped back.

"Nance, meet my niece."

I let my brain juices calm down and then smiled dazedly at the pretty woman who walked in with Uncle Tex.

"Hi Roxie. I'm Nancy, Jet's mother." She shook my hand and then sat down on the arm of a chair in a way that made me think that if she hadn't she would have fallen over. I glanced worriedly at her and her dangling arm, which appeared to be useless. I was about to move toward her to ask if she was all right, when Tex jerked me around toward the espresso counter and my head snapped back again, then again as he yanked me forward.

"Indy, woman, Ally, Loopy Loo, get your asses over here and meet my niece," he ordered and they came forward.

I was right about all of them. Ally was Whisky's sister. Loopy Loo was obviously (for some reason) Tex's nickname for Jet.

Then I was introduced to Lee and I learned the latest news. Lee was now Indy's fiancé and I noticed he had dark brown eyes. Vance, the Native American was next. Then Mace, who I guessed had some native Hawaiian or Polynesian in him and he was almost as tall as Tex. He also had fantastic jade green eyes. After Mace was Matt, a good-looking blond guy that was my height. Last, Eddie. I'd already figured that out, but didn't tell Tex, and luckily the announcement of blood relation to Tex made Eddie's coolness toward me melt a bit.

And finally, Whisky. Or as Tex introduced him, Hank Nightingale.

Hank Nightingale.

Jesus.

Be still my heart.

That was a great, fucking name.

Hank's hand came out. I put mine in his and immediately pulled my bottom lip between my teeth when our skin made contact.

Shit, Roxie, pull yourself together, I thought and took a breath, forced my teeth to let go of my lip and tried to smile (and failed miserably). Luckily, he didn't notice as his eyes were doing a full body scan and then they came up and locked on mine just as Tex jerked me in another direction.

Hank's hand let mine go, but instead of moving away, as the others had, his fingers wrapped around my upper arm and he pulled me gently, but firmly, away from Uncle Tex and toward him. Then more toward him, his hand sliding down my arm. Then more, his fingers circling my wrist. Then more, his hand finding and wrapping around mine. And finally, I was at his side, our shoulders nearly touching.

Uncle Tex looked around, his eyes narrowing on Hank, but before he could speak, Hank did.

"I know you're excited Roxie's here," he said in a low, soft voice that was meant only for Tex and, due to my proximity, me. "But maybe you can get a little control so she doesn't get whiplash."

My heart fluttered and I leaned into him a bit. I didn't mean to. I didn't even want to. My body just did it like it had a mind of its own (it did, of course, have a mind of its own; it just wasn't working at that moment).

My shoulder hit Hank's bicep. The second it did, his hand squeezed mine, and my throat closed with fear that he might drop my hand and move away.

He didn't.

This was good for two reasons. One, if he did, I'd have toppled over like a tree, and two, I liked that he was holding my hand.

Uncle Tex looked at me, then he looked at Hank, then he looked back at me. He took a step back and looked at the both of us. We were standing close. I could feel the heat from Hank's arm burning through my sweater, his hand tight on mine, and I was beginning to feel faint again. My eyes weakly flitted to Uncle Tex's, and when he saw it he grinned.

"Fuckin' A, Roxie. Right on!" Uncle Tex boomed and I stared, not knowing what in *the hell* he was talking about.

"What?" I asked.

Uncle Tex didn't answer me. He looked to Mace and Vance and declared, "You boys gotta learn to move faster or all the good ones'll be *gone.*"

Kristen Ashley

To this, I heard Hank laugh softly next to me. I looked at him and his eyes were back to lazy, but now they were also amused, and, I could swear, behind them was an intensity that made my heart start to race.

I tore my eyes away and looked back at Uncle Tex.

"What?" I repeated.

Again, Uncle Tex ignored me as Nancy moved carefully toward us and grabbed on to his arm. She leaned into him and he took her weight naturally, as if this had happened many times before.

She smiled at me. "Why don't you and Tex come over to my place for dinner? Maybe we can talk Jet into cooking for us."

Without hesitation, Tex turned toward Jet and boomed, "Make those fuckin' brownies with the caramel, Loopy Loo. It's a special fuckin' occasion!"

I jumped at this latest boom and Hank let go of my hand and moved away. I felt his loss like a physical blow and I closed my eyes tight to push it away.

The last time this had happened to me, I'd lost seven years of my life to Billy.

It wasn't going to happen to me again, no way.

No... fucking... way.

I hadn't even gotten rid of Billy. I certainly didn't need the trouble that Hank Nightingale had written all over him.

This trouble was worse. This trouble said loud and clear that Hank would eventually find out about Billy and realize what a fucking moron I was and Hank would never hold my hand again. Don't ask me how I knew this. I just knew this like I knew that Manolo Blahnik made the best shoes in history.

I opened my eyes again and Nancy was watching me.

"You okay?" she asked softly.

I nodded, but replied, just as softly, "I was going to ask you the same thing."

"Stroke," she answered, without hesitation. "Nearly nine months ago."

I moved toward her and then stopped when Eddie came in my peripheral vision.

"I'm so sorry," I whispered, not attempting to get any closer and feeling weirdly scared of Eddie.

"I'm getting better every day," Nancy told me.

I smiled at her. "That's fantastic."

She smiled back. It was a glamorous smile, like her daughter's.

22

"Holy cow, Nancy. Jet and you have the same smile," I noted.

"Don't tell Jet."

"Why not?"

"She won't believe you."

Eddie came in close to Nancy and took her weight from Tex when I heard Indy shout, "Let's have a big old party!"

Tex moved away and boomed, "Now you're talkin', woman!"

I looked at Eddie and he was watching me, his black eyes no longer blank but active. I glanced away, feeling that he knew my secrets, and I wanted to keep them to myself.

It was then I noticed with alarm that the *Witches of Eastwick* had thrown themselves wholeheartedly into planning the impromptu party.

I wasn't sure this was a good idea.

"I'm not getting a good feeling about this," I said to Nancy and Eddie, since he was there.

"I'm not either," Eddie agreed in a tone that made a shiver go across my skin.

Nancy patted my arm quickly then grabbed onto Eddie again.

"It'll be fine," she assured, grinning at Tex.

"I'll make the caramel layer squares," Jet offered, walking up to Eddie, linking her arm through his and putting her head on his shoulder, obviously deciding their tiff was over.

"Damn straight, Loopy Loo," Tex replied.

"I'll get the booze," Ally said, also arriving at our group.

"Where are we having it?" Indy asked, coming up beside me. Lee materialized next to her and his arm went across her shoulders as hers went around his waist. He was looking at me and he kind of scared me too, both in a general way and in an Eddie way.

"It can't be at Tex's place. We'll get cat hair in the caramel squares," Ally remarked, and I saw Hank come up behind her. He wrapped both of his arms around her neck and yanked her back into his chest, playful and rough. Gil would do that to me. Heck, Gil *had* done that to me.

They were close, you could tell. All of them, everyone around me, even Mace, Vance and Matt who'd joined our enormous huddle. They were family, and they'd taken in Uncle Tex as one of their own. This made me simultaneously happy for Uncle Tex, because he finally had this, and sad for me, because I never would.

"Cats!" Tex boomed and turned to me. "Roxie, darlin', you got to meet the cats."

I looked up at him and grinned. "I can't wait." And this was the truth. Uncle Tex had been talking about his cats for years.

"Nancy, you okay with Jet?" Tex asked.

Nancy nodded.

"Good. You all figure it out, tell us where to be. Roxie and me got some catchin' up to do," Tex declared, grabbing onto me. "Darlin' girl, we're goin' to go meet the cats."

Then Uncle Tex dragged me out of the store.

I hadn't taken even a sip of my caramel latte.

⌇

I did have the chance to turn around.

I caught Indy's eye and I mouthed, "*Thank you.*"

She cocked her head and smiled a confused smile before I was pulled through the door. She had no idea what I was talking about, but I didn't care. I had to say it all the same, for my Grams, my Mom, my aunts and myself.

⌇

I didn't look at Hank.

Hank had ceased to exist for me.

He had to.

For his own good and mine.

Chapter 3
Naughty Girl Martini

This is how it got better, and worse.

I met the cats.

There were a lot of them. As in, *a lot*.

Some of them Uncle Tex was getting paid to watch, most of them were Uncle Tex's.

"Is it legal to have this many cats?" I asked, jiggling a laser light on the wall and watching a cat named Petunia, who had splotches of ginger and splotches of white, try to crawl up the wall to get at the red dot.

"Nope," Tex answered, standing by where I was sitting on his couch and gazing at my laser cat play like I was the Master Cat Queen and no one could jiggle a laser light as well as me.

I couldn't help myself. Even with all that was on my mind, I laughed. After all these years, and all our letters, it was good to know Uncle Tex felt the same way about me as I felt about him.

"I thought Hank and Eddie were cops. Do they know about your cats?" I went on.

"Those boys have had bigger fish to fry these past months. What with Indy gettin' kidnapped and shot at all the time and Jet wrestlin' with a loan shark carryin' a knife and runnin' from a crazy rapist."

The red dot arrested on the wall as I blinked at Tex.

"Petunia's goin' loco, darlin' girl, jiggle!" Tex ordered, staring at the wall.

"Kidnapped... shot at... rapist... " I said, or kind of, spluttered.

Uncle Tex turned to me. "It's a long story."

"I think we have time."

"It's actually *two* long stories" he amended.

"I still think we have time."

He sat down next to me on the couch, took the laser light away from me and started jiggling it another direction, trying to get a cat named Rocky interested.

"Rocky's too damn lazy, gettin' fat," he muttered.

"Uncle Tex."

He sighed.

Then he told me two long stories.

<hr>

"Can we call Mom?" I asked.

I'd gotten over Indy and Jet's stories of murder, gunplay, pot farms, strip club mayhem, knife wielding men, rampant kidnapping and assault by taking a shot of Uncle Tex's homemade, gut-dissolving hooch (okay, maybe it took two shots, one for each story).

"Not ready for that," Tex answered.

I nodded. I'd give him time. Hopefully, one day, when my love life was sorted out, we'd have all the time in the world. Then I leaned into him and put my head on his shoulder and, surprise of surprises, he let me.

"You wanna tell me why you're here?" he asked in his soft boom.

I stiffened then sighed.

"Not ready for that," I said. "But soon."

I felt him nod and then he rested his head on top of mine. "Tell me one thing. You through with him?"

He meant Billy.

I closed my eyes then opened them. "I'm working on it."

He nodded against my head. "Good."

<hr>

Uncle Tex took me to get my car so I could go back to my hotel room to rest and get ready for the party. When I got out of his car, he told me that in Denver people wore jeans.

"Give me your cell phone number, so I can get hold of you," I said, talking to him through his open window.

"Don't have a cell."

I stared at him.

Then he slammed War into the 8-track player (yes, I said *8-track*) and hurtled down Broadway with "Low Rider" blaring from the speakers of his bronze El Camino. Uncle Tex, I realized quickly, was kind of living in the 70's and didn't feel like leaving it.

I went to my hotel, asked at reception where the nearest mall was, then drove to Cherry Creek. I went directly to the nearest phone store and bought Uncle Tex a cell phone. He could have his 8-track, but he was also getting a goddamned cell phone. Not having one in this day and age was sheer lunacy. Okay, so Uncle Tex was as close to a functioning lunatic as I knew—Billy notwithstanding—but still.

I went back to the hotel, changed out of my fancy Meet-Uncle-Tex-Outfit and put on a pair of corduroys that were kind of a cross between green and gray and had a silvery sheen, because Denver might do jeans, but I didn't, at least not at a party. Or, I should say, at least not at a party where Whisky would be. Hank may have ceased to exist for me, but he hadn't actually *ceased to exist,* and I was relatively certain he was going to be at the party. A girl had her pride. I kept the turtleneck and boots and threaded a glittery ribbon belt through the belt loops.

Then I turned on my cell.

Nine calls, nine voicemails, all from Billy, all getting steadily angrier and angrier until the last one.

"I'll find you Roxie."

I knew he would. I was counting on it.

One more time.

Then freedom.

※

Uncle Tex picked me up and I gave him the cell phone.

"I've charged it and put my number in it. You can pass it around the party and get everyone's numbers," I told him.

"You should have saved your money, won't use it," he replied.

"Uncle Tex."

"Won't use it."

"Uncle Tex!"

"Darlin' girl, that's sweet but *I won't use it.*"

Kristen Ashley

I crossed my arms on my chest. "Okay then, I'll pass it around the party and get everyone's numbers."

"Knock yourself out."

Uncle Tex never seemed stubborn in his letters.

"Bet Nancy has a cell," I tried.

I could be stubborn too.

Uncle Tex didn't answer.

"So, what were you doing with Nancy this morning?" I asked.

Uncle Tex still didn't answer.

I looked at him. I could see his blush in the dark.

"You like her!" I shouted (in a happy way).

"Shee-it," he muttered.

"Uncle Tex and Nancy, sitting in a tree, k-i-s-s-i-n-g..." I sang.

"How old are you?" he asked.

"Thirty-one," I told him something he already knew

"Act it."

Hee hee.

※

We went to a duplex, the lights blazing on one side. The curtains were open and there seemed to be a million people, shoulder-to-shoulder, inside.

It was all the folks from that morning at Fortnum's, plus Indy's neighbors, a gay couple named Stevie and Tod. There was also a very pretty lady who looked a lot, and dressed a lot, like Dolly Parton (including the bodacious ta-tas) named Daisy.

Into this mix was thrown Indy's Dad, Tom, Hank's parents, Malcolm and Kitty Sue and Jet's Mom's friends, Trixie and Ada.

Add a dash of a Harley guy with long, gray hair in a braid and a rolled red bandana tied around his forehead named Duke (I'd heard about Duke in Tex's letters, he worked at Fortnum's too), a serious stoner named "The Kevster" (The Kevster didn't work at all), a couple of Indy and Ally's girlfriends named Andrea and Marianne, and a bunch of guys; some of them cops, some of them worked for Lee. (I learned Mace, Vance and Matt all worked for Lee at his private investigation service.)

28

Everyone but Daisy was wearing jeans, though Daisy was wearing a jean *skirt* encrusted with rhinestones at the hem, the pockets and along the seams.

Little did I know, this was a recipe for disaster for me.

At the time, I thought this party crush was a good thing. In fact, I was having fun. Uncle Tex had good friends. They seemed to like him a lot and I felt comfortable with them immediately. This meant I could enjoy myself. Maybe a bit too much, and maybe a bit too crazily, considering the fact that Daisy told me a story about her, Ally, Jet and Indy stun gunning some women in a bar that made me double over laughing and nearly pee my pants. Then Tod told me a story about Indy lip-synching with him during a drag show that made me shove him in the shoulder and shout *"Shut up!"* so loud everyone turned to stare. This also meant I could easily avoid Hank at the same time. Well, kind of. It wasn't a big duplex, but I tried real hard.

I was doing pretty well, for a while.

The trouble was it was a good party; nice, albeit slightly crazy. People who enjoyed each other's company and bowls of cashews, and everyone knew cashews equaled good party. Worse still, Indy was at the martini shaker and she made a mean dirty martini. So good, I had three before I even realized it.

Worse than that, and my fatal mistake a couple of hours into the party, I took a bite of Jet's chocolate caramel layer squares while Hank was in the vicinity.

I didn't know, no one warned me.

I bit in.

I chewed.

I closed my eyes in oblivious pleasure.

Then, I moaned.

I couldn't help myself, they were that good.

When I opened them, the Handsome Troop, including Lee, Eddie, Mace, Vance *and* Hank were all staring at me, and Lee and Eddie had lost their scary looks.

Hank was looking at me like he wanted to take a bite out of *me*.

My heart skipped a beat and my head went dizzy.

I covered quickly.

"What?" I asked after I swallowed. "They're good."

Uncle Tex's hand went to the top of my head. "You can tell she's family."

29

Kristen Ashley

Ally came up as Indy whisked empty martini glass number three out of my hand and exchanged it with full martini glass number four, better known to all as Naughty Girl Martini.

"Heard you bought Tex a cell phone," Ally said.

"Yeah!" I replied, maybe a bit more excitedly than a new cell phone warranted, and I pulled it out of my pocket. "I'm getting everyone's numbers for him. What's your number?" I flipped it open, bent my head and hit the buttons that would add numbers to the phonebook.

"I'm not gonna use it," Uncle Tex declared.

"Trust me, you'll use it," I told him.

"Waste of good fuckin' money," Uncle Tex replied.

I looked up and scowled at him.

"I'm telling you, Uncle Tex, you'll use it!" It wasn't so much telling him he'd use it as ordering him to use it.

He grinned. "Darlin' girl, you're cute when you're riled."

"And you're annoying when you're stubborn," I shot back and took a sip of martini (okay, maybe it was a gulp), thus catapulting myself into Naughty Girl Martini Land.

Uncle Tex just shook his head at me like I was funny.

My scowl darkened. "What happens when Nancy wants to get hold of you when you're out in the El Camino? Hunh? What then?"

Uncle Tex's face got red, and it wasn't from anger. Or maybe, I should say, it wasn't *entirely* from anger.

If I'd been paying attention (which I was not, I was too drunk to pay attention), I'd have noticed that all the women in my vicinity, including Indy, Ally, Jet, Daisy and Trixie, smiled, and all the men, including Hank, Lee, Vance, Mace and Eddie, tensed.

"Roxie," I heard a deep voice say from behind me.

It wasn't a voice that was totally familiar to me, but I knew it anyway.

It was Hank.

"Well?" I asked Uncle Tex, ignoring Hank and putting the hand with the cell to my hip.

"Roxanne Giselle, you're cruisin' for a bruisin'," Uncle Tex said in a low boom.

"Ha!" I replied. It wasn't much of a comeback, but I felt Hank behind me and it was all I could come up with.

Tex leaned in. Hank's hand wrapped around my arm and he pulled me away from Uncle Tex's threatening pose and back into his body. I was too drunk for an evasive maneuver, and anyway, I liked the feel of his body against me.

Tex's eyes went beyond me. "Nightingale, maybe you should take her out back and program your number into my new fuckin' phone."

"I'm thinkin' that's a good idea," Hank said behind me.

Sanity returned and I was thinking it was a very, very bad idea.

Too late. Hank was steering me sideways, then forward, through the dining room. He grabbed a jacket off the back of a chair and then moved me through the kitchen and out the backdoor.

＊＊＊

That's when it all began.

The beginning of the end.

＊＊＊

The cold night air outside was like a slap in the face. If I wasn't in Naughty Girl Martini Land, I would have sobered instantly. Unfortunately, I was deep in Naughty Girl Martini Land. So deep, I was skipping dazedly through the Naughty Girl Martini forest and leaping over the Naughty Girl Martini streams, completely oblivious to everything.

I shoved the cell phone in my back pocket and turned to face Hank.

"Uncle Tex is stubborn," I shared, sounding uppity.

Hank had flipped on the outside light and there was a streetlight in the alley behind Indy's house. Both illuminated us and I watched as he walked up to me and threw out the jacket. His arm came around one side of me, his other hand came up on the other side to catch the edge and settle the jacket around my shoulders. Both his hands pulled the jacket closed at my neck and stayed there.

I warmed up immediately, even as I shivered.

"Think that runs in the family," Hank remarked.

"I'm not stubborn!" I retorted, though I knew I was.

"Right," he replied, but his lips were twitching.

"We should go in there, show Uncle Tex how to use his phone. It's good for emergencies and, if the stories he's been telling me are anything to go by, there are a fair number of emergencies amongst you all."

Hank's eyes locked on mine. "Gotta admit, that's the truth."

"Whisky, it's not only the truth, it's an understatement."

His hands flexed and he came closer. My body stilled at his further invasion of my space.

"Whisky?" he asked softly, his namesake eyes going languid, and my heart skipped in my chest.

I ignored his question, his eyes and my heart and leaned back a bit. I wasn't so far gone into Naughty Girl Martini Land to lose my safety bearings *that* much.

I went on doggedly, "From what I read in his letters, Uncle Tex respects you. If *you* told him to use the phone, he might do it."

"I think it might be a good idea if you leave the phone alone."

I tilted my head to the side and narrowed my eyes at him. Before I could say anything, he asked, "Not stubborn?"

"Nope," I lied immediately.

"Right." Then he grinned, full-on this time.

"Stop grinning at me, Whisky. I'm not stubborn."

"Next thing, you'll tell me you're not high maintenance."

I gasped. "I'm not!"

I was. I was totally high maintenance.

His eyes moved over my face. "Jesus. Yesterday, if someone told me Tex's niece looked like you, I would've laughed at them. *Acted* like you, maybe. *Looked* like you, no way."

"What do you mean by that?" I snapped.

"I mean stubborn, full of attitude, a little crazy."

"I'm not crazy!" I *was* crazy, though not as crazy as Uncle Tex.

"Right," Hank said again.

"You've known me, what? Ten seconds? And you think you have me figured out."

"Sweetheart, I had you figured out the minute you walked into Fortnum's."

I felt my breath catch then lock.

With effort, I unlocked it and exhaled. I decided to push the issue. Don't ask me why, it was stupid. Then again, I was a little hammered (okay, maybe a lot hammered).

"And you think I look high maintenance?"

"Eddie called it and Eddie's right," he stated.

Good God. They'd been talking about me.

"So that's why Eddie doesn't like me," I said.

His grin faded, his hands fell away and he moved back.

I didn't like this. I liked his hands where they were. They made me feel warm, and, if I was honest, safe.

"Eddie doesn't have a lot of patience for high maintenance," Hank replied.

"Eddie doesn't know me well enough to throw me and neither do you."

"Eddie'll get to know you and he'll get over it. I'm already over it."

I didn't want him to be over it. I didn't want him to be anything.

This wasn't strictly true, but I was trying to go with that thought as best I could, considering I was highly inebriated.

Hank was watching me and I could tell he was reading my thoughts.

"How long are you staying in Denver?" he asked.

"A while," I answered vaguely.

"How long is a while?" he pushed.

"I haven't decided yet."

"Long enough to have dinner with me?"

Holy cow. I'd read it in Uncle Tex's letters, but now it was right here in front of me. When they wanted something, these Denver boys *did not* fuck around.

I blinked at him.

"What?" I asked.

"You heard me."

I blinked again.

"That isn't a good idea," I replied and threw out my arm for emphasis.

Unfortunately, the hand attached to my arm was still carrying a martini and it sloshed all over the bricks paving the backyard *and* on Hank's jacket.

"Shit! I'm sorry," I said, turning to put the glass on a table and starting toward the door, using this as what I considered a golden opportunity to execute an escape plan. "I'll go and get a towel."

Hank caught my arm and stopped me.

Escape plan thwarted.

"Don't worry about it," he said.

"I got vodka on your jacket."

"It'll clean."

I stared at him. "It won't clean. It's suede. Dammit, it's soaking through. I'll buy you a new one."

"You aren't buyin' me a new jacket."

"I am, this'll be ruined," I told him. "We have to get a towel."

"You're avoiding my question," Hank pointed out.

"You're avoiding the vodka stain!" I returned.

I *was* avoiding his question. I was avoiding it with everything I had.

He drew me closer to him.

"Let's get back to dinner. Tomorrow night. I'll pick you up at six thirty. Where are you staying?"

I shook my head. "Uncle Tex and I'll be playing with the cats."

It wasn't good, but it was the best I had.

He drew me closer.

"Is there a reason you don't want to have dinner with me?" he asked.

Yes, there was a reason. There were millions of them. None of which I was going to share, the biggest of which was Billy.

"No," I lied.

"Where are you staying?" Hank, obviously, could be stubborn too.

"Listen, Whisky, I'm here to see my uncle, then I'm gone."

He drew me even closer, pulling me in front of him so that my breasts nearly brushed his chest. He looked down at me and smiled.

My mind went blank and I stared.

It might sound stupid, but his smile was breathtaking. He had great teeth.

"Sweetheart," he said in a low voice. "You were here to see your uncle until you stepped into Fortnum's and saw me and I saw you. You know it and I know it. You want me to convince you. I'm prepared to do that."

Yowza.

My stomach pitched and I could feel my breasts swell. So much so, I was surprised they didn't poke him in the chest.

I wanted him to convince me. I wanted that a lot. Maybe that was why I said what I said next.

"You have no idea why I'm here."

His face came closer to mine, and for some reason I didn't move.

I really should have moved.

His eyes looking into mine, he said, "No, I don't. But you'll tell me over dinner tomorrow night."

"I don't think so."

"I do."

I started to panic, mainly because I was realizing if I didn't get away, he was going to kiss me.

I pulled at my arm. "I need to go inside."

The hand not on my arm came to my hip and his fingers bit into me, gentle but firm, holding me where I was.

"Where are you staying?" he asked.

My heart started racing. "Let me go."

"I see I have to convince you." He said this like it was an advantageous turn of events that pleased him a great deal.

I was going to say no. I should have been quicker about it, but his hand at my hip pulled mine into contact with his. His head came down and he kissed me.

Good God.

It was true. These Denver boys *did not* fuck around. It wasn't a soft or gentle kiss, a brush or touch of the lips. It was a *kiss* kiss, his mouth opening over mine, his tongue insistent against my lips until they parted (which, I'm afraid to admit, didn't take a lot of insisting) and then his tongue slid inside.

His fingers stopped biting into my hip, mainly because I'd leaned into him. My arms lifted and slid around his neck and my left hand went into his hair. I tilted my head to the side and kissed him back.

I couldn't help it, it was the best kiss I'd ever had. It beat even Billy's finest mouth talents by a mile.

When he lifted his head, I kept my eyes closed and breathed. "Holy cow."

"Where are you staying?" he asked against my mouth.

"Marriott Towneplace Suites on Speer."

"The old Hirschfeld Press building?"

I nodded, still feeling a bit dizzy from the kiss and warm and cozy pressed up against his hard body, even though the vodka-stained jacket had fallen off my shoulders.

"Sunshine, open your eyes," he whispered.

35

I opened my eyes and he was grinning at me.

"Now I have another question," he continued.

Shit.

I'd already said too much.

I fought against the Naughty Girl Martini pull and his hand at my hip slid around my waist and held me close. The other one went to my neck.

I lost my fight against the Naughty Girl Martini pull.

"Why'd you thank Indy before you left Fortnum's?" he queried.

I stared at him for a second, not remembering. Then I remembered.

As this wasn't a dangerous question, I answered, "She brought Uncle Tex to me."

His arm tightened and his thumb slid across my jaw. "How's that? You two are close."

I shook my head. "Until today, I'd never met him."

He blinked, slow.

"Seriously?" he asked.

My hands moved to press against his chest, but he didn't move away. I gave up and left my hands where they were.

"Seriously," I answered. "We've been writing to each other since I was a little girl, but we'd never met. He cut the family off after he got back from the war. He talked only to me and only through letters."

"Christ," Hank muttered.

"He's been writing about you all for months and I know Indy got him off his block and gave him a job. I thought it was time to try and see him and I'm hoping I can get him back to the family."

His eyes locked on mine. "That why you're here?"

It wasn't, not entirely. It was too important to lie about so I didn't answer at all.

"Have you asked him to go home with you?" Hank went on.

I nodded. "Kind of, but he's not ready yet."

"I expect you won't give up."

I shook my head.

"Good girl," he whispered.

His approval felt like he'd wrapped his jacket around me again.

"Will you let me go now?" I requested.

His hand slid along my neck and then into my hair from the bottom to cup the back of my head. "After you promise me you'll be at the Marriott tomorrow at six thirty when I come to pick you up."

"I promise," I fibbed with great remorse. I was going to be nowhere near the Marriott, even though I wished I could be.

He shook his head. "You know I'm a cop?"

I nodded.

"You know Lee owns a private investigation service?"

My brows drew together, but I nodded again.

"You know all the boys on his payroll are experienced bounty hunters?"

My eyes widened. I didn't know *that*.

"Really?" I asked.

"Yeah," Hank answered.

"Why are you telling me this?"

"'Cause you aren't at the Marriott, I'll find you, or one of them will, and they'll bring you to me."

Holy cow.

My throat closed with fear and I swallowed hard to open it. "You're joking."

"Nope."

Boy, was I in trouble.

"Why?" I asked.

"You know why."

I did. I knew why. I knew exactly why.

Fatal attraction.

"Whisky—"

"Sunshine, promise me now and mean it."

I thought about it. I could have dinner with Hank. Then it would be done. Then I'd find a time to tell Uncle Tex my plan, I'd place the breadcrumbs for Billy to find me and go back to Chicago with him. Then, I'd get my stash of clothes and money from Annette and, with Uncle Tex's help, I'd disappear for long enough for Billy to forget me and move on.

In the meantime, I could have a pleasant memory: a nice meal with a handsome guy.

I sighed. "Okay, I promise to be at the hotel."

Kristen Ashley

I thought that'd be it, but his lips came down to mine, his hand at the back of my head tilting my face up and he kissed me again. It was a repeat of the first, but better, if it could be believed.

When we finished, my arms were around his neck again.

"I'm gonna have to ask you to stop kissing me," I whispered, and even to myself I didn't sound very convincing with my request.

He smiled.

"I'm not gonna stop kissing you, but I'll wait until tomorrow night to do it again." His hand fisted gently in my hair and his mouth went to my ear. Then he said, "And, as soon as I can, I'm gonna taste more than your lips."

Good God. My head went dizzy, my breasts swelled again, my nipples got hard and my knees went so weak, I had to hold on tight.

"You're moving too fast," I breathed.

He kissed my neck then lifted his head and looked at me.

"Sweetheart, I intend to move so fast, you'll be dizzy," he promised.

It was way too late for that.

Chapter 4
Eyes Wide Open

I was lying on a couch at Fortnum's, feet up on the armrest, knees bent, eyes closed, arm over my face, not caring if the customers thought I was a nutcase. I was listening to Bruce Springsteen singing "Thunder Road" on my MP3 player, waiting for Uncle Tex to finish work and trying to forget last night.

After Hank took me back inside Indy's house, I accepted martini number five, or Stupid Girl Martini. If memory served, I spent the rest of the evening standing next to Hank, giggling myself silly. And I think I might have even spent some of that time holding his hand.

Good God.

Luckily, before I could get to martini number six, or Puking Girl Martini, Uncle Tex took me back to my hotel. I lay in bed until the room stopped spinning and fell asleep.

I woke up feeling like I'd been run over by a truck. I stood under the shower until I could pry open my eyes without them burning gaping holes into my skull. I did my massive Get Ready Preparations, full-on makeup and flippy hair. I opted for jeans, because everything went with jeans, and I didn't have the brain capacity to pull together a complete outfit. It was a Monday. Hank would be working and I wouldn't run into him. I didn't need to be Glamorous High Maintenance Girl until six thirty that night.

I topped the jeans with a fitted, white, collarless shirt that buttoned up the front and had several rows of miniature ruffles along the chest. I completed this with a Me&Ro choker on my neck and Me&Ro dangly hoops at my ears and a pair of silver ballet flats.

I stumbled into Fortnum's after maneuvering the four lanes of traffic on Broadway and Uncle Tex, Duke and Indy all looked up at me through the line of customers.

"Shit, girl." Uncle Tex grinned as I made it to the counter, cutting in front of everyone and not giving a good God damn.

"Coffee," I breathed.

"Hey, I'm next," the man at the front of the line said.

I turned to him.

"I had five martinis last night and kissed a seriously hot guy I barely knew. *Twice*," I told him.

"You can go first," he replied.

Indy laughed.

I got my caramel latte and found out why Indy hired Uncle Tex. The latte was sublime.

"Uncle Tex, this is beautiful," I told him.

"You got foam on your mouth," he said.

I licked it off.

Duke was staring at me.

Then he looked at Tex. "Couldn't we have, like, maybe a week before the next one rolled in the door?"

"Gotta take life as it comes," Uncle Tex returned with a shrug.

I looked between them.

"What are they talking about?" I asked Indy, taking another sip.

She was digging in her purse. She pulled out a pill bottle, shook out two ibuprofens and handed them to me.

"Tex tell you about Jet's troubles?" she asked.

I sucked down the pills with another gulp of latte. "You mean the rapist and the loan shark and her Dad being in the hospital after being thrown from a moving car?"

The eyes of the customer next to me bugged out of his head.

I ignored him and Indy did too.

"Well," she started, "that all finished up on Friday. You came in on Sunday. Seein' as you and Hank, um… seem to be, um—"

I interrupted her, "Yeah, and…?"

"Well, I think Duke's a little gun shy."

"Gun shy, hell. Hank is fucked." He looked at me. "No offense but you're gonna run him through the mill, I can tell. And no doubt, we'll all get ground up with him."

I blinked.

"I'm only in town for a couple of days," I said.

"I can see it comin'," Duke retorted.

"Hallelujah!" Uncle Tex boomed. "No lag this time. Keep 'im hoppin', darlin' girl, that's what I say."

I looked to Indy.

"I think I might throw up," I told her.

"Hungover?" she asked.

"That too."

She laughed again, but I couldn't figure out what was so funny.

At that point, Daisy powered in the door wearing a hot pink, velour, skintight, Juicy Couture track suit with the top's zipper unzipped to what could only be called the Cleavage Danger Zone, and a braided terry cloth bandana around her forehead, looking like Dolly Parton halfway morphed into Jackie Stallone, but younger.

"Hey Roxie! Popped by to see if you wanted to do a power walk with me while Tex is working," she called out.

My stomach roiled. "I'm going to get a cheeseburger," I replied.

Cheeseburgers with fries were the only hangover cure I knew that worked. It only lasted fifteen minutes after the last fry was chewed and swallowed, but it was fifteen minutes of nirvana.

Daisy frowned. "Sugar bunch, cheeseburgers kinda defeat the purpose of a power walk."

How did these people avoid hangovers? They'd all been right with me, drink for drink. It was unreal.

I figured it had to be the altitude.

"Maybe you can power walk to the burger place and back," Indy suggested.

"Maybe you can power walk to Siberia and stay there," Duke put in.

I turned and scowled at Duke.

"Shee-it," he said when he caught my scowl. "Hank is fucked."

"Hank's gonna be fucked, you ask me," Daisy giggled, and it sounded like tinkling bells.

"I've entered a loony bin," I told another unwitting customer, this one a female.

"It's always like that around here," the customer replied. "That's why I come. It's like walking into a sitcom that could only air on HBO."

I wasn't getting a good feeling about this.

Daisy grabbed my arm and power-walked me the few blocks to a fast-food burger joint on the corner of Broadway and Alameda.

While we were standing in line waiting for my order, which consisted of an ultra-sized cheeseburger meal and four extra orders of ultra-sized fries, she said to me, "All right, tell Daisy *all* about it."

"About what?" I asked.

"About whatever's making your eyes sad."

Holy cow. Was I that obvious?

"Nothing's making me sad," I lied.

She looked at me for a while. The counter guy passed me my bag and then she said, "When you're ready to talk, I'm here, comprende?"

I nodded.

She let it go. Left it at that and I liked her all the more.

Though not enough to share, but I did feel badly about it.

We walked back a lot slower, mainly because I was consuming my ultra-sized cheeseburger meal, and Daisy was programming phone numbers into my cell phone (just in case, her words).

When we got to Fortnum's I handed out the fries, sucked down my Diet Coke (because even if I'd just hoovered through an ultra-sized meal, there was a girlie law that said you had to have it with a diet drink) and ordered another caramel latte.

The customer rush was mostly gone. Daisy and Indy were talking at the book counter, Duke had disappeared and Uncle Tex was alone behind the espresso machine.

"I'm takin' it that your loser boyfriend is your loser fuckin' *ex*-boyfriend since you were holdin' hands with Hank last night," Uncle Tex remarked.

I sighed. "Can we talk about it later?"

"Got a lot of respect for Hank. He's good people," Uncle Tex shared. "Tell me you're done with that weasely motherfucker."

"I'm done with Billy. I've been done with him for a long time. He's just not done with me. I'm having dinner with Hank, but only because he's persuasive—"

"I bet," Uncle Tex broke in.

"It's just dinner. Nothing more, not until I can finish up with Billy."

"Dinner may be just dinner in Chicago, but it ain't in Denver. These boys don't fuck around, you know what I'm sayin'?" Tex asked.

I'd already learned that.

He went on, "Indy was livin' with Lee after 'bout *a day*. Jet was with Eddie from my count, after less than a week. The way Hank's lookin' at you, I'm guessin' less than forty-eight hours."

Good God.

He continued, "I'm your fuckin' uncle and I like that boy enough to say I'd be doin' cartwheels, you end up with him."

Boy, was I in trouble.

"We'll talk about it later, okay?" I requested.

He stared at me awhile then he said, "Hang out in here for a few hours then we'll go someplace and talk. I don't want you wanderin' off and gettin' abducted or car bombed." My eyes bugged out and he shrugged. "It's been known to happen."

Good grief.

I settled into the couch, chose Springsteen and made it through "Candy's Room", "Incident on 57th Street" and was enjoying "Thunder Road", even though my hangover had come back with a vengeance, when I felt movement beside me on the couch and something pressed against my hip.

My eyes opened.

Hank was sitting next to me, his hip against mine.

Shit.

"What are you doing here?" I asked.

For some reason, this made him smile and my stomach clutched.

He plucked the MP3 player out of my hand and turned it to look at the display. His eyes went lazy at what he saw, but he touched it with his thumb and the mega-blast of music powered down to seriously un-rock 'n' roll levels.

Then he leaned down. His fingers found the cord to the earphones, which was resting against my chest. He tugged it and my right earphone popped out of my ear just as his lips made it there.

"You're shouting," he whispered.

Goddammit.

I was such a loser.

"Though, Springsteen is worth it," he finished.

"Don't you have a job?" I asked when his head came up.

His hand went away from my chest and settled opposite my body on the couch by my hip, making him lean into me all the more.

43

I was trying to ignore the fact that, although it wasn't even noon, I'd made a fool of myself at a used bookstore in Denver at least half a dozen times.

"Came by to get coffee," Hank answered.

"Oh."

"Want to have lunch?"

"I'm having lunch with Uncle Tex."

He looked at the coffee counter. I moved my head on the couch seat and looked too. There were four people in line and two people waiting at the end of the counter for their coffee. Uncle Tex was working the espresso machine like a mad man, banging and crashing like each coffee needed to be created with as much violence as possible.

"He might be delayed," Hank noted, looking back at me.

"I just had an ultra-sized cheeseburger meal," I told Hank. "I'm not hungry."

His eyes drifted down my body then up to my face again. It'd been a long time since I'd done it, but I was pretty sure I was blushing.

"Then maybe you'll keep me company while I have lunch," he suggested.

"I don't want to be around food, it'll make me sick. I'm hungover. Probably too hungover even to have dinner. I haven't been this hungover since Purdue beat IU at Ross-Ade my senior year."

"Then we'll have a quiet night."

He had an answer for everything.

Before I could say anything, he commented, "You're a Boilermaker."

"Hoosier by birth, Boilermaker by the grace of God."

It came out of my mouth by rote. I'd been saying it since I was three, nearly as long as I'd been saying, "Go, Cubbies, go". I didn't mean it to be cute, or flirty, or funny.

Hank's look told me he took it all three ways.

I sat up, putting my elbows behind me, so I was somewhat face-to-face with him. "Whisky, don't get any ideas. My reflexes are slow. I'm still not sure about this dinner."

"You're sure."

"I'm *not*. I'm in Denver on personal business, business with Uncle Tex. I don't need you complicating matters."

"What kind of personal business?" he queried.

"Business that's *personal*," I said in answer.

He grinned. "Why don't you walk me to my truck and I'll do some more convincing that you want to carve some time for me out of your busy schedule," he pressed.

"No more convincing!" I shouted, and everyone looked our way, customers and all. I lowered my voice and hissed, "You promised, not until tonight."

"I can wait until tonight."

Good God, I'd walked straight into that one.

"You're an arrogant sonovabitch," I told him, flat out.

What could I say? I was hungover, and, at home, there was another man sleeping in my bed. Okay, so maybe Billy was on the road, looking for me and not sleeping in my bed. And maybe Billy and I hadn't had sex in over a year, even though he tried and was beginning to get pretty pissed-off about my lack of response. But still, I had to sort out Billy before any Hanks entered my future, and *definitely* my present.

"Sunshine, you're sensational even when you're bein' a bitch."

I gasped.

Then I narrowed my eyes. "Don't call me a bitch."

"Let me get this straight, you can call me a sonovabitch but I can't retaliate in kind?"

"That's right."

He smiled again.

I was majorly in trouble. There was no shaking this guy.

Maybe it was because I didn't really want to shake him.

All right, it was time to get serious.

"Whisky, you have no idea what you're getting into with me."

His other hand came down to the couch and he leaned into me, so close his face was just an inch away.

"Roxanne, listen closely. One look at you and I knew trouble was on your heels. I'm willin' to give it time for you to tell me. That doesn't happen, I'm willin' to wade in when that trouble catches up. Right now, I'd be doin' it for Tex and out of curiosity about you. After tonight, I reckon I'll be doing it for other reasons."

Holy cow.

I didn't know what to say, so I did the smart thing for once and didn't say anything.

He went on, "I can understand you protecting yourself, but you have to know, you've no reason to protect me. I have my eyes wide open—"

I was beginning to find it hard to breathe.

"Hank—" I whispered, interrupting him but he kept going.

"And I like what they see."

Yowza.

"I'm in trouble," I said.

"I already know that."

"I'm talking about *you*."

"Good to know you've got your eyes open too."

He didn't even let that sink in. He kissed my nose, moved away, grabbed his paper cup of coffee off the table and he was gone.

"Holy cow," I breathed.

"Sugar bunch, you can say that again," Daisy called. She was sitting on the book counter, legs crossed and leafing through a copy of *Us* magazine. Though her hands were moving the pages, she was looking at the door that had just closed behind Hank.

"Holy cow," I said again.

"We're all fucked," Duke's gravelly voice came from somewhere in the books.

I had the feeling he wasn't wrong.

Uncle Tex got off work and took me to a Middle Eastern restaurant on University Boulevard called Jerusalem. We both ordered the combo platter, which arrived brimming over with rice, baba ghanoush, hummus, fattoush, tabbouleh, stuffed grape leaves, falafel, gyros meat, three kinds of kabobs and pita bread.

"Holy cow. I'm never going to be able to eat this," I said, staring at my plate.

Uncle Tex launched right in. "Then don't eat, talk. What's goin' on with you?"

I started eating.

"Roxanne Giselle—" he began.

"Jeez, Uncle Tex, you sound just like Mom."

His eyes flickered, pain slicing through them, and I wished I'd kept my mouth shut.

"Okay, I'll talk," I said, mainly to take his mind off whatever it was that was hurting him.

I told him about Billy.

Halfway through the story, around about the sledgehammer part, he boomed, pita bread and baba ghanoush flying out of his mouth. "I'm gonna fuckin' *kill* that *motherfucker!*"

I looked around at our gawking neighbors.

"Uncle Tex, calm down," I whispered.

He swallowed, then he demanded, "Finish it!" and he did this circling his fork at me.

I finished the story.

Then Tex said, "You don't gotta be on the run from that asshole. One word to Lee and he'd fix his sorry ass and good."

No way. No way in hell.

"No, Uncle Tex, no words to Lee, to Hank, to Eddie, to Indy, to *anybody*."

"Lee's one badass individual. Lee'd make Hitler shake in his silly, shiny boots, even with the whole German army standin' at his back."

"No," I denied.

"Roxie, darlin', your plan is shit," he informed me.

"I've been working on this plan for years!"

"It's still shit."

I scowled at him. "Uncle Tex, I got myself into this mess. I'm getting myself out."

He shook his head.

"Not gonna fuckin' happen. I'm talkin' to the boys," he said like that was final.

I slammed my palm on the table to get his attention and Uncle Tex's eyes locked on mine.

I took a deep breath and said, "I appreciate your concern and I need your help, but I'm fixing this my way."

"Roxie—"

"No!" I closed my eyes and tilted my head to the table. Then I looked up again. "Uncle Tex, I have to look myself in the eye in the mirror every morning. After I fucked up seven years of my life, do you honestly think I can just hand over my problems to some guys I barely know and be able to wake up and look in those eyes?"

He stared at me.

Finally, he said, "Jesus Jones, but you're a MacMillan."

"Damn right I am," I told him with more than a little bit of pride.

He stared at me some more.

"Fine," was all he said.

I felt my body relax. "Thank you."

"One thing, darlin' girl. I get even the niggliest fuckin' inklin' that this shit plan o' yours is goin' south, and mark my words, it's gonna go south, I'm callin' in the boys."

I felt my body get tense again.

"No," I replied.

"That includes Hank."

"No!" I shouted, now ignoring our gawking neighbors.

"I should fuckin' say that especially fuckin' includes Hank," he amended.

"You do that, I leave," I threatened.

"You leave, I'm siccin' Lee on your ass. He'll send Vance or Mace to track you down. You won't even make it to the Colorado border."

Man, oh man, I was undoubtedly, seriously, officially in trouble.

"Uncle Tex—"

His big, beefy hand came out and enveloped mine. "Just got you in my life, darlin' girl, ain't no weasely-assed motherfucker gonna take you back out. He'll have to split my skull open with that fuckin' sledgehammer before that happens."

The fear crawled up my throat again, mainly because I was worried Billy would do it.

"Uncle Tex—"

"Don't worry, Roxie. Before he cracked open my skull, he'd have to crack open half a dozen other ones. Trust me, I know how these fuckin' guys work. He wouldn't get through the first wave."

"I don't know these people and you barely do," I reminded him.

"Don't need to know much more of them to know what they're made of. Seen a lot of it these past months." He squeezed my hand. "You came to the right place." Then he leaned back in his seat and tipped his head back, "Bring it on!" he boomed.

Good grief.

Yes, I was undoubtedly, seriously, officially in trouble.

Chapter 5
Phone Calls

Uncle Tex took me to my car. I followed him to his house and I helped him clean litter trays. After, we went down to the corner store where he introduced me to Mr. Kumar, his friend and grocery supplier. Then I found out Uncle Tex needed to get ready for his date with Nancy.

On the way back from Mr. Kumar's store, I sang the "Uncle Tex and Nancy, Sitting in a Tree" song again. He picked me up, carried me to my car, set me down on the street, turned around and, without a backward glance, walked back into his house.

Hee hee.

* * *

I went to my hotel and tore through my suitcases. Yes, I had two. I was high maintenance, and high maintenance women didn't go anywhere without at least two suitcases. I was looking for an outfit to wear for my date. I was staring at the exploded suitcases in despair because, even though I had more clothes in those two suitcases than most of the earth's population would own in their lifetimes, I did not have an outfit to wear on my date with Whisky.

My cell phone rang.

I tensed and stared at my purse like it was a living thing out for my blood and I yanked the phone out of my bag, expecting it to tell me Billy was calling.

Instead, it told me Daisy was calling.

In shock, I flipped it open. "Hello?"

"Hey sugar bunch, what're you wearin' for your date?" Daisy asked.

I sat on the edge of the bed. I'd known this woman for less than twenty-four hours and she acted like she'd known me for twenty-four years.

"I've no idea," I told her.

"Call Indy, she'll know. She's good at that stuff. Listen, you gonna be in town awhile?"

What now?

Kristen Ashley

"I don't know," I answered.

"Well, me and Marcus are havin' a party, not this Thursday but next. Would love for you to come."

That was so sweet of her.

"I don't know if I'll be here, but if I am, I'll come," I replied.

"I don't need exact numbers, it's a charity do so it'll be finger food. The people comin' own most of Denver. They can afford to fill their bellies before they show up at The Castle."

The Castle?

Daisy went on, "It's black tie. You got something sparkly to wear?"

"Um…" I didn't. Billy and I didn't normally attend black tie affairs.

"Don't worry, Tod will loan you somethin'. He's a drag queen. He has *the best* closet. Oh! Gotta go, my masseuse is here. Ta-ta!"

"Bye," I said to dead air. She'd already hung up.

I flipped the phone closed and tried to flip off the switch that was making me feel welcome and safe and weirdly at home (the switch didn't work).

I washed my face in order to prepare for my nighttime makeup regime and I was drying it when my phone rang. I looked at it on the vanity, certain that it would be Billy. Instead it said it was Tod, Indy's neighbor.

Holy cow. I knew that Daisy had programmed in Tod *and* Stevie when she was fiddling with my phone. How Tod got my number, I did not know.

I flipped it open. "Hello?"

"Hey girlie. It's Tod. Daisy called, said you might need something to wear to her big bash. Come over, we'll go through my closet," Tod invited.

Oh my God, that was *so* sweet.

"I'm not sure I'm going to be here," I told him.

"You *have* to be here! It's gonna be the party of the decade!" Tod screeched like I just told him I turned down a marriage proposal from Prince William.

"Um…" I mumbled.

"Come over anyway. I'll get out a bottle of sparkling wine and the Yahtzee game."

"I'm going on a date with Hank."

Silence.

Then, "Shit, those boys don't fuck around."

He could say that again.

50

Because I needed help, I took a deep breath and confided, "I'm not sure what to wear."

Tod answered immediately, "Tell me what you've got."

I described the contents of my suitcases. The whole time I spoke, he muttered, "Mm-hmm. Mm-hmm." Then, when I described my black top with the wide, scoop neck, he yelled, "That! With jeans and heels and a rock 'n' roll scarf. Do you have a good belt? Forget it. I'm coming over with belts... and scarves. Be there in ten."

Then he disconnected.

I stared at the phone.

Was he serious?

Holy cow.

He couldn't be serious.

I couldn't worry about it. Time was ticking by and I'd only just begun my preparations. I started on my makeup and just got through the first phase of a five phase production when the phone went again.

My body didn't tense this time. I could see the display saying, "Ally Calling".

I was no longer surprised by this bizarre string of phone calls.

"Hi," I answered.

"Hey chickie, Daisy texted me your number. You got an outfit for your date with Hank?"

Good grief.

"No, but I think Tod's coming over with belts and scarves."

"Good to hear. Tod'll sort you out. How long you staying in Denver?" she asked.

"I don't know," I told her.

"Well, it's October and the Haunted Houses are opening and we're going; all of us, Indy, Jet, Daisy and me. You gotta go. It's hilarious."

"I don't do scary," I shared, thinking she'd understand.

She didn't understand.

"Perfect. Don't worry. The chainsaw man never has a chain on his saw. We'll keep you in the loop. Gotta go. Later."

Chainsaw man?

Before I could ask, she disconnected.

I was staring at the dead phone in my hand when the hotel phone rang. I walked over and picked it up, this time worried that Billy had found me too soon. Or worse, Hank had come early.

"Hello?"

"It's Tod, what room number are you?"

I was silent a second.

He *was* serious. How did he even know where I was?

I didn't want to know.

"Three thirty-three," I said.

Disconnect.

Good God.

Now I knew how Uncle Tex had been so well, truly and quickly ensconced in the fold. These people acted as fast as lightning.

There was a knock on the door and I opened it. Tod walked in carrying enough scarves and belts to accessorize the entirety of the Purdue Boiler Babes Dance Team.

He charged in, tossing everything on the bed.

I closed the door and walked back into the room.

"Tod, he's going to be here in…" I looked at my watch. Then I let out a little scream.

"Calm, calm," Tod said, his hands out in front of him, palms down, pressing the air. "Let's get crackin'. Finish your face, I'll sort through this."

Then, without further ado, he started digging through my suitcases.

I didn't have time to flip out that some guy I barely knew was digging through my suitcases. Hank was going to be there in twenty minutes and I hadn't even moved to phase two of makeup.

I was shading and blending through phase four when Tod walked into the bathroom. "Outfit's on the bed, I unpacked you, because, girlie, you're getting wrinkles in some of your fab-you-las blouses. So I hung them up, unmentionables and PJs in the drawers. You can return the belt and scarf to Indy and I'm borrowing those Manolo Mary Janes for my act this weekend if you're still in town. They fit like they were made for me."

"Sure," I replied, even though it wasn't a request.

We air-kissed and he took off.

I finished the makeup, fluffed out my hair and put on the black top, jeans, a black belt of Tod's, the Manolo Mary Janes and looped once around my neck a thin, long rock 'n' roll scarf made entirely out of silver bugle beads stitched together. I put a wide silver cuff on my wrist, my Raymond Weil on my other wrist and some seriously long hoops dangling at my ears. I was spritzing with Boucheron at six twenty-nine and trying to breathe calmly and reach my Zen zone (and failing) when my cell rang again.

It said, "Jet Calling."

I flipped open the phone. "Hello?"

"Hey Roxie, Daisy gave me your number."

Daisy was a busy little beaver.

"How's your Dad?" I asked.

Jet's Dad had been shot, stabbed and beaten, then thrown out of a moving car on Broadway outside of Fortnum's just days before. They moved him out of ICU that morning and Jet spent the day in the hospital with him.

"A lot better. Breathing, talking, *conscious*," she answered.

I smiled. "I'm glad."

"I hear you're going out with Hank tonight. You got something to wear?"

Cripes! I had four new best friends and I'd known them only a day. Next thing, Indy was going to be calling, asking me to a slumber party.

Before I could answer, the hotel phone rang.

I let out another little scream.

I heard Jet laugh.

"Hank's there," she surmised.

"Ohmigod, ohmigod," I chanted.

"Deep breaths," Jet advised.

"Ohmigod, ohmigod," I chanted.

"It might help if you answer the phone," she suggested, but I could tell it was through a smile.

"Hang on" I said to her.

I took the cell from my ear and picked up the room phone.

"Hello?"

"Hey."

It was Hank.

My legs gave out and I sat on the bed.

"Hey," I replied.

"I'm at reception. What room are you in?"

Kristen Ashley

I did not want Hank in my room. I wanted Hank nowhere near my room. In fact, Hank was already nearer to my room than I ever wanted him to be.

"I'll come down."

He ignored me.

"What room are you in?" he repeated.

"I'll be right down," I said.

His voice dropped low. "Sunshine, I'm gonna ask one more time. What room are you in?"

His voice shivered through me.

"Three thirty-three," I replied.

Disconnect.

I put the cell back to my ear, "Ohmigod, ohmigod," I chanted again to Jet. She was laughing. "Word of advice?" she offered.

"Anything."

"Don't fight it."

Shit.

"Jet… there are things…" I stopped. Then I started again, "I can't—"

She interrupted me, "I can't either, but I really don't need to because Eddie can. It, like, *totally* freaks me out," she confided.

"Eddie adores you. I could tell that the minute I saw you two. And Uncle Tex said so," I told her.

"Yeah. I'm beginning to believe it. It still, like, totally freaks me out."

There was a knock on the door. My eyes swung to the door and I stared at it.

"Ohmigod, ohmigod," I chanted yet again.

Jet laughed again. "Get the door."

I nodded, got off the bed and walked to the door. Then, to focus on something, *anything* that was not what was behind the door, I said, "Uncle Tex is taking your Mom out tonight."

"I know," she replied. "That works out, we could be related."

I knew in an instant I'd like that.

I opened the door and looked at Hank.

He smiled at me.

My knees went weak and I wasn't thinking about anything but Hank.

"Gotta go," I said to Jet.

"Tell Hank I said hi."

54

"Sure."

She disconnected and I flipped the phone shut.

Hank's eyes went to the phone.

"Jet," I told him.

Without a word he walked forward, even though I was in his way.

He seemed bigger than I remembered; taller, broader of shoulder. His presence seemed to invade the room. He was wearing a black leather jacket, a dark gray turtleneck sweater, jeans and black boots.

He looked fantastic.

I quickly moved out of his way. He finished entering and turned. I stood in the door.

"She says hi," I shared.

He grabbed my arm and pulled me out of the doorway and then shut the door behind me. I watched the door close and just barely stopped myself from screaming again.

"Uncle Tex is going out on a date with her mom tonight," I kept sharing.

His hand was still on my arm and now he was pulling me to him. He still didn't say anything.

"If this works out, Jet and I could end up related," I went on, completely unable to stop talking.

He pulled me closer, his hand left my arm and went around my waist. The other hand went to the side of my neck.

"We'll be, like, cousins or something," I carried on.

His face came toward mine. His lips weren't smiling but his eyes were.

My lips and eyes weren't smiling. My body was preparing to have a heart attack.

"Is it cousins? Or would I be her niece? How does that go?" I asked, desperately re-designing my family tree in an effort to avoid what was happening in real time.

"Sunshine?" he said against my mouth.

"Yeah?" I breathed.

"Shut up."

I did.

Then he kissed me.

It was just like the night before. Just as serious. Just as hot. Just as quick to scramble my brain and make me go dizzy.

Kristen Ashley

He lifted his head.

When I could think straight again, I said, "You're supposed to do that after the date is over."

"I'm gonna do it then too," he returned, his arm still around me, his hand still at my neck.

Holy cow.

"I'm sorry, but you Denver people are nuts. I've known you all, like, a day and I just got calls from Daisy, Ally and Jet. Tod actually came over, bringing half of Neiman Marcus's accessory department with him, to help me get dressed. The entire Denver experience is weird. Beyond weird. Denver is 'The Twilight Zone'," I told him.

"We're friendly."

"You can say that again."

He ignored my comment and asked, "You hungry?"

I wasn't hungry. I'd eaten a mountain of food only a few hours before.

If I said no, I wasn't certain what my options were, and since we were in a room that consisted mainly of furniture on which a girl could only find trouble (or, in my case, more trouble), I lied.

"Starving."

It was then the smile in his eyes hit his mouth.

Holy cow.

My phone rang.

"Shit!" I cried, pulling out of his arms and lifting the phone to look at it. "Who could it be now? It has to be Indy."

I stopped talking when Hank plucked the phone out of my hand, flipped it open and put it to his ear.

I stared at him in disbelief.

"Yeah?" he said into the phone.

"Whisky, you can't just answer my phone," I snapped, sounding a lot like Jet when she snapped at Eddie. That was, to say, full of shit. I reached to take it away from him, but he jerked his head away from my reach.

"Hello?" he repeated, sounding far more serious.

My body froze and my heart stopped.

Billy.

This was not good. I thought it would be Indy, Duke, Stevie, Lee, Eddie, or half dozen other people I barely knew who were all of a sudden my friends. Not Billy.

He took the phone from his ear and flipped it shut.

"Who was it?" I asked, wondering if I should ask for CPR pre-heart attack and deciding Hank's lips on mine (again) was not a good idea.

"No answer."

The phone rang again.

I reached for it, knowing now who it was and feeling panic spreading through my body, but Hank stepped away, flipped it open and put it to his ear.

"Hello?" he said.

I moved toward him and got in his space. "Hank," I whispered.

"Is someone there?" Hank said into the phone.

I closed my eyes.

This was not happening.

I opened my eyes again and Hank was watching me. He took the phone from his ear and flipped it shut. "No answer," Hank informed me. He opened it and started pressing buttons.

I knew what he was doing, looking at the received calls. Normally, I would have been angry at his nerve, but I was too busy freaking out at what he might find.

"Give me my phone, Hank."

He got to what he was looking for. "It says unknown caller."

Shit.

Billy was on the road and likely his cell had run out of juice.

"Give me the phone," I repeated.

It rang again.

Without delay, he flipped it open and put it to his ear.

"Hank!" I yelled, making a play for it, but he caught me, snatching me around the waist with his arm and he pulled me up against his body.

"This is Detective Hank Nightingale. Who's calling?" he demanded in a voice that rang with so much authority, if it was me on the other side, I would have answered in a flash.

Billy was going to have a shit hemorrhage. A man answering my phone. A man with a deep, sexy, authoritative, no-nonsense voice and a police title.

"Identify yourself," Hank ordered.

57

He waited. I waited.

Hank was looking pissed-off. I was holding my breath.

He pulled the phone from his ear, flipped it shut one-handed and looked at me.

"No answer?" I asked.

He nodded.

I closed my eyes.

His arm tightened.

I opened them.

"Your trouble catching up with you?" he asked.

I bit my lip. Then I let it go.

"Maybe."

"You ready to tell me about it?" Hank pushed.

I answered immediately. "No."

This made him look more pissed-off.

It might make me a freak, but Hank, normally, was seriously handsome. Hank pissed-off was off-the-charts handsome.

"You're even better looking when you're angry."

Now, *why* did I say that?

He stared at me, and, luckily, ignored my comment.

Then he shared, "I dated a girl all through high school. She was pretty, but when she walked in a room, only I noticed her, not every fuckin' guy in the room. She wore normal clothes, not shit that looks like it comes from the pages of a fashion magazine. She never threw attitude at anyone. She never got drunk, never listened to music too loud, never stayed out after curfew, wouldn't know trouble if it bit her in the ass and wouldn't even know how to keep a secret."

My heart clenched, definite pre-heart attack for sure. I should have asked for CPR.

"You should have married her," I said, sounding uppity.

He let me go, closed his eyes, wiped his hand on his forehead and agreed with me, "I should have married her."

Well!

"If you'll remember, I didn't want to have dinner with you," I reminded him.

He dropped his hand and his eyes locked on mine. "Sunshine, you want to have dinner with me, you want me to kiss you and, later, you're gonna beg me to do other things to you too."

I put my hands to my hips even as the blood rushed to very specific parts of my body. "I don't *think* so, Hank Nightingale. This has officially become the shortest date in history. You want to find your high school girlfriend? Start looking now."

Quick as a flash, he grabbed my waist and hauled me up against his body.

"You want to pretend you don't feel what's between us, be my guest," he said, his face close to mine. "You'll admit it soon enough."

"There's nothing to feel," I lied.

His brows drew together. "Honestly?" he asked.

I scowled at him because even I couldn't utter that lie again.

"You shouldn't have answered my phone," I said.

"I thought it'd be Indy, bein' a pain in the ass, as usual. I didn't know the evil wind was gonna blow through just yet. I was hoping for at least a little time to knock down that guard you got up. Seems I'm gonna have to speed things up a bit."

Speed things up a bit?

We were going Mach Five and I wasn't even certain Mach Five existed.

"Who was on the phone?" he asked.

I kept up the scowl and didn't answer.

"Tell me one thing. Are you in danger?" he went on.

I lost my scowl and felt my body begin to melt.

Shit.

He was worried about me.

Billy had taken a sledgehammer to the door and he'd put his arm to my throat, once. Even after years of me running away and more than a year of no sex, he'd never raised a hand to me after the arm incident. He was intense, that was for certain, but every time I pretended to escape, he brought me back by talking me into it, or at least I let him think that.

I didn't think I was in danger. I was just trapped.

"I'm not in danger, I just have... a situation. I'm fixing it," I told Hank.

"Now isn't the time to lie," Hank told me in his authoritative tone.

"I'm not lying."

At least, I didn't think so. Or, at least, I hoped not.

He watched me for a while. Then he let me go, but grabbed my hand, tossed the phone on the bed and pulled me toward the door.

"Good, let's get some food."

Simple as that.

He trusted me.

Good God.

I yanked hard on his hand and tugged him back into the room. He allowed this until my fingers closed around my Fendi bag, then we were off.

Chapter 6

Hank Speeds Things Up

Holding my hand the whole time, he took me to his black Toyota 4Runner, helped me in, swung in the driver's side and off we went. He drove one-handed and natural, like he was one with the 4Runner. I was beginning to think I was seriously a freak because, for some reason, the way he drove turned me on.

Okay, maybe it was everything about Hank that turned me on.

"Are you a vegetarian?" he asked, thankfully breaking me out of my thoughts of him turning me on.

"I ate three pounds of meat for lunch at Jerusalem's," I answered.

"Combo platter?" Hank guessed.

"Yeah," I confirmed.

"Good choice."

He drove me through what could not be considered the best of neighborhoods, though it also wasn't the worst. He parked in a parking lot and I saw Denver's light rail train slide by. The building he took me to looked like it had been yanked right out of a John Wayne western.

"What is this place?" I enquired.

"Buckhorn Exchange, the oldest restaurant in Denver. Great steaks."

He held the door for me and I saw that the décor consisted largely of dead animal heads, but somehow it seemed cozy, romantic and elegant at the same time. We sat at an intimate table for two with big, high-backed, comfy arm-chairs. Hank ordered a bottle of wine while I looked at the menu. It included rattlesnake, fried alligator tail, Rocky Mountain oysters and elk.

I looked up from my menu to Hank. "Is the ghost of Wyatt Earp gonna walk through the door?"

He grinned at me. "Smart ass."

"No, seriously."

The grin deepened to a smile.

I shut up.

"Let me order," he said and this surprised me. I'd never met a man who ordered for me before. I didn't even know men did that anymore.

What the hell, when in Denver...

"No Rocky Mountain oysters," I replied.

He nodded and kept smiling.

"And no alligator tail," I carried on. "Alligators are cute. I'm not a vegetarian, but I don't eat cute animals. Like lamb. Lambs are cute. We can try the rattlesnake. I think I could eat snake because snakes freak me out."

He stared at me. The smile was gone.

"You think alligators are cute?" he asked.

"They always look like they're smiling. I think alligators are misunderstood. They just want to laze in the sun and swim, but people keep bothering them, forcing them to wrestle and stuff. It's not nice."

He kept staring at me.

"Do you eat cows?" he asked.

"I try not to think of them as cows, like that cute cow, Norman, in *City Slickers*. I think of them as bulls. Bulls are scary."

More staring then, "How about pigs?"

"I heard somewhere that pigs are mean. They aren't like Babe. Babe wore a toupee."

His lips twitched.

"You are definitely related to Tex," he remarked.

"Well... yeah," I replied.

He ordered. When the wine came, we drank. When the food arrived, we ate.

It was good food. So good, I ate it even though I was still full from lunch. Hank ordered steak and it came in one big hunk of meat, which they carved in half at the table and plonked a big old wodge of herbed butter on top of each portion so it melted all over. It was heavenly.

All the time in between eating and drinking, we talked.

I was dreading it, but it came easy.

I found out that Hank was kind of a second generation Coloradan, a definite third generation cop. His grandfather had been killed in the line of duty in New York City, and after, his grandmother had moved the family to Denver where her sister lived.

Hank had gone to the University of Colorado, studying pre-law, and into the Police Academy a couple of weeks after he graduated from college. His Dad didn't want him to be a cop. He wanted him to be a lawyer. But Hank had never wanted to be anything else but an officer of the law, so there you go.

I was learning quickly that Hank kind of did whatever the hell he wanted.

I could tell he was close with his family and he told me he'd known Indy his whole life. Her parents were best friends with his, and when Indy's Mom died young Hank's Mom promised to take care of Indy and make sure she was raised right. Indy and Lee had been in love as long as anyone could remember, but had only gotten together recently. Eddie had been Lee's best friend since third grade and was like a member of the family too.

Hank skied in the winter and played softball in the summer. He listened to Springsteen and had seen him in concert three times, but couldn't say his favorite song or even favorite album. He just liked all that was Springsteen.

This, in itself, said a lot about him.

He was a Rockies fan, a Broncos fan and it was clear he loved his family, Denver and his job.

I told Hank that I lived in Chicago and owned a work-at-home web designing business, but I'd been born and raised in Brownsburg, a town fifteen miles west of Indianapolis. I told him my parents still lived there; my brother was a Park Ranger for Indiana State Parks and my sister worked in hospital administration at a medical center in Louisville. I told him I'd never been to the Indianapolis 500, but I'd been to the time trials, like, a million times. I told him I was a Cubs fan, as were all the family, but we switched staunchly to the Pacers and the Ice for our basketball and hockey needs. I explained I'd rebelled against my family's devotion to the Colts and cheered for the Bears.

I also told him, as was a prerequisite for anyone who lived in the Midwest, I loved REO Speedwagon, though not the power ballads. Just songs like "Roll with the Changes" and "Ridin' the Storm Out". I further told him I liked Springsteen, but had never seen him in concert.

Then I'm afraid I got kind of lost in the discussion and admitted to him I *loved* Springsteen and thought he was a storyteller poet of biblical proportions (but I didn't tell him I thought Springsteen had a beautiful lower lip designed by the gods because I thought that might be sharing too much).

I also waxed lyrical about Mellencamp, maybe a shade too long, but I'd been born in a small town and Mellencamp sang about small towns. I'd also

63

Kristen Ashley

watched a lot of my minutes turn to memories, life sweeping away the dreams that I had planned, and Mellencamp sang about that, too. A girl from Indiana understood those things like no one else. Springsteen might have been able to tear through my heart, but Mellencamp shot straight through my soul.

When I was done talking, Hank was staring again, but this time, his eyes were soft and lazy and I felt a shiver drift across my skin.

I didn't tell him about Billy.

When we were done, I declined dessert because the button of my jeans was digging into my belly. Hank paid and I began to feel relief that the date was soon to be over. If it lasted much longer, I knew I'd lose myself. I even knew I wanted to.

In the end, it wasn't *that* bad. In fact, it was nice. I could almost pretend I was on an actual date, a great date, instead of on the run from a criminal boyfriend who was way too possessive and not afraid of wielding a sledgehammer.

Hank led me out the door and I began to relax thinking he'd take me home, likely kiss me, which would be a lovely addition to a lovely memory, and then we'd be done. It would suck, I'd hate it and I'd regret our timing for the rest of my life, but I was trying not to think about that.

Instead of going to the parking lot, he guided me to the light rail platform.

I stared at him as he bought tickets from a machine.

"What are you doing?" I asked.

"Takin' you downtown."

I blinked. "I thought the date was over."

He grabbed my hand and moved me toward the tracks. "The date is definitely not over."

Shit.

I pulled my hand out of his. "I'm full and I'm tired. It was a delicious meal and thank you, but all that wine and food, I need to go to sleep."

What I needed to do was get out of my jeans and get away from Hank, and not in that order.

He was staring down the tracks, partially ignoring me.

"You'll wake up," he said.

"I'm cold. I didn't bring a coat," I tried.

He took off his coat and settled it on my shoulders. He did the closing the edges with his hands thing again and bent his head to look down at me, standing smack in my space.

64

"Better?" he asked.

"Better" was not the word for it. *"The fucking best"* were the words for it.

Cripes, there was *no* shaking this guy.

"You're in my space," I pointed out.

He got closer. "Yeah."

"Whisky, back off," I warned.

He grinned. "Roxie, relax. We're goin' downtown and walkin' off the food stupor. That's it."

I sighed, or more like harrumphed.

I supposed I could go downtown, see a bit of Denver, walk off the food stupor.

"Oh, all right," I gave in.

He got even closer. Then, I kid you not, he rubbed his nose against mine and then he looked me in the eyes and my breath caught. "It's after that you need to worry about."

Shit.

I was in trouble.

<hr>

We rode the light rail downtown and Hank walked me through Denver. I wore his jacket, and at first he held my hand. Then he dropped my hand and pulled me into his side with his arm around my shoulders.

I allowed this because I decided that to get through the night I was going to pretend to be someone else. I was going to pretend to be the Roxanne Giselle Logan before Billy Flynn, who hadn't yet made a stupid decision that fucked up her life. The Roxanne Giselle Logan who deserved to be out on a date with a tall, handsome guy named Hank Nightingale.

I was going to give myself this one night of pretend.

"You can walk in those shoes?" Hank asked.

"I can play basketball in these shoes," I told him, and I wasn't lying. I'd been wearing high heels since my Mom bought me those little, pink, plastic kiddie go-aheads when I was five.

"Your feet hurt, let me know," he murmured.

Shit.

He was a good guy, through and through.

We walked down 16th Street Mall and the streets were packed with people even though it was Monday night. Bars were hopping, restaurants were jammed, lights were shining. It was gorgeous and alive. He walked me through Writer Square and down to Wazee Supper Club where he bought me a drink and we talked some more.

We were heading back up 16th Street Mall and I knew the date was about to come to a close. It was getting late and Hank had to go out and do good deeds tomorrow. As for me, I had to sort out my life.

Then I saw the horse drawn carriages.

I loved horses.

Okay, it was safe to say I loved anything with fur.

"Just a sec," I said to Hank. I pulled away from his arm around my shoulders and walked to the driver. "Can I pet your horse?" I asked him with a smile.

"Sure," the driver replied.

I walked up to the horse and ran my hand down his satin nose. "Hey, big fella," I whispered to him. He lifted his head with a jerk then settled and nuzzled my neck. I couldn't help but let out a low giggle, mainly because it tickled.

"Likes you," the driver called.

"I smell like food," I told him.

"Likes food too."

I kept stroking and Hank allowed it for a little while and then pulled me away. The horse turned his head to watch me go. So I gave him a little wave and I started up the sidewalk, but Hank guided me toward the carriage.

"What are you——?" I started to ask.

"Get in, we're gonna ride," Hank said.

I stared at him then I stared at the driver.

"No," I whispered.

I couldn't take it. An evening with delicious food at a romantic restaurant, wine, good conversation, a walk through the streets of Denver wearing Hank's jacket, now a carriage ride. It was too much. I couldn't withstand it. I'd never been in a horse drawn carriage. I'd begun to believe I'd never have anything romantic happen to me, except in a scary Bonnie and Clyde type way where I'd end up riddled with bullets if Billy's stink settled on me.

Billy had never taken me on a horse drawn carriage ride. Billy had promised a million romantic promises, but he'd never even bought me flowers. Hell, *none* of my boyfriends ever bought me flowers.

"What's the matter?" Hank asked when my body locked and refused to move.

I felt it happening. I hated it when it happened without warning. My nose was stinging and I was trying to fight it but I just knew I was going to cry.

Hank turned me to him and looked down at me.

My nostrils were quivering.

Shit!

There was nothing worse than the nostril quiver.

I dropped my head.

His hand came to my neck. He cocked his head and bent low to look at me. "Jesus, Roxie, what's the matter?"

"Let's just go," I whispered.

"She okay?" the driver asked.

"Sunshine..." Hank said softly, his hand at my neck sliding around my shoulders and his other hand going around my waist, pulling me to him.

"Let's just go," I repeated, but it was kind of muffled against his chest because my head was still tilted down and my face was pressed against him.

"You want my hankie?" the driver asked.

One of Hank's hands went away then came back to my chin and he tilted my head up. This was unfortunate considering the fact that I was now out-and-out crying.

I slid my eyes to the side so I couldn't see Hank because everyone knew, in an embarrassing situation, if you couldn't *see* the person you were trying to hide from, they weren't actually there.

He wiped my face with a blue bandana and didn't say a word.

"Don't mind me," I said on a sniffle, still looking to the side. "I cry a lot."

Hank didn't say anything.

"I cry at commercials," I told him.

Hank still didn't say anything.

"I cry when I watch *Terms of Endearment,* which I've seen, like, a dozen times," I went on.

Hank stayed quiet.

I took a shuddering breath. "Every time Shirley MacLaine comes out and has that fit at the nurse's station about getting Debra Winger her medication," my throat closed at the memory and I swallowed hard, "it gets me."

"Are you tellin' me you're cryin' because you're thinkin' about a movie?" Hank asked.

I shook my head.

"Then why are you crying?"

Finally, I looked at Hank.

Then, don't ask me why, but I whispered, "Because you're being so nice to me."

For a second, before he could hide it, his head jerked a fraction and his face changed. I didn't get a chance to read it before it went away and his eyes went perfectly blank.

What I could read scared me, in a lot of different ways.

"Has someone not been nice to you?" he asked, and I could tell his voice was carefully controlled.

"Let's just go."

He watched me for a while, one arm still wrapped around my back. Then, he let me go. I thought he was going to give in, but I was wrong. He leaned over, slid an arm behind my knees, grabbed my shoulders and lifted me up.

"What are you doing?" I kind of screamed, throwing my arms around him to hold on.

"We're takin' a carriage ride," he said, carrying me while climbing into the carriage.

This was no mean feat as I wasn't exactly dainty. Uncle Tex toting me around was one thing. Uncle Tex was Paul Bunyon come alive. This was plain crazy.

Hank settled me in the seat without apparent effort and sat beside me.

The driver rushed to his perch and we took off.

"There's just no shaking you, is there?" I asked Hank, my tears gone. I was beginning to feel... I didn't know what I felt.

Hank pulled me into his side. "Nope," he answered.

I crossed my arms and tried to pretend I wasn't feeling whatever it was I felt. Whatever it was felt nice and I couldn't give in to it. I had too much to lose if I did.

Then I looked up at him. "Is my makeup ruined?"

He looked down and smiled. "Yep."

Shit.

I fixed my makeup the best I could with the bandana and my hand mirror and we rode through Denver.

After a while, I settled into Hank's side and relaxed. I couldn't help it, he was solid and warm. Denver was beautiful as I watched it passing by on the clop and the carriage rocked soothingly. Even the most tense, stressed-out neurotic would have relaxed.

After another while, Hank's hand came to my chin, he tilted my head up and he kissed me.

It didn't take a while for me to kiss him back. I just did, right away.

He was a great kisser, and on close inspection, I realized he had a bottom lip that even rivaled Springsteen's.

That shot straight through my heart *and* my soul.

"Boy, am I in trouble," I whispered, looking at his mouth.

His hand went to the side of my head. "Yep."

Shit.

I sat in Hank's 4Runner watching the streets roll by as he drove me to the hotel.

The date was over.

I was trying not to cry again.

It was the best date I'd ever had. It could even be the best date in the history of the world, or at least it had to make the top ten.

I wanted another one just like it. I wanted a dozen of them. I wanted a lifetime of them.

I was only going to get this one.

I should count myself lucky. Some women never had a single date like this.

I didn't feel lucky.

The car stopped and I noticed it was parked in the street.

I glanced around.

We were not at the hotel. We were in a neighborhood. From what I could tell, a nice neighborhood.

I looked at Hank. "Where are we?"

"My place."

"*What?*" I shrieked.

He ignored me and got out.

I stayed rooted to my seat.

This is not happening, this is not happening, I chanted in my head.

My door opened.

I looked at Hank again. "Take me back to my hotel."

He reached in, undid my seatbelt and grabbed my hand, pulling me out of the SUV. "I gotta walk my dog."

We were several steps up his walk when I halted, yanking on his hand. "You have a dog?"

He stopped too and looked back at me. "Yeah."

I loved dogs.

"What kind of dog?" I queried.

"A chocolate lab."

Shit.

I loved labs.

"I'll wait in the 4Runner," I told him.

He tugged my hand, pulling me behind him.

"Whisky, I have to get back to the hotel." I was trying to yank my hand out of his. I was trying, but not succeeding.

He ignored me and kept walking to the house. One story, brick, nicely tended yard, but you could tell no woman lived there. There were no pots for flowers and there weren't any festive autumn decorations in sight. I would definitely have put out festive autumn decorations if I lived there.

I was trying not to think about other things I would do if I lived there when Hank stopped at the door and dropped my hand.

"Whisky..."

He unlocked then opened the door.

A chocolate lab bounded toward us.

"Oh my God!" I yelled and crouched low. "What a cute dog!"

And he was cute. Adorable.

The lab jumped on Hank and he commanded, "Down."

The lab stopped jumping and head-butted Hank in the thighs, got an ear scratch and then came at me. He knocked me on my ass on the front stoop and started licking my face.

"I hope you don't use him as a guard dog," I said, trying to scratch his ears as he jumped all over me.

"I think you can kiss whatever makeup you had left good-bye," Hank noted.

I couldn't help it, I laughed.

Hank went into the house while I got up and played with the dog and he came back with a lead.

"What's his name?" I asked.

"Shamus."

I clapped at Shamus. He came to me and sat on my feet while Hank put the lead on him. The minute the lead snapped into place, Shamus knew the drill and was aching for it. He headed for the sidewalk, snuffling the ground.

Hank grabbed my hand and we followed the dog.

After half a block, it hit me and I declared, "This is not fair."

"What?" Hank asked.

"Don't play innocent with me, Hank Nightingale. You know what. The dog."

Hank dropped my hand and slid his arm along my shoulders.

Then he stopped, and Shamus stopped, though Shamus didn't want to stop. His "come on you guys" glance over the shoulder said it all, and I stopped.

Hank bent, kissed my temple and then his lips went to my ear.

"You try to be difficult and hard, but I can tell you're soft and easy," he whispered.

I jerked my head back and scowled at him.

"I'm not soft!" I snapped.

"You cry at commercials," he pointed out.

This, unfortunately, was true. Worse, I'd volunteered this information to him, just like the idiot I was.

"Well, then, I'm not easy," I went on stubbornly.

"We'll see."

Shit.

⋙⋘

We walked Shamus on a two block loop.

Then Hank let us into his house.

I stood at the closed front door, trying to be obvious about wanting to leave (although I didn't want to leave, I needed to leave) while Hank turned on some lamps.

The front door led to one big front room consisting of a living room to the right, dining area to the left, then a bar and set of cabinets that began a u-shaped kitchen.

It had been redone and looked nice. Gleaming hardwood floors, the kitchen completely refitted with oak cabinets and KitchenAid appliances, deep-seated, cushiony furniture covered in mocha twill and an old beat-up dining room table that looked cool.

It was (somewhat sparsely, but still) decorated in what could only be considered "Colorado". A couple of old Colorado license plates with skiers stamped into them over the doorway to a hall, some Native American artifacts on the tables that looked carefully chosen, two framed prints of New Belgium Brewery beers ("Fat Tire" and "Skinny Dip") over his twill couch.

That was kind of it for decoration. It wasn't like he had an abundance of scented candles and toss pillows, but it was enough to give the place a personality and homey feel. Like he lived there. Like he liked it there. Like he was proud of it and the work he'd done on it.

I thought of it with some nice, sturdy, black iron candleholders with mulberry scented candles and some curtains covering the blinds.

Stop decorating Hank's house, I told myself and crossed my arms to emphasize my thoughts to myself.

"You want a drink?" Hank asked from the kitchen after he'd taken off Shamus's lead. Through the floor and overhead cabinets, I could only see his waist and abs.

As with all things Hank, it was a good view.

Shamus sauntered over and sat on my feet again. I uncrossed my arms and scratched his ears.

"I want to go back to the hotel," I answered.

"You're spendin' the night here," Hank informed me, moving to the end of the counter that delineated the kitchen from the dining area and leaning a hip against it then he crossed his arms.

My mouth dropped open and I stared.

Then I closed it.

"I'm not spending the night here," I said.

His eyes looked lazy again.

My heart started beating faster.

"Come here," Hank called softly.

"No, take me back to the hotel."

"Come here and I'll convince you that you don't want to go back to the hotel."

Good God.

He didn't have to convince me. I was already pretty certain I didn't want to go back to the hotel. But I had to go back to the hotel, for Hank's own good, if not for mine.

"Whisky, I have to get a good night's sleep. I have things to do tomorrow."

I didn't really, but I needed an excuse.

"What things?" he asked.

I kept silent.

Hank went on, "You can come here or I can go over there and get you. Your choice, but I'll warn you, you should probably come to me."

I stared at him and he stared back.

My heart wasn't only beating faster, it was tripping in my chest like a jackhammer.

We kept staring at each other, one beat leading into two, two beats leading into three.

Then his arms uncrossed and he moved forward.

Shamus saw Hank's advance and deserted me (damn dog).

I backed up and as I was standing at the door, in half a step, my shoulders slammed against it.

I lifted my hands to keep him at arm's length.

"Whisky..." I started, but he avoided my hands by bending double, putting a shoulder to my stomach and lifting me in a fireman's hold.

Holy Mary, Mother of God.

"Hank!" I shouted at his back, but he'd turned and was walking through the dining area.

"Put me down!" I yelled, pushing against his waist, but he kept going, through the kitchen and into a dark room.

"Goddammit! Put me down!" I kept at it when he turned and walked into another dark room.

73

He stopped, bent, turned on a lamp and then put my feet on the floor. I would have escaped, but he was right in front of me, and a quick glance around showed that there was a huge bed made out of what looked like logs behind me. *Right* behind me.

"Get out of my way," I demanded. "I'm calling a taxi."

His arms slid around me.

"No taxi," he said, one hand gliding up my back and into my hair to cup the back of my head and keep it steady. "No hotel," he went on, the other arm wrapping itself completely around me so his hand was gripping me at the side of my waist, my body pressed the length of his. "Tonight you sleep in my bed with me."

I looked up at him. In his arms I was quickly losing the will to fight.

"Please," I whispered, the last desperate attempt.

His head bent and, with his lips against mine, he said, "Remember that word. You're gonna be using it a lot tonight."

My stomach fluttered. I felt it and I liked it.

Those were my last coherent thoughts.

He kissed me, his tongue sliding into my mouth. I went dizzy and my brain scrambled. I kissed him back. I wanted to fight it, but I didn't. I probably could have if I wasn't weak. But I was. I'd been weak with Billy and now I was weak with Hank.

My arms went around his neck, my hand slid into his hair. He had great hair, thick and soft and just enough wave.

"You have great hair," I whispered into his ear as his lips trailed along my cheek to my ear.

"You're a nut," he whispered back, sounding like that was a good thing. Then his mouth touched me behind my ear and I shivered.

"I'm not a nut," I went on quietly and turned my head to press my lips to his neck, just above his turtleneck, then I touched my tongue there.

His hand left my waist, went into my shirt and slid up the skin of my side. I was sensitive there, even ticklish, and I squirmed against him.

"You gonna talk through this?" he asked, lifting his head to look down at me.

"Maybe," I answered.

He shook his head and he kissed me again.

I had kind of thought the last kiss was serious as it had a serious effect on me. But I was wrong. *This* kiss was serious. If I thought I was dizzy before, I didn't know the meaning of dizzy.

The kiss was hot and hard and before it was done, I had my hands up his sweater, roaming the skin of his back and shoulders.

He kissed me again, likely to keep me quiet, and I lost any control I had, though there wasn't much to lose.

Then again, so did he.

We were all over each other. Hands inside each other's clothes. Tongues inside each other's mouths. He pulled away and unwrapped the scarf from around my throat and tossed it aside. Before he could come back, I lifted his turtleneck from the waist and pulled it over his head. He shoved me back on the bed but followed me there, his body covering one side of me, his hand going up my shirt, trailing up my belly to cup my breast. He kissed me again and I felt him yank the cup of my bra roughly down and then his hand was skin against skin on my breast.

I arched into it and his hand went away but his finger didn't. It circled lazily around my nipple, his mouth still on mine.

"Let me take my shirt off," I muttered.

"I'm not done," he said, still circling with his finger and it was driving me mad, but in a good way.

I pressed into him. "Whisky, let me take my shirt off," I repeated.

His head lifted and he looked down at me, still circling.

It felt good.

"Why Whisky?" he asked.

"What?"

"Why Whisky?"

I tried to scoot away so I could get my clothes off and, I don't know, maybe attack him, when his thumb joined his finger and he did a roll.

My body stilled and I felt a spasm between my legs.

"Holy cow," I breathed.

"Why Whisky?" he repeated, going back to circling.

"Your eyes," I said. "They're the color of whisky."

He smiled.

I felt a spasm between my legs again.

Then his mouth was on mine.

Kristen Ashley

I was dizzy when he finally moved and pulled my shirt off.

I would have thanked him, but he covered my body with his and used his hands and mouth on me, *all* over me, so I was robbed of speech. Before I knew it my bra was gone. He reached down to pull off my shoes then he yanked down my jeans. Then, without warning, his hands spread my legs and his mouth was on me over my panties.

It was nice. It was better than nice, it was amazing.

Then he whisked away my panties and his mouth was on *me*.

That was even better, *way* better.

In fact, so much better, I felt it coming and I knew it was going to be good.

"Hank," I said and it sounded like a moan.

Then his mouth was gone and he came back over me. I stared at him, lifted my hands to his shoulders and pressed down. I wasn't done so he certainly wasn't done. To my surprise, he resisted and buried his face in my neck, touching his tongue there.

"I was close," I whispered.

"I know," he answered, still resisting the pressure of my hands.

I blinked at the ceiling.

"Why?" I asked.

"I'm not done with you yet."

And he wasn't.

He took me from nearly there to nearly there to nearly there and I tried to get him nearly there but only got so far as getting his belt unbuckled and the top button of his jeans undone. He did pull away to yank off his boots and socks, but that was it.

He had his hand between my legs and I had my hand in the back of his jeans and I was nearly there again, panting against his mouth when his fingers went away and slid up my belly.

My eyes flew open.

"Whisky!" I snapped, bucking and trying to push him to his back to get some leverage on the situation.

I was so turned on, I'd never been that turned on before, my body was humming with it.

He was smiling.

"Don't smile at me, you rat. Finish what you start," I ordered.

He gave me a light kiss. "Ask nice."

76

I growled.

Then I attacked.

It got out of hand then. There was a bit of wrestling, and unfortunately Hank was stronger. I ended up on my back, wrists over my head held by one of his hands, his other hand between my legs again and his mouth at my neck. I was close again and I knew he knew it.

"Let go of my hands, I want to touch you," I demanded.

He didn't answer, but instead ran his tongue along my neck.

"Hank." His name came out kind of whiney.

Okay, maybe a lot whiney.

His hand went from between my legs and my body tensed.

"Please," I said low.

His head came up and he looked at me.

His eyes were hot and intense and I held my breath.

He rolled completely over me. I opened my legs and his hips fell between them as he let go of my wrists. His hand worked at the buttons of his fly and I pushed his jeans down his hips, my mouth at his neck. Then my hand wrapped around him.

"Jesus, Sunshine," he muttered, but there was a smile in his voice.

I looked him in the eye.

I was trying to guide him into me, but he was having none of it.

"I want you inside me, Whisky. Now."

He pulled my hand away and then his hands went to my hips, lifting them, and he stared down at me, but he didn't come inside.

I gave in. "Please."

He slid inside.

It felt beautiful.

My head arched back and my arms wrapped around him.

"Sweetheart, look at me," Hank whispered.

I looked at him. He moved inside me and it felt delicious.

"It starts now," he told me.

I moved with him. I wasn't really focusing on what he was saying, mainly because it was building again and I could feel it coming.

"What starts now?" I asked.

"You and me."

He moved faster, pressed harder, went deeper.

Kristen Ashley

Good God.

"What?" I asked dazedly.

"You and me," he said again.

"Whisky," I breathed, "I'm not keeping up with you."

I was keeping up with him, but not in the way I was talking about. I held onto him, tilted my hips and he went even deeper.

"God, you feel good," I breathed.

"Sunshine, try and pay attention," he replied, sounding amused, and I blinked at him.

He was still moving and I was getting closer all the time.

"Are you crazy?" I asked, not really caring if he was.

"Starting now, there's a you and me."

My arms tightened involuntarily, and other parts of me tightened involuntarily, too.

Hank's eyes went lazy.

"Now, *that* felt good," he muttered.

"Hank—"

He slid in deep.

"Be quiet."

"Hank!"

His mouth met mine.

"Quiet," he said.

Then he kissed me. He moved. I moved. Pretty soon I said his name again (in a moan again), but mainly because he finally let me come.

And it was glorious.

Chapter 7

The End

After we finished, Hank moved away. He pulled off his jeans, positioned me into the bed with the covers over me, slid in beside me and turned out the light.

He lay on his back and rolled me into his side.

Throughout all of this, I was silent and compliant, mainly because I was trying to decide how many types of fool I was.

I was settling on twenty-seven types of fool when Hank spoke, "I think I prefer you talking."

"I'm sleepy," I lied.

"You're thinking, and the way your mind works, that's probably not a good thing."

"You don't know the way my mind works," I told him.

"You've talked yourself into thinking alligators are cute."

"I didn't talk myself into it. Have you *looked* at an alligator? They *are* cute," I retorted.

His body moved with laughter.

"And owls are cute," I went on, nonsensically, ignoring his laughter, or more likely, *because* of his laughter. "I've always wanted to own an owl. Like Florence Nightingale. She carried one in her pocket."

His body kept moving, except I could tell instinctively the laughter had turned deeper.

Then a thought struck me and I got up on an elbow. "Hey, are you related to her?"

I felt his eyes on me in the dark. "Not that I know of."

I settled back down and put my head on his shoulder. "Oh."

He rolled into me and I fell to my back.

His hand went into my hair at the side of my head.

"Are you really sleepy?" he asked.

I wasn't. I was wide-awake and scared out of my wits.

"Um," I mumbled.

"Because if you want to talk, we got shit to talk about."

"I'm sleepy," I said immediately.

His hand slid out of my hair, down my neck, between my breasts and down, to circle my waist. Then, he pulled me into him.

"We'll talk tomorrow," he decided.

I pushed in closer.

I wasn't going to think about it. Not then. Maybe not ever.

I wrapped my arms around him and he held me close.

After a few minutes, I whispered, "Hank?"

"Yeah?"

I pressed my face into his throat. "Thanks for tonight."

His arms went tight.

I woke up and something was crushing me.

I lay there, in the dark, assessing the situation then I remembered.

I was on my back and Hank was at my side. I could feel his breath at my temple, his bicep was resting on my midriff, his forearm curling up my ribs with his hand resting at the side of my breast. His thigh was thrown over both of mine. Adding to this, Shamus was on the other side of me, his head resting on my belly under Hank's arm, like my stomach was a pillow.

Both the human and canine Nightingale boys had me trapped. I'd been feeling trapped for years, but this kind of trapped felt snug and secure.

It was at this juncture that reason returned.

This was not a good thing.

It was *so* not a good thing that it might have been a catastrophic thing.

The thing wasn't even about Billy. I had the feeling that Hank might understand about Billy. Hank was a good guy and it was pretty clear he liked me (okay, so it was *really* clear he liked me).

I wasn't entirely certain I wanted to test this idea, however.

No, it was about sleeping with Hank on the first date.

I was *such* a slut.

What must he think of me?

I might have been able to explain about Billy if I hadn't slept with Hank on the first date. Now, he'd just think I was easy. An easy girl from Indiana who'd fuck criminals and cops without blinking an eye.

I'd even said please.

There was only one solution to this problem.

I had to get out of there.

Immediately.

Not just get out of Hank's house, but out of Denver.

My plan to leave Billy was screwed. I had to abort and start all over again.

I moved and Shamus jerked and sat up.

I froze, listening, but Hank didn't wake.

"Let's go boy, move out," I whispered to Shamus, shoving him a bit and he jumped off the bed. I slid out from under Hank and then stopped again, waiting. He still didn't wake so I got out of bed. Shamus thought it was playtime and wagged his tail, running to the door of the room and back to me.

"Shh!" I hissed. "Come here. Sit!" Shamus did as he was told and I heard his tail sweeping the floor with excitement. He thought we were going to take a midnight stroll, maybe go to a park and play Frisbee. Crazy dog.

I gave him an ear scratch, wishing I could play Frisbee with him. Not at that exact moment, of course, but at some moment, eventually, and it caught at my heart that I knew I never would.

He licked my hand.

That caught at my heart too.

"You're such a good boy," I told him, meaning it and also wishing Hank didn't have a dog. It was hard enough dealing with all that was Hank. Add a dog to the mix and it was nearly impossible.

"Stay," I commanded and Shamus obeyed.

I started searching for my clothes in the dark and tripped over one of my Mary Jane's.

"Shit!" I whispered and looked toward the bed.

Hank hadn't moved.

Thank God.

I found my underwear and jeans, but tripped over Hank's boot on the way to my shirt.

"Fuck!" I snapped and gave up, feeling like a fool, rooting around naked in the dark. Much better to root around in the dark partially dressed.

Kristen Ashley

I put on my underwear and Shamus lost patience with waiting and walked over to me. He leaned his furry body into my legs and I could feel it undulating with the force of his tail wags.

"Sit, Shamus. Be good," I mumbled, doing another head scratch while Shamus settled on my feet.

I was straightening from the dog, jeans still in my hand when the light came on.

My head snapped up and I looked at the bed.

Hank came back from stretching to reach the light and sat up on an elbow, his eyes settling on me. He looked sleepy, hair tousled, chest bared and my breath caught. He might look handsome normally, kickass handsome angry and melt-in-your-mouth handsome when he casually drove his car, but sleepy he was a knockout.

"What're you doin'?" he asked.

"You're awake," I pointed out the obvious.

"The neighbors are awake with all your racket. What're you doin'?"

"I'm leaving."

Uh… not good.

One second, he looked sleepy, the next second, he looked pissed-off.

"What did you say?" he asked.

I looked down, anything not to look at Hank, and pulled my feet out from under Shamus.

"I'm gonna call a cab and I'm leaving."

Deprived of my feet, Shamus got up and pressed his body against my legs again. This was unfortunate as I was trying to put on my jeans, thus hopping around on one leg and avoiding Shamus at the same time. Not exactly graceful, but I had nothing left to lose.

I shouldn't have looked down. Without warning, Hank was there. He jerked my arm pulling me off balance. I dropped the jeans and collided with him and Shamus. Shamus scooted out from between us then pressed against both of us.

Hank was naked. I hadn't had a chance to get a good look at him, what with being entirely too tuned into how turned on he was making me. I knew he had a great chest but my quick glance showed me he pretty much had a great everything else as well.

82

I ignored his great everything else and snapped, "Hey!" trying to pull my arm away but Hank held on tight. In fact, his free hand came up and grabbed my other arm.

"Get back into bed," he ordered, looking down at me.

"I'm going," I told him.

"You're not going."

I was still trying to pull away. I was still not succeeding.

"I am," I replied.

"Why?" Hank asked.

"Does it matter?" I asked back.

"Why?" he repeated.

Jeez, there was just no shaking this guy.

"Let go." I was getting kind of desperate. I dropped my gaze to his chest, raised my hands there and began to push.

He shook me gently to get my attention. It worked. I looked back up.

"Tell me why you're sneakin' out of my bed in the middle of the night," he demanded.

"Hank—"

"Answer me, goddammit!"

Holy cow.

He wasn't pissed-off anymore, he was angry. I couldn't only see it on his face, I could feel it emanating from his body. For some reason, it didn't scare me. He had it in check. It was entirely controlled. I knew that like I knew there were no other jeans in the world as good as Lucky jeans.

It did make me talk, however. I didn't like that he was angry, not at me.

"I'm not a slut," I blurted out.

His hands on my arms relaxed, but didn't go away and he blinked one of his slow blinks.

"Sorry?" he asked.

"I'm not a slut."

God, I sounded like an idiot. Now, I had to explain.

"I'm not a slut. Never have I slept with a guy on a first date. Never. Never. Never."

"Roxanne—" he started to say, but I forged ahead.

"Bil... the last guy, it took, like, three weeks to get to third base and at least a month before we did it. I swear."

"Roxie—" Hank began again, but I kept talking.

"Before him, there was Derek, and we were dating, like, forever before we did it and it was unfortunate when we did because he wasn't very good at it. Then there was Kenny and I don't even remember how long it took before we did it. He was a jerk. Once we did, he dumped me."

"Roxie—" Hank said again and started to pull me against his body, but I had my arms up between us, and like the total idiot I was, I was counting down my ex-lovers on my fingers.

"Then there was Troy. He was a good kisser, like you, but it still took, I don't know, at least *two weeks* before I let him get his hands up my shirt. Wait, Troy doesn't count because we never did it in the end. I saw him making out with my friend Kim and I broke up with him. What a bitch. I forgot about her."

Hank now had his arms around me. Shamus was sitting beside us, his doggie body resting against our legs and I was oblivious to this because I was on a roll.

"Then, there was Scott, he was my first. We dated for at least *a year* until we finally did it. He married the prom queen and now they've got half a dozen kids, no joke."

I stopped and looked up at Hank.

He was looking down at me, angry gone, pissed-off a memory. He was smiling again with only his eyes engaged in the smile.

Had I just recited all my lovers to Hank?

I had.

Shit.

"You finished?" Hank asked.

"I'm an idiot."

Hank bent his head and rubbed his nose against mine. Then he gave me a light kiss.

That was nice, but I still felt like I was now at least thirty different types of fool.

"I'm a slut *and* an idiot," I told him.

"You aren't a slut and you aren't an idiot," he said authoritatively, making me believe that at least he believed it.

Then his hands came up my back and undid my bra.

"No!" I protested. "Don't do that, I have to go."

He ignored me, slid the straps down my arms and tossed the bra aside. Then his hands went down my back. He bent, I felt them go over my bottom and he jerked me up. I threw my arms around him and he turned and deposited me on the bed and he came down on top of me.

His weight felt good on me. Too good.

"Whisky, get off me. I need to go."

His hands were on me and I liked how they made me feel. I liked it a whole lot. His fingers tagged my panties and started to pull them down.

Against my neck, he said, "You still want to go after I fuck you again, I'll take you back to the hotel."

Holy cow.

My stomach did a dip.

I tried to ignore the dip and the subsequent melty feeling. I had to be strong. Or, at least, I had to try to be strong.

"No. No more fucking. I've got to sort out my problem, then if you're still around when it's done, we'll try this again, but we'll take it slow and get to know each other before we, uh… carry on… er, like this."

His head came up and he looked at me. I could tell right away he thought I was funny.

"Sunshine, I know you're crazy, and I have to admit it's sweet, but you're all kinds of crazy if you think I'm waitin' to get inside you again."

Holy cow. The melty feeling graduated to a rolling boil.

"Hank…"

He'd stopped pulling down my underwear at my hips, his hand went to cup my pubic bone and he kissed me.

Shit.

I felt the little, itty bit of strength I was clinging to start slipping away as his tongue moved against mine then Hank broke the kiss.

"Open your legs," he murmured against my mouth.

"I need you to understand," I said, and I did. In that instant, I decided that I was going to tell him everything and I *needed* him to understand.

"You can explain it tomorrow. Now I want you to open your legs."

I kept my legs firmly closed. "What if I explain it to you tomorrow and you don't understand?"

In answer, he kissed me until I was dizzy. After the kiss, his lips trailed down my cheek to my ear.

"Roxanne, sweetheart, open your legs for me," he whispered.

I opened my legs.

I was weak and I couldn't help myself, but truly, at that moment, I would have done anything for him.

He rewarded me immediately. Later, I rewarded him.

Even later still, I'd lost all thoughts about leaving. My back was pressed to his chest, his arm was around me, my arm resting on his and our fingers were laced.

I was half asleep when he murmured, "Whatever it is, I'll understand."

I snuggled deeper and prayed that was true.

My hair was moved away from my face and then a finger trailed down my neck. That finger turning into a full hand as it slid down my side to rest on my hip.

"Wake up, Sunshine."

I rolled to my back. The hand stayed where it was so it moved across to my belly as I opened my eyes.

It was the best wakeup call I'd ever had.

Hank was sitting on the bed, leaning over me. It was still dark outside, although a little light was coming through the blinds, and there was also light coming from some other part of the house through the doorway. I could see he was dressed in a Rip Curl t-shirt and pair of dark track pants that had a wide stripe running down the side.

"You're dressed," I mumbled.

"Shamus and I are goin' for a run. We'll come back, shower and I'll take you out for breakfast."

I blinked.

"Run?" I asked.

"Run," he answered.

"As in, exercise?"

His lips twitched. "Yeah."

"Why?"

"I take it you don't run."

"Only when chased by men wielding chainsaws."

The lip twitch turned into a grin. "That happen a lot?"

"No, but Ally says there's one at the Haunted House she wants to take me to."

The smile died and his brows drew together. "Christ, don't go to the Haunted Houses with Ally and Indy. A few years ago, Indy went berserk and broke through the hay bales they had set up to make the haunted trail and headed into the cornfields. All the employees chased after her, but since they were dressed like monsters, Indy lost her mind. They had to call the cops to settle her down."

I lost him at "cornfields".

"Cornfields?" I whispered.

"Yeah."

"They have a haunted trail through cornfields?"

"Yeah, up in Thornton. Best Haunted House in Denver. Indy and Ally go every year. Why?"

"Cornfields freak me out," I admitted.

Hank was silent.

Then he said, "You're from Indiana. How in *the* fuck can cornfields freak you out?"

"Cornfields don't freak me out. Cornfields at night freak me out. *Haunted* cornfields at night freak me out," I clarified.

"You been to many haunted cornfields?"

"Dude," I said low. "All cornfields are haunted. Trust me. I know." Then I came up on my elbows so I was closer to him and said quietly, "They whisper to you." Then I gave a shiver because, well, the memory of whispering cornfields freaked me out. Indeed, whispering cornfields should freak anybody out.

His arms came around me and he pulled me fully up and pressed my torso against his. I knew he was laughing. I didn't hear it I felt it.

After his body quit shaking he asked, "Did you just call me 'dude'?"

"Yeah. So?"

His hand went into my hair at the side of my head, his fingers sliding through it. This made my scalp tingle pleasantly. He watched his hand move then his eyes came back to me.

"What's wrong with 'dude'?" I asked when he didn't answer.

"We don't have enough time to get into all that's wrong with 'dude', especially when we have more important shit to talk about. And if I stay here any longer, I'm gonna want my exercise in an entirely different way, a way that isn't going to help Shamus keep fit." He gave me a light kiss, which made my lips tingle even more pleasantly than my scalp. "There's coffee beans in the freezer, grinder in the cabinet over the coffeemaker. Help yourself, but I'm takin' you to Dozens for breakfast, so don't eat anything that'll spoil your appetite."

"Okay," I said, staring at his lower lip, fascinated with watching it move while he talked.

"Roxie?"

"Hmm?" I was kind of not paying attention. What could I say? His lower lip was *fine*.

"You keep lookin' at my mouth like that, after I'm through with you, and since I've been doin' most of the work, *you're* gonna have to take Shamus for a run."

My eyes moved to his and then they narrowed. "*You've* been doing most of the work?"

He grinned, but didn't answer.

"Well! Do I have to remind you, Hank Nightingale, that you wouldn't let me touch you the first time and the second time I *tried* to climb on top but *you* flipped me over—"

He kissed me quiet.

"You don't have to remind me," he said softly when he was done kissing me. "I remember every second."

That shut me up, mainly because it took my breath away.

He went on, "I'll be back in forty five minutes, an hour at the most. Wait for me. We'll shower together."

I nodded my head. Although somewhere in my psyche it was registering that he was being supremely bossy, I didn't care, not even a little bit.

"I think I might go back to sleep for a while," I told him. "Wake me up when you get home."

At my words, his eyes got lazy and his arms tightened, bringing my body deeper into his. I got the feeling he was losing his motivation for the run. I looked to the side of the bed and saw Shamus sitting there impatiently, tongue lolling out, tail starting to wag when he caught my gaze.

I looked back to Hank. "Whisky, Shamus is waiting."

Hank kept looking at me; just that, looking at me, his face close, his eyes staring into mine. I felt my breath turn shallow as his lazy eyes got that intense look behind them.

"What?" I asked.

His hand ran up my side.

"Just thinking of you sleepin' in my bed," he said. "It's a good thought."

My throat closed and feelings of panic and happiness surged through me. It was strangely thrilling and frightening at the same time. I swallowed to open my throat then I put my arms around him and pressed my face in his neck.

"Hank," I whispered against his skin. "What I have to say at breakfast I know you aren't going to like. Please, for me, or for the person you think I am right now, don't—"

He interrupted me, "Are you tellin' me you're a different person?"

I shook my head, pulled away from his neck and looked into his eyes. "But once you hear what I have to say, you might think I am."

He stared at me a beat, then all of a sudden he pulled me completely out from under the covers and slid my naked body across his lap. He yanked the covers over me, wrapping them around me to keep me warm and then his hands went into my hair on either side of my head and held me, facing him.

"Sweetheart, I'm thirty-five years old and I've had a fuck of a lot more lovers than you counted on your one hand last night. I've come to the point, with women, that I know what I want when I see it and I haven't seen anything in a long time that interests me as much as you."

Holy cow.

I was trying to process that (and struggling with it) when he continued.

"Not only that, but I've seen a lot of shit in my job and I deal, day-to-day, with the filthy crust eating away at the edge of good civilization. I know good people. I know bad people. I know good people who do bad things and bad people who do good."

I stared at him, wide-eyed, fascinated and speechless as his face dipped closer to mine and he kept going.

"I know what kind of person you are and nothing you say over breakfast is gonna change the fact that, while I'm runnin', I'm gonna think about your fucking fantastic body naked and asleep in my bed."

A shiver slid through me.

"Wow," I whispered.

Kristen Ashley

"So you can stop worrying," he finished.

I nodded.

He watched me for a beat and then his hands went from my head, to my shoulders and then around my back.

"One more thing, Roxanne."

I nodded again, still speechless, still processing and, even though I nodded, I was not entirely sure I could take "one more thing".

"I meant what I said last night, about you and me. I know you're scared—"

"I'm not scared," I lied, automatically and in self-defense.

His arms tightened. "Quiet," he ordered.

I shut up.

"You think we're going too fast."

"*That*, I'll agree with," I broke in again.

He shook his head and smiled. "What you need to get is that it's done. The minute I slid inside you last night, it was done."

That got a belly quiver.

"You said that last night," I reminded him.

"I have to know you get it."

"Why?"

"'Cause whatever it is you're gonna tell me in a couple of hours is gonna make me involved."

"I'm not sure it means that," I objected.

"I am."

"Whisky—"

"I'm already involved."

"I don't think so."

He frowned. "You don't get it."

"You have to let me sort it out myself."

"Been there, done that. I was a bystander the other times and it sure as fuck isn't gonna happen with you and me."

He was talking about Indy and Jet and all their problems.

"You're being very nice, but I have to take care of this my way," I informed him.

"I'm not being nice. I'm protecting what's mine," Hank returned.

My body jerked in shock at his words. I blinked and my back straightened.

"I'm not yours," I said.

90

"You're welcome to think that, but it doesn't change the fact that you are."

This was familiar, too familiar, annoyingly familiar.

Men!

"I'm not yours!" I said and my voice was so much louder, Shamus gave a woof.

"I get it, Roxie, you're tryin' to be independent and strong—"

Oh no, now he was patronizing me. I wasn't a big fan of being patronized. "Don't you dare patronize me, Hank Nightingale. I *am* independent," I said, not claiming to be strong. I knew I wasn't that. "And I'm sick to death of men who think they can..."

I stopped. I didn't want to go too far, too soon.

"What?" Hank asked. When I didn't answer he pushed, "Men who think they can what?"

I scowled at him and burst out in a flurry of (loud) words, "Possess me! Trap me! Make me be where I don't want to be or go where I don't want to go or feel what I don't want to feel!"

After I was done talking, he twisted, my back hit the bed and before I knew it, he was on top of me, staring down at me, his eyes intense.

"Belonging to me doesn't mean I'll make you do anything, it just means I consider you mine for as long as this lasts. It means I protect you. It means I take care of you. For another man, it might mean something different."

His eyes changed. They went funny, the intensity strengthening to something that was mesmerizing.

Then he concluded, "Don't confuse me with another man."

His words dealt my defenses a destructive blow.

Doggedly, I carried on, trying to be philosophical, trying to hold up the ragged remains of what was left of the shield I had around me, protecting me from Hank.

"They say if you care about something, you have to set it free and if it comes back to you, it was meant to be."

"They're full of shit."

Obviously, I failed spectacularly at being philosophical.

I gave up on that and went for annoyed.

"Hank!" I snapped.

He smiled, effectively breaking the moment, and gave me a light kiss. "We'll talk about it over breakfast. I'll promise to listen to you and you have to promise to listen to me. We'll figure it out."

If I could have put my hands on my hips, I would have.

"You're as stubborn as Uncle Tex."

The smile deepened.

"That means you're in trouble," he said.

"I already know that," I grumbled.

He rolled completely on top of me, his body pressing into mine, taking my breath away.

"The minute I saw you walk into Fortnum's, I knew I'd do whatever it took to get you right where you are now. And I'm gonna do whatever it takes to keep you here for as long as both of us get something good out of it."

I bit my lip. What could I say? He was getting to me.

No, if I was honest, he'd already gotten to me.

I couldn't let him know it.

"And you think *I'm* crazy?" I asked.

"Yeah, I do. If you keep pretendin' you don't want to be here, you're definitely crazy and you're lyin' to yourself." He kissed my nose and grinned at me. "Don't worry, I'm patient."

Shit.

He got up, twisted me around until I was right in the bed and bent low to kiss my temple.

Then, without waiting for me to come up with an answer (which I was finding difficult) he was gone.

I heard him leave and didn't sleep. How could I? My mind was a flurry, I was dizzy and Hank wasn't even in the house.

I mentally tugged at my protective shield but I knew it was useless.

Oh well, whatever. So, I had to factor Hank into my plan. It wouldn't be hard, considering I had the feeling that Hank was probably just going to take over the plan and do it his way.

There were worse things, right?

Anyhoo.

I heard a knock on the door while I was burrowing into Hank's pillow and I smiled.

He'd come home, way early.

Poor Shamus. Maybe I'd take him out to play Frisbee later. I didn't know if Shamus actually played Frisbee, but he seemed to be a super smart dog. He'd learn.

I thought that Hank probably didn't take his keys because he knew I'd be here.

I got up, found my panties, tugged them on, grabbed his turtleneck off the floor and pulled that on too.

I left his bedroom and entered another room, a big room that ran the length of the house and had two couches running down the sides, and a wood-burning stove sitting on a stone hearth at the end and a television. I walked through the side door, through the kitchen to the front door. Without looking to see who it was, I opened it, a smile still playing on my mouth.

The minute I saw who was on the threshold, my smile died.

Billy stood there.

Chapter 8
Billy and My Wild Ride

That was the end of Hank and me.

Even though I thought it was the beginning, what happened next would keep Hank further away from me than any flimsy shield I could throw up.

Now I'm sitting curled under a sink in a filthy hotel, gagged and handcuffed to the drainpipe. I hurt, everywhere. I've never hurt so much. My body hurts. My face hurts.

My heart hurts.

Everything hurts.

I hurt, but I wasn't scared.

Billy's gone. The men took him away. I don't know who they were. I don't know where they were going and I don't care. Someone would find me, the maid (if they had one in this fucking place) or the manager when we don't check out. I just have to wait. I wasn't going to die cuffed to a sink.

Though, it was debatable if something important, something deep inside me, something precious, hadn't already died.

Billy kidnapped me. There was no other way to put it.

It wasn't an easy kidnapping for him. I fought it.

It was violent, it was destructive and it was ugly.

After I opened the door and the smile died on my face, he surged into Hank's living room, hands on me.

We went back... back... and then he slammed me into the wall. My skull cracked against it and I hit with such force, one of the New Belgium Brewery prints (the Fat Tire one) fell, crashing down, glass flying everywhere.

Kristen Ashley

"Hank fucking Nightingale," Billy spat in my face, telling me how he found me. He'd looked up Hank.

Shit.

I couldn't talk. Billy's hand was at my throat and it was squeezing.

"I saw him running with his fuckin' dog. A fucking cop. *Detective* Hank fuckin' Nightingale," Billy snarled.

I pushed hard, kicked harder and somehow got him off me.

We wrestled standing. I broke away, starting to run. Billy caught me, whipping me around. More wrestling; a lamp fell, crashing to the floor, tables overturned. Billy got me on the floor, rolled on top of me, his angry face in mine.

"You fuck him?" he asked.

I didn't answer, too scared to speak. I pushed against him, my heart racing and frightened out of my wits, hoping with everything that I was that Hank would come home, and soon. I tried to think of how long he was gone. He'd said forty-five minutes, an hour. It had probably only been twenty minutes, twenty-five, tops.

"I said, *did you fuck him?*" Billy shouted in my face when I didn't answer and then he moved.

I heard the snap of a switchblade and he rolled off me, and before I knew it the blade went into Hank's sweater, slicing through it. I pushed away. Billy caught hold of me by the sweater and it tore more, hanging on me in tatters. I pulled free, got up and tried to run, but Billy caught me by the ankle and I went flying, landing hard on my knees.

I twisted around as he yanked me toward him by my ankle and tried to fight him, but he was too strong. He hit me in the face, one of his silver rings tearing my flesh open at my cheekbone. I saw stars and tried to shake my head clear when he got up, pulling me with him and dragged me through the house, into Hank's bedroom.

"He fuck you here?" he demanded, pulling me up, slamming me against a wall, pushing his body against mine. "Did he fuck you?" he repeated, pushing my face to the side, pressing my bleeding cheek against the wall. "Did he make you come? How many times did he fuck you?" He pulled me away from the wall and slammed me against it again. "*How many times did he fuck you?*" he screamed.

No smooth talk now. No fast-talking, silver tongue.

He was out-of-control, completely.

96

"Billy," I whispered.

He hit me again, so hard my head and body flew to the side, and I went down on my hands and knees. Then he kicked me in the ribs, his boot slamming into my body so hard it pulled me off the floor. Then he dropped down and rolled me over, tore the remains of the sweater off me and forced his thigh between my legs until his hips fell between them, his groin pressing against me.

"I should fuck you, right here, in his bed. Leave a present for him on his sheets."

God, no. Please, God, no, I thought.

I started struggling again. My ribs were burning where he kicked me, my face aching. I could feel the blood there.

Billy didn't notice my struggles.

"I should do it, but we don't have time," he said, and I had just a second to thank God before Billy said, "Get dressed."

He got up, jerking me up with him.

"*Get dressed!*" he screamed.

Shaking and scared, I got dressed.

<hr />

I tried to escape.

He took me to his car, parked out in the street behind Hank's 4Runner. He drove, at first, like a madman, silent, crazy.

I left him to his thoughts. Mine were of survival, then escape.

Once we left Denver, he seemed to calm.

I decided it was time to try to speak, maybe reason with him, maybe talk him around. "Billy, I have to go to the bathroom," I said.

"Shut your fuckin' mouth."

Okay, so I was wrong about him being calm.

He drove, fast.

Close to the Colorado-Nebraska border, we stopped at a gas station.

"Billy, I have to go to the bathroom, see to my face," I said quietly.

He turned to me. He didn't look like my handsome, sweet, dreamer Billy anymore. I didn't even know this man.

"You run, I'll catch you. Make no mistake."

I nodded. I believed him. Still, I was going to try.

He got me the key and I went to the bathroom. There were other cars at the station and the people in them stared at me, but gave us a wide berth.

I looked at my face in the cloudy, pocked, gas station mirror. There was blood running down my left cheek and it was smeared along my face. The cuts weren't bad, but they were there bleeding a lot and the bruising and swelling had already started.

I felt my nostrils burn and I took deep breaths to stop the tears from coming. Tears would leak energy and I needed everything I could get. I forced back the tears, washed my face and stayed in the bathroom as long as I could, hoping someone would call the cops. Hoping I'd hear sirens.

A fist pounded on the door.

"Get your ass out here!" Billy yelled.

I tilted my head back, closed my eyes and took a deep breath. Then I pushed open the door with all my strength and ran straight by Billy, hell bent for leather, no destination in mind. I just wanted attention, to get someone to help. So I ran, screaming at the top of my lungs.

I saw the surprised stares turn to shock, people filling up their cars or waiting in them, stunned immobile at the sight of Billy chasing me. Then he caught me, dragged me kicking and screaming to the car, shoved me in the driver's side, got in with me and, somehow, we rocketed from the station even as I was fighting him.

I saw a man run toward us, but he was too late.

Billy drove wild, fighting me as he drove. I didn't care if we wrecked. I'd take the damage of an accident to my body far easier than I'd take any more damage from Billy.

He pulled over and turned, giving me his full attention.

He hit me again, so hard my mind went blank and I slowed to let my brain settle. When I blinked away the unconsciousness that wanted to envelop me Billy was tying my hands together with nylon rope.

When he was done, he yanked me across the emergency brake until his face was an inch from mine.

"You gotta learn, Roxie. You gotta learn."

I didn't know what he was talking about and didn't want to know.

"You'll learn," he finished, then he pushed me off him, put the car in gear and we took off.

He drove erratically. I thought we were heading toward Chicago, going east, but then he went south. We stopped at another gas station over the Kansas border. He chose one that was desolate. No cars this time, just the attendant. He tied my hands to the steering wheel when he went in to pay. He brought back cheese puffs and a diet drink and I ate with my hands tied. I noticed his wallet was full of bills, bulging with them, and I was too scared of what was happening to be even more scared of how he got so much money.

I didn't think of anything. I kept my mind blank, tried to sleep so my body would be rested, ready to fight, but sleep wouldn't come.

We headed into Kansas, went west for a while and, deep in the night, stopped at a hotel. Billy tied me to the steering wheel again while he checked in. He didn't untie my hands all night, even stood over me while I went to the bathroom.

Lying on my back in the bed, Billy pressed into me, half his body over mine, keeping me from breathing. My ribs still hurt and they hurt worse with his arm tight around me.

He whispered, "You can't leave me Roxie. You're the only good thing I got. You're the only good thing I ever had. I can't lose you. Don't you understand?"

I didn't understand. "Billy, you have to talk to me. What are you running from?"

"We gotta stay clear for a few days. I struck it this time, Roxie. Right before you left, I hit it. Now I can take you to France. Now we can go anywhere. We can go to Italy, Bermuda. You can live in a bikini."

"Billy," I whispered. "What have you done?"

"It's all for you, Roxie. Everything I've done is for you."

I felt the tears crawl up my throat, my nostrils quivering, but I fought it down and laid there, awake all night, Billy sleeping beside me.

I was lying in the bed I'd made for myself.

The next day, more of the same. The only difference was I didn't try to escape and I got a tube of chips with my diet drink.

We headed back east, then north, cut back and then south, then north again.

We didn't talk. Billy was beyond fast-talk now. Even Billy was smart enough to know he'd have to talk three miles a minute to bring me back around.

We were at the Nebraska-Iowa state line when the clock on the dash turned to midnight and we stopped at a filthy motel.

The manager looked at me tied to the steering wheel while Billy checked in. I didn't make a move, didn't try to communicate my dilemma. Thoughts of escape were gone, for now.

Like my Mom said, I needed to be smart. To escape, I needed people. I needed a place to run, a police station, a fire station, a hospital, an all-night café. Something. I had to bide my time, not fight. Maybe make Billy think I'd given up. Billy would have to fuck up somewhere along the line, and I was waiting.

That was when I'd go; escape, find my way home, get my stuff from Annette and disappear. I'd have to leave the country, maybe go to Canada, Mexico, disappear and stay gone for a good long time, maybe forever.

I was my generation's Uncle Tex. I had to cut myself loose. I understood Uncle Tex now. I understood how it felt to feel dirty even though it wasn't you who jumped in the mud. Instead, you'd been pushed, but you were soiled all the same.

I hadn't taken a shower in three days. My hair was filthy, my face and body still ached from the fight, especially my ribs, and I feared they'd been cracked when Billy kicked me. I hurt from being cooped in the car, my hands hurt from being tied together for two days. I lay in bed, Billy beside me again, and my thoughts drifted to Hank.

I'd succeeded in not thinking about him until then. But I was tired, so fucking tired, I couldn't push the thoughts away.

I wondered what he thought when he came home from his run, thinking to find me asleep in his bed; to wake me, shower with me, take me to breakfast, like normal people, like a couple starting out. Instead, he came home to find his house wide open and trashed, me gone.

One date and he said there was a him and me. He was so sure about it. He was so fucking sure he'd made me sure. For twenty minutes, I'd felt good and clean and *free*.

God, how I wished that could be true.

It didn't last, *couldn't* last.

Here I was, unshowered, in a stinking motel, on the run with a criminal, my pretty, designer clothes dirty, no longer my armor. Hank would take one look at me and wonder what in the hell he was thinking. I wasn't what he thought I was. *I* didn't even know who I was anymore.

I felt a single tear slide down the side of my eye when the door splintered and crashed open.

Billy jerked awake and came away from the bed. I rolled the other way as the lights went on.

"Fuck, Roxie, run!" Billy shouted, but I had no time to run. There was nowhere *to* run. They were in the door, cutting off the only escape route.

There were two men with guns. I felt momentarily stunned. I didn't think I'd ever seen a gun, except in a holster carried by a uniformed cop.

Billy charged. I shook free of my daze and tried to make a dash. One went after Billy, but I didn't see what happened because the other one came after me.

Thanks to my fucking, shithead, so-very *ex*-boyfriend, I was hindered by tied hands, wrists rubbed raw by being bound for two days.

I fought all the same.

He easily overpowered me and forced me into the bathroom, cuffing me by one wrist to the pipes under the sink. I was shouting and he shoved his hand-kerchief in my mouth, tying it in place with a cord he ripped from a lamp in the bedroom. This all took him less than a minute. He was a practiced hand at this crap.

Then, without looking back, he entered the grunting, scary scuffle I heard in the other room. No one outside heard me scream before I was gagged. Or it was the kind of place where they ignored it. The scuffle stopped or moved, but one way or another, the bedroom went completely silent.

I sat under the sink, tense and waiting, but minutes ticked by and no one came back for me.

⌁

So there I was. My worst fears had come true.

Billy's stink had settled on me.

I could even smell it.

Part Two

Chapter 9
A High Price

I heard movement in the other room, barely, just a rustling.

I knew someone was there, maybe someone who wasn't supposed to be there.

I kept quiet and held my breath, unsure of what to do. I didn't want the men who took Billy to come back and get me. I didn't think they were good people who were there to explain that Billy had won some magazine's million dollar sweepstakes and just got really carried away with the excitement of it all.

I saw the shadow when it hit the doorway, and without thinking I scooted further under the sink.

"Fuck," the shadow muttered.

Then the bathroom light flipped on.

Vance stood there, Lee's bounty hunter.

I blinked up at him, my eyes adjusting to the light.

It immediately hit me that Vance was a different sort than Hank. He didn't have control over his reactions, maybe didn't want to, and he didn't try to hide his expression from me. Vance's dark eyes were blazing angry and his mouth was tight.

He pulled some keys from his pocket and crouched beside me, his eyes never leaving my face even as his hands went to the cuffs. He freed me from the sink within a few seconds, then he went to work on the cord wrapped around my head, all the while looking at me.

After he pulled the handkerchief gently from my mouth, his hands went back to mine and he worked on the nylon rope while he asked, "You okay?"

I wanted to laugh and ask him how many girls he found beaten up, gagged and cuffed to sinks in sleazy hotels that answered, "Yeah, sure, peachy." But it was anything but funny and both Vance and I knew it.

Instead, I said, "I think he cracked a couple ribs."

His eyes flared, and, again, he didn't try to hide it.

He helped me up from the floor, out of the hotel and then helped me into a black Ford Explorer.

Once I was inside, he skirted the car and swung behind the wheel. Without delay, he started the truck, hitting some buttons on the sat nav after he hit a button on the phone, making it ring inside the truck.

"Yeah?" A voice answered before the second ring.

"Got her. Do you have a lock on my position?" Vance asked, still fiddling with the sat nav.

"Yeah. She okay?" the voice asked back.

"I need the nearest hospital," Vance replied.

Silence, then, "Fuck."

Vance stopped fiddling with the sat nav, reversed the Explorer out of the spot and started driving.

"When you hear the zip code, enter it into the sat nav. Can you do that?" Vance asked me.

"Yes," I whispered, then cleared my throat. "Yes," I said louder.

The male voice gave me the zip code and I entered it. After I did that, Vance took over, pressing a couple of buttons. The navigation system calculated the route and Vance swung a u-ie.

Then the male voice said, "What can I report to Hank and Tex?"

"She's safe. Let me get her checked out. Then I'll call in and you can let Lee decide," Vance replied.

"I'm here," another voice said, a voice I knew was Lee's.

I closed my eyes and leaned my head against the window, humiliation burning deep into my already exposed mental wounds. I didn't know what time it was, but it had to be early in the morning, three o'clock, maybe four, and Lee and his army were at work for me.

"Hank there?" Vance asked.

My already tense body went rock-solid.

"He's not in the surveillance room, he's in my office. Bobby's getting him now," Lee replied.

I let out a breath.

"Tex?" Vance asked.

"Tex is systematically tearing apart the weight machine in the down room."

I almost smiled at that. Almost.

Vance started speaking, "Roxie's been beaten, but looks okay. She thinks he cracked her ribs. I'm gonna get her checked out. Then we'll head home."

I wrapped my arms around my middle and kept my head against the window. I wanted the conversation to end before Bobby got Hank from Lee's office and he made it to the surveillance room. I didn't know how long I had.

"You get Flynn?" Lee asked, breaking into my thoughts.

"No one was there. She was alone and cuffed to the sink in the bathroom. Signs of a struggle. I didn't ask questions, just got her out." Vance's eyes moved to me. "That struggle yours?"

I shook my head.

"Someone came and took Billy, cuffed me to the sink," I said quietly.

"Hear that?" Vance asked.

"I'll get Ike on it," Lee said.

I closed my eyes again. So much for not dragging Lee and his boys into this.

"Roxie?" Lee called my name. I sat there and didn't answer. I knew this was better than being on my wild ride with Billy, but somehow, right then, it felt worse.

"Roxie," Lee said again, his voice softer.

"Yes?" I replied, responding to his tone and to Vance's coaxing squeeze on my knee.

"Talk to Vance, tell him everything that happened. Everything you can remember. Okay?" Lee ordered, again, soft.

"Okay," I said.

"Vance, I want regular call-ins," Lee went on.

"Roger that," Vance replied.

"Get her home," Lee kept issuing orders.

Disconnect.

I breathed a sigh of relief that I didn't have to deal with Hank.

"I don't want to talk about it," I told Vance after I watched him press a button on the phone.

"You don't have to," he said, not looking at me. "Not now. Nebraska yawns before us. We've got time."

I sat there a second and then whispered, "Thank you."

I meant about him rescuing me, not about him letting me be quiet.

I think he knew what I meant.

X-rays showed I had three cracked ribs. There was nothing they could do but wrap me up, and I thought they did this more for my peace of mind than for my ribs. The cuts on my face would heal, they told me, and didn't need stitches.

They didn't like what they saw and gently asked if I wanted them to call in a police officer.

I said no.

I hadn't decided what I was going to do next. I was getting by, minute-by-minute.

Vance loaded me up and we rolled.

Without asking, he pulled off at an outlet mall.

I could have kissed him, but I didn't. If there was anything a high maintenance girl like me needed after being kidnapped and assaulted, it was an outlet mall.

We went into the Levi's store where he bought me a pair of low-rise jeans that were just this short of being as good as Lucky's, a great belt that was so dark brown, it was nearly black and a dusty pink henley. It wasn't D&G, but it would do in a pinch. Then we went into a Body Gap and I got new underwear. Then we went to Designer Shoe Warehouse and Vance bought me a pair of Keds so I could change out of Manolo Mary Jane's.

Vance pulled off at a hotel, and I would have born his first child if he but asked (though I didn't tell him this), when we checked in and I took a shower, using the hotel's shampoo and body wash.

I came out of the bathroom squeaky clean, but still feeling dirty. I threw my clothes in the trash bin, never wanting to see them again (all but the Manolos, because even being abducted and on the run couldn't taint Manolo Blahnik shoes).

I looked at Vance who was sitting on the bed.

"Ready to roll?" he asked, coming up from the bed, all action even though I suspected he'd had about as much sleep as I'd had these past few days.

That was to say, none.

I suspected that Hank or Uncle Tex sicced him on me the minute Hank found me gone.

"I need you to re-wrap my ribs," I said, holding out the bandages to him.

He came toward me. I lifted my shirt to just under my breasts, beyond embarrassment at this point. I mean, he found me handcuffed to a sink with really bad hair. Embarrassment was a now a luxury.

He re-wrapped me, quickly, expertly, no-nonsense, like he'd done it before a hundred times. When he was done, I nodded to him and said, "Ready." But I didn't move.

He watched me for a few beats then stood in my space and looked down at me. For the first time I noticed his eyes were shuttered and he was holding back from me.

Then he asked, "You need time? Lee wants you home, but if you need time, we'll make time. You can get into bed and let sleep heal."

Shit.

Here I was again, with another good, fucking guy.

I couldn't cope.

I swallowed the threatening tears.

"Home is Chicago," I told him. I decided to focus on that and not tell him that I could likely sleep for a hundred years and not be healed.

He kept looking at me but stayed quiet.

"Will you take me to Chicago?" I asked.

He still kept looking at me.

Then he said, "I want to say yes, but I'm gonna say no."

I closed my eyes and felt his hands on my arms.

"Girl," he said softly. I opened my eyes and looked at him. "If I came home and found what Hank found with my woman bein' gone and the man I sent lookin' for her took her further away, there's no tellin' what I'd do. I'm sorry, it's a guy thing. I respect him and I'm not gonna make him show me what he'll do."

I'd had a good look in the bathroom mirror. The cuts had scabbed over, the blood was gone, but the bruising and swelling on my cheekbone and around my eye were worse than ever. I had more bruises on my throat, arms, ribs, hips and wrists. I was an absolute mess. I was hideous. I felt it like a physical thing, inside and out.

"Look at me, Vance. I can't go back to Hank," I whispered and it sounded like a plea, because it was a plea. Hank was goodness and truth. I was secrets and lies. I had no business with Hank Nightingale.

Vance watched me for a few more beats, came to a decision and nodded. "I can give you that. I'll take you to Tex."

My relief was so great, I couldn't help it. I sagged into him. His arms slid around me and I pressed my good cheek against his chest.

"Thank you," I said.

He didn't respond. We stood there awhile, Vance holding me, until I felt warmer and able to move. The minute my body prepared for action, he felt it and stepped away, took my hand in his and guided me to the car.

⌗

We stopped only for lunch and dinner and to fill up the gas tank. I didn't eat much. Vance noticed and made me stay hydrated by buying me bottles of water and handing them to me every once in a while, making me drink.

I tried to sleep, but it wouldn't come.

So when I was ready, on a long stretch of straight road that was all I'd ever known of Nebraska (until now; now I knew of a sleazy motel, a hospital with nice people working there and an outlet mall), I told Vance my story.

As I talked, the cab felt like it was vibrating with the open anger that was rolling off him.

I just kept talking.

He didn't say anything when I was done. He simply phoned it in to Lee's surveillance room.

⌗

Denver loomed bright in the darkness.

Before I knew it, we were exiting off I-25 onto Speer Boulevard, well into the city, when Vance hit a button on the phone and the ring filled the cab of the SUV.

"Yeah?"

"We're in Denver."

"I see you," the voice said. "You're headin' the wrong way."

"I'm takin' her to Tex," Vance replied.

Silence.

Then the voice said, "Hank wants her."

"She wants to go to her uncle. I'm takin' her there," Vance told the voice.

Another beat of silence, then, "Your call."

Vance hit a button and the phone went dead.

"Are you going to get into trouble?" I asked him.

"No."

"You wouldn't lie?" I asked.

"I would," he replied, and I watched his shit-eating grin spread, his handsome face illuminated by the dashboard light. "But I'm not."

That almost made me smile too. Almost.

He pulled up outside Uncle Tex's house and the front door opened before the Explorer stopped. Uncle Tex came out of the house and into the darkness. The outside light came on and I saw Nancy standing in the doorway.

I opened the cab, got out and Uncle Tex was there.

He looked at me, his face lit by the streetlights, clearly showing a battle between relief and fury. Relief won out and he pulled me into his arms.

"Careful, Tex. She's got three cracked ribs," Vance warned from somewhere close.

Uncle Tex's tight arms loosened.

"I'm okay," I said against his chest.

He didn't answer.

"Uncle Tex. I'm okay," I repeated.

Still no answer.

"She needs rest. I don't think she's slept in days," Vance informed him.

I was kind of getting tired of these men talking about me like I wasn't there. Unfortunately, I was so dog-tired physically I didn't have the mental capacity to call them on it. So instead, my head, still pressed against Uncle Tex's chest, nodded and I pulled a bit away.

"Don't know how to thank you," Uncle Tex said, obviously to Vance.

"We'll talk about that later," Vance replied.

Uncle Tex let me go and looked at Vance. I saw that Vance and Uncle Tex were staring at each other and the air around us had somehow changed.

"You got an idea of what you want?" Uncle Tex asked, not beating about the bush, and I hoped that whatever answer Uncle Tex was looking for was the one that Vance gave.

"Yeah," Vance replied.

"Money?" Tex asked.

Vance's face got tight, and I could tell right off that wasn't the right thing to say.

So could Uncle Tex and he changed tactics.

"Roxie?" Tex guessed, and he wasn't addressing me, he was talking to Vance.

My eyes got wide and I stared at Vance, waiting for his answer.

I might have been tired and just rescued from a kidnapping, and I was certainly thankful to Vance for everything he'd done and he was cute and all (really cute, super cute, actually cute wasn't the word, hot was more the word), but I sure as hell wasn't going to be handed over as a gift of gratitude for saving my hide.

And anyway, if anyone could hand me over, it was me and I was done with men. Totally and completely. I was looking forward to a life as a cat lady. I was going to get a dozen cats and a fucking great vibrator, maybe one of those rabbits I heard about, and that was it.

Vance's voice broke into my lonely, but satisfied, plans for the future.

"I'll get what I want from Lee."

"Money," Tex said decisively and he sounded disappointed.

Vance looked at me. Then he looked at Tex. He was deciding if he should share.

Then, he decided. "I want five minutes in the holding room with Billy Flynn before they turn him over."

I looked between the two men. I didn't know what "the holding room" was, but it didn't take a rocket scientist to figure it out.

Holy cow.

I held my breath.

For the first time, Uncle Tex smiled and whatever was in the air evaporated.

"You'll have to stand in line," Tex told him.

"I think I've earned one of the first cracks," Vance returned.

Holy cow. Holy cow. Holy cow.

"Vance——" I started, but stopped when his eyes locked on me.

He wasn't hiding his reaction again. He looked angry, beyond angry. I realized immediately that he actually *had* been controlling his reaction. *This* was his real reaction and it scared the living daylights out of me.

"A man raises a hand to a woman, he needs a lesson," Vance declared.

I opened my mouth to say something, but there was nothing to say. What he said was downright, bottom line true.

Vance got in my space and put his hands on my shoulders, and whatever I was going to say flew from my brain. He looked down at me and his eyes changed. The anger was still there, but I watched as whatever was fighting for its place was concealed from me.

"Talk to Eddie," he urged, his voice quiet, his expression now under control and hidden. "Press charges. The kidnapping took place in Colorado at a cop's house. Billy Flynn is fucked."

He didn't wait for my response, and my heart stopped when he grabbed my chin, pulled my head to the side and kissed my cheekbone, right where my scabs were. Then he turned, walked around the hood of the Explorer, swung into the driver's seat, and he was gone.

"Let's get her inside." Nancy was there and had her good hand on me. It was stronger than I expected it to be. She turned me toward the house, her face filled with concern.

Uncle Tex's arm came around my shoulders as I saw lights rounding the corner down the block.

I froze.

It was dark, but I could see in the streetlamps it was Hank's 4Runner.

"No," I whispered, panic flying through me.

"Roxie?" Uncle Tex asked. He and Nancy stopped with me.

My eyes flew to Tex. "I can't see Hank."

Uncle Tex glanced at the oncoming car. "Darlin' girl..." Tex started, and I knew he didn't agree with me.

"No! No, I can't see him and... and he can't see *me*. Not like this. Please, please, please," I chanted.

The SUV was close. I had no time. I stopped chanting, shook off Nancy's hand and Uncle Tex's arm, and I ran.

I went into the house, tearing through it, to the room at the back.

I threw the door closed. It was Uncle Tex's bedroom.

I ran to the windows, cats flying everywhere, sensing my panic, and I pulled the drapes. Then I went back through the dark room to the door, feeling the knob for a lock but there was none. I put my back to the door and slid down it, sitting with my shoulders pressed against the door.

I heard the voices, Uncle Tex's a soft boom, Hank's deep voice controlled and patient, Nancy's butting in every once in a while. The boom got louder, and then I could tell, even though I couldn't make out the words, that Hank's control slipped.

I put my hands over my ears, pulled my knees up and rested my forehead on them, but I could still hear the voices. I could feel Hank's impatience and I knew Uncle Tex was trying to protect me.

I started humming.

God, I was so tired. So, fucking, tired.

I couldn't give in to the exhaustion.

I hummed, forcing the voices out of my head, and I planned.

Get my clothes from the hotel.

Get my car.

Go to Chicago.

Go to Annette's.

Get my money, my stuff and escape.

There came a soft knock at the door and I stilled.

"Roxie, honey, it's me. Nancy."

I got up slowly from the door and opened it a crack. She was alone.

The voices were gone.

"Where's Hank?" I asked.

"Lee and Eddie are here, they've got him outside. Let me in, baby doll," she said gently. I opened the door enough so she could slide in and I closed it right behind her.

She switched on a light and then turned to me. "Eddie and Jet went to your hotel today. It's good having a cop in the family." I watched as she smiled a mother's satisfied smile and my heart wrenched at the sight. I'd never seen my Mom smile at Billy and me like that. Never.

Nancy kept talking. "Eddie explained to management and they checked you out. Your car's outside. Jet and Indy brought in your stuff. They're making up the second bedroom right now."

I was leaning against the door, trying to hear what was happening outside, and at the same time trying not to hear.

"We all think you should go home with Hank," Nancy said softly. "Even Tex."

I shook my head, looking at the floor.

"I'm going to sleep for a while, then I'm going to go," I told her.

Nancy got close to me. She leaned against the door with me, more for real support than moral support, I could tell.

She reached out and grabbed my hand. "Where are you going to go?"

"I don't know." I was still looking at the floor. "Away."

"You should know, Hank wanted to look for you. Jet told me. Lee and Eddie talked him out of it. When he got to his house…" she stopped. "Baby doll, look at me."

I looked at her. Her green eyes were kind, and I felt my nostrils start to burn and I sucked in deep breaths to control the tears.

She continued talking. "When he got to his house and you were gone, it wasn't good. Tex knew exactly what had happened and told them about this Billy person. Lee was worried what Hank would do if he caught up with you and Billy was with you. Tex told me that Lee and his boys can do things Eddie and Hank can't do. Still, it took a lot to talk Hank out of coming after you."

I realized that Nancy thought I was upset that Vance had come after me, not Hank.

"It's not that," I told her.

"What is it?" she asked.

I looked at the floor again and swallowed.

She squeezed my hand. "What is it, honey?" she asked, her voice so soft, I could barely hear her.

My nose started burning and so did my eyes. I closed them, hard, and blinked the tears away.

"I'm dirty," I whispered in a voice lower than hers. "He's good and clean and wonderful and he deserves better than me."

"Oh baby doll," she whispered and she moved, sliding across the door, her hand letting go of mine and her arm coming around me. "You gotta know that's just not true."

I stood there and let her hold me as best she could. She was smaller than me and she'd had a stroke, but she was still stronger than me. So was Jet. So was Indy. So was Ally.

Everyone was stronger than me.

Hank needed someone like them. Someone who knew good from bad, was strong enough to stand for the good or turn away from the bad.

And that was not me.

Kristen Ashley

John Mellencamp sang an old adage, "*You gotta stand for something, or you're gonna fall for anything.*"

Mellencamp was right.

Miracle of miracles, I didn't cry, and finally I said, "I have to go to sleep."

She pulled away and looked at me closely. I could tell she didn't like what she saw.

Even so, she sighed and let me be.

"I'll see how Indy and Jet are doing with that bed. You want me to send them in here?"

"No!" I said it louder than I needed to, but I liked these people and spending any more time with them would make it harder to leave. "No. I want to be alone. I haven't been alone in three days."

She nodded, but I could tell she still didn't agree. "I'll knock on the door when the coast is clear."

I took her hand and gave it a squeeze. "Thank you," I whispered.

She reached up, kissed my cheek then slid out the door, not opening it any more than she needed to. I found myself hoping, again, that Uncle Tex and Nancy worked out.

I turned out the lights and resumed my position on the floor, shoulders against the door.

I heard Nancy talking to Indy and Jet, their voices a murmur, and I couldn't hear what they said.

Then there was quiet.

I waited.

A long time passed and there was a knock on the door.

"Roxie?" It was Uncle Tex.

"Yeah?"

"It's just you and me, girl. Everyone's gone."

I didn't answer.

I closed my eyes and rested my forehead on my knees.

It wasn't with relief, it was with heartbreak.

❧

I sat in the dark for a little while longer, and when I felt ready I came out.

Uncle Tex made me eat half of a frozen pizza and made me drink three shots of hooch. The whole time he watched me silently. I could tell he wanted to say something, but he kept his peace.

I left him in front of the huge, old console TV in his living room and went to the second bedroom.

The double bed was made with fresh sheets, an old, mint-green, chenille blanket smoothed over the top. My suitcases were on the floor against the wall. My pajamas had been cleaned and were folded and resting on the pillow.

I fought back the tears (again), changed into my pj's and slid into bed.

I still had my plan, and tomorrow I was going to carry it out.

I didn't know what was happening to Billy and I didn't care. He was dead to me.

I didn't know where Hank was and I tried not to care. He wasn't dead to me, but we were over. This I knew like I knew MAC cosmetics were the best quality for the price by a long shot.

Finally, I slept.

⚜

I woke when the covers moved and it wasn't me that moved them.

For a moment, I thought it was one of Uncle Tex's cats. Then the bed moved in a way that it would have to be the biggest cat in history.

Or a human.

A strong arm slid around me and I was pulled back against a warm, hard body.

I froze then I tried to pull away.

"Don't," Hank said to the back of my head.

Shit.

I stopped pulling away, but my body was tense.

"How'd you get in here?" I whispered.

"Tex let me in."

I closed my eyes.

Betrayed by my own flesh and blood.

"Well, he's certainly not invited to my next birthday party," I stated.

Silence.

"I'm okay, Hank. Really. You can go," I told him, or more like lied to him.

More silence, and he didn't move.

"Actually, I'd rather that you went," I continued. "I'm feeling the need to be alone."

"That's too bad, 'cause I'm not feelin' that same need."

Jeez, he was stubborn.

"If memory serves, I was the one who was just abducted. I'm not sure your feelings count about now," I told him, sounding so uppity I was borderline bitchy.

His body got as tense as mine. I felt it like a warning.

Then his mouth came to my ear. "I feel the wraps," he murmured, his hand running gently along my ribs. "And I know the way Vance found you. I'm sorry you went through that, Sunshine."

I didn't answer and waited. I expected he wasn't done.

I wasn't wrong.

"But I came home from a run the morning after the best date I'd ever had, a date with a girl who talked about pigs wearing toupees, who could quote Springsteen lyrics, who whispered to horses and who grew up in Indiana and was scared of cornfields. I came home thinkin' that I was gonna make love to that girl, shower with her, get her breakfast, get her to trust me and finally, start to get to know her better. Instead, I found my house a disaster, what I could only assume was her blood on the wall in my bedroom and she was gone."

Dear God. How'd my blood get on the wall?

Hank must have been out of his mind. Uncle Tex must have been out of his mind.

I closed my eyes and sucked in a breath.

"Was that your blood?" he asked.

I let out my breath. "Well, I tried, but unfortunately, I was the only one who ended up bleeding."

I should have stayed silent, or, possibly, I shouldn't have been flippant. For one reason or the other, the air in the room changed so much I found it hard to breathe and it had nothing to do with his arm tightening around my ribs.

"Hank, my ribs," I whispered.

Instantly, his arm loosened and his mouth went away from my ear. I waited while he got control. The air changed back to normal and he spoke again.

"I guess I'm sayin' that my feelings do count about now," he finished.

"I'm sorry. I'll pay for any damage or cleaning of your house," I said.

He ignored my totally stupid comment. "You told me you weren't in danger."

Shit.

I had said that.

"I wouldn't have left you alone if I'd known you were in danger," he went on.

Good God, he thought it was his fault.

"It wasn't your fault, Hank. I didn't think I was in danger," I told him.

And it was true, I didn't think I was.

I thought Billy loved me. He was crazy and possessive, not to mention crazy possessive, but I never thought he'd even hit me, much less beat me up and threaten to rape me on another man's bed. I never thought he'd drag me across country, on the run from what had to be bad guys, and put me in even worse danger from them than I had from him.

How lucky was I that they didn't take me with them or shoot me on the spot?

How fucking lucky was I that they left me cuffed to a sink?

I never thought, growing up with dreams of being a corporate goddess with two closets full of clothes and another one dedicated to shoes, that I'd end up like this.

My tense body started shaking.

"Oh shit," I mumbled.

He felt it coming and he turned me. I resisted but he did it anyway.

"Shit," I repeated as it came over me. "Shit, shit, shit."

I was face-to-face with him and both Hank's arms went round me as the tears arrived, great, wracking sobs.

Dammit, I *hated* when I cried. I was so fucking weak. And anyway, crying hurt my ribs.

I put my hands over my face and, pain or not, had no choice but to let loose.

"I'm so s-s-stupid," I stammered between crying hiccoughs, taking my hands away from my face. "Billy scared me, what with the sledgehammer and all, but I was so stupid. I thought I could play games."

"Sledgehammer?" Hank asked but I ignored him.

"I thought I was smarter than him. Uncle Tex said my plan would go south. It's so south, it's in the next fucking galaxy!" I shouted.

"Let's go back to the sledgehammer," Hank suggested.

I pulled away and started to roll out of bed. I was nearly out when Hank tagged the camisole top of my pajamas and pulled me back into bed.

"Let go!" I cried.

"Roxanne, calm down."

I struggled against him. "Hank, let me go!"

Surprisingly, I won the struggle. It didn't occur to me he wasn't going to wrestle with me when I had three cracked ribs. I jumped out of bed and ran to my suitcases, my breathing labored with that minimal effort.

"I have to go, like, now," I announced, even though I was in no shape to go anywhere.

Hank was out of bed and getting in my space.

"Come back to bed," he said.

"No, I have to go."

He was blocking my way every way I turned, and herding me back to the bed.

"Get out of my way!" I shouted.

"Where are you going to go?"

I made a split-second decision, "Mexico!"

"Mexico?"

"My money will go further there. I could start a franchise, like a convenience store or something. I'll be the *gringa* queen of my village."

I was still trying to dodge him when his hands caught my hips and he held tight.

"Don't tell Tex you're gonna buy a franchise, he'll go ballistic," Hank advised.

What he said made me stop and I stared up at him stupidly in the dark.

"What's wrong with franchises?" I asked.

"They're the death of America," Uncle Tex boomed from the next room and both Hank and I froze. "Now, will you two keep it the fuck down? The walls are paper thin and you're disturbin' the cats!"

We both stood stock-still for a moment and then I started laughing. I couldn't help myself. I laughed so hard I thought I'd crack another rib. I started to bend double, but my forehead collided with Hank's collarbone. Still, I didn't stop laughing.

Hank, I noticed vaguely, didn't laugh at all.

His arms went around me and my laughter quickly turned to tears again. I put my arms around him. I didn't want to, but if I didn't, I wouldn't have been able to stay standing.

Finally, when I'd gotten some control, I said quietly, "I thought he loved me."

Hank's body had relaxed when I'd wrapped my arms around him, but at my words it went still again.

"I promise, I didn't think I was in danger," I continued.

He began to stroke my back with one hand, holding me with the other arm. Something had changed in the way he was holding me but I was too worn out to notice it.

"I believe you," he said.

I swallowed because I knew he did and that meant a lot.

"Thank you," I whispered, for like the millionth time that day.

"Do you love him?" Hank asked.

I nodded against his chest and the air changed again, and, again, I was too exhausted to notice.

I didn't mean that I loved Billy *now*. I meant I had loved him, once upon a time when the fairytale could still turn real.

I didn't love him anymore. I didn't hate him either. I just didn't want him anywhere near me. I didn't even want to think about him.

I stood there in Hank's arms and let the tiredness seep through me.

It was like he felt it, he was so tuned into me, and he guided me to the bed.

I didn't resist.

We both got in and he held me again.

I didn't resist that either.

Sleepily, to take my mind off my thoughts, or maybe to teach myself a lesson, I quoted the lyrics to Mellencamp's "Minutes to Memories".

"Mellencamp," Hank muttered.

"Yeah," I whispered. "I should have listened closer."

Hank's head moved, he kissed my neck and then he settled.

I waited until his breathing evened.

Then, when I knew he was asleep, I whispered the part of the song where Mellencamp explains about the wise old man in the song's vision. About how that vision was hard to follow. About how the young man in the song did things his way and paid a high price. About how, years later, he looked back at his conversation with the old man and he knew the old man was right.

And oh man, was he right.

I went silent.

Then, after a while, it hit me and I started to sing, thinking it was a secret, my secret, my song. In another life, a life without the last three days, a life where Hank came home from his run before Billy found me, it could have been Hank's and my song.

Springsteen's words.

I sang so quietly, my voice was barely a whisper and I changed just two of the words.

It was the first verse of Springsteen's "Because the Night".

I hummed the second verse, and in the middle of humming I fell asleep in Hank's arms.

Because I was asleep, I never realized Hank wasn't.

⌘

It felt like I slept for a week.

When I woke up, Hank was gone.

Chapter 10
MP3 Torture

It was daylight when I rolled out of bed. My body protested with aches and pains, letting me know early that they felt like hanging around for a while.

I didn't know where Hank went, but I figured to work because it was nearly noon.

I went to the bathroom and saw that either Indy or Jet had put my toiletry bag on the sink. I crushed down another wave of remorse that these kind people would not be in my life but for a few treasured memories. Then I swept the thought aside, brushed my teeth and washed my face.

I surveyed myself in the mirror. The swelling was gone and the bruises were purple, green and yellow. Not a good color combination and I was doubtful that Calvin Klein would use them in his spring line.

I walked into the living room and saw Uncle Tex on the couch his feet up on the coffee table, a bowl of popcorn resting on his belly and a Bruce Lee movie running quiet on the console TV.

He looked at me when I came in. "Hey darlin' girl. How you feelin' today?"

"Coffee," I replied.

He grinned. "I can do coffee."

I sat in a loud, green, white and yellow daisy-printed, vinyl chair at his kitchen table. He got me a cup of coffee and sat with me

"Hank still sleepin'?" he asked.

"Hank's gone," I replied.

He looked at me funny. "What do you mean, gone?"

"Probably at work."

He stared at me.

"I didn't hear him go," he noted.

I shrugged and looked out the window.

"You mad at me that I let him in?" he asked.

"A little bit," I answered truthfully.

"You wanna talk about it?"

Kristen Ashley

I shook my head.

"You wanna talk about anything?"

I shook my head again.

"All right, girl. I'll give you today. Tomorrow, we're talkin' about it."

"I'm leaving town as soon as I shower and get dressed," I said.

"How's Hank feel about that?"

"I don't know. I don't care," I lied about the second part.

Silence.

I looked from the window back to Uncle Tex. He was staring at me again. It appeared he was finding it hard to keep his peace.

Then he said, "So be it."

I was surprised he gave in so easily. Surprised and relieved, and maybe a little sad. I got up and kissed the top of his head, took my coffee mug and headed to the shower.

o

❧

I stood on the sidewalk, Uncle Tex next to me, my suitcases on the ground either side of him, staring at my car.

"Well, I'll be," Uncle Tex said. "Never seen that before."

I slowly turned my head to look at him. He kept staring at my car.

Then he went on, "Can't say this is the best neighborhood, but *four* slashed tires? That has to be a record."

"Uncle Tex—" I started.

"Welp!" he boomed, bending over to pick up my suitcases. "Guess you aren't leavin' today."

I had a sneaking suspicion my four slashed tires had nothing to do with this being a bad neighborhood.

Uncle Tex walked into the house with my suitcases and didn't look back.

I turned back to my car and stared at it.

After a while, I heaved a huge sigh and I went into the house.

❧

I was sitting on the couch, feet up, watching *Independence Day,* and Will Smith was seriously kicking some alien ass.

124

Uncle Tex had been fielding phone calls for the last hour. Jet called. Indy called. Nancy called. Daisy called. Eddie called. Eddie called again. Eddie called a third time. Every time, Uncle Tex covered the mouthpiece and boomed out a name, making the covering of the mouthpiece action moot.

Every time, I'd get tense, thinking it was Hank. Worried it was Hank. *Wishing* it was Hank. Then, when it wasn't Hank, I'd shake my head and Uncle Tex would make some ludicrously bad excuse for me and hang up.

Another phone rang and I knew it was my cell. Uncle Tex was sitting next to me and he stared at me while I ignored my purse ringing on the floor by the side of the couch. Then he got up, grabbed my purse, rooted through it and pulled out my phone just as it stopped ringing and stuck it out at me.

I shook my head.

"Maybe it was Hank," he said.

Shit.

He knew I was waiting for Hank to call.

I shook my head again.

He flipped open my phone and started pressing buttons. He did this for a long time. Then, my phone started making alarming noises and I couldn't help myself. I yanked it out of his hand.

"Stop that!" I snapped.

"Find out who phoned," he ordered. "Maybe Hank's tryin' to get hold of you."

"He knows your number," I pointed out.

"Maybe he doesn't want to talk to me. Maybe he just wants to talk to you," Tex suggested.

"Well, I don't want to talk to him," I shot back.

Uncle Tex stared down at me and then walked in front of the coffee table, his shins pushing my legs aside, forcing me to sit up. He sat on the coffee table right in front of me, blocking my view of Will Smith and making me worried about the future of the coffee table when his bulk settled on it.

"You're in my way," I told him.

"Look at me, girl."

I tried to look around him at the TV.

"Roxanne Giselle Logan, look at me."

I looked at him. I'd had years of "Roxanne Giselle Logan". I was conditioned to do what I was told after my full name was uttered by an authority figure.

"What?" I clipped, totally uppity.

Okay, so I was conditioned to do what I was told, but I was uppity enough to do it with ill grace.

He leaned forward and his eyes were bright. So bright, they were fevered, and something about them scared me.

I held my breath and waited for what was coming next.

"You're at a crossroads, darlin'. You got two paths to go down," he informed me.

I stared at him and he continued.

"I was at your crossroads once. I chose the wrong path. Once you go down, it's fuckin' impossible to find your way back."

I let out my breath, but only to suck another deep one in and hold it.

His beefy hands settled on my knees and he got closer. "Halfway down my road, a six year old girl wrote me a letter."

Oh shit. Oh shit.

"No," I whispered but the word wasn't audible, only my mouth made the form of the word but without sound. My breath caught with something fierce and I knew, pretty soon, I was going to lose all control.

With effort, I sucked air in my nose, keeping the tears at bay.

"She didn't stop me from losin' my way, but she stopped me from losin' myself."

"Quit talking," I whispered, and I heard the words come out this time, but Uncle Tex ignored them.

"Now, I got a chance to return the favor."

"Please, Uncle Tex, don't."

I felt my nostrils quiver.

He still ignored me.

"This life is made of good turns and bad turns. Few months ago, I did a good turn. I took a bullet for Indy. The last three days, Lee paid me back."

I closed my eyes.

"Look at me, darlin' girl."

I opened my eyes.

"Lee'd put himself in front of a bullet for his brother, make no mistake. Hank was fuckin' beside himself when he came home to find you gone. I thought he'd tear Denver apart lookin' for you. Lee nearly had to lock him in his safe room to keep him from comin' after you."

"Please, stop."

"You had your bad turn, Roxie. Open your fuckin' heart and let Hank be the good."

We stared at each other awhile. Somehow, I didn't cry.

Then, I nodded and opened my phone.

With shaking hands, I went to my received calls, my heart beating, hoping it was Hank.

It wasn't. It was my friend Annette from Chicago.

"Annette," I told Uncle Tex.

His hands left my knees.

"Not Hank?" he asked, openly surprised.

I shook my head.

He got up and sat down beside me.

"He'll call," he said.

I lay on the bed in Uncle Tex's extra bedroom and listened to Joni Mitchell on my MP3 player while I stared at the ceiling.

Independence Day was over. Eddie had called again, and so had Stevie. I didn't talk to either of them.

Hank had not called.

Uncle Tex was down at Kumar's buying stuff to make pigs in a blanket and macaroni and cheese for dinner.

I shut down Joni singing about drinking a case of you because I knew I was just torturing myself. I picked up my cell and called Annette.

Annette had given up web design to open a head shop in Chicago called, appropriately, "Head". She sold bongs, pipes, incense, blankets with Celtic knots and pictures of Jimi Hendrix printed on them, psychedelic posters, tie-dyed t-shirts and hemp clothing. To her surprise, it was a huge success, most likely because she was a nut the caliber of Tex and it made her store fun to hang out in, just like Fortnum's. After she got too busy and couldn't do it anymore, she hired me to run the website. She sold bongs on five continents.

She had curly, ash-blonde hair, milky green eyes and was tall, taller even than me. She was a good friend. She was nice to Billy's face, never letting on that she'd once gotten so angry on my behalf (yes, after my recounting the sledge-hammer incident), she threw a yard glass at a wall, smashing it to smithereens.

"Yo, bitch!" she answered on the second ring. This was nothing to be alarmed about. This was how Annette answered the phone all the time.

"Hey," I said, quietly.

Then I burst into tears. Then I told her my story, *all* of my story.

"Holy fucking Jesus H. Christ," she said when I was done.

"I know."

"He hasn't *called?*"

"Annette!" I cried. "Billy kidnapped me and beat me up. This is not about Hank!"

"Billy's probably been whacked and his worthless, dead body is being eaten by red ants on some sand dune in Utah, goddess willing. Billy's the fucking past, this Hank dude is the future, baby."

I told you Annette was a nut.

"I'm coming home as soon as I get my tires fixed," I said, skirting the issue of Hank.

"When's that gonna be?"

"Uncle Tex has a friend who's picking up the car tomorrow. It can't take that long to change four tires. I figure I'll be on the road tomorrow night. Then I'll pick my stuff up from your place, and if you and Jason can come with me to the loft, just to make sure it's safe, I'll close it up. Then I'm going to Mexico."

"Fuck that shit," Annette said. "Jason and I were going on a long weekend camping in Michigan. We'll make it a longer weekend and bring your shit to Colorado. We'll leave tomorrow. What do you want from the loft?"

"Annette," I said low. "I've made up my mind."

She ignored my warning tone. "Well, I'm un-making it up."

"You can't come out to Colorado. What about Head?"

"I have to beg my staff to leave at the end of the day. I got no problems with Head coasting along. I could join a commune for six months and they wouldn't even know I was gone."

This was true. Annette's staff was like the staff in Nick Hornby's *High Fidelity*. Their whole life was Head. If someone threw a live grenade into Head, they'd fight each other for the opportunity to throw themselves on it. It was scary.

"You aren't talking me out of this," I told her.

"Sure I am. That's what friends do when their friends turn into idiots and make stupid decisions on the fly," she retorted. Then she shouted, "Road trip!" and disconnected before I could say another word.

I flipped my phone shut and stared at the ceiling.

I realized I lived on a small island of sanity while all else around me was bedlam.

I was about to torture myself with "Both Sides Now", or really go for the gusto and switch to Van Morrison's "Into the Mystic" when a knock came at the door.

"Yeah?" I called.

"Dinner's ready," Uncle Tex boomed.

I set aside my MP3, rolled off the bed and headed out of the room.

⊰⊱

It was late.

Uncle Tex and I had eaten our blanketed pigs and macaroni and cheese. Later, we had some cookies-and-cream ice cream. Even later, after-dinner drinks of Uncle Tex's moonshine.

We finished watching Letterman. I got up from the couch and announced, "I'm going to bed."

I looked down at Uncle Tex. He had the phone (a rotary phone, by the way, its cord strung across the living room) sitting on his lap and he was glaring at it so hard I thought laser beams were going to shoot from his eyes and burn it to cinders.

"'Night," I said when he didn't answer.

He looked up at me. "He's gonna call."

I smiled at him. Even I knew it was a sad smile.

I'd had a short conversation with Nancy, but I figured she'd soon be family, so she'd be safe. Eddie had called again, so had Indy. I didn't talk to either of them.

Hank had not called.

I knew what it meant. I'd known it even before I went on my date with him.

It was dark in my room. He couldn't see me last night, battered face, bruised body, but he knew. He could smell it on me. He dealt with people like Billy every day. I was Billy's girl, even if it was once upon a time.

Hank didn't want that stink in his bed.

I bent down and kissed the top of Uncle Tex's head again.

"He's gonna fuckin' call," Uncle Tex growled.

I touched his shoulder and walked away.

I got into the bed and lay there for a while.

Then I got out my MP3 player and found the song.

I listened to "Because the Night" from Springsteen's Live 1975/85 box set.

Then I listened to it again.

On the third time around, I started crying. Not huge wracking sobs. Even with the paper-thin walls, Uncle Tex would never hear me.

Then I shut off my player, wiped my face on my pillow and went to sleep.

Chapter 11

Pretend World of Bubble Gum Goodness

I rolled out of bed feeling better than I had the day before. The aches and pains were subsiding.

The mirror in the bathroom showed me another gruesome concoction of bruising colors on my face, but at least they were fading. The marks around my neck, arms and wrists were still visible, but not nearly as angry.

I wandered into the kitchen, poured myself a cup of coffee and saw Uncle Tex's note saying that he'd gone to work and would be home around one.

I was wandering back to my bedroom, having visions of a morning spent performing more musical self-torture, when I glanced sideways out the picture window in Uncle Tex's living room.

I stopped dead at what I saw, coffee cup arrested halfway to my lips.

A huge truck was stopped in the middle the street, and hovering in the sky, dangling from what looked like a crane, was my car in straps.

Regardless of the fact that I was wearing nothing but a pair of pajamas (strawberry colored bottoms with cute powder blue and turquoise retro stars printed on them and a strawberry camisole with turquoise lace), I threw open the door and ran, barefoot, to the sidewalk.

"Hey!" I shouted at a big, black guy in dirty blue coveralls who was at the truck's levers. "That's my car!"

"Taking it in to change the tires," he replied, not stopping from his maneuvering of my car, which was floating precariously in the air over the flatbed truck.

"Can't you change the tires here?" I yelled over the noise.

"Tex wants me to do it in the shop. Told me to give it a tune up and detail while I got it."

I was going to *kill* Uncle Tex.

Kristen Ashley

"It doesn't need a tune up. I had it serviced before I drove out here," I informed him.

He shrugged.

I scowled at him.

He ignored me.

I saw a car approaching and turned to watch as Hank's 4Runner rolled up the street.

I forgot about my no-longer-earthbound car and stood frozen watching Hank park.

Shit.

Shit, shit, shit, shit, shit.

Hank got out, his eyes on my car in midair, and walked to me.

He looked good.

He wore jeans, boots and a wine-colored henley. There was a gun and badge attached to his belt. All that was missing was the white hat.

He stopped next to me, eyes still on my car.

"What's goin' on?" he asked, not looking at me.

I realized, belatedly, that it was warm as a summer's day outside. Still, I was standing on the sidewalk in my pajamas and I hadn't done anything with my hair.

Shit.

"That's my car," I shared.

Hank looked down at me and I just caught myself from holding my breath.

"What happened?" he asked.

"Uncle Tex slashed my tires."

Hank stared at me.

"He didn't want me to leave," I explained.

Hank stared at me another beat then his eyes moved on my face; then to my throat, my arms and my wrists, taking in the bruises. I almost bit my lip, but forced myself to stay still under his scrutiny. Then his eyes moved to mine.

"We have to talk," he said.

Damn tootin', we had to talk.

He turned and walked to the porch. I followed him.

He stopped at the porch, not attempting to go inside. I found this odd but I stopped with him.

"You want coffee?" I asked.

132

"I'm not stayin' that long."

I blinked at him, confused.

Then it hit me.

His eyes were all wrong. They weren't sexy-lazy or alert. They were distant and disinterested.

I felt my breath start to come faster, like I'd run a race before I'd run the race. And the fact was I wanted to run, run as fast as I could, as far away as I could get.

"What's up?" I tried to act like I didn't feel like I wanted to curl up and die.

"You've been dodgin' Eddie," he said.

I blinked, confused again, but he went on.

"You can't protect Flynn, Roxanne. I've already filed. He broke into my house and trashed it."

"Protect?" I said, unable to form a full sentence.

"Eddie's comin' by this morning to take you to the station so you can give your statement, file charges if you want, or not. Your choice. But even if you go home, I'm still following through. And since we found out Flynn is wanted in Boston, Pensacola and Charleston, once we find him and deal with him here, he's gonna be a busy guy."

I couldn't speak.

I wasn't surprised that Billy was wanted in three different cities, four counting Denver, even though it was news to me.

No, the reason I couldn't speak was because Hank thought I was protecting Billy.

"Hank—"

He interrupted me, "I found your scarf at my house. Indy's got it."

Automatically (and inanely) I said, "It's Tod's."

"Indy has it," he repeated, looking away. He watched the crane settle back into position, my car in the flatbed. Then he looked at me, eyes blank, like Eddie's were the first time he saw me. "Gotta get back to work," he said. "Take care of yourself."

At his dismissing words, I moved suddenly. It was involuntary but I jerked back, just at the middle, like he punched me in the stomach.

Immediately, his hand came out to grab my arm and his brows drew together.

"Are you okay?" he asked.

I stared at him then nodded my head. "Fine," I lied.

He watched me a beat, then two. It was my time to say something but I couldn't think of what to say.

"Talk to Eddie," he said.

I just stared at him and didn't say a word.

I watched as his eyes grew hard and he let go of my arm. "Suit yourself."

Then he walked away.

I watched him go, watched the flatbed truck go and watched the street for a good long while before I turned and walked into the house.

I set my cup on the coffee table and stood in the living room.

Petunia, the ginger and white cat, rubbed my legs. I sat down on the floor, the better position to pet her.

Then I curled up on the floor, on my side, my knees to my chest. Petunia walked on top of me and sat on my hip. Perched there, she cleaned her foot.

This is how Eddie found me when he opened the door.

"Jesus," he muttered.

I rolled to my back and Petunia scampered.

I stayed flat on the floor and looked up at Eddie.

"Hi," I greeted him.

"You okay?"

No, I was not okay. I was anything but okay. I was so far away from okay that okay was in another dimension.

"Peachy," I said.

"Why are you lyin' on the floor?" he asked.

Because the best guy I'd ever met thought I was some stupid, idiot woman who would protect an outlaw even after he'd beaten me and kidnapped me and dragged me through three states. Because that same guy was about goodness and justice and wanted nothing to do with a woman like me. Because that fact broke my heart and pissed me off and I wasn't sure which one I felt more. I thought.

"I felt like having a rest," I answered.

Eddie took a second to process this then he asked, "Did you talk to Hank?"

I nodded my head.

"I'm here to take you down to the station to file charges against Flynn."

"Okeydoke," I replied, rolled over and carefully got up, holding my ribs.

When I was up and looked at him, he was staring at me with undisguised surprise.

"Sorry?" he asked.

"I said 'okeydoke'. Can you hang on while I get ready?"

He kept staring at me, then, slowly, he nodded.

"It takes a while for me to get ready. Maybe you want to come back."

His eyes went guarded. "I'll wait."

"That's cool. Coffee's in the kitchen," I told him and then went to the shower.

I'd never pressed charges against anyone. I'd never even been to a police station except on a fieldtrip in sixth grade. I wasn't sure what the dress code was.

I took a shower. I blow dried then parted my hair deep on the side and smoothed it into a severe ponytail secured at the nape of my neck. I caked on the makeup to try and hide the bruising (this, for your information, didn't work). I wore a skintight, camel-colored, pencil skirt that came down to just below the knee and had a slit up the back, topped with a red jersey t-shirt and on my feet, sexy, red, spike-heeled sling backs. Finally, I tied a jaunty scarf around my neck.

I looked like Faye Dunaway's Bonnie in *Bonnie and Clyde*, but without the beret or shotgun and with a little more flair for color.

I walked out and Eddie was on the sofa, drinking coffee and watching a ballgame.

"Ready," I announced and went to the TV. "You want me to turn this off?"

Uncle Tex's TV had to be thirty years old. It had no remote. It was likely considered a priceless antique in some circles. It definitely belonged in a museum.

I turned and looked at Eddie. He was giving me the once-over.

"Eddie?" I called when he didn't answer.

His eyes had kind of glazed over, but he came to and looked at me.

"Let's roll," he said.

I almost didn't get up into his fancy, red truck because my skirt was so tight, but I made it.

We drove to the station in complete silence.

He parked and I twisted gingerly to undo my seatbelt. He stopped me from twisting back around to get out when he put a hand on my arm.

"You should know somethin' about what's happenin' with your boyfriend," he said, looking me in the eyes.

I blinked at him.

"Boyfriend?" I asked.

"Flynn," he replied.

My back went up. "That would be my *ex*-boyfriend," I informed him.

He stared at me, then ignored what I said and went on, "You repeat any of this in the station, I'll deny it."

It was my turn to stare at him.

He continued, "Lee's got one of his boys lookin' for him. Not only that, he's put a bounty on Flynn so not only is Ike lookin' for him, *and* the cops, but also every bounty hunter in about eight states. Lee'll probably get him before we do. Hank has given Lee orders and Tex has agreed." He paused and watched me. "Do you understand what I'm saying to you?"

I didn't so I shook my head.

"Flynn's going to the holding room before he's turned over to the police. Vance has called dibs. Vance gets first crack after Tex has his shot. Hank's bowed out but you know that by now," Eddie explained.

Oh, I knew that last bit, for certain. Hank had been pretty clear that morning.

I also understood what Eddie was telling me. Billy was going to this "holding room" and they were going to beat the shit out of him. I felt badly for Billy, but I figured what comes around, goes around.

"Do you understand now?" Eddie asked.

I nodded my head.

"You got anything to say about that, say it now, to me. I won't like it but I'll put in your word. Right now, it's up to Tex and Vance to take into consideration what you have to say."

"What do you mean?" I asked.

"I'll talk to Lee about havin' Flynn taken directly to the cops, no holding room. You should know, I doubt he'll listen. It wasn't easy for him to watch his brother, or Tex, go through that."

Well, poor Lee, I thought.

It wasn't a nice thought, but then again, I wasn't having one of my better days. In fact, I wasn't having one of my better weeks.

"Let me get this straight," I started. "You think I'm going to ask you to protect Billy?"

"That's right," he replied.

I turned fully to him. It kind of hurt my ribs, but I did it all the same. I wanted to have his full attention.

"First off, he tried to strangle me. Then he took a switchblade to the sweater I was wearing. Then he hit me. Then he dragged me through Hank's house."

Eddie's eyes had been guarded, but the guard slipped at my words.

I ignored it and carried on, "Then he kicked me in the fucking ribs, threatened to rape me on Hank's bed and kidnapped me, bound my wrists, drove like a fucking crazy man for two days, tied me to the steering wheel any time he left the car and made me go to the bathroom with my hands tied while he watched."

Eddie's guard was gone. Now, his eyes were glittering.

"That's just plain rude," I told him. "I won't even get into the two bad guys with guns or sitting on a stinking bathroom floor handcuffed to a fucking sink, not to mention the fact that I didn't get a shower in three days. I threw away my cutest pair of Lucky jeans because of that guy!"

My voice was getting louder. It was filling the cab, and I didn't care.

I threw up my hands and looked at the ceiling of the truck. "I mean, jeez! I broke up with him, like, I don't know, *years* ago! A woman locks you out with your suitcases in the hall, get a fucking *clue!*"

Okay, now I was shouting.

"Roxanne—" Eddie said.

I ignored him. "Then, Uncle Tex is back here, all freaked out and Hank... whatever. And Lee's boys are running all over the fucking Bible Belt," I stopped and looked at him. "Are Nebraska and Kansas in the Bible Belt?" I asked but I didn't wait for an answer. "Anyway, doesn't matter. I don't know what this holding room is, but I don't care. Do whatever. Billy's a memory. I just don't want to know."

Then I turned, opened my door and jumped out of the truck.

It would have been a great exit, except I kind of wobbled on my heel a little bit when I landed.

I started walking without waiting for Eddie, but he caught up to me.

Kristen Ashley

"Hang on there, *chica*," he said, grabbing me by the waistband of my skirt. It was quite a catch since my skirt was so tight. He must have had a lot of practice doing that.

I stopped and glared at him. "What?"

He looked down at me, his eyes still kind of glittery, and I could tell he was making up his mind about something.

Finally he said, "I think I need to have a chat with Hank."

"Don't do me any favors," I snapped. "Hank's a memory too. I'm going to file charges, get my car and blow this crazy burg. Denver is Looney Tunes Town. I don't care if it's October and feels like July and I can see the mountains every day. This place is nuts and since I'm half MacMillan, coming from me, that's saying something."

Once I finished, I pulled away and stomped into the station.

My Mom would have been proud.

The room was filled with desks, chairs, couches and people. Most of the people stared at me openly when I arrived. I ignored this, straightened my shoulders and followed Eddie to a desk. All around me was a hive of activity; people walking around, talking, phones ringing, doors opening and closing.

Eddie sat me next to a desk so I could talk to a nice, older man named Detective Jimmy Marker.

I told my story while Eddie stood beside us, watching and listening.

Every once in a while I'd look at Eddie. Sometimes I scowled at him. Sometimes I'd raise my brows in the silent question of, "Don't you have anything better to do?" After about the third eyebrow raise, he smiled at me like I was funny.

Fucking crazy, Denver men.

Around about the end of when Detective Marker was taking my statement, I felt Eddie tense.

I scowled up at him, but he wasn't looking at me. He was looking toward the door.

I followed his gaze and stopped breathing.

Hank, Lee and Vance were standing in the door, all of them looking at me.

138

Hank's eyes were blank. Lee's were the same.

Vance grinned at me.

With a superhuman effort, I ignored Hank and Lee and grinned back at Vance.

"Excuse me," Eddie murmured and walked away.

I turned to Detective Marker. "Do you have everything you need?" I asked.

"Yep," he said, but he was looking at Hank too, and for some bizarre reason, he was smiling. Smiling huge, like he found something supremely hilarious.

I was so totally right about Denver being a loony bin. Everyone was crazy.

"You have my card?" Detective Marker asked after he'd looked back at me.

I nodded. "I may be on the road. You'll have to call my cell if you need anything else."

"You'll come back to testify?" he asked.

I gave him a look.

"You'll come back to testify," he muttered.

I got up, shook his hand, hooked my purse over my shoulder and walked across the room.

Everyone in the room watched.

Hank, Lee, Eddie and Vance were in a huddle. Vance broke off and walked over to me. The other three turned to look.

"Hey, girl," Vance said when he arrived in my space, seriously in my space.

I didn't back away.

"Hey. I need a ride back to Tex's. Can you take me?" I asked him.

"First, I'll take you to lunch."

I didn't want lunch. I hadn't had breakfast or even any coffee, but my stomach was clenched tight knowing Hank's eyes were on me. I was torn between throwing myself at his feet and begging him to understand, and jumping on him and scratching his eyes out.

Instead, I kept my eyes on Vance and said, "Sounds good."

Vance turned to The Huddle.

"Keys," he called to Lee.

Lee threw him a set of keys and Vance caught them. I avoided Hank's gaze. Vance grabbed my hand and we walked out.

I was concentrating so hard on not tripping or doing anything else idiotic that I didn't realize the pulse of the room had changed when Vance grabbed my hand.

I also didn't catch the look on Hank's face when he saw Vance take my hand, which was good because if I had, I would have tripped for sure.

⁂

Vance took me to Lincoln's Road House, a motorcycle bar skirting an off-road on I-25.

He settled me at a high barstool at a table. I glanced around, thinking that perhaps I should have changed my outfit. Denver was definitely a jeans town, and at Lincoln's Road House jeans were practically required.

I noted that optional were black leather chaps.

Vance bought me a beer and a pop for himself. He got some menus and sat across from me.

"How're you doin'?" he asked, watching me closely.

"My life's a total shambles, my body still aches and I'm pretty certain I'm going to have a scar on my face to remind me daily of this precious time in my life," I told him. "How're things with you?"

"Better than you."

"Vance, honey, that isn't saying much."

He smiled.

I crossed my legs, looked at my menu, and noticed Vance move out of the corner of my eye. I glanced at him, but he was looking over my shoulder. I turned around and saw Mace enter the bar from the back.

Mace did a chin lift to Vance, got himself a beer and then came over and sat beside me.

He gave me a once over and remarked, "Nice outfit."

"Thanks," I replied.

"I thought you were on a stakeout," Vance said to Mace.

"Matt relieved me. I hate stakeouts. Fucking boring," Mace returned. "Any word from Ike?"

Both Vance and Mace's eyes slid to me.

I was taking a pull from my beer and I waved my free hand at them. I set the beer on the table and said, "I know about the holding room and the planned ass-kicking. I'm all right with it."

Mace looked at Vance. "I think I like her."

"Take a number," Vance replied.

Good God.

"Is anyone going to feed me?" I blurted to stop them talking about liking me.

Vance did his shit-eating grin then we ordered.

My purse rang so I opened it and grabbed my phone. It said, "Annette Calling". I flipped it open.

"Hey," I said.

"Hey," she said back.

Oh no.

Annette didn't give her normal greeting. This meant something was wrong.

I got tense. Since I got tense, I felt both Mace and Vance get tense.

"What's wrong?" I asked her.

"Well, Jason and I are on our way out there. We're in bumfuck Iowa, goddess almighty. Iowa."

She stopped, as if there were no words for Iowa, so I prompted, "And?"

"Well, we went by your place and it was kind of trashed."

I got even tenser. Vance and Mace were watching me.

"Trashed?" I asked.

"Yeah. Your laptop was there and it didn't look like anything was missing, but a lot of stuff was broken. Your furniture was slashed. I'm no expert, but it looked like someone was looking for something. I got most of your clothes and some other stuff I thought you might want."

I closed my eyes, put my elbow on the table and head in my hand. "Thanks, Nettie."

"We're gonna see if we can power through. We'll get a hotel or something when we get there. I'll call you tomorrow."

"Okay. Be careful and… thanks."

"Later." Then she disconnected and I flipped the phone shut.

Vance and Mace were still watching me.

"Trashed?" Vance asked.

Kristen Ashley

"My loft. A friend went by to pick up some of my stuff. She said it looked like someone was looking for something. She said nothing was missing that she could tell. She even got my laptop so they couldn't have been there to rob me," I told him.

Vance looked at Mace.

Mace peeled off mumbling, "Gotta make a call."

I ignored Mace and asked Vance, "Should I be worried?"

He stared at me.

"I should be worried," I said.

His hand came out and grabbed mine. "It was probably the people after Flynn. They already proved they have no interest in you. You likely have nothin' to worry about."

I nodded but I didn't much appreciate him using the word "likely".

Then I saw Vance looking over my shoulder again. He let go of my hand, but dropped his head and smiled at the table when my phone rang again.

It said, "Indy Calling".

I took a deep breath and answered it.

"Where the fuck are you? I called home a fuckin' million times," Uncle Tex boomed.

"Sorry, Uncle Tex, I should have called you. I went with Eddie to the station to press charges against Billy. Now, I'm having lunch at Lincoln's Road House with Vance and Mace."

I felt the hairs rise on my neck and turned. That was when I saw Mace standing in the back doorway talking with Lee, Eddie and fucking Hank.

"Fuck," I said, turning around.

Vance was smiling at me.

"There's nothing to smile about!" I hissed at Vance.

Vance's smile went wide.

"What the fuck are you talkin' about?" Uncle Tex boomed in my ear.

"Nothing," I answered, the hair raise going to goose bumps as I felt Hank's eyes on my back. "Where are you?"

"At Fortnum's. Spent all day listenin' to fuckin' Indy, Ally and Jet goin' on 'bout how you're still hung up on that stupid, weasely motherfucker that kidnapped you. Told 'em they were all fuckin' nuts," he said. Then he asked, "You aren't, are you?"

I blinked at the table just as the waitress came and set down our food.

142

"What are you talking about?" I asked.

"Apparently, Hank told Lee and Lee told Indy and Indy told every-fuck-in'-body that you're still in love with that fuckin' asshole."

My body went completely still. Then, slowly, I turned around and looked at Hank.

Or, to put it more truthfully, scowled at him, eyes narrowed and everything.

Hank caught my scowl and raised his brows.

My eyes narrowed to slits.

Then I turned back to the table.

"No... I... am... not... in ... love ... with ... Billy... fucking... Flynn," I enunciated every word.

After I finished, Vance actually threw his head back and laughed. I scowled at him too.

"Didn't think so," Uncle Tex muttered.

"Get my car back, Uncle Tex. I'm leaving the minute I get home," I demanded.

"No, darlin'. You gotta straighten things out with Hank."

"Not a fucking chance."

Tex was silent.

"You sure?" he finally asked.

"Very sure," I replied.

More silence.

Then he enquired, "How're you feelin' about Vance?"

Lord have mercy.

"Good-bye," I replied.

Before I could hang up, he said on a rush, "You stay the night, we'll call your Mom."

My breath caught in my throat.

"We?" I asked.

Mace sat down next to me, threw Vance a look and then started eating.

Uncle Tex said in my ear, "Yeah, you 'n' me."

"You'll talk to her?" I asked low.

He paused. Then he said, "Yeah."

Instantly, I agreed. "I'll stay the night."

I felt like doing cartwheels, but Uncle Tex had moved on. "Have fun with the boys. You're cookin' dinner tonight."

"Fine by me. We'll celebrate. I'll make something fancy."

"Sounds good. I'm feelin' like fat, juicy pork chops with that rice with the vermicelli stuff in it, like on TV. The San Francisco treat."

I watched Vance eat a fry, stuck in a moment of stupefied silence.

Once I tugged myself out of my silence, I asked, "The San Francisco Treat?"

"Yeah," Uncle Tex said. "I'll go to the store."

"I was thinking something fancier, like, beef wellington. That's everyday food, not food you eat after talking to the sister you haven't spoken to in decades."

"Fuck that. Next thing you'll want champagne instead of hooch. I'll go to the store. You get home in time to cook. And since you're with Vance, give him a good look-over. If you don't like what you see, have a look at Mace. I don't know Mace all that well, but he seems a good sort."

"You *are* joking, right?" I asked my uncle.

"Fuck no. Those boys are the shit," he answered. "Hank would have been my choice, but he fucked it up. Matt and Bobby are taken. Ike's on the road and he's a scary motherfucker. You don't like Mace or Vance, I'll introduce you to Luke. Lee says Luke's a serious badass, but he's been recoverin' from a gunshot wound so I haven't seen him in action. Still, I heard Indy sayin' she thinks he's cute. You'll just have to go easy on him for a while."

Good God.

Uncle Tex, the matchmaker.

"You're nuts," I said.

"That's what they tell me." Then he disconnected.

I flipped my phone shut and stared at it for a second. Then I curled my fist around it, threw my hands up in a "Goal!" gesture and shouted, really loud, "Woo hoo!"

Everyone turned to stare, everyone including Lee, Eddie and Hank, who were now standing at the bar.

Whatever.

Nothing could pierce this piece of happiness. Not even Hank.

I grinned at Vance.

"Seems your luck just changed," Vance commented.

"Dude, Uncle Tex is gonna talk to my Mom tonight. First time they'll have talked since he got back from Vietnam."

Vance's eyes flashed then they warmed. Then, he reached out and traced the curve of my ear.

"Good news," he murmured.

"You better believe it," I agreed.

I heard the loud thud of a beer bottle hitting a counter. I turned in time to see Hank's back as he left.

I looked to where Eddie and Lee stood at the bar.

Eddie was smiling at me. Lee was glowering.

I turned my back on them, trying to pretend none of this affected me.

Which it did, like, a lot.

But I'd decided, just then, with the happy news that Uncle Tex was going to call my Mom, that I was going to live in a pretend world of bubble gum goodness.

At least until I drove over the Colorado border, then it was Joni Mitchell and Van Morrison all the way through Nebraska.

Chapter 12
Hank and My Wild Ride

"Hi Mom," I said.

Uncle Tex was sitting across from me at his dining room table, his leg bouncing, his hands running up and down his thighs, his eyes wild.

We'd had our pork chops and rice and Tex had had three shots of hooch and two beers. I thought he was primed, but he looked like he was going to spontaneously combust.

"Hey there, honey. What's up with you?" Mom said in my ear.

I smiled reassuringly at Tex.

"I have two pieces of really good news," I told her.

"Yeah? I can always use good news."

"Well…" I drew it out, "Billy and I are done. He's gone. Really gone this time."

My Mom was silent.

Then she breathed, "Oh sweet Jesus." Then, she took the phone away from her mouth and I heard her shout, "Herb! Herb, come here! Roxie's broken up with Billy. Oh sweet Jesus. The sweet Lord Jesus heard my prayers."

Mom carried on like this for a while.

I waited patiently, mainly because I was accustomed to this behavior from Mom. Mom went to church on Sundays and she was a Christian for sure, but she only invoked the sweet Lord Jesus on special occasions (of which there were many) that demanded a bit of a flair for drama.

Such as this one.

The phone was jostled and my Dad was there. "Roxie?"

"Hi Dad."

"Is it true? Did you finally get rid of that sum 'a bitch?"

"Yeah."

I wasn't going to tell them about my wild ride with Billy. I needed to pick a good time for that, like after they'd had three shots of Uncle Tex's hooch. Anyway, I didn't want anything to color the upcoming semi-family reunion.

"Thank fuckin' God. I always hated that bastard," Dad said.

My Dad wasn't one to hold anything back.

"I know. You didn't really keep that a secret," I told him.

"So did your brother," he went on.

"I know."

"And your sister."

"I *know*," I stressed.

"And your mother."

I rolled my eyes to the ceiling. "Jeez, Dad, I *know*."

"And Mrs. Montgomery from down the street. The minute she laid eyes on him, she told me he was a bad seed."

Good grief.

Billy was, of course, a bad seed, but Mrs. Montgomery thought everyone was a bad seed. She even said Holly Newbury was a bad seed, and Holly was Sister Holly now and taught at St. Malachy Elementary School.

"Dad," I said warningly.

"This is good news, Roxie. Good news."

I decided to change the subject, mainly because Uncle Tex looked about to burst, and if I didn't get this show on the road, who knew what would happen?

"Is Mom still there?" I asked.

"Yeah. You wanna talk to her?"

"Dad, listen, is she sitting down?"

Silence then, "No."

"Well, get her to sit down. Dad, I'm in Denver."

Silence again.

I went on, "I'm sitting across from Uncle Tex right now. He wants to talk to her."

There was a hesitation, then I heard his hand go over the mouthpiece, but I still could make out the words. "Trish, you need to sit down."

"What?" my mom asked in the background, and I could hear the Mom edge of "What Has Roxanne Done Now?" in her tone.

"Roxie's in Denver, with Tex," Dad told her.

I heard a short, but loud, scream.

"He wants to talk to you," Dad continued when Mom finished screaming.

"Sweet Jesus. Sweet Jesus," Mom chanted.

I smiled at Uncle Tex.

Tex abruptly stood up, ready to escape. I stood too, prepared for this, and carrying the phone with me, I blocked his way. His eyes were wilder than ever.

"Uncle Tex, take a deep breath," I advised.

"I'm handing the phone over to your mother," Dad said in my ear. "You ready?"

"Yeah," I told him and looked at Uncle Tex. "You ready?" I asked.

He shook his head.

"Tex?" Mom said hesitantly in my ear.

"Hi Mom, it's still me. Hang on, here's Uncle Tex."

Tex was taking in deep breaths then pursing his lips and blowing them out in quick bursts like he was a woman in labor practicing Lamaze. I handed the phone receiver to him and he stared at it like it was a living thing. Then he took one more deep breath, snatched the receiver from my hand and put it to his ear. I set the phone on the dining room table.

"Trish?" Tex said in a soft boom.

I felt a melting warmth spread in my belly. I got up close, rested my forehead against my uncle's big, barrel chest and wrapped my arms around his middle. He may not have needed me to hold him, but I needed it, I needed it badly.

"Yeah, it's me. How's things?" Tex asked.

I heard my Mom talking to Tex. Her voice sounded high and I couldn't make out what she said. After she talked for a while, I felt Tex's body relax and he put his hand on the back of my neck.

"Me and Roxie just had chops and rice. We been spendin' a few days gettin' to know each other. She's a good kid, Trish. You done good with her. How's Herb?"

Mom talked again and I heard a knock at the door. I pulled away, got on tiptoe, gave Uncle Tex's fuzzy cheek a kiss and walked to the door.

I still had a smile on my face when I opened the door.

The smile faded and my mouth dropped open at what I saw.

Hank was standing there, still wearing his jeans, boots and wine-colored henley but now he was also wearing his black leather jacket.

"What are you doing here?" I asked but he didn't answer.

He walked in and I jumped out of his way because if I didn't he would have walked right into me.

Hank looked around the room, searching for something.

Uncle Tex stood holding the phone receiver to his ear, eyes on Hank.

Then Hank grabbed my purse off the coffee table, came back to me, took my hand and dragged me out the door, slamming it behind us.

Through the slam, I could hear Uncle Tex's booming laughter.

Holy cow.

What *on earth* was going on?

"Hank!" I yelled, trying to pull my hand from his, but he was dragging me along the sidewalk toward his 4Runner.

"Hank! Stop! What's going on?"

He took me to the driver's side, opened it, bent, picked me up and I let out a cry.

It was like I didn't make a noise. Hank put me on the seat and then entered behind me so I had to scoot over to the passenger side, double time. Before I could do a thing, even buckle my safety belt, Hank threw my purse in my lap, started the car and took off.

"Take me back to Tex's," I demanded. He ignored me so I carried on. "What are you doing? Take me back to Tex's!"

He still didn't say anything.

"We'll just see about this," I snapped, opened my purse and dragged out my phone. Who I was going to call, I did not know, but I was going to call someone.

I barely got the cell out when Hank plucked it out of my hand and tossed it on the dash, *his* side of the dash, far away from me.

I stared at it. Then I stared at him.

"Well!" I huffed because I couldn't think of anything else to say. My heart was hammering in my chest and my mind was in a tizzy.

Then I figured out what to say.

"This is crazy. You're crazy. Denver's crazy. All you boys skipped right over the last century, didn't you? I think even the last million years! You're cavemen," I rattled on. "I do not *believe* you just dragged me out of Uncle Tex's house. He was talking to my Mom!"

"Quiet," Hank finally spoke.

"Fuck quiet. God! Why didn't I get in my car and get the hell out of here when I had the chance?"

"That's a good question," was Hank's answer.

That shut me up because I seriously didn't want to go there.

I buckled my seat belt, crossed my arms on my chest and tried to devise a plan.

I was still in my skintight skirt and heels. I couldn't run. I still had three cracked ribs. I couldn't fight. I didn't want to fight Hank anyway. Hell, I didn't want to run either.

What was I saying? I thought.

Then I forced myself to stop thinking altogether.

Before I knew it, he parked in front of his house. I sat in his 4Runner, arms still crossed, not moving as he walked around the hood of the car.

He opened the passenger side door, leaned in, unbuckled me and pulled me out. He dragged me up his front walk.

"I want to go back to Uncle Tex's," I told him.

"You're not goin' back to Tex," he replied in his authoritative voice and opened the door.

Before I could say anything else, Shamus was there and leaping all over Hank and me as Hank pulled me inside.

"Hi fella. Hey there, boy," I cooed, bending to give him a quick scratch behind the ears. I was pissed-off at Hank for abducting me, but I saw no reason to take it out on Shamus.

It was a *very* quick scratch because Hank closed the door behind us, locked it, grabbed my hand again and then carried on dragging me, straight to the bedroom.

That was when I started fighting, pulling at my hand in his. "Hey! Where are you going? Let go of me!"

He didn't stop.

"Hank, goddammit!"

He finally stopped once we'd reached the bedroom. He also let me go. He switched on the light by the bed and I turned to run, but he caught me by the waist, somehow doing this gently, and pulled me around so I was pinned between him and the bed.

Then he shrugged off his jacket and tugged off his henley.

My eyes bugged out and I stared at his bared chest.

Good God.

"What are you—" I started to say but he interrupted me.

"In deference to your ribs, you can be on top this time."

My mouth dropped open.

Kristen Ashley

Then my eyes went back in my head and they narrowed on him.

"I don't *think* so," I snapped.

He caught me at the hips, pulled me to him and kissed me.

I did resist. I'm not *that* weak. It's just that my resistance didn't last long.

When his mouth left mine to trail down my cheek to my neck I said, "You're a jerk."

He moved away a bit, pulled my t-shirt free of my skirt, yanking it over my head, and dropping it on the floor.

Then he looked into my eyes.

My hammering heart thundered in a swell and then stuttered to a halt when I saw the look in his eyes. They were not distant or disinterested. They were something else, something I'd never seen on him, or anyone, before.

"Yeah," he agreed, and his voice echoed the look in his eye. "I am."

Then he kissed me again.

Needless to say, it went wild after that. What could I say? This was Hank.

We were all over each other, hands, mouths, tongues. He pulled my skirt up, bunching it at my waist, turned us both around and sat down on the bed, his arms around me, taking me with him. He fell back, rolled me over carefully then came away, yanked down my panties and tossed them aside. He bent low, spread my legs and his mouth went there.

"Good God," I breathed and I slid my hands into his hair.

He took me to the edge. I was panting, pressing my hands in his hair and nearly there when he pulled away. Instantly, I came up. My hands went to his shoulders, pushing him to his back. I undid his buckle, unbuttoned his jeans, slid them only as low on his hips as was needed and climbed on top of him. I had my hand wrapped around him to guide him inside, but his hands went to my hips. He bucked, ramming into me, and my hand flew away from between us.

My back arched when he filled me. I gasped and Hank kept bucking.

It was Hank and my wild ride and it was far more satisfying.

He didn't make me do all the work. He was strong; his hips were power-ful and I just held onto his shoulders and enjoyed the ride.

It was delicious.

When I came, his hands slid up my back, pressing me down, and he cap-tured my moans in his mouth.

A few minutes later, I returned the favor.

Afterward, I had my face pressed into his neck, and he spoke, his voice deep and hoarse, "Say my name."

I hesitated, not sure what he was asking. Did he think I didn't know who he was? Did he think I imagined myself with Billy?

"Hank," I whispered, my heart in my throat.

"That isn't what you call me."

My stomach fluttered but I kept silent.

His arms tightened around me and I felt his muscles clench as he sat up, taking me with him. He settled on the edge of the bed, me still straddling him, my hands at his shoulders. I looked down at him and he was looking up at me. He didn't take his arms from around me.

"I talked to Eddie," he said.

"I figured that," I told him.

He dropped his head and kissed my throat, then kept his face there.

"Christ, Roxie, I'm sorry," he said against my throat.

I closed my eyes and my arms tightened reflexively but I didn't say anything. What was there to say? The last twenty minutes had been the best apology in the history of mankind.

He tilted his head back again. "You need to call Tex and let him know you're spendin' the night with me."

I shook my head.

I was glad he didn't think I was some sad, lost woman in love with an abuser, but I also wasn't ready to pick up again with Hank.

"You need to take me back to Tex's."

His eyes got lazy. "You aren't goin' back to Tex's."

I stared at him and I figured he was right, mainly because behind the lazy in his eyes was the intense and I knew to get what I was trying to tell myself I wanted, I'd have to fight. Since I didn't really want it anyway, I wasn't prepared to fight.

He rolled me to the side and my head hit the pillow. He reached across me, grabbed his phone and handed it to me.

I called Uncle Tex while Hank moved away and pulled up his jeans, but didn't button them. He then pulled down my skirt.

"Yo!" Uncle Tex boomed in answer.

"Hey, Uncle Tex. I'm with Hank."

153

I heard a chuckle. "Yeah, I saw that. These boys are *the shit*," Uncle Tex replied.

I sighed. "I'm not coming home tonight."

"Not surprised. Get Hank to bring you to Fortnum's tomorrow. I'll put a key under the mat if you need to come home."

"How'd it go with Mom?" I asked.

"She and Herb are comin' out in a few weeks."

Hank was up on an elbow, leaning over me and, I couldn't help it, I smiled at him. His eyes went soft and his hand went to my neck. He stroked my jaw and I bit my lip.

Silently, I shared my happiness and silently, he accepted it.

I mentally shook myself out of the moment.

"That's good," I said to Uncle Tex.

"Gotta go, told Nancy I'd call her. She's not gonna believe this, you and Hank, me calling Trish. Fuckin' A, but things don't stay borin' around here for long."

"I love you, Uncle Tex," I blurted, then closed my eyes, wondering if that was too much for him.

There was silence, then, "Darlin' girl."

That's all he said before he disconnected.

I opened my eyes and hit the off button on the phone. Hank took it from me and put it in its cradle.

Then he looked at me. "Have you eaten?"

I nodded.

"Did you have dessert?"

I shook my head.

He knifed up, grabbed my hand and pulled me up after him. "Get dressed, let's go."

<hr />

He took me to a place called Gunther Toody's. A gimmick restaurant designed for family dining and to give the feel of a 50's style diner. Neon, chrome, vinyl and waitresses in white uniforms covered in slogan buttons wearing shocking red lipstick.

Hank ordered a burger and cheese fries. I got a chocolate malt. The malt was the thickest, biggest, best malt I'd ever had in my life.

I was staring out the window, sucking on the straw in my malt, trying to catch a thought. Everything had been happening too fast. I couldn't keep up. I didn't know what to do next, where to go, what to think.

The only thing I did know was I needed to slow down, catch my breath, heal my body and get myself safe. I didn't figure Hank was safe. Denver certainly wasn't safe, at least not emotionally. Neither was Chicago, if I was honest.

I felt Hank's foot nudge mine, taking me away from my thoughts and I looked from the window to him.

God, you're handsome, I thought when my eyes settled on him.

I sighed and realized I was still seriously in trouble.

He was done with his food and his plate was pushed away. He was watching me.

"There are things to say," he told me.

I supposed there were, but I not only didn't want to say any of them, I didn't want to hear any of them either.

I wasn't going to get a choice.

"You told me that you loved him," Hank said.

I blinked.

"Loved, lov*ed*, deh, deh, deh," I said. "Past tense."

Hank leaned forward and took my hand. "Sweetheart, I asked, 'Do you love him?' and you nodded, not past tense."

Oh.

I remembered that.

Shit.

I leaned forward too. "I'd just been rescued from a crazy man and hadn't slept in days. I was so tired, I didn't know what I was saying or doing."

His hand squeezed mine. It was the only acknowledgement he gave that he understood and he was sorry, but I knew he understood and he was sorry. A man like Hank probably didn't apologize a lot and I'd already got one straight out from him that night.

I looked back out the window.

"I'm glad we got that straightened out," I said to the window, and I was. It would be good to have a clean break, leave things settled and good rather than ugly and bad.

His hand gave mine a little tug and I looked back at him.

"We'll go back to where we left it," he stated. "We'll have to deal with Flynn when they find him, but you and I can go on from here."

I shook my head. "No, my friend Annette is bringing my stuff to Denver as we speak, and as soon as I get it and my car, I'm going."

"Sunshine—"

"No, Hank. There's no going back. I'm not mad at you for thinking I'm an idiot, because, well, I am an idiot. I'm just not an idiot about that. It's that… I have to get my life sorted out and that's going to take a while. You should… move on."

His eyes flashed dangerously.

"Move on?" he said the words slowly.

I nodded. "Yeah, it's nice that we'll end on a good note and not a misunderstanding," I told him.

"Roxie, we're not ending."

"Yes, we are. You're a good guy…" I stopped and realized that was just it. He was a good guy. I was a nut, my house had been trashed, my ex-lover was wanted in four states and still at large, God knew where, and the thing we were both skirting around was that I was tainted. He knew it. I knew it. Even if he knew I didn't love Billy anymore, the fact that Hank would even think that let me know all I needed to know about what he thought of me.

"It's over," I finished.

"Sorry, wasn't it you that I was fucking an hour ago?" he asked, his eyes narrowing.

I scowled at him.

"It isn't over," he said.

My brows drew together. "It is. I'm leaving tomorrow."

He watched me for a second then let go of my hand, pulled his wallet out of his back pocket, threw some bills on the table and got up, shoving his wallet back in his pocket. He pulled me out of the booth and, holding my hand, guided me to the door with a chin lift to our waitress before we went through it.

Once we got outside, he dropped my hand and put his arm around my shoulders and pulled me into his side.

Well. He was taking my ending things really well.

Although I knew I should be relieved, it kind of pissed me off.

At the 4Runner, he opened my door for me and I turned to him, deciding to keep things on a positive bent and be polite.

"Thank you for understanding."

He looked down at me. "I don't understand," he said.

"Excuse me?"

"Roxie, you aren't going anywhere. I just have to convince you to stay."

I blinked at him.

"I'm leaving tomorrow," I said (again).

He moved into my space. I moved back, and he pinned me against the inside of the door.

"Then I gotta convince you before tomorrow."

"You won't be able to do that. My mind is made up," I told him, pressing on his chest with my hands to push him back.

"A few days ago, you didn't even want to have dinner with me. In less than twenty-four hours you were in my bed. I'll be able to convince you."

Well! He was certainly sure of himself.

Of course, what he said was true (all but the convincing me part), but still.

"Take me back to Uncle Tex's," I demanded.

He grinned. "You aren't going to Tex's. You're comin' home with me."

I made a huffy noise.

So I guessed this meant he wasn't taking my ending things with him really well. In fact, he wasn't taking it at all.

Hank kissed me.

Then, still feeling dizzy, I went home with him.

꿈

I was on my back. Hank had lifted my legs at my knees so they were tucked into his sides. He was up on his elbows so his weight wasn't on me. With my legs bent and his leverage, he was sliding deep inside me, deeper than anyone had ever been.

I had my eyes closed, feeling him move, my arms wrapped tight around his back.

I let him seduce me again (honestly, it didn't take much) and was memorizing everything, the smell of him, the feel of him, the taste of him, the strength of him. I'd need to keep these memories for a long time.

He pulled out and broke his rhythm, his body tense. I could feel him but he wasn't coming inside.

My eyes opened. "Hank?"

His head dropped and in my ear he murmured, "Stay."

Holy cow.

My entire body spasmed.

"Don't," I begged.

"Promise me you'll stay," he whispered.

I moved, tightening my arms and wrapping my legs around his back. "Whisky—"

When I used his nickname, he slid deep inside and kept going, finishing me off.

<hr>

After we were done, he held me against his side and made me tell him what happened with Billy, from the minute he left for his run, to the minute he got into bed with me after I came back.

He listened without saying anything, but his body was speaking for him, getting tense; his hand, which was stroking my back, going still every now and then, sometimes flexing and biting into me.

Then he made me tell him about the sledgehammer incident.

He said something then. "I'm gonna kill that motherfucker."

"That's what Uncle Tex said," I told him.

After that, he made me tell him about my plan to get rid of Billy.

In other words, we had the conversation we were meant to have over breakfast five days ago.

"That wasn't a very good plan," he said to me.

"I know that *now*," I replied.

He told me he knew my place was trashed. Mace had told him at Lincoln's Road House.

"You're not safe to go back there," he said.

"I'm going," I returned.

"We'll see."

Jeez, there was just no shaking this guy.

"You *do* know that there's this little thing called the Nineteenth Amendment giving women the right to vote?" I asked.

"I heard of that," he said, and there was a smile in his voice.

"And there's this whole movement called fem... in... is... im," I said it slowly, like he was a dim child. "Where women started working, demanding equal pay for equal work, raising their voices on issues of the day, taking back the night, stuff like that."

He rolled into me, which made me roll onto my back. "Sounds familiar."

"Do you have an encyclopedia? Maybe we can look it up. If the words are too big for you to read, I'll read it out loud and explain as I go along," I offered.

He got up on his elbow. "Only if you do it naked."

I slapped his shoulder.

He ignored my slap, threw his thigh over mine and settled in.

I sighed.

Shamus jumped up and walked around on the bed like it was the floor for a bit, laid down with a loud, doggie groan, his back pressed the length of my side.

I sighed again. "You Nightingale boys are hard to shake."

"Remember that," Hank murmured, and wrapped his arm around my waist as if to prove the point.

Chapter 13

This Is Gonna Be Fun

The next morning Hank woke me up and made love to me, catching further at my heart by paying special attention with his mouth and hands to the fading bruises on my neck, arms, hips, even my wrists, like he could erase them and their memory with his touch.

Man, was I in trouble or what?

When we were done, both of us still breathing heavy, Shamus gave a whine and moved up and down the side of the bed, not taking his eyes off Hank.

"I gotta let him out," Hank said, giving me a light kiss on the mouth and moving gently away from me.

I nodded and rolled onto my side, pulling the pillow to my middle.

I watched Hank tug on his henley and jeans and walk barefoot out of the room. I heard a door open and close. Then something weird happened.

I closed my eyes slowly, languidly, coming down from the high that was Hank's lovemaking, and when I opened them, Billy's face was right in mine.

I jerked straight up in bed, still holding the pillow to my middle, and screamed Hank's name. The scream was loud; it was shrill and it echoed through the house like a gunshot. I scooted up the bed, clutching the pillow and getting to my knees. My back hit the headboard when Hank ran into the room.

"Jesus Roxie," he said, looking at me. I had no idea I was deathly pale and as wild-eyed as Uncle Tex was last night.

I was staring at nothing. Billy wasn't there. My eyes moved to Hank and he sat on the bed, his hands coming to me, taking the pillow away and pulling me into his warm, solid body.

"Holy fuck. Fuck, fuck, fuck. I'm seeing things. I could swear Billy was right here," I told him, and I could feel my body trembling.

He swore under his breath and pulled me across his lap, wrapping the sheet around me and tucking my head in his neck.

"I'm going crazy, or crazier. God, I swear he was right here. I could see him plain as day," I whispered against his neck, twining my arms around his middle.

"It was a flashback, sweetheart. Victims of violence get them all time."

I was still shaking and I felt the tears crawling up my throat.

"Dammit," I choked, burrowing into him, trying to get him to absorb me, or trying to absorb some of his strength into me, I didn't know which. I felt the wetness on my cheeks transferring itself to his skin. "I'm so fucking weak."

"I shouldn't have brought you back here. I was worried about that."

I shook my head, tears still coming. "It's me. I'm weak."

"It isn't you, it could happen to anyone."

I knew it wouldn't happen to Indy or Ally or Daisy or anyone he knew. They were made of sterner stuff than me.

"I'm sorry," I said quietly.

"Why?"

"I feel stupid."

"Christ, Sunshine, give yourself a break."

I nodded, but didn't agree.

He held me until I quit shaking, his arms tight around me. Then he stood up, taking me with him and set me on my feet. He bent and picked up my panties from the floor, silently handing them to me. I put them on while he dug in his drawer and pulled out an olive-drab thermal, long sleeve shirt with a kickass skull in tan emblazoned on the back. It was a Lucky thermal and it was sweet. He yanked it over my head, I shoved my arms through and it fell over my hips.

"Let's go get Shamus," he said.

He guided me to the backdoor, holding my hand the whole time, and opened it. Shamus bolted inside. Then Hank walked me to the kitchen, let go of my hand and started to make coffee.

"Feed Shamus, will you?" Hank asked.

He told me where to find the stuff. The sleeves of the Lucky thermal went over my hands and I wiped the remains of the tears off my face with them. Then I pushed them back up my forearms and looked around the living room.

It was tidy. The Fat Tire print was gone. The Skinny Dip print had been repositioned to center over the couch. Everything was where it was supposed to be. The broken lamp hadn't been replaced, but any remnants of it were swept away. It was like Billy hadn't even been there. Instead, it looked like when I first walked in after Hank's and my date.

I looked away before I started decorating again, took a deep breath and made Shamus his breakfast. While I did this, Shamus jumped around me in happy anticipation of being fed. When I set his bowl on the floor, he shoved his face into the wet food, his body still moving with his wagging tail.

"He's a happy dog," I told Hank, staring down at Shamus and wishing my life could be as simple as his. Food, happy. Walk, happy. Hank, happy.

Okay, maybe my life could be like that, or a version of that, but I wasn't going to go there.

Hank got in front of me and then smack in my space, backing me up until my bottom hit the counter. He got so close I could feel the heat from his body.

His hands came to either side of my neck and he looked into my eyes.

"How you doin'?" he asked.

I nodded. "Better. Sorry about that."

"If you apologize again—"

"Sorry. Sorry... um, sorry!" Oh God, I couldn't quit saying sorry.

Hank smiled at me. "Shut up," he ordered.

"Okay," I replied.

"Put your arms around me."

I was so weirded out by that morning's experience I immediately did as I was told.

He got even closer. "How'm I doin'?"

I blinked up at him. "Pardon?"

His hands slid down my shoulders and linked around my back. Then he rubbed his nose against mine.

I hated it when he did that, mainly because I loved it when he did that.

"Convincin' you to stay," he went on quietly.

Shit.

"I'm leaving today, Hank."

His eyes got lazy.

I hated it when they did that, mainly because I loved it when they did that.

I gave my foot a little stomp, both to show him I was serious and to show myself.

"You think I'm staying!" I snapped.

"I know you're stayin'," he replied.

I rolled my eyes to the ceiling then brought them back to him. "I'm going to have coffee, make you French toast for breakfast and you're going to take me back to Tex's. Then I'm going to get my car, find Annette and go."

"French toast sounds good." He obviously felt like ignoring the rest of what I said.

Whatever.

"Do you have bread, eggs, maple syrup?" I asked.

His head dipped and went to my neck. With his lips there, he said, "Probably."

"Powdered sugar, cream cheese?" I went on.

"Probably not," he answered, mouth still at my neck.

Oh well, I'd make do. "Move back, I'm going to get started."

His head came up and he was grinning at me.

I rolled my eyes at him and heard him laugh softly.

He let me go and stepped away.

I walked to the coffee and pulled open the cabinet above it, figuring that was where the mugs would be because that's where I'd keep the mugs. The mugs were there and I took out two.

"How do you take your coffee?" I asked.

He came up behind me, pressed my hips against the counter and his arms went around me, his mouth going back to my neck.

"Black," he answered, just before both his hands went under the shirt. One went north, one went south.

"Hank!" My body jerked but there was no getting away from him. "Let me go."

"Call me Whisky and I'll let you go," he muttered against my neck.

Good God.

I ignored his request and shouted, "Let me go!"

One hand went into my panties, the other hand cupped my breast.

Oh shit.

Ten minutes later I was pressing my back against his body and holding onto the counter for dear life. My head was tilted back resting on his shoulder, my forehead was pressed into his neck. He'd tilted his head forward and he was listening to me gasp.

The fingers on both of his hands did a delicious swirl.

"Call me Whisky," he murmured.

I didn't delay and did what he asked.

Then he took care of me, orgasm number two of the day, and I hadn't even been awake as many hours.

He held me, my back to his front, his arms wrapped around my midriff, while I recovered.

Once my breathing evened he asked, "Scared of my house anymore?"

My belly melted and I let out a quick breath from my nostrils. Hank was trying to erase the bad memories by giving me good ones.

God, he was *such* a nice guy. Though, he was a nice guy in a seriously sexy way.

I shook my head.

He kissed my neck. "You feel like stayin' yet?"

Jeez.

He might be a nice guy but he sure was a stubborn one.

I shook my head.

"Stubborn," he murmured, his mouth behind my ear.

"I was just thinking that about you," I told him.

I felt his smile rather than saw it.

"This is gonna be fun," he said.

I doubted that.

We had French toast. We had a shower. Hank took me to Tex's and I heard him on the phone in the kitchen while I did the whole getting dressed production.

I called Annette and she answered with a sleepy, "Yo bitch." She was in Denver and she told me she and Jason were catching up on sleep and we arranged to meet later at Fortnum's.

I called Uncle Tex at the store (he was still not using his cell phone) and got the address for where my car was. Then Hank took me to get my car.

I thought this was fishy, Hank being so nice, taking me to my car, considering I intended to drive off into the sunset with it. But I wasn't going to look a gift horse in the mouth, especially Hank's mouth. His mouth was mesmerizing.

The guy in dirty blue coveralls was sitting behind the counter, flipping through the paper.

"I'm here to pick up my car," I told him when he looked up.

He looked at Hank, then back at me. "Sorry, can't give it to you."

I stared at him. "Why?"

"Some cops came in a while ago, towed it to the impound. Said it was evidence in a crime."

My body went still. "What crime?"

He shrugged.

My head turned slowly to look at Hank. He was looking pleased with himself.

That was when my body turned slowly to face Hank. "You know anything about this?"

His lips twitched. "Might do."

My hands fisted at my sides, I stomped my foot and let out strangled noise.

Hank did a full-on smile, tagged me around the waist and pulled me into his body.

"Told you you were stayin'," he said.

"I... you..." I stopped and made the strangled noise again.

One of his arms wrapped around my waist, the other one slid into my hair.

"God, you're cute," he said.

"You're a jerk," I replied.

He shook his head, then bent it and kissed me dizzy.

I blinked up at him when he was done.

Then he said, "This *is* fun."

⌖

Hank took me to Fortnum's and everyone was there; Indy, Lee, Ally, Daisy, Uncle Tex, Duke, Jet and Eddie.

It was like they were waiting for the show.

I stomped in and Duke opened his mouth to speak but I put up my hand.

"I don't want to hear it. So, yeah, you called it. I put you all through the mill. It wasn't like I *wanted* to be assaulted and abducted," I snapped at him.

"I was just gonna say, good to see you safe," Duke told me.

"Well..." I huffed, the wind out of my sails, "Thank you."

He shook his head at me like he wondered about my sanity. I couldn't say I blamed him. I was beginning to wonder about my sanity, too.

"You're welcome," he replied.

Hank stood close to my side and I looked up to him. "Don't you have to go to work or something? Interrogate suspects? File reports? Testify in court? That kind of thing," I asked, sounding uppity.

He put his arm around my shoulders and dipped his face to mine, his eyes smiling, his mouth not. "It's Sunday, I only interrogate suspects on weekdays if I can manage it."

My head jerked. "It's Sunday?"

"Yeah."

Shit. I'd been away a week.

"My life's a shambles," I whispered.

He squeezed my shoulder, and, for some reason, I felt reassured.

I had no time to process my feelings of reassurance as Daisy bellied up to us, looking up at Hank. "Back off, big boy. You've had her long enough. We got girl talk."

Then she grabbed my hand and pulled me into the shelves of books. We turned into the P-Q-R-S section, and I noticed Ally, Indy and Jet had followed us.

"So, you're back with Hank." Indy was smiling.

"I'm leaving town as soon as I can get my car," I told her.

Her smile faded.

"Where's your car?" Jet asked.

"Hank had it impounded," I answered.

Indy's smile came back.

"He doesn't want me to leave," I explained unnecessarily.

"You are so not gonna leave," Ally said, she was smiling too.

I looked at her. "I'm gonna leave." I said it and meant it.

"You are so not gonna leave," Ally repeated.

Indy came closer to me. "Roxie, you should know, once, when Hank wanted a motorcycle, and his Dad told him he'd have to buy it with his own money, Hank got, like ten jobs. He worked himself to the bone, getting up early, working late nights. He even did it and went to football practice and games. In the end, he got that motorcycle."

"Hank drives a motorcycle?" I asked.

Ally ignored my question and shared her own story, "Yeah, I remember when Hank decided he was going to buy a house in Bonnie Brae. He wanted to be close to where he grew up and have a place in a neighborhood where he could

Kristen Ashley

teach his kids how to ride their bikes on the sidewalks without fear of a drive-by. Property values were out the roof. No way to buy there on a cop's salary. Everyone expected he'd give it up. When he found his place, it was a total dump. No one wanted it, except to buy it for the lot and scrape it. Hank paid more than it was worth and fixed it up himself."

I was kind of lost in thoughts of Hank teaching his kids to ride their bikes when Daisy called, "Earth to Roxie."

"What?" I came to.

"Why do you want to leave?" Daisy asked.

"It's too complicated to explain," I told her.

They all looked at each other then looked at me.

"It is!" I cried.

"Whatever," Ally said, dismissing my life's complications with a single word. "Are you gonna go to Frightmare with us tomorrow night?"

Good God.

"Frightmare?" I asked.

"Yeah, the Haunted House in Thornton. It is *the shit*," Ally shared.

"I'm not good at doing scary," I replied, thinking I'd had enough of scary in the last week, thank you very much.

"Oh, it's all in fun," Indy coaxed.

I turned to Indy. "Hank told me you went berserk and broke through hay bales and they had to call the cops. That doesn't sound like fun."

Ally and Indy looked at each other then burst out laughing. They were doing it so hard they doubled over with it. Jet, Daisy and I watched them.

They finally sobered and straightened.

Ally wiped a tear from her eye and muttered, "I remember that year. Good times."

"You're all nuts," I declared.

"You got that right, sister," Jet mumbled.

"Well, I'm going. It sounds like a hoot and you could use a few giggles, am I right, sugar?" Daisy asked, looking at me.

She was right. Too right. Scary right.

"Okay, fine," I gave in. "My friends Annette and Jason are in town. Can they come?"

"The more, the merrier," Ally, clearly the Haunted House ringleader, said.

168

Again, I knew I was in trouble, but this was a different kind of trouble.

A tall, very thin woman turned the corner at the back of the shelves, carrying an armload of books. She jerked to a halt when she saw us. Obviously she'd been in her own world.

"Hi," she said, surprise at the existence of other human beings on the earth still on her face.

"Hi," we all said back.

She waited a beat and then said to me, "Glad you're okay."

I blinked at her. I had no idea who this woman was.

"Thanks," I replied.

She shelved a book and wandered away.

"Who was that?" I asked Indy.

"That's Jane. She's worked here for years. She's kind of… odd," Indy answered.

Uncle Tex had told me about Jane. Quiet, addicted to romance and detective novels. Her life was devoted to Fortnum's, reading, writing her own novels that were never published, and not much else.

Daisy grabbed my hand, taking my mind off Jane. "How's everything else? You hangin' in there?"

Her cornflower blue eyes were kind but sharp. I knew from just her look she didn't miss a trick.

I told them about seeing the vision of Billy in Hank's bedroom that morning. I finished with, "Hank said it was a flashback."

Jet, Ally and Indy watched me, all smiles gone. They were looking concerned.

Daisy, on the other hand, nodded. "Yeah, I got those after I was raped."

My hand clenched in hers.

"You were raped?" I whispered.

"Long time ago. Flashbacks lasted awhile but they went away. The mind heals just like the body, but it takes its time. It's good you got a decent man to see you through it. Helped me that, during that time, I found my Marcus."

I sighed.

No one believed me when I said I was leaving town, and I knew they wouldn't believe me when I told them Hank wasn't my man, so I stayed silent.

We heard a shout from the front of the store.

"Jumpin' Jehosafats! This place is fuckin' *great!*"

That would be Annette.

All the girls' faces were frozen with incredulity at the yell.

"That's my friend, Annette," I told them, broke away and walked to the front.

Annette and Jason were standing a few feet inside the door. Jason was Annette's partner, same height as Annette, light brown hair and dark brown eyes. He always smiled like he meant it and was never in a bad mood.

Annette and Jason looked at me when I arrived, and I realized Jason could have bad moods under extreme circumstances because the minute he saw me, his face went hard.

Annette stared.

"Hey," I greeted, smiling at them.

Annette looked at Jason then turned on her heel and walked out the door.

On the sidewalk outside, hands clenched and arms straight, she threw her head back and screamed at the top of her lungs. Then she started kicking the sidewalk like she was kicking dirt and punching the air like she was hitting a punching bag, all the while emitting loud, nonsensical, *angry* mutterings.

I turned to all the folks in Fortnum's. "She's a little crazy."

No one said a word. They were all staring out the door.

Annette walked back in.

"I'm gonna *kill* that motherfucker," she announced.

"I think that's the consensus," I told her.

"No, no, no. I'm gonna rip his dick off, shove it up his nose and parade him through the streets naked and dickless, *then* cut his head off."

The entire store was silent.

"Annette, honey, I thought you were a pacifist," I reminded her in a placating voice.

"Have you *seen* your face?" she shot back.

"Um… yeah. It's already a lot better."

At my words, her eyes bugged out.

Holy cow.

Wrong thing to say.

Quickly, I offered, "Let me introduce you to everybody."

I did the introductions. Annette gave Uncle Tex a big old hug, and when I finished with Hank, she looked him up and down, turned to me and nodded while she drawled, "Nice."

Hank's arm slid along my shoulders and he pulled me into his side.

Annette and Jason took this in and Annette smiled huge. Then she said, "*Very* nice."

I looked up at Hank and his lips were twitching.

Shit.

Then, Jason came forward, took my hand and asked Hank, "Do you mind?"

He pulled me away from Hank's arm and into both of his own, gave me a tight hug, shoving his face in my neck.

The room, having recovered from Annette's outburst, went silent again.

I felt the tears hit the backs of my eyes and slid my arms around him.

"Jason, I'm okay," I whispered. "I'm fine. I'm here. It's over."

He didn't let me go. I heard Annette give a loud, hiccoughing sob (Annette was a crier, just like me) then her arms came around both of us.

We stood like that for a while and I heard Hank say softly, "Jason, Roxie's got three cracked ribs."

Jason's arms loosened and he and Annette stepped away. Immediately, Hank slid his arm across my shoulders again and pulled me tight to his side.

"Annette tells me you're a cop," Jason noted, looking at Hank.

Hank nodded.

"You'll get him?" Jason asked.

Hank nodded again.

Jason looked at him for a few beats then he nodded too and I watched the tension ebb from his body.

Everyone was quiet after that.

"All righty then!" Indy exclaimed into the ensuing silence. "Why don't we all get lunch?"

"That sounds great. I could eat a horse, but gotta unload the car first. We got a boatload of your shit," Annette said to me. "The old Subaru is draggin'."

"You can take it to my place," Hank told her.

I froze.

No. No way in hell, I thought.

"No," I said out loud.

"Cool," Annette ignored me. "Should we follow you there?"

"We'll all go," Ally, all of a sudden, was there. "Many hands make light work."

"No," I repeated, slightly louder this time.

"Let's go, I'm starved. The sooner we get this done, the sooner I can eat," Eddie said as he and Jet walked up to us. He had Jet in a hold much like the one Hank was using on me.

"No," I said again, even louder.

"Where are we going to lunch? I vote Las Delicias," Indy put in.

"We had that yesterday," Lee said.

Indy smiled at him. "Every day is Las Delicias day."

"No!" I said for the fourth time and it was nearly a shout.

Daisy linked her arm in mine, pulling me away from Hank. "You can ride with me, sugar. We got shit we haven't talked about yet."

It was Hank's turn to freeze.

"Don't worry, Hunkalicious, we'll be right on your tail," Daisy assured him and guided me to the door.

"Don't mind Tex, Jane and me! We'll just stay here and work!" Duke shouted to us as we walked out the door.

"Thanks, you're a doll!" Indy shouted back.

I looked back in dread at Uncle Tex, but he was grinning.

Daisy took me to her Mercedes, which was parked in the back, while everyone scattered to their own vehicles.

I sat in the car, staring unseeing out the window while she started the car.

"Sugar, you look scared as a jackrabbit," Daisy remarked.

"I am scared," I told her. "My car has been impounded and I can't get home. I can't get anywhere. Now my friends are essentially moving my shit into the house of a man I've known for a week. It's official. As of today, I met him a week ago."

"Seems longer," Daisy muttered.

She wasn't wrong.

"Relax," Daisy said. "One thing I learned, this life is a wild ride and you got to just go with it."

I turned to her. "I need a moment to think. I need a moment to plan. I need a moment to myself."

"That's just when it all goes wrong, when you have time to think. And you got an eternity of lyin' alone in your coffin. Now you best be spendin' your time with good folk and a handsome man. Come when you're eighty and wonderin' where your life went, you won't thank yourself for cuttin' loose and leavin' a good thing behind, comprende?"

I opened my mouth to say something, but Daisy didn't let me.

"Trust me sugar, I—" then she stopped talking, her eyes got big and she looked beyond me, out the side window.

I turned to see what she was looking at, and in my window was a man, bent over and looking in.

Not just any man, one of the men who took Billy.

He tapped on the window with a gun.

"Get out of the car," he said, looking at me.

"Please tell me that's a flashback," I whispered.

"That ain't no fuckin' flashback," Daisy replied.

She slammed the car in reverse and sped backwards on a vicious tug of the wheel, curling sideways. The bad guy jumped out of the way of the bumper and Daisy nearly rammed into Eddie's truck, which was pulling down the alley behind us.

The man with the gun ran to a car on Bayaud and got in as Daisy took the turn onto Bayaud. The other man who'd come to take Billy, the one who tied me to the sink, was driving the car. They shot away from the curb after us.

"Oh no. No, no, no. *Shit!*" I shouted.

I looked behind and saw that they followed and Eddie turned in behind them.

"You know these boys?" Daisy asked.

"They're the ones who took Billy."

"Mm-hmm," she mumbled, shifting up and staring in the rearview mirror as she ran the red and turned onto Broadway.

Cars honked and swerved as we cut into traffic. I held onto the dash with one hand, the ceiling with my other, and braced my body as best I could. When we were rocketing down Broadway, I chanced another glance behind and saw that the two guys and Eddie had taken the red light, too. To my further despair, I saw a Subaru pulling up the rear, its end dragging under a load and two mountain bikes strapped to its roof.

Shit.

Cars were swerving everywhere, honking, and I could see angry faces through windows.

A Crossfire and Hank's 4Runner both zoomed out of parking spots at the front of Fortnum's and joined the chase.

Then the bad guy in the passenger seat leaned out the window and aimed the gun at us.

"Holy cow! He's gonna shoot!" I yelled just as we heard gunshots and a "ping, ping, ping" as the bullets hit the trunk of our car.

"They shot me! They shot my Mercedes! Those fuckin' bastards!" Daisy squealed and she hooked a right down some narrow road with parked cars on either side, barely enough room for us to drive down.

A car was coming toward us and Daisy leaned on the horn.

"Get out of my way, motherfucker!" she shouted, leaning forward squinting through the windshield like she was nearsighted and nearly resting her huge bosoms on the steering wheel.

At the last possible moment in our scary game of chicken, the car swerved into an open spot and we flew by. I looked behind us and saw the rest of the cars in our convoy fly by too.

"Drive to a police station," I said to her.

"What?" she asked, still laying on the horn.

"Take your hand off the horn and drive to a police station!" I yelled.

She stopped honking her horn and I heard my purse ringing.

"Shit!" I snapped.

"Put your seatbelt on. Fuck the phone. Belt. Now!" she ordered.

I did as Daisy instructed. She hung a left, running a stop sign, and then two blocks down, she took another left, thankfully through a green light, and got onto a two-lane road. My phone finally quit ringing and Daisy weaved in and out of traffic, honking her horn liberally and staying out of the line of a clean shot.

We took several more turns. I kept glancing behind us. Eddie's truck had fallen back. The Crossfire was behind the bad guys, Hank behind the Crossfire.

Daisy took another turn and we were in the parking lot of the police station Eddie had taken me to the day before.

I watched out the back window as the bad guys kept going. The Crossfire stopped on a squeal of tires. Hank's 4Runner shot past it and kept after the bad guys. Indy jumped out of the Crossfire and the minute she closed the door, it took off on another squeal of tires.

Then I could look no more.

Daisy executed what could only be described as a Bo-and-Luke-Duke-General-Lee stop on a squeal with the back half of the Mercedes swinging around and rocking to a halt. The red truck came in behind us, Annette's Subaru following it.

Two squad cars flew out of another exit, sirens and lights flashing.

Eddie didn't bother to park. He stopped behind us, got out of the truck, Jet getting out the other side. She immediately started running toward the entrance of the police station. Indy was there, holding the door for her. Eddie jogged toward us.

Daisy and I climbed out of the car.

"Get into the station. Now," Eddie ordered, and I realized Jet and Indy already had their orders.

Daisy and I didn't quibble. She threw her keys to Eddie, he caught them in midair, and we hoofed it into the station, joining Jet and Indy. Annette and Jason came in not a minute later.

"What the fuck just happened?" Jason snapped.

Okay, so I'd learned of another situation that could take away Jason's good mood.

I told them about the bad guys.

"Those fuckers shot my Mercedes," Daisy said when I was done talking. She was shaking, maybe with rage, but I figured it was something else.

I put my arms around her and she reciprocated the gesture.

"Those fuckers shot my Mercedes," she whispered.

"I'm so sorry," I whispered back, feeling the weight of her fear settling firmly on my shoulders.

She held on.

Eddie walked in. His dark eyes, glittering with anger, went first to Jet and then they came to me.

"You okay?" he asked me.

I nodded.

"Daisy?" he prompted.

She took her cheek from my chest and nodded, but she didn't let me go.

Eddie watched her a beat and then said, "I'll call Marcus."

Something changed in the air. I saw it in Daisy's face and in Jet's, but I didn't know what it was.

Eddie looked at me. "You know those guys?"

I shook my head but said, "They took Billy."

"Billy isn't with them now," he noted.

I just stared at him.

"Fuck," Eddie finished.

He could say that again.

—※—

I was sitting on a couch in the room where I gave my statement to Detective Marker.

Daisy was by the door being held by a good-looking, dark-haired man that I knew had to be her husband, Marcus. He was ignoring some very weird looks he was getting from all the cops in the room.

Indy was six feet away, talking to some handsome black man in uniform. Jason was standing with them. His face still had not morphed back to the good-natured Jason I knew.

Jet was sitting on one side of me, Annette on the other, and we were all holding hands.

Eddie was talking on the phone.

Then, some guy who was on another phone yelled, "Yo, Eddie!"

Eddie put his hand over the receiver and lifted his chin.

"Hank got 'em," the guy said.

Eddie's eyes slid to me.

"Thank the goddess," Annette breathed.

I stared at Eddie and felt my chest squeeze.

Before, I thought I was leaving town to guard my heart.

Now, I had to leave town to guard my friends.

—※—

What seemed like forever later, Hank and Ally walked into the room. Ally had been in the 4Runner with Hank and he'd taken her with him, hell bent on going after the bad guys. This was talked about by the cops like it wasn't a big deal, and I got the impression they all knew Ally was the kind of girl who could handle herself in a crisis.

I could tell from across the room that Hank's body was taut, he was wired and he was seriously and completely pissed-off.

He scanned the room until his eyes fell on me and then he came straight to me.

I got up from the couch.

He stopped in front of me, toe-to-toe, totally in my space.

He tilted his head down and looked me directly in the eye.

"You're stayin'," he declared in his authoritative voice.

Shit.

Chapter 14
"She's the One"

I was lying on top of the covers of Hank's bed, wearing my dusty lilac, stretchy nightie with the black lace on the bodice and hem. It was a little risqué for hanging out in Hank-the-guy-who-I-was-telling-myself-I-was-trying-to-shake's bedroom, but fuck it, these days risqué was my middle name.

Shamus was lying on his belly beside me. His head on my stomach, his eyes closed, content as I scratched his ears. "Born to Run" was playing on the stereo in Hank's bedroom and I'd just finished writing a letter to a friend in Atlanta, but did not share any of the recent goings-on. That would have to be a phone call.

I had put my stationery aside. I was staring at the ceiling and trying to decide how my life had descended into such madness and obviously avoiding blaming myself in an attempt to save what was left of my sanity.

It was like someone in a suit walked up to me and gave me a certificate, which stated "Roxanne Giselle Logan, Your Life is Fucked".

⌖

I'd spent the afternoon at the police station.

First they took everyone's statement. Then Daisy and I identified the two bad guys in a line up. It gave me a chill up my spine to see Sink Man again, so close he seemed *right there*.

Luckily, Hank was right there, too, standing behind me, his strong hand warm on the back of my neck.

After that we went back to the big room with the desks and phones and people. Hank didn't come with us, but everyone was still there. Vance and Mace had arrived and both were looking grim. Or at least Mace looked grim. Vance looked pissed-off.

They were talking to Lee, but before they peeled off, Vance approached me, stared me in the eyes, his burning so deeply I felt the heat on my face.

"Don't worry," he said low.

Then he and Mace took off.

Yowza.

I wasn't certain what he meant. All I knew was that whatever it was, he seriously meant it.

After that, everyone else took off. I tried to follow but Lee caught my arm and held me back.

"You stay here, wait for Hank," he ordered.

Eddie stood beside him. Jet and Indy stood beside their respective men. I looked at them.

"I need to—" I started.

"You need to wait for Hank," Lee cut me off and his tone brooked no argument.

I felt the need to argue, even though Lee scared me a bit.

"You don't understand. Uncle Tex—" I told him.

"We'll talk to Tex," this time Eddie cut in.

I felt another presence behind my back, so I turned and there stood Malcolm, Hank and Lee's dad, a handsome, older version of them both. I'd met him briefly at Indy and Lee's party a week ago.

"Come on, Roxie. Let's get you a cup of coffee," Malcolm invited.

Shit, shit, shit.

Coffee with Hank's dad after I'd been chased through the streets of Denver and shot at.

Shit.

I gave Lee, Indy, Eddie and Jet one last glance and a small smile. Then I nodded to Malcolm and went with him.

He got me coffee, or what could loosely be described as coffee. I'd never again take coffee for granted after having one of Uncle Tex's orgasmic creations. We went back to the big room, its activity beginning to fade. He sat with me on the couch.

"Let me tell you what's goin' on," Malcolm said to me.

I looked at him. His eyes were open and unguarded and infinitely kind. I realized two things straight off. One, this man had raised two pretty fantastic sons and an amazing daughter, and I could tell the reason for that was because this was a good man. I also realized that he had been dragged into the mess that was the last week of my life right along with everyone else. The first thing humbled me, the second embarrassed me.

I tamped down the embarrassment, focused and said quietly, "I'd like to know what's going on."

His eyes registered approval of my comment and I felt like I passed an important test. Not only that, I got an "A".

He started talking. "They're interrogating those men. Jimmy Marker and Danny Rose are doing it. Jimmy and Danny are veterans, good at what they do, and friends. Hank can't be involved because of you."

I nodded, he continued.

"Hank's watchin', two way mirror. First, we want to know what happened to Flynn and if he's still at large. Then, we want to know who they're workin' for and why they came after you."

I nodded again. I wanted to know all of that too.

"Hank wants you here, where he knows you're safe and he can get to you. Will you do that for him?"

I swallowed, wondering if Malcolm knew how huge his question was.

Then I nodded again.

He patted my thigh.

"Good girl," he said.

I did it again, passed another test and got another "A".

I took a deep breath and he continued.

"This is a family affair, Roxie, in more ways than one. Now, I'm gonna explain how that works. No one kidnaps a cop's girlfriend out of his house then puts her in the path of a bullet. The whole department is gonna work until we get these guys and make you safe. Lee and I'll do whatever we can to that same end. You have my promise on that."

I tried not to focus on the fact he called me Hank's girlfriend. Instead I focused on something that was even scarier. I liked this man. He was Hank's dad and had made Hank into what he was now and what he was to me. I didn't want him to think badly of me.

"I'm sorry all of this is happening," I said to him. "You must think—"

He squeezed my knee and interrupted me, "No offense, honey, but you don't know what I think."

I waited, quiet, knowing he wasn't done, and for some reason, I was even more scared. I might have passed a few tests, but someone had shot at me that day. That probably wasn't number one on a father's list of the kind of girl he wanted his son to be with, especially a son like Hank. It occurred to me I could

Kristen Ashley

be Hank's "Billy", the girl that made his parents wince and get sad faces when they saw us together.

Malcolm continued, "The only thing I want in this life is a piece of happiness for those I call my own. I know my boy. He doesn't fuck around when there's somethin' he wants, excuse my language."

I did a hand gesture to excuse his language. It wasn't his using the word "fuck' that was making me freak out.

"It's pretty damn clear Hank wants you and that boy doesn't make stupid decisions," Malcolm carried on. "He's smart, he's controlled and he's decisive. If he wants you, there's somethin' to want and that's all I need to know."

I looked at him, feeling funny. It wasn't a bad feeling. It was a good one, a *really* good one, and that scared me even more.

"You remind me of my dad. He doesn't bullshit either," I told him.

"Sounds like I'll like your dad," Malcolm said, and he said this like it was a done deal that he'd meet my dad.

I had visions of Malcolm meeting Dad and it made my heart skip a beat.

Mom and Dad had never met Billy's parents. Neither had I. Billy never even talked about them. He would close up the minute they were mentioned. I'd learned not to push.

My parents would like Malcolm and they'd *love* Hank. I could hear Mom calling Sweet Jesus all the way from Brownsburg, Indiana at the mere thought of me with a guy like Hank.

"Thank you for telling me all of this," I said to Malcolm.

He smiled at me and his smile was just as drop-dead gorgeous as his son's. "My pleasure."

We sat for a while longer, talking about Denver weather, and then we started talking about sports. He told me it took a while for him to warm to the Rockies. He'd been a Mets fan. I teasingly congratulated him for at least remaining faithful to the National League. Then I told him I thought there was nothing better in the world than eating a hotdog and drinking a beer in the humid sun at Wrigley Field. After I finished with that, Malcolm gave me another one of his smiles, making me think I'd passed another test.

Then Hank walked into the room and I stopped talking.

His eyes settled on us and he didn't take them away as he walked across the room.

"What'd they get?" Malcolm asked when Hank arrived.

182

Hank grabbed my hand, pulled me up, stood close and didn't drop my hand. Malcolm rose as well.

"Not much, they're not talkin'. I called the Chicago PD yesterday to have them check Roxie's apartment. Prints from the apartment match these guys, and Chicago tells us these boys are linked with a bigger operation. We're waitin' for reports on the prints they lifted in the hotel in Nebraska to check if we can place them there too. We don't hold much hope for that. The place was a shithole. Filthy, prints everywhere. They didn't get much except partials from around the sink. It'll be Roxie's word that puts them in Nebraska."

After he said that, his mouth got tight at the thought of me and the sink.

I stared at him. I had no idea that anyone had gone back to that hotel in Nebraska, and I certainly had no idea the cops checked out my loft in Chicago.

"What are you talking about?" I asked.

It was Malcolm that answered. "The minute Vance found you, Hank and Jimmy've been runnin' what's become a three state investigation."

Holy cow.

"Well, Hank hasn't been runnin' it, at least not officially," Malcolm went on as if I was going to hightail it to Internal Affairs and snitch on Hank's efforts to keep me safe.

Before I could react to what Malcolm said, Hank tugged my hand.

"Let's go," Hank said, nodding to his father, obviously done talking.

"Where?" I asked.

He looked down at me. "Home," he answered.

I pulled my hand from his and gave Malcolm a kiss on the cheek. When I pulled away, I saw Malcolm's eyes crinkled at the corners in a smile that didn't reach his lips and I figured, somehow, I'd got another "A".

I turned back to Hank. He grabbed my hand again and we left.

When we got in the 4Runner and Hank had it on the road, he asked, "How're you doin'?"

"Not good," I answered honestly. "You?"

"I'm angry," he said, just as honest.

"I can tell." After a beat I sighed, huge and loud, and looked out the side window, trying hard not to cry.

"Roxie," he called.

"What?" I asked, still looking out the window.

"I'm not angry with you."

Kristen Ashley

"I know."

I believed him. Still, I felt like a total and complete pain in the ass.

"I like your dad," I offered as a change of subject.

"Good," he replied and, for the first time that afternoon, I felt some of his anger had slipped away.

He parked in front of his house. There were familiar cars lining the street, including Uncle Tex's El Camino.

When we walked into the house, we were assaulted by the smell of garlic, the sounds of Led Zeppelin and an overexcited chocolate lab.

If that wasn't overwhelming enough, the place was filled. Indy, Jet, Ally and Annette were sitting at Hank's dining room table playing cards. Kitty Sue (Hank's Mom) and Nancy were in the kitchen cooking. I could hear (just barely; Led Zeppelin was kind of loud) a ballgame playing on the TV in the other room.

"Yo bitch!" Annette greeted when we walked in. "And, um... dude," Annette went on, looking at Hank.

"Is everything okay?" Kitty Sue asked, her eyes on Hank. She was holding up a wooden spoon that looked like it was coated with spaghetti sauce.

Nancy moved toward me and gave me a one-armed hug.

"Bet you're hungry," she said into my ear.

Hank answered his Mom while I relaxed into Nancy's hug and nodded to her. She moved away and Uncle Tex was standing behind her.

"For fuck's sake, girl. We don't want it borin' but this ain't the god-damned *French* fuckin' *Connection*," he boomed, and I could tell he was trying to make a joke, but he didn't think the situation was all that funny.

I grinned at him, but it was weak.

He put his big hand on the top of my head for a second then took it away.

I grinned at him again, this time it was stronger.

"We got all your stuff in, it's in the extra bedroom," Ally announced and I turned to her.

"Nancy and I packed your things at Tex's and brought them over," Kitty Sue added, and I looked to her in total shock. I opened my mouth to say something, something like, "Are you fucking insane?" but then Tex caught my look and started booming.

184

"No lip, Roxie. Hank wants you with him, you're stayin' with him."

Good God.

They'd moved me in with Hank.

Uncle Tex was right. It'd been a week, and there I was, all moved in with Hank.

Shit.

I stared at Jet and she was giving me a look that was half smile, half grimace. She knew my pain. She'd had to move in with Eddie during her troubles, and even though her problems were through, she still hadn't moved out. I could tell she wasn't going to do a thing about my current situation though, likely because she agreed with everyone else.

I made a strangled sound and looked back at Tex. I was beginning to get angry.

"Do I not have a say in this?" I asked Uncle Tex.

"Nope," he responded.

My eyes narrowed. "Excuse me, but I think I do."

"You can have your say when people aren't shootin' at you," Tex returned.

Jason, Lee and Eddie walked in from the TV room to catch what was likely to be a more spectacular show as I squared off with Uncle Tex.

"That's just it. They were shooting at me, but Daisy was with me. They could have shot her. They did shoot her car!" I snapped. "Seems to me everyone would be a heck of a lot safer if I was far away from here."

"You ain't thinkin' straight," Tex said agreeably. "That's understandable."

I stomped my foot. I was no longer beginning to get angry, I was out and out angry.

"I *am* thinking straight. If something happens to someone because of me, I wouldn't be able to live with myself."

"Nothing's going to happen," Hank said from beside me, cutting into the conversation.

I turned to him. "Yeah? You sure about that?" I asked.

His eyes got hard. "Yeah," he said slowly, staring at me. "Yeah, I'm fuckin' sure."

Holy cow.

The way he said it, the way he looked, made me believe him.

Almost.

"Hank, that mouth," Kitty Sue said in a mother's tone. Even with the tension flowing between Hank and me, I had to admire Kitty Sue telling off her grown-up, super-macho, badass cop son for dropping the f-bomb.

Then she announced, "Spaghetti's ready, let's eat."

The conversation was over, and so was the show.

Even though I didn't want it to be, I really had no choice.

⚘

We ate. We did the dishes. We played Scattergories. Uncle Tex took Nancy home. We had sundaes smothered in hot fudge sauce and topped with whipped cream and a cherry. We did the new dishes. Kitty Sue went home, Hank and Lee both walking her to her car.

This I found so sweet I felt my breath constrict in my chest and caught Indy's eye. Her eyes were bright and warm and something flowed from her to me, like an invitation to a sisterhood that only we two could share. I wanted to accept, more than anything I'd ever wanted in my whole life, even Corporate Diva-dom, closets stuffed with clothes and a front row seat at the Chanel Winter Runway Show in Paris.

Hank and Lee came back and the moment was lost, but the promise remained, and I felt so moved by it I barely said another word the rest of the night.

We played more Scattergories. We listened to Indy and Ally telling stories of Haunted Houses past and I began to get more and more freaked out at this Haunted House business. It didn't sound fun. It sounded frightening. It sounded crazy. It sounded totally out-of-control.

Hank noticed me getting tense and pointedly put away the Scattergories game.

Everyone took the hint. Hugs were exchanged then they all left.

"You've gone quiet," Hank commented after he'd closed and locked the door.

"I was shot at today," I answered, thinking I had a good point even though I was lying.

He walked up to me. "That's not it."

He was right, that wasn't it. How he knew that, don't ask me, but it was like he had a cord and he'd plugged it into me the minute he first laid eyes on me. It had been that way since the start. This freaked me out and made me feel

186

centered and safe all at the same time. Don't ask me how it did this, I couldn't tell you that either.

"It's nothing," I said. "I need to call Daisy."

Surprisingly, he let it go, saying he had his own calls to make.

I called Daisy and she told me she was fine and not to worry about her.

"They fucked with the wrong girl when they fucked with me. Mark my words," she threatened.

I marked them. She sounded serious. Daisy might be sweet-as-pie and cute-as-a-button, but I got the definite sense she could open one major can of whoop ass.

⌇⌇

Hank's house had three bedrooms. The master, at the side of the house next to the kitchen with a small, three quarter bathroom attached, and there were two bedrooms at the back, off the living room, separated by a full bath. One of these rooms was what appeared to be a weight room-slash-junk room, made more so by my boxes and suitcases.

Annette and Jason had brought my stashed clothing and had also packed up most of my clothes. They'd also got my shoes, my jewelry case, my high school yearbooks, photo albums and some picture frames filled with photos of family and friends, and then carted it all out to Denver.

Apparently, they thought I was going to stay for a while.

The other bedroom was Hank's office. It had an old comfy looking couch, a table with TV, a desk, his computer and a bag filled with bats that was lumpy at the bottom with what appeared to be softballs sitting in the corner. I figured that room was his lair. He'd disappeared there when I called Daisy and I didn't disturb him.

After I called Daisy, I got undressed and ready for bed. I found Hank's CDs in the TV room, picked Born to Run because I was in Hank's house and that demanded Springsteen, and Shamus and I settled in with my lilac, embossed stationery.

I had set aside my stationery. I was amusing myself (not) by thinking how my life was certifiably fucked and "She's the One" had just started playing when Hank arrived.

He stopped at the side of the bed and stared down at me. He did this for a while. So long, it made me uncomfortable.

"What?" I asked.

"Been waitin' a long time to meet the girl in this song."

I felt my body still at the importance of what he just said.

So did Shamus. His head came up and he looked over at Hank, too.

The lyrics to this song weren't cryptic. Even so, somehow to me they collided with the thundering, unbelievably cool music that told what I considered the real story. Starting expectantly and then exploding, and then drawing out to a beautiful, vibrating climax.

Every girl would secretly want to be "the one", even though she might lie to herself that she did not. It was a man's view of the woman he desired, and even loved: bitter, sweet, defiant, admiring and fucking sexy as hell. Regardless of all that, the chorus was a repeat of "she's the one", present tense, which said it all.

"Whisky," I said quietly because I didn't know what else to say.

He tugged off his t-shirt, dropped it on the floor and turned out the lamp. I heard rustling in the dark while he took off the rest of his clothes and then the bed moved as he got on it.

He lay down beside me, but didn't touch me, and we both stayed still in the dark.

I waited for him to touch me, turn into me, something, but he didn't, and Shamus settled his head on my belly again.

To cover my confusion (and disappointment, if I was honest) I asked, "What's the deal with Daisy's husband, Marcus?"

Hank answered, "He's bad news. Runs guns, has a stable of girls and deals drugs as a hobby."

I got up on my elbow and turned, looking down at his shadow in the dark, wondering if I should laugh.

"You're joking," I said, and I really hoped he was.

"Nope," he replied, and my hope died.

Holy cow.

I didn't want Daisy to be married to a bad guy. I really liked Daisy. I wanted Daisy to be married to someone like Hank.

I asked, "Well, how does that work, with Daisy being one of the clan?"

"Daisy's a new addition. She's only been around the last few weeks."

I gasped at this piece of news. It was almost as unbelievable as knowing her husband was a crime lord.

"But I thought you'd all known her for ages."

"She took to watchin' out for Jet when she had her problems and she stuck. Marcus isn't a part of it, and somehow it works."

Boy, these people were nuts.

"What's the deal with Marcus and Eddie?" I asked.

"Eddie wants Marcus in prison and has been workin' to make that happen for a long time. Marcus doesn't want to go to prison. They hate each other."

That did not sound good.

"I don't see this working for long," I noted. "What happens when Eddie puts Marcus in jail?"

"Daisy knows the score, and so does Marcus," Hank told me. "It's not your problem and it isn't mine. When that happens, we'll all deal."

For Hank, it was simple as that. There was something very cool about that.

Even so.

"I don't think it's that simple," I shared.

He sighed and turned to me, but, I noted, he still didn't touch me. "Roxanne, I like Daisy, hard not to like her. But she's made her choice. Something happens to Marcus, and she reaches out her hand to 'the clan' as you call it, I expect everyone will take hold."

"Including you?" I asked, needing to know the answer to that as much as I needed oxygen.

"Including me."

I felt something settle in me. It wasn't in my belly, my heart or my mind. It was everywhere. It was in my soul.

Hank got up, walked through the dark room and turned off Springsteen in the middle of "Jungleland".

He lay down beside me and again didn't touch me.

"Whisky?"

"Yeah?"

"Nothing."

I was stymied. I wanted Hank to touch me. I didn't want to admit it, but there it was.

I'd never touched him. I had, but I'd never made the first move.

Kristen Ashley

I lay there some more.

Oh, fuck it, I thought, and rolled into him.

My hands went to his chest and my lips went to his collarbone. His arm curled around my waist. Shamus got the hint, jumped off the bed and meandered out of the room.

"Thought you were never gonna do that," he muttered, and I could swear he sounded relieved.

I didn't answer. I was busy, or at least my mouth was.

I explored his collarbone and neck with my mouth and tongue, then I kissed him. He let me taste him, even tease him, allowing me control of the kiss, and it was heady stuff.

Then I moved down slowly, discovering his chest and abs with my hands, mouth, teeth and tongue. The whole time he stroked my hip, bottom and back, but otherwise, he didn't touch me.

I took my time, enjoying the feel and taste of him, and his response, which consisted of the tightening of muscles, low groans (my favorites) and sometimes his fingers would bite into me if I did something he really liked.

I dipped lower, taking him into my hand, and then into my mouth.

His hand slid into my hair.

"Fuck," he said low.

I knew he liked what I was doing. I could tell and it turned me on. So much that I went gung ho, giving him all my best moves and making up new ones. All of a sudden his hand left my hair. Both his hands went under my armpits and he yanked me up onto his body.

Mm, seemed it was time to get serious.

I sat up, moving to the side, saying, "Let me take off—", but he pulled me back over him and pushed me up so I was straddling him. His hands went to my underwear and gave them a vicious tug. My hips jerked forward, the material tore and then my panties were gone.

"Whisky," I whispered, stunned that he just tore off my underwear (maybe he *was* part caveman, except a really good-looking one and without all the hair), but I had no time to process this. His hands were at my hips and he pushed down just as his hips lifted up and he slammed into me.

It felt great, unbelievably great, and I nearly lost track of what I was doing. I bit my lip, controlling my desire to let him take over and bent forward, kissing his neck under his ear and asked, "Hank, please. This time let me."

190

Partly I did this because I wanted to give him something, but partly I did this because it was fucking well my turn.

His grip loosened at my hips, which I took as his affirmative answer, and I started moving slowly, exploring his neck with my mouth all the while. When it was time to stop playing, when I knew we both wanted more, I pulled up but didn't go down, thinking to give him a taste of his own medicine.

In his ear I said, "I want my car back."

"Sunshine," he groaned, his hands biting into me.

"Promise me Hank."

He laid still, and just when I thought I had him where I wanted him, his hands tightened and he flipped me to my back and took over, pushing in deep and then grinding.

"Whisky! It's my turn!" I cried, wrapping my arms around him and lifting my hips into his.

"Don't use sex to manipulate," he told me.

I stared at him in the dark.

"You do it all the time!" I said.

"I'm good at it." He quit grinding and started moving. I couldn't help it, I moved with him. "And I don't do it with anything that's important."

I ignored his arrogance and the fact he was full of shit. The night before he'd used it to try to manipulate me into staying. If that wasn't important, I didn't know what was.

I decided, instead, to go back to the matter at hand, or at least one of the matters at hand. "I want my car back," I demanded but it came out kind of breathy.

"Quiet," he returned.

"I want my car back," I repeated.

He kissed me. I went dizzy. He kept my mouth busy so I wouldn't talk, and my body busy so after a while I *couldn't* talk.

Then I felt it. I twisted my head and tensed, breathing into his ear, "Whisky, I'm going to..." I didn't finish. He lifted my legs with his hands behind my knees, pounded into me and I lost the ability to speak.

When he was done, he rolled to his back, taking me with him. I lay on top of him for a while, my head on the pillow next to his, my forehead pressed to his jaw.

Finally I said, "That wasn't fair."

"The first time *you* touch *me*, it's so you can ask me for your car so you can leave me. I didn't feel much like playin' fair."

"Hank—"

He interrupted me, "You were callin' me Whisky a few minutes ago when you intended to make me do what you wanted by takin' me in your mouth."

I realized then that he was angry and I came up on my elbows.

"Are you angry?" I asked, even though I knew he was.

"You *are* 'She's the One'."

I gasped.

"I am *not* 'She's the One'," I snapped.

"You're completely 'She's the One'."

"Am not!" I shouted.

"Please tell me we aren't havin' this ridiculous conversation," he asked, sounding exasperated.

"You started it," I returned.

"I see. We *are* having this ridiculous conversation."

I made a strangled noise.

He rolled me onto my back, his weight moved and he reached over me, switching on the light. He settled on his side, towering over me and looked at me.

Before he could say anything I said, "I want my car."

"You aren't leavin'," he replied.

"No. I'm not. I just want my car."

"Then you aren't gettin' it until I know you won't do anything stupid. Like leave."

I scowled at him. "I said I wouldn't leave, I won't leave."

"I hate to say this Sunshine, but I don't trust you. You think alligators are cute and you got friends who'll drop everything to drive across country to bring you your stuff and that's because you got a heart bigger than the state of Colorado and what happened today flipped you out. Not, I'm guessin', what happened to you, but what happened to Daisy while she was with you. I give you back your car and you're gone."

He was so right.

I *hated* that.

"It's *my* car."

"You're *my* woman and I don't want you off on your own with Flynn and God knows who lookin' for you."

My body froze. "Billy?"

Hank stared at me and I knew he'd said more than he intended.

Then he muttered, "Fuck."

I felt fear steal through me.

"Hank, talk to me," I whispered.

His thigh moved over mine and he pinned me to the bed. "Roxanne, you're safe. No one's gonna harm you."

"Talk to me," I said, louder and slightly more hysterical this time.

Hank sighed. "Got word before I came into the bedroom. Jimmy got one of those boys to talk. Flynn got away from them."

Good God.

My body jerked and Hank's arm went around me, pulling me into him.

"No one's gonna harm you," he repeated.

"Hank, he knows where you live. I have to get out of here."

"Roxanne, listen to me."

I started squirming, totally panicked, trying to escape.

"Roxanne, dammit," he swore, but I didn't quit struggling.

He dropped to his side and rolled me into him, wrapping his arms around me, pinning mine to my body and he tossed a heavy thigh over mine. He was so strong, resistance was futile so I stilled.

"He hurt me," I told Hank's neck.

"I know."

"He'll do it again."

"No he won't."

I lay there breathing heavily, more from anxiety than my struggles.

"I'm scared," I admitted, and it took everything I had left to do it.

Hank's arms and leg tightened. "I know."

After a few minutes of internal struggle, I relaxed into him and he let go, reached out and turned off the light. Then he fell to his back, me partially on top, partially in his side, keeping one arm around me.

I tried to keep my mind quiet. Luckily I was exhausted so it worked. I'd think about it tomorrow. Or not at all. I was thinking not at all sounded good.

"I'm not your woman," I said, drowsy.

"You are," he returned.

Jeez.

There really was no shaking this guy.

"I'll die. I'll go with Billy. I'll do whatever so no one gets hurt," I promised.

"It won't come to that," he gave me a promise in return.

"I want my car," I went on, stubborn.

"We'll talk about it tomorrow night."

"I'm going to be at the Haunted House tomorrow night."

I heard his head move on the pillow. Probably he was shaking it because he thought I was a total idiot.

"You're a nut."

Okay, he was shaking it because he thought I was a nut.

"No I'm not," I said.

He didn't answer.

I lay there for a long while. I felt the tension leave his body, his hand now relaxed on my hip and I figured he was asleep.

"I didn't start touching you to get something out of it. I did it because I wanted to," I told his sleeping self.

"That's good to know," he replied, his voice low and sounding tired but definitely not asleep.

I jerked up on my elbow. "I thought you were asleep!"

"Nope."

Shit.

I settled back down.

"I really do think you're a jerk," I said, though even I could tell I didn't mean one word of it.

"For not being asleep?" Now he sounded both tired *and* amused.

"Well... yeah."

"I wasn't asleep when you sang 'Because the Night' either."

Holy cow.

I jerked up on my elbow again. "Please tell me you're kidding."

"Nope," he said again.

Shit. Shit. Shit.

I rolled away. He rolled with me, caught me around the waist and pulled me back into his body.

"Now, I have to leave," I said.

"Why?"

"It's embarrassing. My singing sucks."

"It sounded good to me."

"That's because you like me."

He kissed my neck.

Then he settled behind me and said, "Yeah."

Chapter 15

My Day with the Boys

I heard Hank's phone ringing. He muttered an oath and leaned over me to pick up his cell from the nightstand.

"Yeah?" he answered, his voice husky with sleep.

My eyes flickered open. It was still really dark.

My eyes shut again and I curled into Hank. Shamus pressed into my back.

"Where?" Hank asked.

He seemed resigned, not tense. Since he wasn't tense, I figured my world was not about to come crashing down so I didn't get tense.

Then he said, "Got to take care of somethin' at home, then I'll be there." Another pause, then, "Yeah."

I heard the beep of him disconnecting the call.

"Whisky?" I whispered.

There were more beeps. Hank was making a call.

"Just a minute, sweetheart," he answered then he talked into the phone. "Jack? Hank. I need to go out and I need protection for Roxie."

He stopped talking. I got up on my elbow and pulled my hair out of my face. Shamus gave an enormous doggie groan of protest.

"Fuck," Hank said then paused. "Yeah. I'll take her there. Twenty minutes, tops."

Another beep as he disconnected.

"What's going on?" I asked, looking at his shadow in the darkness.

He moved. The light came on and I blinked. Shamus jerked to his belly and surveyed the scene, preparing for all doggie possibilities open to him: early walk, early breakfast or some sort of pets and cuddles.

"There's been a homicide and it's connected to a case I'm on," Hank told me. "I've got to go to the scene. I need to take you to Lee's offices. You can go back to sleep there. I'll pick you up later."

I blinked again, but not because the light burned my eyes.

Lee's offices?

No way in hell.

Kristen Ashley

"I can go to Uncle Tex's," I suggested.

He shook his head, pulled away, got out of bed and walked to the dresser.

"Please don't argue. I want to be sure you're safe and Lee's boys can keep you safe. Get some stuff together. A change of clothes, whatever you need for the morning. We have to leave now."

Was he serious?

"Now" wasn't an option for me. He knew I was high maintenance. He'd said twenty minutes, and some of that was travel time. I needed to choose an outfit, I needed hair stuff, body stuff, makeup. I needed twenty minutes just for the outfit.

"Now?" I asked.

He pulled on some white boxer shorts, came back to the bed and tugged me out of it.

When he was standing in front of me, he bent and kissed my nose.

"Now," he answered.

Shit.

Hank carried his workout bag that he'd emptied for me to pack and held my hand as we walked up some steps to some offices. I had the handle of Shamus's leash in my other hand.

Shamus was beside himself with glee, his doggie body trembling with it. He was on an adventure.

I was beside myself with despair. I couldn't be left alone without protection.

I'd come without a fight mainly because I'd caused enough worry and mayhem. I didn't need to have a big argument with Hank when he needed to go to work. Furthermore, he was right. Uncle Tex was huge and tough, but Lee's boys could be commissioned to keep the Pope safe.

Not to mention, Hank had said please.

We walked into some offices. The lights were out in the room we entered, but there was an inside door open. A light from the hallway there lit the space and I could tell it was a reception area.

Hank and I walked down the hall. It had several doors leading off of it.

198

A man came out of a room halfway down the hall, but stood in the open doorway. He was built like a truck, but perhaps slightly more solid.

"Safe room's open and ready," he said to Hank. His eyes came to me briefly, then he went back into the room and the door closed behind him.

Not much of a welcome.

Hank took me toward the end of the hall and into a room. It was sparsely furnished and not decorated. A double bed, a reclining chair, a TV and a bookshelf full of books and DVDs. Another door led off of it.

I let go of Shamus's lead and he got busy exploring his new space.

Hank dumped the bag in the chair.

"Sleep," he said after he turned to me. "I'll be back before you wake up."

"Okay," I replied. He had things to do, important things that involved crime and justice. I reminded myself that now was not the time to cause a fuss.

He walked to me. I noticed his eyes were lazy and I held my breath. His hand came to the side of my neck and he gave me a light kiss.

Then he was gone.

I took off my jacket, under which I was wearing a pair of jeans and my lilac nightie. I took off my shoes, the jeans, turned off the light and got into the bed. Shamus got in with me, walked around on the bed for a while, getting the lay of the land. He settled on his side, his back pressed to my side and we both fell asleep.

⌐◈¬

Shamus jerked and jumped off the bed. I rolled over to see what he was up to, but he was already halfway across the room.

I looked toward the doorway and a man was standing there.

For a second, I stared at him, confused, because I didn't know what was going on.

Then I remembered.

Even so, I continued to stare at the man.

It didn't take much to know this was another one of Lee's boys. Not Big Truck Dude. This guy was tall but lean, wearing black cargo pants, a black, skintight t-shirt and black boots. He had black hair, cut close, and the absolute best facial hair I'd ever seen on a guy in my life. A thick, black mustache that grew across his lip and down the sides of his mouth, shaved clean and precise. He looked like Harley Man morphed with Just Plain Hot Man.

"Hey," I said to him.

One side of his mouth went up in a sexy half-grin.

Good God.

"Dog wants out. Hank's delayed. Go back to sleep."

I nodded, stunned silent at the amount of information he was able to share using the fewest words possible.

He stepped aside. Shamus walked through the door, tail wagging, and he closed it.

I laid there for a second, thinking there was no way in hell I was going to get back to sleep.

Then I went back to sleep.

<hr/>

I woke up, again felt confused, again realized what was happening and I got out of bed.

I tried the inner door and found it was a bathroom. I hauled my shit into it, did my mega-morning-preparations (even though I forgot my body wash, I found an unopened bar of Irish Spring under the sink, and I forgot my hair-smoothing lotion so I had to make do with just my finishing wax). I hadn't done half bad with my outfit, considering I was half asleep. Rich forest green, low rider corduroys, oatmeal, shawl-necked cashmere cardigan that I wore without a shell, belted at the waist with a wide chocolate suede belt and matching suede flats.

Once I was done, I walked through the other room to the door, needing coffee, needing food, needing to check on Shamus and needing to know where Hank was.

I tried to open the door, gave it a yank, my hand slipped off the handle and the door didn't move.

I stared at it and tried again.

The handle didn't twist and the door still didn't move.

I was locked in.

I felt panic edge through me.

"What the fuck?" I whispered.

Then I heard a disembodied, "Roxie."

I looked around searching for the source of the sound.

It came back. "This is the control room. Hang tight. We're bringin' someone in."

"What?" I asked, feeling stupid, talking to the room.

"We're bringin' someone into the holding room. We need you to hang tight. Once he's secured, we'll come and get you."

"Holy cow," I whispered. Then I panicked.

"It's not—" I started to say.

"It isn't Flynn," the voice interrupted me.

I let out a deep breath. Then I took in a sharp one, realizing he knew why I was panicked.

Okay, whatever, it's not like my life being certifiably fucked is a secret, I thought.

I sat on the arm of the reclining chair and listened to see if I could hear them bringing in whoever. I couldn't.

Then the door opened and Just Plain Hot Guy was standing there.

I got up.

"Hey again," I greeted.

He did one of his half-grins.

"Hungry?" he asked.

I nodded.

He stepped sideways and did a sweeping gesture of his arm, telling me to precede him.

Man of few words.

I walked out. He fell into step beside me and we walked down the hall.

"I'm Roxie," I told him.

"I know," he replied.

Well, there you go.

"And you are...?" I prompted.

He looked at me. His eyes were dark but I noticed they were also blue. Indigo.

Good God.

"Luke," he said.

"Nice to meet you, Luke."

He did another half-grin.

I tripped.

It turned into a full grin.

Shit, shit, shit.

We made it to the end of the hall. At the door, he stopped and put his hand on the handle.

"Our receptionist will go out and get you some food. Whatever you want," he told me.

I nodded, thinking that was nice; visions of Aunt Bea from "The Andy Griffith Show" tumbling through my head. He opened the door and I walked through and stopped dead.

The woman sitting behind the gleaming reception desk was as far away from Aunt Bea as you could get. She looked like she'd just walked off a runway; high cheekbones, shiny blonde hair, ten pounds underweight, absolutely beautiful.

"Hi, I'm Dawn," she said brightly when she saw me. There was a smile on her face that I noticed didn't reach her eyes. She did a full body scan and then her smile turned smug.

Bitch, I thought.

"Hi. I'm Roxie," I replied.

"I know," she said this like it was a joke.

"Breakfast," Luke cut in, clearly having other things to do, and those did not include common niceties like introductions or hanging around listening to Dawn being a bitch.

"Um…" I was feeling funny about giving her my order.

"Coffee?" Luke cued me.

"Yes… a skinny caramel latte?" I asked, unsure.

His eyes moved to Dawn and so did mine. She'd lost her smug smile and looked peeved. It was pretty clear she didn't feel like running out to get me a caramel latte.

"What else?" Luke asked, looking back to me.

"I don't know. A scone, a muffin… something like that." I felt tremendous pressure. Perhaps I should order plain fruit and unsweetened granola and ask them where I could do my morning yoga, though I didn't practice yoga.

"Got that?" Luke asked Dawn. He was done and it was time to move on.

She nodded, grabbed her purse out of the drawer and skedaddled, walking like she was on a catwalk, one foot in front of the other, her ass swaying under the skirt of her expensive, tailored suit.

Bitch, I thought again, watching her go.

"No comparison," Luke remarked after the door closed behind Dawn, and I turned to him.

"Excuse me?" I asked.

"Dawn's a man eater. You're not. No comparison," Luke answered, and I didn't know how to take that.

"Is that good?"

The half-smile came back. "Most men prefer to do the eating."

Holy fucking *cow.*

"Uncle Tex told me you were shot," I blurted out, desperate to get off the subject of Just Plain Hot Guys eating *anything.*

"Yeah," he replied.

"How're you feeling?" I asked, although it was a stupid question. He looked healthy and fit; *very* healthy and fit.

"Alive," he answered.

That kind of said it all.

"Well, I'm glad for that," I told him because I couldn't think of anything better to say.

Before he could answer (not that he was going to answer), the door opened.

I turned and saw Lee and Marcus come in.

"Oh shit," I muttered before I could stop myself.

Luke got close. I could feel his heat against my back.

I stood stock-still.

Marcus's eyes settled on me.

"Roxie," Lee said.

He walked to me and bent to kiss my cheek.

Wow.

A cheek kiss from Lee.

It was a multiple "holy cow" day for sure.

"Hi Lee," I whispered.

Lee's eyes moved to Luke, crinkled at the corners to show his amusement, just like his Dad's, and he stepped aside.

"Did you meet Marcus yesterday?" Lee asked, his eyes moving to me.

I shook my head.

"Marcus, this is Roxanne Logan," Lee introduced us.

Marcus put out his hand and I took it.

Before he could say anything, I said quickly, "I'm so sorry I got Daisy shot at. I like Daisy. She's been really nice to me. She's wise and she's funny and she has interesting taste in clothes." Marcus looked at me and didn't say anything so, of course, I carried on like the idiot I was. "And I'm sorry about her Mercedes getting bullet holes in it. It wasn't her fault. She's a good driver. I mean, she kept her cool, kind of, except when we were playing chicken and... um... other times."

Oh my God, someone had to stop me from talking.

I went on, "And if she ever gets shot at again, I'm sure she'll probably get away."

Luke's hand settled at the back of my neck.

I shut up.

The hand stayed there.

"Daisy tells me you've had it rough," Marcus noted.

I nodded. Luke's hand tightened.

Marcus stared at me and a shiver slid across my skin. He was handsome, that was certain, but there was a hardness behind his eyes that was chilling.

"Your troubles are over," he stated with a finality that caused the shiver to go into a full body tremble.

I blinked at him.

"Let's go to my office," Lee cut in. His eyes were now serious and they were on Luke.

Marcus still had hold of my hand. He gave it a firm squeeze that felt like a promise. Then he let go. Lee touched my shoulder and they walked out of the room.

Luke's hand came away from my neck and I turned to him.

"What just happened?" I asked him.

"Marcus entered the picture," Luke answered.

"What?"

"Three things," Luke said immediately, surprising me. I wasn't sure he could enumerate three things in Luke Speak. He went on, proving he could. "One, the police can track down your trouble, that trouble is put away and it's over. Two, we can do it, your trouble is taken to the holding room, taught a lesson, then handed to the police and it's over. Three, Marcus can do it, that trouble is dead. I'm hopin' for number two."

I focused on number three.

"Dead as in not-breathing-anymore dead?" I asked.

"That's the only kind of dead there is," he replied.

"Holy cow," I said.

He stared at me.

"Why?" I asked.

Luke didn't answer, but I knew why. Marcus didn't blame me for what happened to Daisy. He blamed Billy and whoever else was involved in this mess. I'd seen Marcus holding Daisy the day before. Whatever he was, criminal king-pin, gun dealer, pimp, he loved Daisy. Someone put her life in danger and that someone was going to pay.

"Maybe I should talk to him," I suggested to Luke.

The half-grin came back. "Although that would be entertaining, it's not gonna happen."

"Why not? Maybe I can persuade—"

"Roxie," he interrupted me.

"Yeah?"

"Be quiet."

I stared at him and then heaved a big sigh.

Being quiet might be a good thing.

He put a hand to the small of my back, propelled me toward the hallway door and then took me to the control room and Shamus.

<hr />

"This is *cool!*" I shouted when I entered the control room.

Shamus ran to me and jumped up on me, his body aquiver with excitement. I just avoided him cracking three more ribs, gave his head a good rub and then gently pushed him off. He sat on my feet, tongue lolling.

"Hi, I'm Monty," a man with a blond military cut stood and smiled at me, offering his hand. I took it, we did a shake and I tried not to wince when nearly all my bones were crushed.

Monty was slightly older than most of Lee's boys, but no less fit. He was also slightly more in tune with social nuances, like saying hello.

"What is all this stuff?" I asked, looking at all the monitors on shelves on the wall, DVD recorders under them, knobs, buttons and racks of electronic equipment. It looked like they could strap me in and we could go to Mars.

"This is the surveillance room. We run security through here and... other things," Monty shared.

I looked at the monitors.

I gawked at the monitors.

"Hey! That's Fortnum's! And so's that... and that... and..." I trailed off.

Dear God, they had nearly every corner, the front and back of Fortnum's monitored. I watched Uncle Tex banging away at the espresso machine at the same time he seemed to be carrying on an argument with Duke.

Monty flipped a switch and Uncle Tex's voice boomed into the room.

"I don't want to listen to no fuckin' Hank Williams, Jr.! You got Johnny Cash, I'll listen to Johnny Cash. If not, put Cream back on, turkey!"

Monty flipped off the switch.

"Holy cow," I breathed.

"We monitor Fortnum's twenty-four, seven," Monty said.

"Best part of the day surveillance shift," Luke put in.

I tried to think of the time I'd spent in Fortnum's. Almost none of it had gone without some embarrassing incident.

I looked at Monty and Luke. Luke was wearing his half-grin. Monty was smiling flat out.

"Shit," I said.

"Have a seat," Monty invited, the smile still playing about his face. "You can eat your breakfast in here. I'll show you what we do."

"Where's Hank?" I asked, sitting next to Monty, looking back to the monitors. Shamus moved to settle at my feet.

"Hank's indefinitely delayed," Monty replied, but I wasn't listening. One of the monitors showed a visual of the room I'd slept in.

I turned in horror to Monty.

"Did you watch me sleep?" I asked.

He nodded. "Hank's orders. Constant surveillance. If we aren't with you, we're watching you."

"But... I was just down the hall," I said, mortified that they had watched me sleep, and I hoped I hadn't drooled.

"One thing I've learned, you can never be too careful," Monty replied.

Okay, so, maybe he was right about that.

Monty took my mind off the alarming news that they had watched me sleep and told me what they did in the control room; some security, mostly investigation. Then Dawn showed with my latte and a blueberry muffin. The latte was cold and had hazelnut syrup in it. The muffin was crap. I didn't say a word and ate the muffin while we listened to the police band radio and Monty taught me some of the codes.

Then he turned down the police band. I sipped my latte and we watched the monitors.

About half an hour later, I was losing the will to live and the control room had lost its coolness. How could these guys do this day in and day out? It was stupendously boring.

The phone rang.

"Thank God!" I yelled before I could stop myself. I was happy that something, anything, was happening. I didn't care if it was the dry cleaners calling to say Monty's shirts were ready to be picked up.

Monty shot me a grin then looked at Luke while he reached for the phone. "These girls like their excitement."

"Thank fuck," Luke muttered his reply.

I didn't know what that meant but, I suspected, at least, that it was good.

"Yeah?" Monty said in the phone. Then he said, "She's right here." He turned to me. "Hank."

I took the phone and put it to my ear.

"Hey," I said, dipping my head and feeling weird in that little room with Monty and Luke having nothing to do but listen.

"How're you doin'?" Hank asked and I felt a thrill race through me at the sound of his voice.

"Monty and Luke and I are hanging in the control room."

Silence.

"Hank?"

"I thought you'd watch a DVD or something."

"No, they're teaching me police codes."

More silence.

"Dawn brought me a latte and muffin. Luke said I could have whatever I want so she ran out to get it for me," I said this because I didn't have anything more exciting to say.

"Bet Dawn liked doing that," Hank replied, apparently knowing Dawn.

"She didn't seem tickled pink," I told him.

I heard Hank's soft laugh and another thrill raced through me.

"I'm gonna be a while. You gonna be okay?" he asked.

"Sure," I said.

"I'll be there to get you as soon as I can."

"Okay."

Silence for a beat, and then, "Am I talkin' to Roxanne Logan?" he asked.

"Well… yeah. What's the matter?"

Another beat of silence. "Nothin', sweetheart. I'll see you soon."

I got my third thrill and then he disconnected.

I handed the phone to Monty. He replaced it into the receiver and then he touched a button and said, "Brody, come to the control room." After that, he settled back in his chair.

"Who's Brody?" I asked.

"Our computer guy. You can go with him for a while. Change of scenery."

I gave him a relieved smile.

There was a knock on the door and Luke got up and opened it.

A man walked in wearing black jeans; his dark hair needed a cut and he was head-to-toe in disarray. He wore Buddy Holly glasses and his body was absolutely *not* the normal lean muscle of one of Lee's boys. His black t-shirt said in white lettering, "I upped mine, up yours!"

"Jeez. This is Roxie. Wow. I've wanted to meet you, like, for days!" he shouted when he saw me.

"Hi," I said, surprised at his reaction to me.

"You're, like, famous. It was crazy around here when you were kidnapped. Everybody was running around, the phones ringing off the hook, Dawn was in, like, *a total snit*, worse than usual. I was running every computer check possible. Hotel registrations, airlines, credit cards. Lee paid me a *bucketload* of overtime. Every time Vance reported in that someone had seen you at a gas station or whatever, the whole place went *wired*. When Vance called in that someone saw you tied to a steering wheel, Hank was so pissed-off, he put his fist through the wall in the down room. I saw it. It was *insane*."

I felt the blood run out of my face.

"Brody," Monty said, his voice low with warning.

"What?" Brody asked, looking at Monty, completely lost in the excitement of it all. Then he caught the hint, his exhilaration faded and he looked at me. "Oh yeah. Right. Sorry. Well, glad to see you're okay and everything."

He didn't sound glad. He sounded like he would have preferred the place still to be *wired*.

"Why don't you take Roxie to your office? Show her what you do," Monty suggested.

"None of the confidential stuff, right?" Brody asked.

Monty shook his head and it wasn't hard to read that Brody was trying his patience.

"Right," he confirmed.

"Okay. Come on," Brody said.

I waved to Luke and Monty as I followed Brody out of the control room. They didn't wave back but they did both smile.

Brody took me to another door down the hall and into a room that had four cubbies in the middle, all of them with computers and filing cabinets.

"I do my stuff here. Credit checks, employment checks, stuff like that. I also have other projects that are more fun, but I'm not allowed to talk about them to anyone, even Hank's girlfriend," Brody told me.

I stopped next to what was his cubby. It was decorated profusely with a variety of energy drink cans, big grabs of chips and candy wrappers with the odd action figure thrown in for class.

I looked at Brody. "Did Hank really put his fist through a wall?"

Brody brightened. "Yeah! They haven't fixed it yet. Do you wanna see?"

I bit my lip and shook my head.

Holy motherfucking *cow*.

Hank, Mr. Control, had put a fist through the wall. For me.

Shit.

Brody went on, "He was real upset. Your uncle was super upset, too, but he mostly yelled. No offense, but I thought it was cool. See, Dawn's got a thing for Hank now that Lee's taken, and she knows she isn't gonna get anywhere with Vance, Mace or Luke. She's been trying to get something on with one or the other of them, like, *forever*. Always flirting, even though she has a boyfriend. She was, like, *totally* pissed when she found out Hank had a girlfriend, especially when he went all ballistic. Me and everyone else were thrilled. Dawn thinks her shit doesn't stink. She may be pretty, but everything about Dawn stinks. It's great working here, except you can't tell anyone about the cool stuff you do. Everything's great, but not Dawn. So, we all were happy that Hank really likes you, because we like Hank, but we don't like Dawn. We weren't happy that you were kidnapped or anything."

Well! I just *knew* Dawn was a bitch.

I didn't share my thoughts and gave him a smile.

"Thanks," I said.

None of the other computers were taken so I asked him, "Can I check my email on one of these computers?"

"Sure. Let me set you up," Brody replied.

I checked a week's worth of email, sending replies, deleting junk and doing a few changes and updates through the administration panels of some of my websites.

A little later, Dawn came in with a couple of pizzas and sodas and Monty and Luke took turns joining us, having a break from the monotony of surveillance. Monty chatted about his wife and family. Luke didn't say much, but Brody and I made up for it. Dawn didn't join us at all, likely for fear that the cheese on the pizza would give her instant cellulite, but she came in, face set and hard, to clean up afterward.

Once the door closed behind her, Brody gave me a huge grin.

I was logging out of one of my sites when Brody walked behind me and saw what I was doing.

"You do websites?" he asked.

"Yeah, I'm a designer."

"Cool beans!" he yelled. "Show me one of your sites."

He rolled his chair next to me and we trolled through a few of my sites. Then he showed me a game the computer team had loaded called "Diablo". It was a role-playing game where you got to be a character and went on quests through scary, devastated lands, caves, deserts and cities. You picked up gold, armor, weapons and magical spells and fought bad guys. It was kickass.

Brody networked the game then rolled in his chair back to his cubby. I picked the assassin character because she had the best outfit and we started playing it.

What seemed like minutes later, but was actually hours, we were in a battle to the death with a whole bunch of orcs and trolls and I shouted, "Yeah! Go Brody! Kick his ass!"

"Don't stand there! Move away. He's killing you!" Brody yelled.

I chanced a quick glance at my stats. The bad guy *was* killing me.

I panicked.

"I'm out of health potions. Retreat! Retreat! *Give me some of your health potions!*" I screamed.

"I don't have any potions. Run, bitch, *run*," Brody squealed.

The red ran out on my health and my assassin was transported, stripped of everything we'd earned, back to the starting camp.

"I'm dead! Fuck, they killed me! They fucking killed me," I wailed, jerking my hand from the mouse and rolling my chair back in disgust.

Brody had gone quiet.

I looked at him and saw he was looking at the door.

I turned my gaze to the door, and it was opened. Hank, Lee and Luke were all standing there in various amused male poses, watching us.

Shit.

"What?" I asked, deciding to go with uppity.

"Enjoying yourself?" Hank asked, his mouth twitching.

"No," I said angrily. "I'm dead. Now I have to run all the way back to my lifeless body and get my stuff. The orcs and trolls will be hanging around and we'll have to fight them and I can't do that without my good armor. I'll have to use the crappy stuff I have stashed in my trunk. I had a really good sword and helmet and now they're gone. That just plain sucks."

Hank stared at me.

Then he said, "You do know I don't know what the fuck you're talkin' about."

"Diablo," I replied, like that explained it all.

Hank just kept staring at me.

"Nothing. Forget it." I turned to Brody. "Will this run on my laptop?" I asked.

"Sure, if you've got a good one," Brody replied.

I looked back to Hank. "We need to go to the mall. I've got to buy this game."

"Maybe we'll do that tomorrow, Sunshine."

"Now!" I snapped.

"Uh-oh," Brody said. "I've seen this before. It's not pretty. Soon she'll be playing all night on the Internet."

My head swung back to Brody. "You can play on the Internet?" I breathed.

"Now's a good time to shut up Brody," Lee warned.

Hank walked into the room and grabbed my hand. "Let's go, warrior princess. Time for dinner."

"I wasn't a warrior princess, I was an assassin," I told him.

Hank smiled at me.

My heart fluttered.

I rallied. "Anyway, we just had lunch," I said as Hank pulled me out of the chair.

"Five hours ago," Luke put in.

I stopped and stared at Luke, openmouthed.

"No shit?" I asked.

Luke shook his head, the amused male pose still in full force.

"Holy cow," I whispered.

The game had sucked five hours out of me and it felt like five minutes.

I turned to Brody. "I don't think Diablo is good for me."

"Some can take it, some can't. It's the will of Diablo," Brody replied.

I nodded at the profound sageness of his reply.

Hank tugged me toward the door and I could swear he was laughing.

"Later," Brody called as we walked out.

Chapter 16

Prayers

Hank went to get Shamus and I went to the safe room to pack my stuff.

I was standing at the reclining chair, shoving the last bits into the bag when Shamus ran to my side.

"Hey boy," I said, bending at the waist to give him an ear scratch that turned into a hand wash from Shamus's over-excited tongue. Apparently, the last five hours away from me had been doggie-traumatic for my furry chocolate boy.

"Ooo," I cooed. "Did Auntie Roxie leave you with the scary, badass dudes in the boring room? Poor fella."

I felt Hank's heat at my back before his arm slid around my middle and I straightened. His chin came to my neck and shifted my hair then his lips were there. Shamus sat on my feet.

"Have a good day?" Hank asked against my neck.

I shivered and turned in his arm. His head came up and I looked up at him. Shamus shifted to sit with his body leaning against both of us.

"Yeah," I told Hank, surprising myself because I meant it.

"Good," he said, and I could tell he meant it too.

I looked at him. He looked his usual handsome but tired. He hadn't had a full night's sleep, interrupted or not. He hadn't had his food delivered, even by a snotty bitch. He hadn't spent his afternoon being a make-believe, kickass assassin and killing make-believe orcs. He'd spent his day being a real life cop and going to ugly crime scenes.

"How was your day?" I asked, knowing the answer.

"Shit," he replied.

Yes, I was right. I knew the answer and I felt something happening to me, something drawing me to him and, against the directives of my mind (if not my heart), my body leaned into his. His other arm came around me.

"I guess it's not fun, going to the scene of a homicide at three o'clock in the morning," I said softly.

"No. As many times as I've done it, it's still not fun."

As many times as he'd done it.

Before I could stop myself, I lifted my hand and, with my middle finger, I traced the lower edge of his bottom lip. I watched my finger touch him and then I looked into his eyes.

"I'm sorry, I whispered.

His eyes changed. I couldn't describe it; they warmed, softened, and I felt the change in a physical way, straight to the deepest depths of my belly.

Then his head bent toward me, my hand slid across the stubble of his cheek and he kissed me, no messing around. It was full-on hot and heavy with lots of tongue.

When he was done, his mouth trailed to my ear as I held on tight, trying to recover from the kiss. My hand that was at his lip was around his neck, my fingers in his hair, my other arm was wrapped around his waist.

At my ear, his voice hoarse with something, passion, maybe just emotion, he murmured, "I want to fuck you right now. I want to slide inside you and erase this shitty day."

"Whisky," I breathed, not intending to say anything more. His words had robbed me of speech.

Did he honestly think I could do that for him?

One of his hands went under the hem of my sweater and into the waist-band of my corduroys. The other one slid over my behind and he pressed me into him. I could feel his hardness against me.

Yes, I guessed he thought I could do that for him.

And that thought overwhelmed me.

It all hit me then. His job, his responsibility, three o'clock phone calls, a gun on his belt, the shit he saw, the people he dealt with. After a day of that, going home to his house and his dog and, once there, he would be alone. No one to talk to about it or just help him forget.

It seemed ludicrous, a man like Hank being alone. He could be with any-one he chose.

He probably didn't even care.

But *I* cared.

Oh shit.

I was seriously in trouble.

Before I could process how much trouble I was in, his tongue traced the curve of my ear and I melted further into him. He twisted, taking me with him. Shamus scurried away from our legs and then moseyed to lie down by the door.

Hank started backing me to the bed.

"Hank," I said, but he didn't answer. He pushed me away from him and undid my belt. It fell to the floor and we stepped over it. His hands went into my cardigan, opening it and then he pressed my almost naked torso against his.

Then I remembered something, and ice shifted into my boiling veins.

"Hank, they have cameras in here."

"I don't care," he replied.

Oh no.

He couldn't mean that.

Could he?

"I think they even have microphones," I went on.

"I don't care," he repeated.

He *did* mean it.

The backs of my legs hit the bed and I wasn't prepared for it. I fell back and he came down, his knee settling on the bed between my legs. He was on top of me a moment and then rolled to the side, pulling me with him, sliding his thigh between my legs as his hand at my ass slid my crotch along its length. His mouth went back to my neck.

Oh my, but it felt good.

Even so.

"I don't want them watching," I said.

"They won't watch. They'll turn off the cameras."

I wished that was true, but I'd spent time in that room and after a while, you'd watch *anything*.

"No they won't," I said. "I know what it's like sitting in there, it's boring as hell. They'll totally watch."

His head came up, and in his authoritative voice, addressing the room at large, he ordered. "Turn off the cameras." And his mouth went back to my neck, clearly thinking that was that.

Good grief.

"They aren't going to do it," I told him.

His tongue slid down my neck to touch at the base of my throat.

"They'll do it," he said against my throat.

"They won't. You have to go check."

His head came up and he looked at me like I'd just asked him to pop out and fetch me some Russian caviar.

"Seriously?" he asked.

"Yeah," I answered.

He pressed my behind, putting me in intimate contact with his rock-hard crotch.

"Sunshine, I'm in no condition to go check."

Mm, it would seem he was right.

I thought about it then I made my decision. I'd hate it, but I'd do it, with conditions.

"Okay, but just in case they're watching, we have to do it with as many clothes on as possible and you have to be on top so they won't see me."

He stared at me a beat before he buried his face in my neck and I felt his body move with laughter. Then his lips slid along my cheek again and he kissed me, still laughing.

Then he kept kissing me.

I knew two kinds of Hank Kisses. The light kisses and the make-you-dizzy kisses.

These kisses were a third kind of kiss. His hands roamed my bottom and back and I realized these kisses weren't leading anywhere. They were cuddling-with-Hank kisses; softer, sweeter, slower, still lots of tongue, but mostly just-be-together-and-touch-while-you're-necking kisses. They made me a different kind of dizzy.

After a while, he stopped kissing me and rubbed my nose with his.

Then he said, "Let's go get something to eat."

I looked at him.

"We're not gonna do it?" I asked.

"No. I appreciate your sacrifice Sunshine, but if you're not comfortable, we're not gonna do it."

I hugged him, grateful, burrowing my face into his neck.

He was *such* a good man.

"Thank you," I whispered.

He kissed the top of my head.

"I'll erase your day after I get back from the Haunted House," I offered.

His hand went to my chin and lifted it up so I was looking at him. His eyes had that look in them again, the soft, warm look that made my stomach pitch.

"I'm gonna hold you to that," he said.

I found I had no problem with that at all.

We dropped Shamus off at his house and he took me to a restaurant called Reiver's that was on a street called Gaylord, which was in Hank's 'hood. We sat at the bar and Hank ordered for us. Our beers had just been delivered when my purse rang.

I yanked out my phone, flipped it open and put it to my ear. "Hello?"

"Yo Bitch!" Annette yelled into my ear. "Get shot at today?" she asked.

I looked at Hank and mouthed "Annette." I watched the sides of his lips turn up then to Annette I replied, "Not yet."

"Girl, Jason and I are *in love*," she said.

I smiled at the phone. "I already know that."

"No, I mean with Colorado. We've been mountain biking all day. It's unbelievably amazing," she told me.

"I'm glad you're having fun."

"Fun? This isn't fun. This is nirvana. The trails here kick... fucking... ass. Sofa-King *phat*. Bitch, I'm opening Head 2, Electric Boogaloo in Denver. There's a store across the street from Fortnum's that's for lease. I'm not fucking joking. I'm calling about it tomorrow."

Holy cow.

I wasn't sure this was good. In fact, I was pretty sure this wasn't good. I didn't want Annette moving to Denver.

As for myself, I was in Denver-limbo. I couldn't leave. I wasn't going to stay.

I'd had a day without incident, time to settle, get my mind around things. I'd cleared my email, did some work, felt my life wasn't totally out-of-control.

And I knew what I eventually had to do.

The signs were all there, the right ones. Lee's cheek kiss, Kitty Sue making us spaghetti, Indy's unspoken invitation to the Sacred Sisterhood of Nightingale Women, me getting straight A's on Malcolm's Test.

It wasn't that, it was me.

Things with Hank were good. Fucking fantastic actually, but that wasn't going to last. I knew that like I knew The Gap's clothing sizes ran small. I was damaged goods and when things settled down and Hank had a minute to think, he'd realize just what I was and that he could do better. I wanted to be long gone before that happened.

My plan was simple. I was going to ride the wave, get safe and not cause any (more) trouble and then I was getting the fuck out of Dodge.

I knew I'd lost my heart, it was too late to protect that, but I wasn't going to give it time. I wasn't going to be there when the warm, soft look in Hank's whisky eyes turned cold.

I came out of my thoughts and re-entered the phone conversation.

"Annette—" I started to say in protest.

"No talking me out of it. Jason and I are both agreed. Anyway, we really like your friends."

I looked at Hank. "They aren't my friends, they're Hank's."

"They're everyone's friends," Annette declared as I watched Hank's eyes flicker with controlled frustration. Annette went on, "We're coming down the mountain now, then we'll shower and get some food. We're supposed to meet at Ally's at eight thirty. See you there."

She disconnected.

I flipped the phone shut.

"Annette's thinking of moving to Denver," I told him.

Hank's hand came to my knee, his eyes registered approval. "That'll be good."

I bit my lip.

Hank watched my mouth.

"Shit," Hank muttered.

"What?" I asked.

"I don't like your look," he said.

"What look?" I asked.

He leaned into me and his hand slid up my thigh to rest at the side of my hip.

"Rewind," he said, his face close to mine. "Let's go back to the Roxie of fifteen minutes ago. The sweet one who didn't argue and did what she was told. I like her."

Well!

"That isn't the Real Roxie. The Real Roxie argues, never does what she's told and is a pain in the ass. This Roxie is Freaked-Out Life-in-Danger Roxie. You don't like the Real Roxie then give me back my car and I'll go home to Chicago," I told him.

His eyes went lazy. "I like Real Roxie too."

My eyes narrowed. He grinned.

Then he went on. "I was just enjoyin' the sweet one."

Then he took my hand, lifted it and pressed my middle finger to his lower lip reminding me what I'd done in the safe room and showing me how he felt about it. I held my breath as his mouth opened and his tongue touched my finger.

"Good God," I whispered, staring at his mouth and completely forgetting about my snit.

"Black bean dip," the bartender announced, oblivious to the public fore-play, pulling us out of the moment and putting a bowl of dip and some corn chips in between our beers.

My eyes slid to the side and I saw a table of three women. All three were staring at us openly. Or more to the point, staring at Hank. Their faces all showed identical expressions of sweltering hot lust to the point of being openly carnal.

I yanked my hand away from Hank's and reached for a chip while I collected myself. I heard Hank's soft chuckle before he took a pull of his beer.

Fucking Hank.

My phone rang again, I grabbed it as I dipped in the chip and flipped it open. "Hello?"

"Hey girl," Ally said. "Where are you?"

"I'm at Reiver's with Hank," I replied.

"Excellent! We were all going out to get some food, too late for you two. How about Annette and Jason?"

"I'm sure they'd like to go," then I gave her Annette's number.

"Cool. I'll call," she told me. "Listen, tell Hank not to worry. I know he's got to work tonight. Tell him Carl is going to be there and so is Jason. We've got enough stun guns to go around and Daisy's bringing a bodyguard."

My body went still.

"Stun guns?" I asked.

"Yeah," she answered, as if they were accessories akin to a handbag or a belt.

"Bodyguard?" I stayed on target.

She laughed. "Just saying, you're covered. See you at eight thirty. Wear something warm and gym shoes. Gotta be prepared to run. Later."

"Run?" I said into the dead phone.

I sat there a second then flipped the phone shut and slid it on the bar.

Hank was watching me.

I put the loaded chip into my mouth. I chewed. My eyes widened and I think I had a mini-culinary-orgasm.

After I swallowed, I breathed, "This stuff is *great*," then I dipped in another chip.

Hank's hand caught my wrist with the chip halfway to my mouth, my mouth all the way open to receive the chip. My eyes moved to him.

"Stun guns? Bodyguards?" he asked.

I closed my mouth and told him what Ally told me.

He let go of my wrist and sat back. His elbow went to the bar and his hand went to take a swipe at his forehead.

"Christ," he muttered.

I ate my chip and ignored him. Then I ate another one.

He looked at me. "You wouldn't feel like going back to Sweet Agreeable Roxie for a while, going to the station with me tonight, hanging out while I work?"

That sounded about as fun as sitting in the control room. I wasn't all-fired sure about this haunted house business, but I wasn't going to hang out watching my nails grow at the station while Hank worked.

I shook my head.

"Fuck," he said.

"We need to go back to your place," I told him. "I have to change clothes. Which reminds me, I need to call Vance."

Hank did a slow blink. "Why do you need to call Vance?"

"He bought me some clothes and some Keds. Ally mentioned I need to wear gym shoes and the only ones I own are the ones Vance bought me. I need to pay him back."

"I'll pay him back," Hank answered immediately.

I dipped another chip. "No, I'll pay him back. Do you have him programmed into your phone?" I put the chip into my mouth and held out my hand for his phone.

"You aren't callin' Vance," he said, taking his own chip.

"Why not?"

He chewed and swallowed. "Because you aren't."

I stared at him, thinking I was beginning to get angry. "Why not?"

"Because I don't like the idea of you talkin' to Vance."

Okay, I was definitely beginning to get angry.

"Why not?" I repeated.

"Vance is a player and he's playin' you."

It was my turn to blink.

"I don't think so," I said.

"He is."

"He is not."

"For Christ's sake, Roxie," he said, and I could tell he was beginning to get angry too.

"Don't 'for Christ's sake' me, Hank Nightingale. Vance is not playing me."

"What was happening at Lincoln's then?"

"Lincoln's?"

"When he was holdin' your hand."

Oh.

That.

"We were having a moment."

Hank's control slipped and his eyes went hard.

I watched, scared and fascinated at the same time.

"And when he was touchin' your ear?" he asked.

Mm, there was that too.

"We were having *another* moment," I answered.

Hank's control slipped more and his entire face went hard. He looked to the bartender as he slid off the barstool

"Watch this," he ordered the bartender, motioning with his head to our stuff on the bar. My purse and phone were sitting there as was our food.

The bartender looked at the gun and badge on Hank's belt and nodded. Hank grabbed my hand and pulled me off the barstool.

"Hey!" I snapped, but he dragged me out, around the corner and down the side of the building. All the while I tried to pull free. All the while I failed.

221

He pushed me up against the side of the building and I saw I was wrong about Hank's control slipping. One look at him and I realized Hank's control was *gone*.

Any smart girl would have kept her mouth shut. I was not a smart girl. It was an established fact, especially recently, that I was an idiot.

"I cannot believe you just dragged me out of the restaurant," I hissed.

Hank got close. "Remember when I told you that you bein' my woman meant I protected you and kept you safe?"

"Yes," I was still hissing.

"Well, this time, that comes in the form of me tellin' you what to do and what you're *not* gonna do is talk to, or see, Vance again."

Holy Mary, Mother of God.

I was no longer beginning to get angry. I was pissed the hell off.

"You *did not* just say that to me."

"I sure the fuck did."

"Take it back!" My voice was rising.

He got closer. One of his hands was at the bricks at the side of my head, the other one was at his hip. His chest was nearly against mine and his head was tilted to look down at me.

"Vance means something to me," I told him.

Um... not the right thing to say.

"You barely know him," he said.

"I barely know you," I retorted angrily.

Strike two. *Definitely* not the right thing to say.

"I've had my cock inside you. I'd say you know me a fuck of a lot better than you know Vance."

At that nasty comment, I put my hands to his abs and pushed hard. His body jerked but moved back into my space instantly.

"Don't be coarse," I clipped.

"Roxanne—"

"He rescued me from the sink! He took me to the hospital! He got me clothes when I had to get rid of the ones I was wearing because I couldn't bear to keep them on a second longer. He got me a shower because I hadn't had one in *days*."

"Roxanne—"

"No, Hank—"

"Roxanne, be quiet."

"No!"

His hand went from his hip to cup my jaw and his face dipped so close it was all I could see.

"Don't you think I wanted to be the one to rescue you from that fucking sink?" he growled, his voice low and dangerous.

My stomach clenched as I realized what had brought on his anger.

I stared at him and finally kept my mouth shut.

"Do you have any fucking *clue* how hard it was to wait for Vance to call in witness reports, every fuckin' report worse than the one before? You runnin' from a bathroom at a gas station, bloody, screamin' and fightin' to get away. Tied to a steering wheel. Eatin' fuckin' chips with your wrists bound. *Christ!*"

The last word was an explosion. I winced and jerked as if it had a physical impact on my body.

He pulled back and took his hand away from my face but I grabbed it and tugged on it.

"Hank, listen to me," he was looking at the wall over my shoulder, trying to regain control. When I said his name, his eyes moved to lock on mine and I felt a shiver run through me at the anger still there.

I went on, "After he found me, I asked Vance to take me back to Chicago."

At that, Hank's eyes flared.

I shook my head and continued, "He wouldn't do it. He said he wouldn't do it because he respected you and you'd sent him after me. He said he wouldn't do it because he didn't want to make you show him how you'd react if he didn't bring me back to you."

I watched him work to get control, a muscle moved in his jaw. All the while, he kept his beautiful eyes on me.

I felt the burning in my nostrils and took a deep breath to keep the tears at bay.

When I saw he had control, I whispered, "I'm glad it wasn't you who found me. I couldn't have… I wouldn't have been able to live with it if you saw me that way."

At that, his arms slid around me.

"Fuck, Roxie," he said over my head.

I put my arms around him and sucked back more tears.

Kristen Ashley

I hated it. I hated it with everything I was, but I was so right. This Billy business was going to be between Hank and me forever. I felt anger shoot through my body and if Billy had walked up just then, I would have ripped his head off.

It wasn't fair. It wasn't fucking fair. I hated people who whined about what wasn't fair, but if anything wasn't fair, this sure the hell wasn't.

A fair life would have brought Hank to me without anything between us.

I took a broken breath, the tears still threatening. I closed my eyes, pressed my cheek against Hank's shoulder and prayed. I prayed for this all to be over soon so I could go, so I could pick up the pieces of my life.

I prayed for Hank too, so he could move on and find someone he deserved, someone strong and smart and good. Someone he could talk to about his day. Someone who made him grin. Someone who liked his dog. Someone who put mulberry-scented candles in his house. Someone who had powdered sugar in the cupboard and cream cheese in the fridge so she could make him better French toast than I'd made, the special kind with the sweetened cream cheese spread in the middle.

Someone who didn't get shot at.

Someone who didn't get kidnapped.

Someone who didn't make him put his fist through a wall.

Someone who hadn't spent nearly seven years of their life sleeping with a criminal.

Someone better than me.

Hank pulled slightly away but kept his arms around me.

I looked up at him, pushed my prayers deep down where he couldn't see and I smiled at him.

"Can I call Vance now?" I asked.

"I'm payin' him back," Hank answered.

I sighed.

"Stubborn," I grumbled, giving in.

A hint of a smile came into his eyes and he rested his forehead against mine.

"Sunshine?" he called.

"Yeah?"

"Whatever I saw you thinkin' just now..."

Shit.

I hadn't hidden it fast enough.

I held my breath.

"Get it out of your fuckin' head."

"Hank."

"Promise me."

"Hank!"

"Roxanne," he used his authoritative voice.

"So. What? Now you're gonna tell me what to think?" I asked, pulling my head back and taking my hands from around him and putting them on my hips.

He shook his head.

"You just said—" I started.

"Okay, think whatever you want."

"Well, thank you," I said, uppity.

He grinned.

His mouth came to mine. "But consider yourself warned. Your mind wanders down that path again, I'll be forced to turn it to other things."

Before I could respond, he showed me what he meant. He kissed me, deep.

My brains scrambled, and then I wasn't thinking anything at all.

Chapter 17
"Frightmare"

Hank took me to his place and I changed my shoes. Then I rooted through his drawers and pulled out a University of Colorado sweatshirt and I switched out of my lush cardigan into the sweatshirt.

"I'm confiscating this," I told him when I walked into the kitchen.

He was leaning, hips against the counter, writing notes one-handed on a pad that was sitting on the counter to his right. He looked at me and then his eyes dropped to the sweatshirt, which was so big it was almost a dress.

Then they got lazy.

"Come here," he said low.

"No, we have to go. I'm gonna be late."

"Come here," he repeated.

"No! You have to get to work."

"You can come here or…" he started.

I knew where this was going.

"Oh, all right," I gave in.

I went to him.

He kissed me dizzy. It got heated, there was some groping and we went to Ally's late.

⌐≈⌐

We walked into Ally's and nearly everyone was there but Daisy.

"Yo Bitch!" Annette yelled at me. "Yo dude!" she yelled at Hank.

Hank smiled at her.

She gawked at him, momentarily stunned by his smile, then turned to me and nodded her head slowly.

"Nice," she drawled.

I rolled my eyes.

"Like the sweatshirt," Ally remarked, leaning back and taking me in, then she introduced me to her boyfriend, Carl. He was good-looking; tall, blond,

Kristen Ashley

blue-eyed and grinning at Hank. A knowing grin that made me feel slightly bothered, but, weirdly, in a good way.

"We need to talk," Hank said to him.

"I figured that," Carl said back.

Hank leaned down and wrapped an arm around my waist sideways. I looked up at him and he gave me a light kiss.

"Have fun," he said against my mouth.

Then he and Carl walked out the front door.

"What's that all about?" I asked, watching the closed door as if I had x-ray vision and could see through it.

"That's Hank telling Carl he'll make him into an instant girl if anything happens to you," Ally explained.

"Good God," I murmured.

"Don't worry. Nothing's gonna happen to you," Indy said.

The door opened and Daisy arrived. Or, I should say Daisy *arrived*.

She was wearing a skintight, faded denim jumpsuit, the crotch to bosom zipper unzipped to maximum cleavage potential, rhinestones adorning the outer sides of her legs, up her hips, waist, sides, and down the inside of the sleeves. She was wearing matching platform, high-heeled, faded denim boots heavily encrusted with rhinestones. She had a pink chiffon scarf tied around her neck and her platinum blonde hair was teased out to peak volume.

"Yo Bitch!" Annette yelled, completely oblivious to the fact that Daisy looked like she was about to step onstage in Vegas.

"Yo, sugar," Daisy replied.

"I thought I told you to wear gym shoes," Ally said, peeved that her Haunted House instructions were not carried out to the letter.

"I don't *do* gym shoes, comprende?" Daisy told her, giving her a squinty look.

Yowza.

"It's your funeral," Ally shot back, totally unaffected by the squinty look.

Holy cow.

Daisy's eyes came to me. "Honey bunches of oats," she said, "your man is outside having an *extreme* conversation with her man." A toss of her head indicated Ally.

"I know," I told her.

She nodded and looked around. "All right then, who brought the stun guns?"

Shit.

⌖

Carl, Ally and Indy rode in Carl's Pathfinder.

If you could believe this, Annette, Jason, Jet, Daisy and I followed in the back of Daisy's limousine. Daisy's bodyguard drove.

"I fucking *love* Denver," Annette said, staring out the window and sprawling in the luxurious space, completely at home, as if she rode in the back of limousines every day.

"You gotta stay until Thursday, sugar, come to my do. I'm having a fancy soiree," Daisy invited.

"We... are... fucking... *there*," Annette accepted.

Jason looked at me and closed his eyes in good-natured frustration. When he opened them I was smiling at him. We'd shared these looks a lot over the years.

Then I turned to Jet. "What's Smithie's?"

"Pardon?" she asked.

"Smithie's. I overheard you say when you came into Fortnum's the day I met you that you worked there."

She grinned at me. "Well, officially, I don't work there anymore."

"You let Eddie win," I guessed.

"Eddie wins a lot," she confirmed.

I found this sobering information, considering the fact that I figured Eddie was a lot like Hank.

"What is it?" I asked.

"A strip club. I was a cocktail waitress there."

"Cool!" Annette cried.

Jet smiled full out to Annette and we all sat in the limo dazzled for a moment by her smile.

"My sister is a stripper there," Jet went on. "She debuts tomorrow night. You can all come if you want. I can get you VIP passes."

"Sugar! That would be hot!" Daisy screeched with excitement then did a glance sweeping around all of us. "Her sister is Lottie Mac."

"Queen of the Corvette Calendar?" Jason asked, clearly intrigued.

"Fuckin' A," Daisy replied.

I stared around them. It was like they were talking in a different language.

"You want to come?" Jet asked me.

"Love to," I answered.

She grabbed my hand, squeezed and let go. Through the hand squeeze I felt something pass between her and me. The hand squeeze wasn't about me going to watch her sister strip. It was her giving me strength. I was reminded that just over a week ago she'd been through a trauma much like mine. She'd almost been raped and her Dad was still in the hospital. She knew my pain in many different ways; hers was nearly as fresh.

"I see you took my advice about Hank," Daisy said, taking me out of my thoughts.

I looked to her. "No, I'm leaving as soon as they find Billy and all of this is over."

The limo went deathly quiet.

"Come again?" Daisy asked into the silence.

I sighed and looked out the window. "You wouldn't understand."

"Try us," Jason prompted softly.

I sighed again, this time, deeper and louder. I explained my Hank-deserves-better-than-me philosophy. After I stopped talking, there was more silence.

"Come again?" Daisy repeated.

"I knew you wouldn't understand," I returned.

"I understand," Jet said.

I looked to her.

"Hank doesn't see shades of gray," she continued.

I blinked at her. "What?" I asked.

"You think he doesn't see shades of gray. You think he sees black and white. Good and bad. Crime and justice. He doesn't see shades of gray. You're gray."

I swallowed. That was so *it*.

"Jet, sugar bunch, I don't think Roxie's gray," Daisy put in gently.

"She's gray. And you're gray too," Jet replied, just as gently.

Daisy was silent because Daisy was definitely gray.

I felt my nostrils start to burn, bit my lip and looked out the window. I was trying hard, but I felt tears leak out the sides of my eyes.

"Roxie, you're about as fucking gray as the fucking sun. I'm sorry, Jet, but I've known Roxie for years and she isn't fucking gray," Annette declared.

"I'm not saying gray is bad or that Roxie's gray. Just that I understand how she's feeling and that she *thinks* Hank'll *think* she's gray."

"She isn't gray," Annette repeated.

"I know that, but she thinks Hank'll think she is," Jet returned.

"She isn't fuckin' gray." Annette was getting heated.

"I know that!" Jet was getting heated right back.

"I'm going to have a talk with Hank," Jason cut in, and I could tell by his tone he meant to do it, and soon.

"Don't you dare," I said to Jason, my head swiveling to him.

"Are you crying, sugar bunch?" Daisy asked.

I shook my head even though I was.

"Oh God, I'm sorry. I just wanted you to know I understood." Jet grabbed my hand again.

I wiped away my tears with my other hand. "It's okay. I know you didn't mean anything by it."

"Roxie, look at me," Jet urged.

I turned to her and tried to give her a smile, but it was weak.

"It's okay," I repeated.

"I'm not very pretty," she said suddenly.

I blinked at her. "Excuse me?" I asked.

"At least, that's what I thought," she carried on like I hadn't said anything.

How could she think that? She was flat out pretty.

"Don't you look in the mirror?" I asked, not meaning to be a bitch but... seriously.

"I thought once Eddie saved me he'd lose interest in me because he's so good-looking and I'm... not."

"You're loopy," Annette told her.

I kept staring at her and her hand squeezed mine.

"Eddie saved me a while ago," she whispered.

I felt my throat close.

"Jet..." My voice was barely audible.

"Hank sees gray. You may think he doesn't, he may act like he doesn't, he may even say he doesn't. But he does. I promise." Her voice was just as low.

"I'm still leaving," I said.

She nodded. "I understand that too."

"Thank you."

"Though, you aren't leaving," she said.

"I am," I said back.

"You *think* you are, but you aren't."

"I am!" I said, kind of loud.

She just shook her head.

I glanced between Jet and Daisy. They were both grinning at me.

"Denver people are nuts," I told Annette and Jason.

"I know. Don't 'cha love it?" Annette replied.

We were at the front of the line to the haunted trail, the doors to the trail in front of us. Each side of the door held a flaming torch. A man wearing full ghoul makeup and a big, hooded black cloak was standing in front of the door, glaring at us, completely "in character".

It was dark, it was cold and I was already scared out of my mind.

We'd had troubles from the start.

First, the haunted house was out in the middle of nowhere, and the night was dark. Only the haze of Denver lights could be seen in the distance. This totally freaked me out.

Daisy's limo caused a sensation when we pulled into the parking lot. Then Daisy caused a sensation when she alighted from the limo. It wasn't the thing to wear a skintight, rhinestone-encrusted jumpsuit with high-heeled, platform boots to a haunted house in the middle of the country. People stared. They didn't know if she was Dolly Parton, if she was a Dolly Parton impersonator, or if she was some other important personage. Someone even approached her and asked her for her autograph.

"Well, aren't you sweet?" Daisy squealed on a tinkly bell laugh and signed the piece of paper and then, before handing it back she kissed it with her frosty pink lipstick.

After that, we found out there were no weapons allowed. They tried to confiscate not only the stun guns, but also the full-blown gun Carl wore on his belt.

When Carl flashed his badge (Carl was a police officer too), the big guy who seemed to be head of security got all policy on him. Carl got a hard look on his face, took him aside and they had words. Carl came back and said the worst eight words in the English language for me at that moment: "We're goin' to the front of the line."

We walked in front of everyone to the front of the line.

Due to our *situation* they were giving us a wide berth. Before letting us in, they were waiting longer between the party in front of us and keeping the party behind us well back.

Carl had explained my stun gun to me. I had it shoved in the back of my cords under Hank's sweatshirt. It didn't feel comfortable there, but I found I liked having it, even though I doubted I'd use it.

Indy, Ally, Daisy and Jet all carried one. They'd had only one extra, and without a word Jason took it and gave Annette a look. She pouted for a second then pretended she didn't care.

"All right, huddle," Ally ordered.

We all went into a huddle.

"Everyone got a partner?" she asked.

Indy linked her arm with mine.

I looked at her and then my eyes swung, panicked, to Carl.

He gave me a "don't worry" nod, but I didn't think he got it. I wasn't worried that bad guys would shoot me. No one in their right mind would attack me here. There were hundreds of people all over the place and very stringent security.

No, I was worried that Indy would go berserk on me.

I didn't have time to switch partners as Ally kept talking. "No matter what, stay with your partner."

Oh shit.

Shit, shit, shit.

Ally continued, "We all stick together. Someone gets caught or cornered, say by the hooded hangman or the crazy, bloody surgeon, we all go back and save them. Never leave a man behind. Got me?"

Oh shit!

Shit, shit, *shit!*

"Got me?" she shouted.

We all nodded.

"Repeat it," Ally ordered.

We all muttered, "Never leave a man behind."

She nodded to us, "Good." Then she linked arms with Carl and said to the ghoul, "We're ready."

The doors creaked open and my heart started beating so hard I could feel it in my throat.

Annette and Jason were partners, and so were Daisy and Jet (with Daisy's bodyguard trailing them). Indy was with me. Ally was with Carl. We entered in that order.

It was pretty cool. Scary, but cool. They'd obviously put a lot of effort into it. Great monsters with fantastic makeup, good props, excellent scenery, eerie, scary, dark and the monsters popped out just in time to give you a thrill. It wasn't as bad as I thought. Indy and I were caught unawares a couple of times and we screamed, scooted forward, then giggled our asses off.

We hit the open area with the hangman's section and the character there, swinging a noose in his hand like a lasso, cottoned on immediately to the scaredy-cats in the bunch. He approached Indy and me and in a guttural voice whispered, "Ooo, I like these girlies."

We both froze, standing stock-still and staring at him and then we both screamed at the tops of our lungs. Carl and Ally saved us, pushing us forward in front of them, Ally laughing herself silly.

We left some haunted caves and entered an open area that was a maze of cornfields.

"Oh shit," I said, my heart starting to race again.

Indy had my arm in a vice-like hold and she was glancing around, ever vigilant, trying to prepare for the next scare (a wasted effort; these people knew what they were doing).

"What?" she asked.

"I don't like cornfields."

She stopped and stared at me.

"But you're from Indiana," she said.

Then, out of nowhere, the cornfields moved and Corn Husk Man jumped out at us. He swiped at us with hands made of dry, creepy husks. We both

234

jumped back in sync, shrieked like raving lunatics, and then Indy took off running, *backwards*, dragging me with her. We forged through Carl and Ally, knocking Ally on her ass. Indy was yelling at the top of her lungs and I started laughing so hard, I couldn't control it. Not only at Indy, but Ally going down on her ass. I was bent over with it, running doubled and trying at the same time to pull Indy back.

A monster caught us on the retreat and came out growling. Indy and I stopped dead then screeched like mad women right in his face. I whirled her around, our arms still locked and we went back the way we came.

We rocketed, still screaming, by Carl, who'd followed us, then by Ally who'd gotten up. I slammed into Ally on the run and she went down flat on her ass again.

I was giggling, looking behind, Indy dragging me forward and I shouted breathlessly, "Sorry!"

We both skirted Corn Husk Man and ran flat out, giggling and screaming, to the end of the corn maze. We stopped, doubled over, trying to catch our breath, holding onto each other but still laughing. My ribs ached, just a little bit, but I didn't care. I hadn't laughed that hard in years and I didn't remember the last time I'd had that much fun. We were in an open field. The front of our party was long gone. Ally and Carl would catch up, I was certain.

It couldn't have been a second, or maybe two, later before we heard the chainsaw.

And I could say that there was nothing more terrifying, fake haunted trail or no, than being in an open field, in the dark, in the middle of nowhere and hearing the sound of a chainsaw.

Indy and I looked at each other, and, in unison, our heads moved and we looked over our shoulders at the chainsaw man who was coming toward us.

"Run!" I shouted.

At that point, it was every woman for herself.

Indy and I pushed off each other. She went to one side, I went to the other. I was watching her when I felt my feet hit something soft. The edges of the field were made out of foam rubber. I bounced off it and fell to my knees jarring my ribs, my breath still gone, but nevertheless I was twittering like an idiot. I got up and ran, hell bent, toward Indy.

She'd made it a lot further, but then a monster jumped in front of her. She went sideways to avoid him, hit another patch of rubber and bounced off it, went down rolling, straight into the monster.

He toppled over her and it looked like they started wrestling. Indy was out-of-control screaming and struggling, half terrified, half laughing. The monster was hindered by a big costume that was a lot of shredded material. They swiftly got all tangled up, a flurry of arms, legs and costume.

I stopped dead and bent over laughing, holding my stomach, giggling so hard I was pretty certain I was going to pee my pants. I should have helped but I couldn't. It was simply too damned funny watching Indy and the monster rolling around in the dirt like that.

Then I was tackled. I went down hard.

I was stunned and winded. The fall jarred my ribs and it hurt. The arms around me were strong and not messing around. I couldn't imagine the monsters were allowed to touch you, much less tackle you. Maybe we were in trouble for running around like crazy people. Maybe we were being ejected.

I struggled, turned and stilled at what I saw.

Billy had me.

Shit!

I screamed, not a giggly scream, a real one and it pierced the night, filled with genuine terror.

"Shut the fuck up," he ordered, got up, yanking me with him.

No way.

No fucking way.

This wasn't going to happen to me again.

And anyway, he'd screwed my chances with Hank. I *wanted* Hank. Hank was the best thing that had ever happened to me in my whole, stinking life.

Fuck Billy.

I reared back and punched him in the face.

It hurt my hand, like a lot, but when he staggered back, I didn't hesitate.

I turned and ran.

Indy had come untangled with the monster, but he was rolling around, still tied up in his costume. Indy was on her hands and knees, looking up at me, face pale. She'd heard my scream.

She looked back toward where Billy was. I skidded to a halt next to her.

"Billy!" I yelled, hauling her up. "Let's go!"

We ran together, holding hands. We got around a corner, another one, into another scene with some hay bales.

Billy caught up with us and did another flying tackle. We all went down and rolled around in bales, both Indy and I fighting, kicking, scratching.

"Hey! What're you doing?" A monster came up and yanked Billy off of us.

Billy whirled around and nailed him in the nose.

"Hey!" the monster shouted again, but it was muffled as his hands went to his nose.

Indy didn't wait. She tugged me along and I heard a scuffle behind us as the monster kept on Billy.

We ran through more trail, straight by monsters and entered a house. Billy caught up with us there. He pulled Indy away from me, threw her aside and she went flying. He picked me up, starting up some dark stairs, half carrying me, half pushing me.

When we were halfway up, Indy attacked him from behind. He took the blow of her body hitting him full force, his body jerking forward. He dropped me and I fell on the stairs, my lower back crashing against the edge of a step, my elbows slamming into a stairwell.

Billy spun around and caught Indy with his arm. She fell back and I watched her tumble down.

I got up, clawing at Billy to get around him to Indy.

"*No!*" I shouted.

He kept pushing me up the stairs.

We entered a scene at the top with strobe lights, a surgical table and fake blood everywhere; fake severed hands and legs dangling from the ceiling on chains and a man in a bloody lab coat. He came at us to scare us, but stopped when I planted my feet and rushed Billy, catching him in the belly with my shoulder and sending him sprawling back against a wall. I pulled back and started pummeling him.

"You…" I hit him in the face, "Are…" I hit him with my other hand, "Not…" I hit him again, this time, in the body, "Gonna…" I hit him again, "Hurt…" I punched him in the jaw, "*My friends!*"

I was wild. Billy was cowering to try and protect himself from my raining blows.

The bloody surgeon yanked me off him.

"What the heck…?" he started to say but didn't finish.

Carl came barreling up the stairs at the same time the head of security came into the room through the exit.

Billy saw them and pushed off the wall. He tore through the bloody surgeon and me and took off, not back to the stairs, not through the doorway at the end, but he threw himself out a window.

The bloody surgeon ran to the window. Carl and the security guy ran to the door. I ran to Indy.

She was halfway up the stairs. Ally was with her.

"Are you okay?" I asked when I got to her.

"Fine," Indy replied.

I stopped, realizing my body was in full tremble and I was struggling to catch my breath.

"Are you okay?" I asked again, staring at her.

She took me into her arms. "Honey, I'm fine."

I kept trembling.

"You sure you're okay?" I asked again, tears in my voice, tears burning my eyes, tears crawling up my throat.

Ally's arms came around us both.

"I'm fine, perfectly fine," Indy assured me.

I kept trembling.

"Shh, girl. You're safe," Ally whispered.

The lights came on and we stood there. We heard footsteps and then the others were there. Annette joined the huddle then I felt Jet burrow in. I didn't know how we did it, but we managed to do a group hug on the narrow stairs.

All except Daisy and Jason.

"God fucking *dammit*," I heard Jason yell.

"What the fuck good are you?" Daisy shouted at her bodyguard.

I ignored them and held onto my friends, crying and trembling.

<hr />

Hank opened the door to his house one-handed, his other one held mine.

Shamus came at us, but before he could do his doggie welcome, Hank commanded, "Stay!"

Shamus skidded to a halt and sat, his doggie head swinging in confusion back and forth between the two humans.

Hank pulled me inside, locked the door and walked me into the kitchen. Only then did he drop my hand.

He went to the light switch. I went to the freezer.

I grabbed a towel, put ice in it then put it on my hand.

After he turned on the light, Hank shrugged off his jacket and threw it over a dining room chair, gave Shamus a head scratch and walked to me. He stopped close, his hand came up and he pulled something from my hair. It came back down and there was a piece of straw between his fingers.

"Wrestling in the hay bales," I said, staring at the piece of straw.

When I looked to Hank, his mouth was tight.

Billy escaped. It wasn't hard. It was pandemonium, people everywhere, milling about and not knowing what was going on as the lights had come up. He'd easily slipped away.

They closed early and the cops came. I talked to the people who ran the haunted house, including the guy who was head of security. Carl had already told them my story and they were kind and understanding. It was close to closing anyway, they promised me, no harm done. They seemed more worried about me than anything. The monster who got hit in the nose had only had it bloodied, not broken.

Malcolm and Detective Marker came together and got there quickly, using a Kojak light.

Malcolm walked right up to me, kissed the side of my head, put his arm around my waist and didn't let go. I was leaning into him when Hank arrived.

Hank came up to us, interrupting our conversation. He pulled me away from his father, turned me into his arms and held me, tight.

"How're your ribs?" he asked.

I nodded that they were okay, but didn't answer verbally. I was lost in his arms, taking what I could, wrapping my own around him.

The rest of the interview went on with Hank's arms around me and my cheek resting against his shoulder.

Lee and Eddie showed simultaneously. There were a lot of meaningful glances with glittering angry eyes between the men.

Indy went home with Lee, Jet with Eddie, and Ally went back with Carl. I gave Indy, Jet and Ally hugs before they went.

Daisy took Annette and Jason back. Hank and I walked them to the limo. People were standing around it, staring at Daisy like she was an unknown rock star, likely mistakenly thinking this fuss and muss was about her. I gave out more hugs and they left. Daisy and Jason still looked pissed. Annette looked worried.

Hank put me in his 4Runner and we drove home without a word exchanged between us, both of us lost in our thoughts.

There, in his kitchen, I looked at Hank.

"He could have hurt Indy," I said.

"Yeah, but he didn't," Hank replied.

"He could have."

"He didn't."

"Hank—"

"Let me tell you something about Indy."

I closed my eyes and looked away.

"Look at me, Sunshine."

I opened them and looked back.

"You said you'd die, you'd go with him, before you let anyone get hurt. Remember that?" Hank asked.

I nodded.

"There's no way in hell India Savage would let that happen."

"I barely know her," I whispered.

"You're wrong about that." His arms slid around me. "You know her because she's just like you," he said.

That was one of the nicest things anyone had ever said to me.

Tears filled my eyes.

"Whisky." My voice broke on his name and I shoved my face in his chest. I dropped the ice on the floor and clutched onto his sweater at either side of my face.

Then it hit me and it hit me hard. I pushed away, out of his arms and stomped my foot.

"*That fucking asshole!*" I screamed.

Shamus woofed.

My eyes turned to the dog. He was standing at the edge of the cabinets, his body tense, staring at me.

"Sorry Shamus," I said.

At his name, his tail started wagging and he came and pressed against me. I leaned down to give him a body rub and picked up the ice. I tossed it underhand into the sink and kept rubbing Shamus's body but looked up at Hank.

"I'm going to fucking *kill* that motherfucker," I announced.

Hank stared down at me.

"He pushed Indy down the stairs," I continued.

"Roxie, calm down."

"I'm not going to fucking calm down. I'm going to hunt that bastard down and murder him."

"Oh fuck," Hank rocked back on his heels, his eyes went to the ceiling, his hands going to his hips.

"What?" I asked.

"Nothin'."

"What?" I asked louder.

His eyes came back to me. "You aren't huntin' anyone down."

"Well… no," I said, staring at him like he was crazy. "I was just saying that because I'm mad as hell. I wouldn't begin to know how to hunt him down."

"Let me handle it," he said.

"Okay."

"Seriously."

I straightened from the Shamus Body Rub and Shamus sat on my feet. "I said okay."

"Indy comes to you with any bright ideas, you say I'm handling it," Hank ordered.

"Okay," I replied.

"Jet, Daisy, my fuckin' sister, any of them come to you with grand schemes, you tell them I'm handling it."

"Okay," I repeated, my brows drawing together, thinking maybe he'd gone a little 'round the bend. "Whisky, are you all right?"

"I know how those women work. You want to get even with Flynn, you're angry, and they'll talk you into it."

"Hank, I said I wasn't going to—"

"It won't even seem that way. They'll make it seem like it's *your* idea."

"Whisky."

"Tex either."

Good God.

"Hank, I said *oh…kay*."

"Promise me."

Jeez!

"Hank!"

"Just do it, Sunshine."

I sighed. He *had* gone 'round the bend.

"Okay, I promise."

He stared at me a beat then took in a breath. Then his fingers slid into my hair on either side of my head and he did a little shake. Pieces of straw came out; not a lot, four or five and I watched them float down.

"I'm sorry," I whispered as I watched the straw settle on his tiled floor.

He used his hands on my head to tilt it up to face him. "I don't want to hear you say you're sorry again."

He didn't say this nice or sweet. He said it angry.

I swallowed and stared.

Then I said uncertainly, "Hank?"

His hands went to the sides of my neck. "You aren't the cause of this, Flynn is. Got me?"

I nodded.

"I'm not angry at you. I'm just angry," he explained.

"Okay," I said, for like the billionth time in the last five minutes.

He moved on to another subject and I had to admit, I was relieved. "How's your hand?"

"It hurts like a mother," I told him.

I watched as his anger slid away and he smiled at me. I smiled back. We shared a moment of happiness at the thought of me getting my own back, even a little bit, with Billy. His arms came around me and he pulled me to him, his hands drifting down my back, fitting my body to his.

Shamus backed out from between us and sauntered to his doggie bed in the TV room. He was a smart dog, quickly learning the drill between Hank and me.

"How's everything else?" Hank asked, his voice had changed, sounding slightly husky.

I didn't have to ask what he meant. His hands and tone were doing the talking.

I tilted my head back to look at him and slid my arms around his waist. "I'm fine."

"You owe me," he said.

I blinked at him then remembered.

"Oh. Yeah."

He gave me a light kiss. "Let's get you a hot shower, some ibuprofen and we'll go to bed."

I nodded.

"Then you can erase my day," he told me, turning and tucking me into his side, his arm around my shoulders. We started walking to the bedroom.

"Maybe you should erase my night," I suggested.

"No, I'm thinkin' you should erase my day."

"My night was worse than your day," I said.

"I had a full shitty day. You just had a half a shitty night."

This was true.

"Okay, I'll erase your day," I gave in.

He hit the lights as we walked out of the kitchen.

Chapter 18

Tangerine and Chocolate Wedding

I was lying on my belly, my arms around a pillow, fast asleep, when I felt the sheet slide down my back; low, lower, lowest. It came to rest at the top of my behind.

I twisted my head around sleepily and looked at Hank's shadow in the dark.

"Whisky?" I called, still groggy.

"Quiet, sweetheart. I want to check something."

Then the light went on.

I blinked at him. He was sitting on the edge of the bed, wearing a pair of jeans and nothing else. His eyes were on my back.

"That's a new one," he muttered to my back.

I looked over my shoulder. I couldn't see much of anything.

"What is it?" I asked.

His hand came out and his finger traced something that ran across my lower back. "You were movin' like you were tender last night. Now I know why. The mark hadn't formed then, but now you've got another bruise."

"Oh." I turned around, snuggled back into the pillow and explained, "Billy dropped me when Indy jumped him on the stairs. I landed funny."

I closed my eyes, thinking that was that and deciding I'd catch a bit more shuteye.

Hank had different thoughts.

He tagged me at the waist, gently moved me around and then slid me across the bed, pulling me upright. I was sitting, facing him, the side of my hip against his.

I brought the sheet with me and I pulled it up to cover my breasts.

"What?" I asked when I looked at him.

"Don't get used to this shit. This isn't your life. After this is over, you go back to normal," he replied.

I watched him and felt my gut twist. It was time to begin to show him what he would not be missing when I went away.

"Hank," I said quietly. "I don't have a 'normal'. I've been with Billy for seven years."

I thought he'd look at me in disgust, horror, or at the very least, shock. Instead he wrapped his hand around the back of my head, tipped it down and kissed my forehead. Then he let go and looked me in the eyes.

"Then I'll show you normal."

I stopped breathing.

Hank didn't notice. He got up and went to his dresser.

"Hate to tell you this Sunshine, but I can't leave you home so you're gonna have to walk Shamus with me. Get dressed, we gotta get this done. One of the cases I'm working is heatin' up and I need to get to the station."

Then he sauntered into the bathroom like he hadn't just rocked my world.

I stared after him.

I still wasn't breathing.

"You have your choice today," Hank called from the bathroom. "Fortnum's or Lee's offices. Both are safe, but you can't leave either."

Then I heard an electric shaver.

I let go of my breath.

Shamus ambled over, sat down beside the bed and stared at me, tongue lolling and looking like he was smiling. I grabbed his head, kissed the top of it and gave him a head rub. He leaned up and licked my cheek.

Hank walked out of the bathroom, still shaving, and looked at me and Shamus.

"Sunshine," he said, his voice low with warning, telling me to get a move on.

"All right, all right! I'll get dressed." I sounded uppity.

I'd think about his complete non-reaction to my dire admission later. I had a decision to make. Crazy Fortnum's and what might happen there while Lee's boys were watching, or Lee's offices, meaning Dastardly Dawn, the boring room and Diablo, better known as eight hours of my life sucked away.

I pulled the sheet with me when I got up and wrapped it around me in a voluminous toga. Then I stomped, with a fair bit of attitude (just to make a point, even though there was no real point to be made), out of the room to the other bathroom.

Shamus followed me.

What I didn't know was, so did Hank's eyes.

And another thing I didn't know. He was smiling.

⌐≼≽⌐

I picked Fortnum's and I regretted it the minute I walked through the door.

"Get over here!" Tex boomed at me.

"Shit," I muttered.

Hank's hand slid around my waist and his fingers gripped me reassuringly.

"What?" I snapped at Uncle Tex.

"You know what. People are shootin' at you. A week ago, you were kidnapped! What's goin' on in that fuckin' head of yours?" Tex shouted.

There were over a dozen people in line, waiting for coffee or sitting in the couches and chairs. Duke was behind the espresso counter, and so was Jet. Jane was at the book counter.

They all started to stare.

"It wasn't my fault!" I returned.

"Not your... not your fuckin'..." Tex spluttered. "You have no business goin' to a goddamned haunted house when you got lunatics chasing you. I'm callin' your mother!"

My body went still. Everyone's eyes turned to me.

"Don't you dare call my mother!" I yelled.

Everyone's eyes went to Tex.

"I'm callin' Trish. No!" Tex's voice blasted across the room when I opened my mouth to speak. "Shut your pie hole. I don't wanna hear it."

There was a collective gasp and everyone's gaze came to me.

My eyes narrowed and I leaned forward. Hank's fingers were biting into my waist now, not for assurance but to keep me from launching myself at Uncle Tex.

"You did not just tell me to shut my pie hole!" I shouted.

The eye swivel went to Tex.

"You heard me right, girl," Tex boomed.

I turned to Hank.

"Take me to Lee's office," I demanded.

"Don't you do that, Nightingale. I want her here so I can keep an eye on her," Tex bellowed.

Hank was grinning.

"I'm thinkin' I don't have to worry about Tex giving you any crazy ideas," he remarked.

I frowned at him.

He gave my still-frowning mouth a light kiss then started to leave.

"Don't expect me to erase your day tonight!" I shouted at his back.

He turned at the door and winked at me then he was gone.

I turned to the woman nearest me and said, exasperation dripping from my voice. "Men!"

She was staring at me. "Are people really shooting at you?"

I looked at her. "Well… yeah," I admitted.

"Honey," was all she said on a shake of her head, that one word speaking volumes, then she turned back in line.

⌖

Annette, Jason and Daisy strolled in two hours later.

I was sitting on a couch, nursing my second coffee. Uncle Tex was experimenting on me. The first one was an almond mocha with cinnamon sprinkled on the coffee grounds before brewing. This one was snickerdoodle with a hint of vanilla. Both were divine.

"That space across the street is phat," Annette announced, throwing herself on the couch next to me. "We've put in an application. I'm, like, jazzed." She turned to Tex and yelled, "Americano, big man!"

"Gotcha!" Tex boomed back.

He scowled at me, apparently not over it yet, and then started banging on the espresso machine.

Daisy sat across from us while Jason went to the espresso counter.

"There's some space for let down the street. I'm thinkin' of startin' a beauty parlor, like in *Steel Magnolias*, except not in a garage," Daisy shared. "I gotta find somethin' to do with my time. I thought I'd do charity work but I'm doin' this fundraising party and the women on my committee all got sticks up their asses. They wouldn't know fun if someone beat them over the head with it, and believe me, I've thought about it."

I believed her. I also believed she might be moved to do it.

Jet came over and sat with us.

"That's cool," Annette said to Daisy after she smiled at Jet. "I'd let you do my hair."

Jet looked at me with wide, frightened eyes and gave a firm shake of her head that said clearly, "no, no, *no*".

I had no time to react, as Daisy started talking. "Oh sugar, aren't you sweet?" Then she gave a tinkly laugh.

The bell over the door went and our eyes turned to see who came in.

Luke was standing there. He'd changed nuances of his overall look. Still all black, his t-shirt skintight, except this time with long sleeves. Instead of just plain boots he had on black *motorcycle* boots, and instead of cargo pants, he had on jeans. As a fashion maven, I appreciated the subtlety that still managed to pack a punch. As a woman, I just appreciated him.

"Jumpin' Jehosafats, I think I just creamed my pants," Annette whispered, staring at Luke.

Luke's eyes locked on me. He lifted his hand and crooked his finger.

"I was wrong about before. Now, I've *definitely* creamed my pants," Annette breathed.

I got up and walked to Luke.

He put a hand in the small of my back and propelled me into the books.

We turned right, into the biography section, and stopped.

"Got plans tonight?" he asked.

I blinked at him. "I'm going to a strip club," I answered.

His eyes flashed, momentarily showing his surprise.

Then he gave me one of his sexy half-grins.

My heart stopped beating for a second.

"Why?" I asked.

"I'm your date," he replied.

My heart stopped beating for five seconds.

Then I breathed. "Excuse me?"

"You're not on camera, you're with me," he said.

"Excuse me?" I repeated.

Kristen Ashley

"Hank called. His case is bustin' open. He's busy. I'm assigned to you."

I blinked, twice. "Excuse me?" I said yet again.

The grin came on full-fledged and he moved into my space.

"I'm your bodyguard."

Holy cow.

"You don't leave Fortnum's unless you're with me," he said.

Holy fucking cow, cow, *cow!*

I struggled for a second and then decided not to fight it. I wouldn't win anyway.

First off, Lord knew I needed a bodyguard. Second, Hank obviously set this up. Last, no way, *in hell* was I going head-to-head with Luke.

So, I said, "Okay."

"Outside this store, you don't do anything unless you can see me."

"Okay."

"You aren't anywhere unless I'm close enough for you to touch me."

I gulped at any thought of touching him.

"Okay," I said, but it sounded kind of strangled.

"We straight?" he asked.

I nodded.

"Roxie, listen to me," Luke ordered.

I stared at him. If I listened any closer, my ears would start bleeding.

"I know you're Hank's woman and I don't give a fuck. I also know the stories of the two who came before you, Indy and Jet. You mess around, do something stupid, put my ass on the line, you answer to me. Got that?"

I nodded again. I definitely got it.

"You don't want to answer to me," he warned.

I suspected he was right, but I had to ask, out of curiosity. "What would…" I cleared my throat, "answering to you entail… exactly?"

"You don't wanna know," he replied.

I nodded and decided I didn't.

He got closer and his indigo eyes went funny.

"I'd never raise my hand to a woman," he assured me.

I nodded again and let out the breath I was holding.

"Therefore, I'd have to get creative," he finished.

Good God.

"I promise to be good," I said quickly.

250

"One more thing."

Shit.

"Yes?" I asked, even though I seriously *did not want to know.*

"For the record, I like Hank," he told me.

"Um…" I muttered, not knowing where he was leading with this and I still *did not want to know.* "I'm glad to hear it."

"Things don't work out with you and Hank…"

I waited while he paused, my eyes wide, my lips parted, my heart thumping.

"You can erase *my* day."

Oh… my… God.

He smiled at me in a way that I didn't know if he was serious or playing with me. Then he moved out of my space, but lifted his hand and touched his finger to the tip of my nose. I blinked again, shocked at his words, shocked at his touch, shocked that it was gentle and sweet. It didn't go with his badass attitude.

Then he was gone.

I stumbled out of the bookshelves like a dying man in a desert would stumble into an oasis.

"You okay?" Annette asked from across the room.

"No," I answered.

"Cream your pants?" she asked.

The eyes of the two customers at the espresso counter, both male, came to me in avid curiosity.

"I don't think so," I replied.

"Oh, you'd know," Annette returned.

I bumbled over to the couches and collapsed.

"What'd I tell you about this place?" one customer had turned to the other, they were obviously friends. They were both looking at Annette, Daisy, Jet and me sitting on the couches.

"I don't even like coffee and I've decided I'm a regular," the other one said.

"I don't make tea!" Tex boomed threateningly at him and he jumped.

I closed my eyes, trying to think positively. At least Monty's day wasn't going to be boring. Instead of being mortified, I thought of it as my way of paying back Lee's boys for all the headaches I'd given them.

"I hope you're having fun!" I shouted to the room.

In my head, I heard them laughing.

What I didn't know, in a suite of offices in Lower Downtown Denver, they *were* laughing.

⁓⁂⁓

Daisy went out and got us all bagel sandwiches for lunch. Daisy, Annette and Jason decided to stay the day with me at Fortnum's so I wouldn't get bored.

We spent the early afternoon helping Jane go through boxes and boxes of books. We spent the late afternoon behind the espresso counter while Uncle Tex taught us how to make coffee drinks. It wasn't rocket science, but Uncle Tex was a drill sergeant and Daisy kept gabbing about everything under the sun and over-frothing the milk.

After we learned how to make coffees, Lee and Indy walked in.

Indy smiled at me but I could tell something was wrong.

My first thought was Hank.

My heart clutched and my eyes flew to Lee. Hank was his brother and they were close. If something had happened to Hank, in the line of duty or because of me, I should be able to tell with one look at Lee.

At least I thought so, but Lee's face was closed tight.

I felt like someone put their hand to my throat and squeezed.

They arrived at the espresso counter and Lee looked at me.

"Can I talk to you, please?" he asked.

I swallowed, nodded and walked from behind the espresso counter. He sat on a couch with me and put the sole of his boot up on to the edge of the table. I sat with my legs crossed under me, sideways on the couch, facing him. I looked at his posture. He was sitting exactly the way Hank was when I first laid eyes on him.

Before I could stop myself, I said, "You're just like your brother."

"Sorry?" he asked.

"Nothing."

Lee watched me closely and I could swear he was reading my mind. Finally, he muttered, "Fucking hell." His gaze was still on me.

"What?" I asked.

His eyes crinkled. "I like this," he said, as if to himself, obviously pleased about something, pleased and amused.

252

"Is Hank okay?" I ignored what he said and got to what I considered was the matter at hand.

Lee's eyes focused on me again. "Yeah. Why?"

"You looked serious when you walked in. I was, um, worried."

The corners of Lee's lips curled up slightly. "He's fine, busy. He wanted me to come talk to you."

I nodded. "What do you like?" I asked, going back to what he said earlier.

"Sorry?" he repeated.

"You said, 'I like this'. What do you like?"

He didn't hesitate, but said straight out, "You're in love with Hank."

My eyes bugged out of my head. "What?" My voice was high and didn't sound like my own.

He leaned into me. "It's good Roxie."

I wasn't sure, but I thought I'd started panting.

Lee went on, "Hank dated a girl in high school. She was sweet, but boring as hell. Hank's women have all been boring. You..." he paused, "aren't boring."

Good God.

First, I wasn't sure I wanted to think about Hank's women. Second, well, second was obvious.

"Please, let's not talk about this," I begged.

Lee watched me some more and gave in, but he did it with another eye crinkle.

Then his face got serious. "We've got information."

Shit.

Maybe I wanted to talk some more about me being in love with Hank and not being boring, whatever the hell that meant.

"What?" I asked in spite of myself.

"You know a man named Desmond Harper?" he asked.

I shook my head.

"Big player in Chicago. Mostly drugs," Lee explained. "Flynn was a cog in his very large wheel. Flynn stole from him, big take. Harper is not happy."

"Shit," I whispered.

"He wants his money back."

"How much?" I asked.

"Half a million."

Kristen Ashley

"*Fuck!*" I shouted and everyone at the espresso counter looked over at us. "Half a million dollars?"

Lee dropped his foot and turned to me. "Roxie, calm down."

"Half a million dollars and he bought me cheese puffs and took me to that sleaze bag motel? I'm gonna fucking *kill* that motherfucker!" I yelled.

"Roxie—"

I slammed my fists on my knees. "The least he could have done was bind my wrists with velvet rope. He sure could have afforded it. Stupid jerk."

"Roxie."

"Do you know…?" I interrupted conversationally. Well, more like loony-tunes conversationally, but still. "He never paid any rent. Never bought groceries. What a *dick!*"

"Roxie."

"What? Was he selling drugs?" I asked.

"I don't know," Lee answered. "Listen to me, Roxie—"

I rambled on, "Probably. Probably to little kids. How could I have been so fucking *blind?*"

"Please listen to me."

"I'm an idiot. I'm ten times an idiot. God, I could just *die.*" Then I forged ahead because the last comment was too close for comfort these days. "Not die die, as in not-breathing die, but die figuratively, if you know what I mean."

Lee was grinning.

"What?" I asked as if I hadn't just been on a long-winded rant.

"Definitely not boring."

I made a noise that sounded like "harrumph".

Lee took his opportunity. "I have good news."

I nodded. I very much wanted to hear good news.

"Marcus set a meeting with Harper. He flew out to Chicago last night and spoke with him this morning. Harper now knows you aren't involved. Not only that, Marcus has warned him off. He's given you his protection and whether you, or Hank, want it, it's now there."

I took in a deep breath and let it free.

Maybe Marcus was gray too.

"Now I have some bad news," Lee said.

I tensed. I very much did *not* want to hear bad news.

"Vance and Mace have been in the wind."

"Excuse me?" I asked.

"After the car chase, Vance came to me to tell me he was going to ground, hoping to find out what the fuck was going on with you. I assigned Mace to move with him. They've been tracking and listening. Preliminarily, their assignment was to find out as much as they could, and ferret out Flynn or anyone else who came to town lookin' for you. They got tuned into Desmond Harper at about the same time the police did."

I nodded.

Lee kept going, "Flynn's been making Harper unhappy for a while. Now Harper's not unhappy, he's angry. When his boys got nabbed, something else he's not pleased about, he assigned two more to come after Flynn."

I nodded again.

"And Flynn is after you."

I blinked then asked, "And?"

"They figure they'll get Flynn when he comes after you again. No matter Marcus's warning, Harper isn't callin' them off. You could get caught in the crossfire."

"No," I breathed.

"Don't worry about it. You're protected. Luke's assigned to you. Vance is still out there, trying to find Flynn. He's good, Roxie, very good. Because of that, I've pulled Mace."

I started to panic. "Lee, I need to go. I need to get out of here. I can't ask you to—"

"You go I'll come after you personally."

My breath caught at his tone. There was no doubting he meant it

"But, this is a lot, you're doing too much," I argued.

"It's a family thing."

I stared at him. "I'm not family."

He gave me a look.

Then his eyes, dark brown, warmed into melted chocolate. I watched him, mesmerized, and he reached out and playfully tugged a lock of my hair. He got up, walked to Indy, wrapped an arm around her and kissed her upturned lips. He spoke softly to her for a second and then he was gone.

"Guess we're done talking," I said to Indy as she sat beside me.

She put her hand on my leg. "Welcome to the family," she replied in a teasing voice.

Jeez.

There was no shaking these guys, any of them.

"You okay after last night?" I asked.

"Yeah. You?"

"Yeah. I guess Lee isn't mad at me for putting you in danger," I said.

"You didn't put me in danger, and anyway, Lee likes you. He told me that Vance told him you were a rock after he found you. Other women, they've had other…" she stopped. "Let's just say, you impressed them."

I stared at her, floored.

"Want a coffee?" she asked.

"I want a drink," I answered.

"Whisky?" she teased.

I hit her in the arm jokingly. She got up to get a coffee and I sat watching her go, not quite able to shove down the warm feeling stealing over me.

It was nearing closing time when my purse rang.

I was sitting behind the book counter with Duke.

I grabbed my phone, flipped it open and put it to my ear. "Hello?"

"Hey Sunshine."

My heart fluttered.

"Hey Whisky," I said softly.

"How's your day?" he asked.

"Pure and complete lunacy. But I now know how to make espresso drinks. Yours?"

"We're close to something. I've spent the day putting an operation together, we're goin' in tonight. It'd be good if you didn't get shot at or attacked in the middle of it."

I smiled at the phone. "I'll do my best."

"Good. Lee and Indy have got a key to my place. Ask her to give it to you. There isn't much food in the house but there are delivery menus in one of the kitchen drawers."

"Thanks, but Luke and I are going to Smithie's tonight. Jet's sister's debut. Maybe the gang will go out to dinner before."

Silence.

Then, "Sorry, I thought I heard you say you were going to Smithie's to-night."

"You did."

"Roxanne," his voice was low and discouraging.

"Hank," I tried to mimic his tone and failed.

More silence while I suspected Hank fought for control. "Did anything Tex said to you this morning penetrate that stubborn fuckin' brain of yours?"

Hank obviously lost the fight for control.

"I promised Jet I was going," I told him.

"I'm sure she'll understand."

"Hank."

"You aren't goin'."

I ground my teeth.

Then I said, "I'm going, Hank. Billy Flynn is *not* controlling another fuck-ing *second* of my life."

Another beat of silence then, "Shit, you're stubborn."

I think I got to him.

"Damn straight," I replied.

Then he said, "I spent all day tryin' to concentrate on work, and when I wasn't concentratin' on work, I was tryin' to concentrate on handlin' your shit. Instead, I found I spent most of the day concentratin' on all the ways I want to fuck you breathless."

I went breathless at his words and nearly dropped the phone.

"You're damn lucky you make me hard just rememberin' the taste of you, or I'd think you were a major pain in the ass," he declared.

Holy cow.

"Whisky."

He talked over me as he gave in. "Try not to burn down Smithie's. Smith-ie is a good guy. He doesn't deserve whatever mayhem he's got in store tonight."

I couldn't help myself, I smiled at the phone. "I promised Luke I'd be good."

"You're good all right."

I wasn't sure what he meant by that, but I found it made me both annoyed and my nipples went hard.

Hank carried on, "You get home before I do, don't wear anything to bed. I won't be in the mood for obstacles."

I was sure what he meant by that and I felt a spasm between my legs.

Finally he said, "Stay safe."

"You too," I said back, my voice soft even though we'd had an argument. I didn't know what his "operation" was about, but I didn't want to hang up the phone with him on angry words.

More silence. So much that I got confused.

"Hank?" I called, wondering if he was gone and didn't disconnect or if something was wrong with my phone.

"I'm here," he replied. His voice had changed, gone husky.

"Hank," I said again, and even though I didn't mean to let it show, a lot could be heard through my saying his name.

"See you later, Sweetheart." Then he disconnected.

I flipped the phone shut and noticed Duke looking at me.

"You're all right," Duke told me on an approving nod.

"I am?" I asked.

He turned to me, leaned a hip on the counter and crossed his arms over his black, leather vest.

"You are. These boys need women who can take the heat without meltin' like butter, and sometimes that heat is fiery. They need women who can give back their shit so they don't walk all over 'em and get bored out of their fuck-ing skulls. And they need women who can go soft when the situation demands, because they get hard knocks on a regular basis, sometimes literally, and comin' home to somethin' soft is the only way to cope."

Holy fucking cow.

"You think I'm a woman like that?" I asked him.

"I think there are a fair few women like that in the whole fuckin' world. And yeah, you're one of them."

Um… wow.

"I'm not, you know," I whispered.

He glared at me. "You made a mistake with your old boyfriend. Don't make another one."

"Duke—"

"You told Hank that Flynn wasn't gonna control your life and still, you're lettin' him."

I felt the wind go out of me, like I'd been punched in the stomach.

He leaned into me. "Get smart girl. You don't, you'll only have yourself to blame."

Before I could retort, the bell over the door went and Tod and Stevie waltzed in.

Tod was carrying what looked like a scrapbook gone amok. It was way overstuffed and there were bits of paper and other stuff sticking out of it everywhere. He walked to the book counter and slammed it down.

"Glad you're okay, girlie," he said, giving me an across-the-counter air-kiss. Then, obviously on a mission, he yelled, "Indy, get over here!"

Stevie came around the counter and gave me a genuine cheek kiss.

I was feeling funny about my conversation with Duke. Where everyone else had failed, somehow, what Duke said got to me. No one ever likes it when someone thinks badly of them, and of all the folks I'd met in the last week, outside Jane, I knew Duke the least. Yet I found this driving need not to disappoint him, and I felt I had.

Indy, Daisy, Jet and Annette walked up to the counter. Jason had long ago disappeared into the bowels of bookshelves and had not returned.

Tod flipped open the book. Where he opened it, one page was full of fabric swatches stapled to it; the other one had only two, an orange and a brown.

"Ally tells me you settled on pink and ivory for your wedding colors," Tod said to Indy accusingly.

"Yes," Indy confirmed. "And?"

Tod pointed at the orange and brown swatches. "I thought we'd decided on tangerine and chocolate."

I made a gagging noise at the very idea of a tangerine and chocolate wedding.

Stevie gave me a look that said both, "I agree" and "Not now".

I felt a touch on my shoulder and saw a hand there. I followed the arm attached to the hand and saw Duke was beside me, he gave me a shoulder squeeze and walked away.

I felt relief slide through me. Duke wasn't angry with me. I closed my eyes and leaned against the counter. I opened them when Tod started speaking again.

"I'm calling an Emergency Wedding Summit. Tomorrow night," Tod announced then his eyes shifted to Annette. "Who're you?"

"I'm Roxie's friend, Annette."

He took her in, top-to-toe. "You going to Daisy's gathering?

She nodded.

"Got something to wear? It's formal," Tod went on.

She shook her head.

Tod swung his eyes to me "Do you have something to wear yet? Or have you had time to shop in between shootouts and running for your life?"

I shook my head, too. I wondered how Luke was going to feel about shopping tomorrow. I was pretty certain Luke wouldn't be too happy about that. Furthermore, according to Luke Rules, I was not to be anywhere that I couldn't see him or wasn't close enough to touch him. That meant Luke would have to sit in the dressing room with me.

Shit, shit, shit.

I shoved the thought aside, deciding to worry about it later, and looked to Annette. "We'll go shopping tomorrow."

"Fuck that," Tod cut in. "You're shopping at The House of Burgundy. Tomorrow night." Tod glared at Indy. "They're coming to the Wedding Summit. After that, we'll get everyone situated with party outfits. Do not *even* argue. We have to have a meeting of the minds about this pink and ivory business."

"It's *my* wedding, Tod," Indy pointed out.

"Girlie, you think I've been supplying you with champagne, shoes and accessories for the last God knows for how many years *for my health?*" Tod snapped. "It's payback time."

"Oh dear," Jet said.

Annette laughed.

Daisy emitted a tinkly giggle.

I sent Indy a commiserating look. She didn't catch my look. She was glaring at Tod.

I figured Luke would probably like the Wedding Summit-slash-Drag Queen Closet Trawl a helluva lot less than shopping.

For the first time that day, I smiled.

The bell over the door went and we all turned to see who it was.

Luke was standing there.

"Oh my," Tod whispered. "I think I just creamed my pants."

"Tell me about it," Annette agreed.

"Dinner," Luke declared in Luke Speak.

"Gotta go," I said, grabbing my purse.

"We're meeting at Smithie's, nine o'clock," Jet called after me.

I nodded to her, waved at everyone and stopped in front of Luke. "I'm ready," I told him.

He did a full body scan.

Then he did his sexy half-grin.

I heard some noises that sounded like moans behind me.

Luke wrapped his fingers around my elbow and propelled me to the door.

"Wear something sparkly!" Daisy yelled as the door swung closed.

Shit, but I was *in trouble*.

Chapter 19

Denver Men Are Men

Luke took me to Lincoln's Road House (clearly the Nightingale Investigation Team hang out) for dinner, where, not surprisingly, he didn't say much.

Also not surprisingly, I babbled on enough for the both of us.

Then he took me to Indy's to get Hank's key.

She was in a bit of a dither about the evening's dress code as demanded by Daisy, and loath to ask Tod for another loaner for fear her Tangerine and Chocolate Wedding would turn into an even bigger nightmare.

We spent half an hour sorting through Indy's closet and drawers for something "sparkly" for her to wear. We'd almost cracked it when Luke walked in.

Without a word, he grabbed my hand and dragged me out of the house to the company black Explorer.

Guess he was done waiting.

I, on the other hand, did not have trouble with sparkle. I was the Sparkle Queen.

At Hank's, I washed my face and put on Drama Night Makeup, heavy on the charcoal eye shadow and black kohl eye liner, dark raspberry lipstick on lined lips and glitter dust on my collarbone and shoulders.

I wore a black top that was tight across the midriff and bosom, loose around the waist. The thin sleeves and low, scooped neckline were designed to look torn, not finished. One sleeve fit over my shoulder, the other one fell off by design. The torn bits were adorned here and there with glittery jet beads, a hint of sparkle. I put on a pair of tailored, slightly tight, wide-leg, low-rider, black trousers with a sharp crease. The trousers had a thick line of black beading all the way around my upper hips. I wore a bunch of spangly, thin black bracelets and dangly jet earrings. I put my hair up in a messy knot, secured with bobby pins on the ends of which were baby, black rhinestones, and I let lots of tendrils float down. I finished off with a spritz of Boucheron.

Kristen Ashley

I walked out of the bathroom, all done up, to see Luke's long, lean body stretched out on Hank's bed, his hands crossed behind his head, eyes closed.

Shamus was sprawled and asleep beside him.

"Good God," I whispered.

His eyes opened, his head turned and he did a slow body scan.

Then his lids lowered to half-mast. "Fuck," he murmured low.

I pulled myself sternly into recovery.

"You ready?" I asked.

His eyes went to my feet. "You aren't wearing shoes."

"Damn! I knew I forgot something. Hang on."

I ran to the weight room slash junk room and tore through boxes and suitcases until I found what I wanted.

I walked into the living room carrying my shoes, a little red suede bag and a wrap. Into the bag I transferred the necessities; running back to the bathroom for lipstick, lip liner and extra sparkle powder for emergency re-application, and put in credit cards, money, phone and the VIP passes Jet gave me.

I sat on a couch and slid on one of my (four) pairs of sexy, Jimmy Choo shoes (online auction, brand new, nearly full retail price but worth every penny). These were pumps. Pointed, red suede toe and matching suede four-inch spiked heel. The body of the shoe was red snakeskin.

The shoes were *hot*.

I settled a red pashmina around my shoulders, flipping an end around my neck.

Luke was standing at the door.

"Ready," I said.

Luke didn't move.

Then he asked, "You know what I said in the store today?"

"You said a lot in the store," I told him. He hadn't said a lot of words, but all of them had a lot of meaning.

"The last part."

My eyes got big and I nodded.

"I was fuckin' with you," he told me.

I let out a breath. "I thought so," I said.

"I've changed my mind."

I wasn't keeping up with him. He wasn't exactly going fast but I still wasn't keeping up with him.

"I don't understand."

"I've decided I wasn't fuckin' with you."

Holy Mary, Mother of God.

"Are you *flirting* with me in Hank's living room?" I asked.

"I don't flirt," Luke declared.

I crossed my arms on my chest. "Seems like flirting to me."

"Flirtin' is me tellin' you that you have pretty eyes. I'm not tellin' you that. I'm tellin' you, it doesn't work with Hank, I want you in my bed. That isn't flirtin'."

I stared at him.

He was right, that sure as hell wasn't flirting.

Then I scowled at him.

He was entirely unaffected by the scowl.

I looked to the ceiling.

"Denver men are nuts," I told the ceiling.

He walked forward, grabbed my hand and pulled me toward the door.

"Denver men are men," he declared.

Good grief.

<hr/>

There was a line out the door and around the building when we arrived at Smithie's. It was controlled by big, black leather jacket-wearing bouncers and a red velvet rope.

Luke parked illegally right at the front door.

"Hey! You can't park there," a bouncer, clearly feeling the need to risk his life, said to Luke, peeling away from his station to confront us.

I opened my purse to pull out the VIP passes and noticed the bouncer got close to me. Luke's hand went flat against his chest, keeping him at a distance, while his other hand went to my arm and he moved me close to his side.

"Don't," Luke said, his deep voice sending a shiver down my spine.

I could only see Luke's profile, but whatever the bouncer saw made him say, "I guess you can park there."

I pulled out the passes and showed them to the bouncer. He escorted us to the doors and opened them for us.

The minute the doors closed behind us, I rounded on Luke.

Kristen Ashley

"He was only doing his job," I snapped.

"So am I," Luke replied.

Not much I could say to that.

"Yoo hoo!" We heard. "Over here!"

Tod was waving at us.

I took in the club, thinking it would be seedy and gross.

It was actually nice; clean, new furniture, expensive, flashing disco lights, shiny, reflective stage, gleaming silver poles, red neon behind the bar and stage. All the male staff were dressed in neck to toe black and looked like they could work for Lee.

The place was packed, wall-to-wall people. There was loud music and dancers on the stage, gorgeous girls with oiled, mostly-naked, spectacular bodies. They were making a killing, bills poking out, willy-nilly from their g-strings.

The only women I saw in the room, other than myself (and the dancers), were my friends.

Luke's fingers curled around my hip and he propelled me, part in front of him part beside him, to the tables occupied by our party, situated at the right side of the stage.

Indy, Ally, Daisy, Annette, Jason, Jet, Tod and Stevie were at two connected round tables. Nancy, Uncle Tex and Nancy's friends Trixie and Ada were at two others with three people I didn't know. One was a tiny woman with dyed black hair with one-inch, steel-gray roots and a cigarette dangling from her lip, the other a huge, hairy man who made Tex look sane and civilized. The last was a big black woman with an enormous afro and tawny brown eyes.

I pulled the wrap off and Daisy squealed, "Sugar, you sure can put the sparkle on."

"Thanks." I grinned at her. "So can you."

And she could. She was sitting and all I could see was her head to her cleavage, but she was covered in sparkle. Her hair was even sprayed with glitter-spray.

"Are those Jimmy Choo's?" Tod asked, staring at my feet.

"Yeah," I told him.

"I have the perfect song for those shoes. I don't know what it is yet, but I know I have it," Tod replied.

"You can borrow them," I said.

"Girlie, you are my new best friend." He sent me an air-kiss then aimed a meaningful glance at Indy.

I saw Uncle Tex glaring at me, clearly thinking a night out at a strip club was also not the chosen past-time for a woman being stalked by a lunatic ex-boyfriend.

Nancy appeared not to agree. She gave me a wink and a wave.

I called my hellos to everyone else and Jet got up and grabbed my hand.

"These are my friends, Lavonne, Bear and Shirleen," Jet said and then turned to the table. "This is Roxie and Luke."

"Holy shit but you girls go for the gusto. Look at this fuckin' guy. Sorry, honey but you ain't hard on the eyes," Lavonne informed Luke. Then she squinted toward me through the smoke. "Well done, girlfriend."

"We're not together," I told her.

She blinked. Her eyes lowered to Luke's hand, which was still at my waist. Then she squinted back at me.

"You aren't?" she asked.

"Bodyguard," Luke said.

Lavonne's eyes got huge. "You famous?"

"No, I just have a stalker ex-boyfriend who keeps trying to kidnap me and bad guys who are after him. Luke's here to make sure I don't get caught in the crossfire."

"You gonna make sure we all don't get caught in the crossfire?" Bear asked Luke, butting into the conversation.

"My only focus is Roxie," Luke answered with brutal honesty.

Bear grunted and rolled his eyes.

"That's plain enough to see," Lavonne said, her lips curling up in a grimacing smile, the cigarette still dangling precariously there.

Before I could say anything, Luke's fingers bit into my hip and he pulled me back and stepped in front of me. Around Luke's body, I could see a big, black guy jogging up to us, his eyes on Jet.

"Your sister's gettin' cold fuckin' feet. You gotta go back there and talk to her. I got fuckin' important people here. I got a fuckin' *senator* here. She can't back out. She can't..." he trailed off when he caught sight of Luke in his peripheral vision and he turned, full body, to face Luke. "Who the fuck are you?"

"This is Luke. He's——" Jet started.

"I know who he fuckin' is. He's fuckin' trouble," the black guy said, not taking his eyes off Luke. "Get *the fuck* outta here."

I could swear I saw the air around Luke start shimmering.

Oh shit.

I stepped around Luke and (do not ask me why) said in a girlie, airhead voice, in other words, using lingo punctuated by exclamation and question marks where they did not need to be, "Hi! I'm Roxie! Jet's friend?" I put my arm through Luke's and leaned into him, resting my head briefly on his shoulder. "This is my fiancé, Luke? He's not here to watch the dancers! Really!" I smiled up at Luke. "Are you, pookie?"

Luke looked down at me and gave one of his half-grins and shifted his body, so instead of my side leaning into him, half of my chest was pressed against him.

I pursed my lips, gave him a quick scowl then rearranged my face and looked back at the black guy with a smile.

"We're just here to watch Lottie's fantabulous debut!" I announced.

The black guy stared at me. "I know who you fuckin' are too. Lottie's been talkin'. Shit, everyone in Denver knows who you are. This ain't your fuckin' fiancé. You're sleepin' with Nightingale. Fuck!" he shouted. Then he turned to Jet and pointed a finger in her face. "Somethin' happens, I blame you."

Then he stalked off.

Jet looked at me. "That's Smithie. He's really a big softie."

Maybe Uncle Tex was right. Maybe Jet *was* a bit loopy.

Smithie came jogging back with his finger pointed at me.

"You dance?" he asked.

I stared at him. "Dance?"

He jerked a thumb to the stage.

"Holy cow," I breathed.

"She doesn't fuckin' dance," Luke answered for me.

Smithie threw up his hands and looked at Jet again. "Another fuckin' one of these guys. What's wrong with strippin'? Fuck!"

Annette called from the table. "I dance! Do you have amateur night or something?"

Smithie turned to her. "You don't need fuckin' amateur night, woman, you need to know how to fuckin' move. You know how to move?"

Jason was looking pale.

"I know how to move," Annette answered.

"You'll be drivin' a Porsche in a month."

"I don't want a Porsche. I want a condo in Breckenridge," Annette told him.

"For that you gotta do lap dances," Smithie said.

Jason started to look sick.

"I'm not sure I want to do lap dances," Annette said.

"Suit your-fuckin'-self. You wanna just dance, fuckin' come in tomorrow. We'll get you set *the fuck* up!"

I didn't know Smithie, like at all, but even I could tell he was excited.

I tugged on Luke's arm and he looked down at me.

"Do something," I hissed.

"What?" he asked.

"I don't know. *Something.* Jason looks like he's going to be sick."

"Not my problem."

"This is cool!" Annette yelled.

"Good God," I muttered, momentarily forgetting myself and resting my forehead on Luke's shoulder.

"Babe," Luke said low.

My head jerked up.

Shit.

I stepped away from him.

"Good idea," he mumbled.

I turned to the table and announced, "I need a drink."

"Get over here and sit next to Shirleen, girl," the black woman said to me and I walked over and sat down, throwing my wrap on the back of the chair and my purse on the table.

Luke followed and stood behind me.

"Someone get this girl a drink. What you drinkin'? I got me an appletini. You ever have an appletini? So smooth, get you fucked up before you can blink."

"An appletini sounds good," I agreed. Fucked up sounded even better.

She started snapping her fingers and, as if by magic, a waitress arrived. The waitress was wearing a cute, black camisole with "Smithie's" written across the front in fancy, red script, a tiny red miniskirt and a pair of kickass black strappy sandals. The outfit was the shit.

Kristen Ashley

"Get my girl an appletini, me too," Shirleen ordered then swung her big 'fro back to me and said, totally nosy, but somehow getting away with it. "Jet's been tellin' me you got man trouble."

"You could say that."

"Tell Shirleen *all* about it."

"Which man are we talking about? The scary ex-boyfriend who won't let me go? The bad guys I don't know who might accidentally shoot me? Or the good man I have that I'm afraid to lose?"

Shirleen stared at me. "How many men you got, girl?"

"Just those," I said. I looked up at Luke then back to Shirleen. "So far."

"Well, then, we got all night, unless you're really here for the show."

I shook my head. "I'm just here for Jet."

"Start talkin'," Shirleen demanded.

So I did.

〰️

Three appletinis later, I was definitely feeling loose.

Jet had talked Lottie out of her nerves. Tod had talked me into letting him try on my shoes (they fit). We all spent a lot of time talking about which song he should sing in his drag show while wearing my shoes. No one was able to talk Annette out of dancing. Uncle Tex decided he was talking to me again (but just barely). And Shirleen had sorted out all my problems by telling me she'd known Hank since he was a little boy (what? were there only, like, two dozen people who lived in Denver?) and if I let him go I needed to have my head examined (whatever).

The place was wired. Brody would have been beside himself. The longer we waited for Lottie to dance, the more the anticipatory vibe grew until the air was electric.

Then the lights went low.

Smithie took the stage.

"Gentlemen... fuck..." he looked at us. "And ladies. I give you *Lottie Mac!*"

A roar tore through the massive crowd.

Holy cow. If I was Lottie, I'd have had cold feet too.

The lights went out, I heard Smithie mutter another "fuck" while he tried to get off the stage in the dark. Then the lights went on and Jet's sister was there.

She was as pretty as Jet, bigger boobs, more makeup and a body to-die-for. She wore a killer gold bikini, heavily embellished with beading and sequins that I'd sell my firstborn child just to touch and a pair of strappy, gold sandals that she danced in like she was in bare feet.

And she could *dance.*

To say the girl could move was an understatement of tremendous proportions. She worked her body, she worked the stage, she worked the poles and she worked the crowd. Not like this was her first night on the stage dancing, but like she'd *invented* it.

A hush came over the crowd, total, reverent silence throughout the first song.

When the first song segued into the second, the crowd came out of its stupor. They all started to cheer, to chant, to undulate.

Everyone at our tables was right along with them. My hands were over my head, I was shouting, "Woo hoo!" and "You *go* girl!" After Lottie executed an upside-down pole slide with one leg up in the air and one leg wrapped around the pole, Shirleen and I turned to each other and did a high five, such was our excitement for the beauty of the overall sisterhood.

Lottie was the master. She worked it until the final notes of the song. Then she stood stock-still, reached behind her back and tore off her bra. You got a nanosecond of a glimpse of her magnificent breasts then the lights went out.

When they came back on, the regular girls were there and Lottie was gone.

The crowd went wild. Everyone sitting surged to their feet and screamed, including me.

I barely got my ass back on the chair when I felt something at my ear and I heard Luke say, "Let's go."

I turned to him and he was right in my face.

"Did you see that? That was great!" I yelled. "I want to dance. I want a bikini like that. She's my hero!"

The crowd was still roaring, chanting, clapping, begging for Lottie to come back. I could barely hear, they were so loud.

Luke's fingers curled around my arm. "Let's go," he repeated.

Kristen Ashley

"But... I'm having a good time," I said.

He pulled me out of the chair. "This place isn't safe. We're going."

"Luke."

He pulled me close, probably so I could hear, the roar was still deafening. They were chanting Lottie's name and had begun stomping their feet.

I looked at Luke and there was no sexy half-grin or flirty look in his eyes. His face was serious.

"You want to answer to me, you keep this shit up. Now, we're going."

I gulped, nodded, grabbed my bag and wrap and moved to walk away.

That was when I felt it. The crowd wasn't only wild, they were *wild*. Lottie had whipped them into a frenzy. Two songs weren't enough. She could dance until her feet were bloody and it wouldn't be enough.

I noticed that the others had realized it too. Tex was already moving Nancy out. He glanced back at me and boomed, "Go!" Trixie and Jason were helping Ada, with Tod and Stevie leading the way. Indy, Jet, Ally and Annette were sliding around the stage and heading toward a side door.

Shirleen, Lavonne and Bear were settled in with drinks like they were sitting in their living room. I thought they were completely oblivious to the possible danger, except Shirleen yelled to me, "Go with your bodyguard, girl, Shirleen will be okay. This ain't no place for a pretty child like you. They get one look at you, they'll tear you to shreds."

I nodded, really not feeling in the mood to be torn to shreds.

While Luke pulled me with him, I heard Shirleen shout, "Come see Shirleen! Jet'll bring you. You're welcome any time!"

I noticed the crowd was pressing in. The bouncers pushed through and started lining the stage.

Luke stopped and he bent to my ear. "Get close to my back, hold on to my belt, keep your head down and move with me." I nodded. "Let's go," he finished.

My fingers curled into his belt, I fitted my body to his back and he pushed through the men pressing towards the stage. We got halfway to the door when Luke stopped.

"Where you takin' this sweet thing?" someone I couldn't see asked.

"Step aside," Luke said in a voice full of warning. I figured the man would just step aside. At Luke's tone, anyone in their right mind would step aside.

272

"Don't feel like—" the guy, voice now belligerent (and to my thinking, pretty fucking stupid), started to say, then I felt Luke move swiftly and economically.

He started forward again.

"Watch your feet," Luke said to me.

I looked down and we stepped over the man who was now unconscious on the floor.

We didn't have any trouble going forward then. We were given a wide berth.

Luke put me in the Explorer, rounded the hood and got in beside me.

While he was starting the car I said, "I'm worried about my friends. And Lottie. That didn't feel good."

"That wasn't good," Luke replied, hitting a button on the on-dash phone.

It rang in the cab once and Luke was reversing out of the spot when we heard, "Yeah?"

"Tell Lee his woman is in another situation. Smithie's."

"Got it," the voice confirmed.

"Eddie's woman too," Luke said.

"Got it."

"The sister as well."

"Check."

"Out," Luke finished.

I heard the disconnect.

I stared at the phone.

"That's it?" I asked.

"My assignment is you, not them," Luke explained.

"But—"

"Lee'll take care of it."

"But—"

He switched gears and put the Explorer on the road. "Quiet."

"But, my friend Annette is in there."

"I thought her man was with her."

"Yes, but Jason can't lay out a guy like you!" I yelled, getting panicked. "We have to go back."

"We're not going back."

"We have to go back."

No answer.

"Jason's a pacifist. He's a liberal. He's a *vegetarian*. In a normal situation Jason could handle himself, but that wasn't a normal situation. You're, like, Superman. You have great facial hair. No one'll mess with you. We have to go back!"

"Babe?"

"What?"

"Shut up."

We stopped at a light and I pulled my phone out of my purse and called Annette.

"Yo Bitch!" she answered.

"You okay?" I asked.

"Yeah! Chaos! It's fuckin' cool. They, like, *love* Lottie. She's doin' an early encore. I can't wait. Wasn't it *the shit?* Lottie told me Daisy showed her all of her moves. They're gonna teach me."

"Are Indy, Jet and Ally okay?"

"Well… yeah. We're all drinking champagne in the dressing room. Tod and Stevie left, not really their gig. Jason just got in. He got Jet's mom and the old lady to the car. We're groovin'."

I closed my eyes with relief then opened them again.

"I'll talk to you tomorrow," I said.

"Later." Disconnect.

"They're fine. They're drinking champagne in the dressing room," I told Luke.

No answer.

"It sounds like everything's cool. Maybe you overreacted."

Still no answer.

I was beginning to feel like I was missing out. All my friends were still back there, drinking champagne and I was heading home. I wanted to drink champagne, or at least have another appletini. Anyway, I liked Shirleen. She was hilarious.

So I said, "Maybe it's okay. Maybe we should go back and drink champagne. Lottie is going to dance again and I'd like to see it. I'm sure it's safe."

That was when I saw two squad cars, lights flashing, sirens whirring, speeding toward Smithie's.

I watched them fly by us and kept turned in my seat, looking out the back window, hoping they'd also fly by Smithie's.

They turned in.

Luke pulled forward through the now green light, and half a block up he slowed to let another squad car take a left onto our road and it flew by us, too.

"Shit," I muttered.

"You were sayin'?"

Jeez.

I let us into Hank's and Luke made me stand at the door while he checked the house. Once he was done, we flipped on a bunch of lights and he took me to the backdoor where he let out Shamus. We stood together silently at the backdoor while Shamus did his business and then moseyed back into the house. Luke closed and locked the door and turned to me.

Shit.

Alone with Luke.

"You want coffee?" I asked.

"Yeah," he answered.

We walked back to the kitchen. I ground the beans and made a pot of coffee.

I had no idea how long Hank was going to be and Luke was obviously staying until Hank got home. It might be a long night. We'd need a lot of coffee.

When it was set to brewing, I turned to Luke and he was leaning with hips against the counter, arms crossed on his chest, watching me with his eyes half-mast.

Shit.

I decided to start an unsexy conversation.

"Where were you shot?" I asked.

"Gut," he answered.

Holy cow.

Even I knew a stomach wound was serious business.

"Are you okay now?"

"You already asked me that."

He was right, I had.

I found myself getting angry. I didn't know why.

"Well that just sucks!" I snapped. "They get the guy who shot you?"

"Yeah."

"Good!" Then I found myself getting mother hen. "You should wear protective stuff, like one of those vests. You should probably be wearing one now. Who knows what could happen in your line of business. It should be standard issue."

"I was wearin' a vest. They were armor-piercing bullets."

I gaped at him. "Aren't those illegal?"

"It wasn't exactly a law-abidin' citizen who shot me."

After he said that, his eyes dropped to my legs and I realized Shamus was sitting on my feet and I was absently stroking his head.

"The dog's claimed you," Luke noted.

"He's a friendly dog, he likes everyone," I told him.

"He isn't sittin' on my feet."

This was true, he wasn't.

I looked down at Shamus. Shamus looked up at me. I gave him a full head rub with both hands. He licked my wrist then leaned into my legs.

When I straightened and looked at Luke, he had on one of his half-grins.

"What?" I asked.

"Hank doesn't stand a chance."

"What does that mean?"

"Not that he'd want to," Luke went on as if I hadn't spoken.

"Excuse me?"

Luke pushed away from the counter and came at me.

I braced, not knowing what to expect.

He got in my space, reached around me, opened a cupboard and pulled down a mug. He set it on the counter beside me and tilted his head down to look at me.

I was holding my breath.

"You can go to bed," he said.

"I can?"

"Yeah."

"But what about you? What are you going to do?"

No answer.

I went into good hostess mode. "I can't go to bed with you awake and forced to hang around. That'll be boring."

"I'm used to it," he told me.

"Still," I replied.

"Go to bed," he commanded. Definitely commanded, no other way to put it.

I wasn't the kind of girl who listened to a command.

"I'll keep you company," I offered.

"Babe," he said, his eyelids lowering again. "Hank's got no worries with me movin' in while things are good between you two. I don't move on another man's woman."

Well, that was good to hear.

He went on, "If I were you, I wouldn't push it."

Good God.

"I'll go to bed," I decided.

"Smart decision."

I slid out from in front of him, said goodnight, and Shamus and I went to the bedroom. I took off my clothes and makeup and then was left in a quandary about what to do next.

Hank told me he wanted no clothing obstacles when he got home and the way Hank spoke to me that afternoon, I didn't want any clothing obstacles either. But I wasn't sure it was a good idea to be naked while Luke was in the house. What if something happened and he had to come in?

I compromised. I put on my lilac nightie with the black lace but no underwear.

Then Shamus and I got into bed, and after tossing and turning for a while (both of us), we fell asleep.

Chapter 20
Gray as the North Pole

Shamus jerked and jumped off the bed.

Automatically, I moved into the warm space he left behind just as I felt the bed depress when Hank settled into it.

His hands came to my body immediately and pulled me to him.

I felt like I'd been asleep for hours. I opened my eyes a crack and it was pitch dark so I closed them again.

Hank's mouth touched my shoulder.

"Whisky?"

"Yeah," he said, his lips against my shoulder. His hand was at my waist, skimming down the fabric of my nightie to my hip.

"How did your thing go?"

His mouth moved down my shoulder, effectively pushing aside my hair and his tongue touched the skin at the back of my neck. I trembled and my body warmed.

"We got 'em," he said against my neck.

"That's good," I replied on another tremble.

He pulled the fabric at my hip up and then his hand moved, his thumb pressing in to tag my underwear, except it wasn't there so his hand slid across my naked hip.

Then it froze.

"Jesus," he muttered.

It didn't freeze for long. His fingers gripped me. He turned me and pulled me into him with his hand at my bare ass.

Then he kissed me. Not a lazy-necking kiss. He went whole hog.

I was breathing heavy and my body was in full throb when his lips disengaged from mine.

He rolled us over, got on top and his hips fell between my legs when I opened them.

He kept his mouth on mine, making me dizzy with his kisses while his hand slid between us, his fingers finding me, making me dizzier. I wrapped a leg around his waist, my arms around his back, using them as an anchor to press my hips into his hand.

He touched me as he kissed me and then one of his fingers slid inside.

"Hank," I breathed, before I nipped his beautiful lower lip gently with my teeth because I could not stop myself. If someone paid me ten million dollars not to, I would still have done it.

Without warning, his hand slid away and he was inside me.

He started moving, rocking deep, pounding hard. It was unlike any time before. I got the sense there was control; if there wasn't he might have hurt me, but there was just not much of it.

I liked it. No, I *loved* the thought of making him lose control.

I lifted my knees and hips, encouraging him to lose more. I started panting, my body jerking with each of his thrusts. I whispered in his ear, running my hands across the skin of his back, stroking the damp hair at his nape.

Then there was no way I could talk.

We breathed into each other's open mouths until I felt it and every muscle in my body clenched, even the secret ones, and I moaned against his lips just as he groaned against mine.

After, he let his body weight rest on me for half a minute before he rolled us over, still connected, him on his back, me on top.

My face was pressed against his neck and his hands were on my bottom.

"Holy cow," I whispered against his neck.

His fingers dug into me but he didn't answer.

A little later he asked, "Did I hurt you?"

"Not even close," I responded.

His hands roamed up my back. One wrapped around my waist, one slid into my hair.

He turned his head and murmured in my ear, "Jesus, Roxie, you undo me."

My body stilled, and for once, I was silent.

I didn't know how to process this information. I didn't even know how to process the fact that Hank would share it. It was an admission of grand proportions, especially for a man like Hank. It was an admission bigger than the one I'd made that morning. It was the kind of thing that was said that changed lives.

Finally, I said, "I thought you were just jazzed after catching the bad guys."

"That's part of it," he replied. "Most of it was knowin' when I was done, I'd come home to you."

Good God.

"It helped that you weren't wearing any underwear," he finished.

That did seem to be the impetus that speeded things up a bit.

He rolled us to our sides and his hand went to my jaw. "We have to talk," he announced.

"We are talking," I pointed out.

"Not after-sex talk. We need to have a conversation."

Oh no.

I wasn't ready for a conversation, at least not the kind of conversation he seemed to be talking about.

"It's late. You have to be tired. I don't—"

"I know you're pullin' away even as you get closer," he told me.

I started shivering because this was getting plain old scary.

He was so tuned into me it was unreal.

"Hank—"

He still didn't let me talk. "I don't like sayin' it just as much as you aren't gonna like hearin' it, but I understand one thing about Flynn. I don't like you pullin' away."

My breath caught in my lungs.

"Don't say that," I whispered.

His hand gripped my waist. "It's not that. It'd never be that. There's no way I'd ever hurt you, sweetheart."

My body was shivering like I was cold, and Hank's arms wrapped tight around me.

"We're different, you and me," I told him.

"I know, Sunshine."

Even though he agreed, I kept on. "We're something else."

Something special, I thought, but did not say.

"Roxie, I know."

"I've never been with Billy how I am with you."

"Sweetheart—"

"And because of Billy, I can't have you."

It was his body's turn to still. "Sorry?"

I was so freaked out; I was on a roll and let my mouth run away from me.

Kristen Ashley

"This'll always be between us. You knowing about him, what he's done to me, how I let him, comparing yourself to him, me comparing us to what Billy and I used to have. It'll color us forever. It'll make it go bad."

"Roxanne—"

"It's too soon. I was meant to have time, after I got rid of Billy, time to feel good about myself, time to feel worthy, time to feel clean again. But you saw it, you're in the middle of it now and I *hate* that. I've gotten used to his stink on me. I can't allow his stink to settle on you."

"Roxanne, be quiet for a second and—"

I pressed my face in his throat. "It's not just protecting you from seeing me under that fucking sink, Hank. Even without you seeing that, you'll always know that I'm gray. You'll always be white and, now, for you, I'll always be gray."

If his body was still before, it was hard as rock now.

"Roxanne." His voice was as solid as his body, solid and sharp. My name cut through the air like a cleaver. It was filled with warning, so filled it was dangerous, but I was lost in making him understand.

I ignored the warning and went on, "We were over before we even began."

I barely finished the sentence when he rolled, his weight settling on me and pushing me into the bed.

"Quiet!" The word hit the room like a gunshot, and it shocked me so much my mouth snapped shut.

Even in the dark I could feel his eyes on my face.

Then he said, "You've been talkin' to Jet."

I nodded but didn't speak.

"Jet and I were havin' a conversation about an internal struggle she was having. We were talkin' about some people we know, friends we both like, friends who deal drugs and run games and likely murder other people."

Holy cow.

What friends were those?

And what conversation was he talking about?

I didn't have a chance to ask.

Hank continued, "What I said about them in no way... Roxie, hear this right fucking now... in no way does it transfer to you."

"Hank—"

282

Now he was on a roll and he was angry.

Way angry.

"You need to learn to give yourself a goddamned break. You're so fuckin' hard on yourself, I wouldn't even begin to be able to make you feel as badly about yourself as you do. Even if I wanted to. Christ!"

"You don't understand," I told him.

"I think I fucking well do," he fired back.

"No you don't!" I pushed at him, but he wouldn't budge, so I carried on anyway. "You didn't see us together, when we'd visit my folks, the looks on their faces. My friends who'd try to be nice to him even though they knew he was a piece of dirt. I knew they wondered about me. Why was I with him? What was wrong with me?"

"What was wrong with you?" he asked.

My head jerked like he smacked me in the face.

Then I started struggling. "Get off me, I'm going home!"

He caught my wrists and held them over my head. "Answer my question, what was wrong with you? Why were you with him?"

"I thought he loved me!" I shouted. "He promised me everything. He was full of grand dreams. He was going to show me the fucking world. I was young and stupid and believed him."

"So, you're sayin' that you're stupid because you believed a pack of lies some shithead fed you?"

"Yes!"

"It's *you* who's wrong in this scenario, just because you loved someone, and since you did you trusted him to tell you the truth?"

I blinked in the darkness. I hadn't thought of it that way.

"That's what love's all about, Roxanne. You love someone, you trust them always to tell you the truth."

"Hank, please, get off me," I begged.

"Did he get you to deal drugs?" Hank asked.

"*What?*" I screeched.

"Did you deal drugs with him? That's what he did. He was a drug dealer. Smack."

For some reason, the last word he said jarred me out of the moment and I became confused.

"What's smack?" I asked.

I could almost hear Hank's teeth grinding. "Jesus. You don't even know what it is. How in the fuck can you think you're gray?"

Then it hit me.

"Oh... *smack*." I said with dawning understanding.

"What is it?" Hank asked.

"Drugs," I answered.

"What kind of drugs?" he persevered.

I thought about it, trying to remember what they were referring to on the TV cop shows when they mentioned it. I didn't want to sound uncool that I didn't know what it was, but I kind of didn't.

For some reason, as I was silent and trying to think, Hank's body started moving like he was laughing. His hands loosened from my wrists and he buried his face in my neck.

"Sunshine, you're a nut."

Yes, definitely laughing.

"Are you laughing?" I asked just to check.

He rolled off me, to his side, but took me with him, his arms locking around me.

"Smack is heroin," Hank's voice still sounded amused.

"Oh God. Sid Vicious died of an overdose of that," I told him.

"Yeah, a lot of people die of overdoses of that."

It took me a moment to realize that our conversation had taken a drastic, and very weird, turn.

I felt it important to keep on target.

"I don't deal drugs, Hank. I design websites."

"I know," he replied and lifted a hand to run his fingers through my hair at the side of my head before he tucked it behind my ear, and then his arm locked around me again. "Roxie, people in six different states have been bringing up your name and no one knows who the fuck you are. On my desk, I got copies of employment records, apartment leases, phone bills and credit card statements a mile high with your name on them. I can track your life for the last four years and none of it was even a little shady. Whatever Flynn did, he protected you from it. Every piece of paper and every report that comes in shows you're as pure as snow. You're about as gray as the North Pole."

Oh... my... God.

"You checked up on me?" I asked, horrified.

"I checked up on Flynn. Doing that meant I had to check on you, since the only thing we got, except arrest reports and his name linked to various pieces of scum, is the trail he left through you."

I tried to process that, but Hank interrupted my processing by asking, "Did you know he was dealing drugs?"

I closed my eyes in despair.

Here we go, I thought.

I took a deep breath and I admitted, "I had no idea. At first I didn't care. Then I knew he wasn't out all day doing good deeds, but I didn't ask questions. I just didn't want to know."

I thought that said a lot about me and none of it was good.

Hank replied quietly, "You've just proved my point, Sunshine."

"What point?"

"You didn't work with him. You didn't even know what he was about. The only thing you did was fall in love with an asshole. He lied to you and you believed him because you loved him. It's easier for other people to see what kind of guy he was. They didn't care about him, they only cared about you. You haven't lived a life of crime. You just lived with a criminal who lied to you about who he was. All this time, you've been living a normal life, Roxie. You aren't to blame for letting the wrong guy into your heart."

I didn't say anything because there was nothing to say.

Except he was wrong.

He just didn't get it.

I didn't want a cop boyfriend who was forced to run checks on my old leases and phone bills to track down an ex-lover on the run. It was humiliating, pure and simple.

When I was silent, Hank kept talking.

"Roxie, it would be different if you let him stay in your heart. But you didn't do that. Eddie told me that you tried to turn him out years ago. You were a woman alone doing the best she could, but sweetheart, you're not alone now."

"I don't want to talk about this anymore," I said, and all of a sudden I didn't. Not that I wanted to talk about it before. Just that since we were, I didn't want to do it anymore. I was exhausted. It felt like I'd run a hundred miles without even an energy bar to see me through.

His hands moved to stroke my back. "All right, Sunshine, we won't talk about it anymore."

Kristen Ashley

His fingers trailed soothingly up and down my back.

Honestly, it was too much. I couldn't cope.

He was such a good guy and there just seemed nothing I could say to get him to back off and leave me be.

It didn't matter that I didn't actually want him to back off and leave me be.

It was about me caring about him so much that I wanted him to have something better than me.

I prepared to move. "I think I need to be alone. I'm going to go sleep on the couch."

His fingers stopped moving and his hands pressed against my back. "No you aren't."

"Please, Hank. I need to be alone. I have to think."

"That's the last thing you have to do."

"Really Hank—"

"Quiet, go to sleep."

"Seriously."

"Roxie, quiet."

"Oh for God's sake," I snapped.

I lay there, angry, or trying to convince myself I was angry. What I did know was that my body was wound up and tense.

Hank just kept his arms around me and kept his silence.

Then I spent some time trying not to think, but everything he said was tumbling around in my head. All I could do was think.

Through this, Hank kept his arms around me and kept his silence.

When I stopped trying to stop thinking, I stopped thinking altogether and fell asleep.

Hank's arms were still around me.

Chapter 21
There Was Just No Shaking This Guy

"Wake up, Sunshine."

I opened my eyes as the light switched on and I blinked, temporarily blinded.

Then I saw Hank's thighs, upright, at the side of the bed. They were encased in black track pants with three thin stripes running up the sides, the outer two white, the inner one dark gray.

I decided no one should be upright, especially Hank. He'd had, like, two hours of sleep.

I closed my eyes again.

"No waking up," I mumbled.

I rubbed my face into the pillow and turned away from the light.

The bed moved when Hank sat on it. Then the covers slid down to my waist and Hank's hand rested there.

"Get up, sweetheart, Shamus needs his walk."

I felt his lips touch my shoulder, then the bed moved again and he got up.

I was lying mostly on my side, but partially on my belly. I felt Shamus in front of me and I squinted my eyes at him. He saw me squint. His tail wagged, he edged up to me and rested his chin on my waist. He blinked twice and then closed his eyes again.

Since Shamus closed his eyes, I did too.

Clearly Shamus was in no mood to walk. Shamus shared *my* mood, which was to sleep more and forget my life was a disaster. Though Shamus's life wasn't a disaster and he probably didn't comprehend that mine was, but if doggie brains could comprehend such complex situations, I felt pretty certain he would commiserate and let me sleep.

I'd fallen asleep again when I was suddenly pulled across the bed, flipped and lifted, an arm behind my knees, one at my waist.

"What the hell!" I screeched, grabbing onto Hank's shoulders as he walked the few steps to the bathroom, carrying me. He dropped my legs and set me on my feet in the bathroom door.

I tipped my head back and frowned at him. He kept his arm around my waist and was grinning at me.

His hair was damp from a shower and he looked awake, alert and refreshed.

I found this supremely annoying.

"How can you be bright eyed at this hour? You've barely slept," I asked. I didn't know what hour it was. All I knew was that it wasn't a good hour.

He kept grinning.

"Conditioning," he answered. "Get dressed. I have to get to work, but before that we have to walk Shamus, have breakfast and then you have to spend an hour doing whatever it is you do that, in the end, makes you look no more cute and sexy than you do right now."

I stared at him.

Was he serious?

"Excuse me?" I asked.

"Get dressed, Roxie."

"I'll have you know that I've spent years honing my getting-ready routine to a fine and practiced art, and when I'm done with it I look far better than I do right now."

"No you don't."

My mouth dropped open.

He wasn't only serious, he was insane.

I'd been perfecting my high maintenance toilette since I was twelve years old. My family was always yelling at me to get out of the bathroom. I never left the house without at least two coats of mascara, a shimmer of blush and one lipstick and one lip gloss, just in case I changed my mind sometime during the day as to which was more appropriate for my outfit.

"Yes I do," I told him. "When I wake up my eyes are all squinty and my face is all blotchy and my hair is always a mess."

He pulled me into his body and tilted his head down so his face was an inch from mine. "I see you're in the mood to argue, but I have to get to the station, so can we argue while we're walkin' the dog?"

Before I could answer, he rubbed his nose along mine. He let me go, turned me around to face the bathroom, put his hand to my ass and gave me a little shove. I whirled around to glare at him and say something smart, or at least say something, but he was already walking away.

Shamus sauntered into the doorway of the bathroom and sat down, tail wagging and his tongue rolled out.

"Whatever," I muttered and grabbed my toothbrush.

We didn't argue while walking Shamus. I pouted and practiced my cold shoulder while trying not to think about my life's spiraling descent through the seven depths of hell.

My cold shoulder didn't work literally or figuratively. Hank ignored it completely and slung his arm around my neck, making me walk pressed against his side.

I also managed to think of nothing but my downward life spiral through the depths of hell, and by the time we made it back to his house I had waltzed through the fourth depth of hell and was careening headlong into the fifth.

Hank left me to my thoughts and my getting ready routine. While he scrambled eggs and made toast, I showered.

I was standing at his bathroom sink applying blusher when he brought me coffee and a plate of food. They were good scrambled eggs. A hint of garlic and some cheese, and the toast was toasted perfectly: not too light, not too brown and with a generous coating of real butter and grape jelly.

I found it immensely irritating that Hank was even a good fucking cook.

I ripped off a chunk of toast angrily with my teeth and chewed while Hank watched me. He was leaning against the bathroom doorway, feet crossed at the ankle, plate in his hand, forking up some eggs.

"What now?" he asked, his eyes lazy and amused.

"Nothing," I answered with my mouth full.

"You have jelly on your face," he told me.

My eyes flew to the mirror.

Shit.

I rubbed it off, put down my toast and took a sip of coffee.

He walked into the bathroom, kissed the side of my head and walked out.

Kristen Ashley

Fucking Hank.

⌖

We were parked behind Fortnum's and I had my hand on the door handle when Hank stopped me and turned me to him.

"You want to tell me what's buggin' you?" he asked.

"No," I answered.

His eyes smiled but his mouth didn't.

How he could smile, I did not know. Even if it wasn't a full blown smile, to my mind there was nothing to smile about.

"Is this about our conversation last night?" he went on.

"No," I repeated. This time it was a lie.

It was *totally* about our conversation last night. I couldn't get it out of my head, any of it. Last night, he'd made sense. In fact, everyone made sense, Daisy, Duke, everyone. I wanted to believe, even tried to believe.

In my heart, I couldn't.

Deep down, I knew I had to protect myself from that time. The time that happens in any relationship when your judgment was called into question. Then where would I be? What would I say? I didn't have solid moral ground to stand on, and Hank was a pillar of solid moral ground. Any relationship had to have equality. Ours did not. He was clean and good. I was dirty, and if not bad, then at least dubious. Who wanted to be the dubious girlfriend?

Not me.

That said, I spent more of my time thinking about him telling me that I undid him than my moral dubiousness.

"I can't believe you can cook," I snapped, deciding to focus on something other than the matter at hand.

His smile went away and he did a slow blink. "Sorry?"

"You're a good cook," I said.

"You're angry because I can make eggs?"

"Well… yeah," I said not caring, even a little bit, that I sounded demented. Demented was good. No one wanted a demented girlfriend.

"Sunshine, I can scramble eggs and I can cook meat on the grill, that's the extent of my cooking skills," he told me. "Feel better?"

"You make good toast too." I made it sound like an accusation.

He stared at me a beat then threw his head back and laughed. Out and out laughed. I'd never seen him laugh, not like that. I'd *felt* him laugh, and I'd heard him chuckle, but I'd never watched him laugh. He was good-looking all the time, sometimes better than others, but when he laughed he was beautiful.

This did not make me happy, so I scowled at him.

He caught sight of my scowl and snatched me across the cab into his arms and buried his face in my neck.

"You're a nut," he said there.

Enough was enough. I had to end this. I didn't want to, I *had* to.

Okay, so Hank didn't get it. And neither did anyone else. So they all thought I was a crazy person and I would disappoint a lot of people if I broke it off with Hank. That didn't matter. What mattered was I knew what I was doing and what I was doing was for Hank.

He deserved better than me.

I should point out that I didn't really know what I was doing, but I thought I kind of did.

So I announced, "I'm moving back in with Uncle Tex. He's a big guy. He has a shotgun. He can protect me until this mess is over."

Hank's head came up and he was smiling at me like I was being cute and adorable. "You aren't movin' back in with Tex."

"Yes I am."

"Let's forget for a second that no way in hell would he let you. *I* won't let you. First, I want to make sure you're safe and the only way to do that is for me to make you safe. Second, Tex is an ex-con. Something happens, he has to use that shotgun, there'll be uncomfortable questions as to why he's got a gun."

Shit.

I didn't want Uncle Tex to have to answer uncomfortable questions.

"So I'll move into the safe room until this is over," I tried.

"Lee won't let you."

"Why not?"

"Because I won't let him let you."

I scowled at him some more.

Fucking Hank.

There was nothing for it. It was now or never.

"Okay then, I'm breaking up with you. Trust me, Hank, it's for your own good. I know you don't understand, but one day, when you're with a nice woman who makes you French toast with sweetened cream cheese spread in the middle, you will."

And I hope she's boring, boring, boring, I thought, but did not say because it wasn't nice and I didn't really mean it. I didn't want Hank to have boring, but if I was honest with myself I didn't want him to forget me either.

I made this announcement on a wave of bravado and a seriously painful stomach clutch. In fact, I was almost certain I was going to vomit.

He shook his head and his smile didn't change. Even though I was breaking up with him, he *still* was looking at me like I was cute and adorable.

"You're not breakin' up with me," he said.

The nausea left me and I blinked at him. "I am," I told him.

"You're not."

"Hank, I *am*."

"Sunshine, you are not."

"You can't tell me I'm not breaking up with you when I'm breaking up with you!" I said, fairly loudly.

"I think I just did."

I looked at the ceiling of the cab. "I *do not* believe this," I told the ceiling.

There was just no shaking this guy!

Hank's hand moved to my chin and he forced me to look at him. "Roxie, I have never met a woman more annoyingly stubborn than you."

Well!

He ignored my flashing eyes (and I was sure they were seriously flashing) and went on, "You've got some fool idea in your head that you're protectin' me and you're fired up to keep it there."

"It isn't a fool idea," I retorted.

"It's beyond a fool idea," Hank shot back.

Well!

He ignored my grinding teeth and his grin came back. "Lucky for you, I'm as patient as you are stubborn."

"You're not patient. You're more stubborn than me."

"That works too."

"Hank, you have to listen to me—"

"On this subject, no I don't."

"Hank—"

"Let's get you inside, I've got to work."

"We have to talk."

"We'll talk later."

"We need to talk now."

His arms tightened and he pulled me out of my seat and across his lap. His arm went around my waist as one hand slid into my hair and tilted my head down to look at his face. It was a tight fit and we were super close. His face was all I could see.

"When Fortnum's closes, I'll come and get you. We'll go home. We'll make dinner. We'll make love and afterward you can try and convince me that we're not gonna work. When that doesn't happen, I'll convince you we are. Then, we'll probably make love again and then we'll sleep. How does that sound?"

It sounded fucking great.

Jeez.

I was definitely in trouble. In fact, I was so in trouble you could tattoo it on me.

I gave up.

Temporarily.

"I'm going to Tod and Stevie's tonight. Emergency Wedding Summit, and then Tod's helping me with an outfit for Daisy's party."

His body started shaking and I realized, belatedly, he was enjoying this. He actually thought this was fun. My stomach was tied in knots and Hank was entertained.

"How exactly were you thinkin' you were going to manage to break up with me and go back to Chicago when you have no car, a car full of your shit is in my house and you've got a more active social life in Denver than I have?" he asked.

"They're *your* friends," I snapped.

"Too late, sweetheart. You can't scrape them off either. Although, it would be amusing to watch you try."

Good grief.

Whatever.

Time to cut my losses.

"Don't you have to get to work?" I asked, sounding uppity.

"Yeah," he said.

Kristen Ashley

He gave me a light kiss, but the look in his eyes told me he'd have liked to have done more.

He slid me back to my seat. I got out and charged ahead. He caught up with me and grabbed my hand.

I sighed.

We walked into Fortnum's hand in hand, and it was packed.

Hank tensed. He did a scan of the crowd and relaxed when he decided it was safe. He yanked my arm so I fell into him and he kissed me, deep but swift.

Then he grinned down at me with approval while I stared up at him, my body leaning into his, my head completely dizzy.

Then he was gone.

It was a little after noon when she walked in. I wouldn't have noticed her if she wasn't looking around in hopeful expectation. It wasn't that she wasn't pretty, she was. But there was just nothing about her that made you keep looking at her once you first noticed her.

She was wearing a long sleeved, v-necked, blue t-shirt, jeans and boots. She had strawberry blonde hair, peaches and cream skin and warm, brown eyes.

As I'd done while people watching many times before, I mentally redesigned her outfit so that it would pack a bigger punch, get her noticed, give her some flair. Better belt, definitely. A funky necklace would help. Some cleavage for certain. And a different pair of jeans; ones that weren't utilitarian but that made a jeans-like fashion statement. She had a great figure and she needed to learn to work it.

She was looking at Uncle Tex (or, kind of staring at him in horror), then she caught my eye, decided I was the safer bet for whatever was on her mind, walked up to me and smiled.

"Hi. Do you work here?" she asked.

"I do today," I answered, smiling back.

I was sitting behind the book counter.

When Hank dropped me off, Indy, Uncle Tex and Jet were the only ones working. The place was jammed and there were empty coffee cups everywhere. They weren't even keeping up with the crowd and had no time to clean up. I gathered the dirty dishes and started washing, happy to have something to take my mind off my thoughts.

Not that I could have thought anything. Lynyrd Skynyrd's "Gimme Three Steps" was blaring from the radio when I hit the sink and Skynyrd played for the next two hours.

Once the crowd died down, Indy gave me a quick training session on the book counter cash register (Uncle Tex was strictly espresso and didn't do book sales) so she and Jet could go see Jet's Dad in the hospital. They were going to swing by and get us some lunch on the way back.

The girl looked to Tex then back to me.

"Does India Savage still own this store?" she asked.

"Yep. You looking for her?" I replied.

She blushed and her eyes slid away. "Actually..." she hesitated then looked back at me, "I'm looking for a friend of hers. Hank Nightingale. Does he come in here?"

I stared at her.

Holy cow.

I felt something twist inside me, something painful.

"Yeah," I said quietly. "Hank comes in here. Do you know him?"

"We, um... dated a while back. Then I moved to New Mexico. Now I've moved back and I thought I'd look him up. He and Indy, well you know, they're close..." Her voice trailed away before she brightened with determination. "I'm Beth," she introduced herself.

"Roxie," I replied.

She looked at me and her eyes did a quick sweep. I was sitting on a stool, my legs crossed and a bit away from the counter, leaning my elbows on it. I was wearing a fitted, boat-necked, black sweater and worn-out, vintage Levi's. I had an intricate, chrome mesh choker around my neck and a matching wide bracelet over my sweater at the wrist, and round-toed, black suede, platform wedges with kickass magenta binding and sling-back strap.

"Have you worked here very long?" she asked.

"I don't really work here, I'm filling in."

I felt badly for her. This couldn't be easy and she didn't even know I was sleeping with her ex-boyfriend. I didn't know how to tell her, or even if I should. I decided I shouldn't, especially considering the current circumstances.

"Listen," I began. "Do you want me to give Hank a message?"

"Um, yeah. Could you tell him——?"

The bell over the door went. She turned, I looked over and we both saw Hank walk in.

Damn.

His timing was shit.

As he walked in, it hit me even more than normally how good he looked. Jeans that fit so well they might be illegal in a few states. Gun and badge on a killer, dark brown belt with a heavy, matte silver buckle. An olive brown sweater with half zip and a high collar, the hem tucked in behind the belt, untucked around the rest of his waist, sleeves shoved up his forearms.

He could have been in a fucking catalogue and he didn't have three stylists to make him look that way. It came naturally.

His eyes were on me, warm and lazy, the edges of his lips turned up in a sexy smile.

Shit, shit, shit.

"Hank——" I started, but it came out quiet and croaky. He rounded the counter as I cleared my throat. "Hank," I said, louder this time, but he was there.

I'd come away from the counter and tilted my head up to look at him. Even though Beth was standing there, and before I could stop him, he wrapped his hand round the back of my head and gave me a light kiss.

He hadn't even looked at her.

"Thought I'd take you to lunch," he said softly, his eyes looking in mine, his hand still around my head. He'd moved away barely an inch.

Shit.

I cleared my throat again, even though I didn't need to, and said, "Hank, you remember Beth." Then my eyes slid to the side.

He let me go and straightened, turning to Beth, and I watched him. For a second, he seemed blank, like he didn't remember her and my breath caught in my throat.

Then he smiled. Not the sexy lip turn, but a friendly, genuine smile. "Beth. Jesus. What're you doin' here? I thought you lived in New Mexico."

Beth looked between Hank and me. She was blushing, big time.

"I moved back to Denver," she replied.

Hank shifted into my space and his arm went around my shoulders, unconsciously doing a man-brand move, not having any idea why she was there.

She went from just blushing to looking like she'd plunge a knife in her gut if one was handy. I searched the counter just in case there was a letter opener within reach.

"That's great," Hank said, still oblivious.

"Hank," I cut in. "Beth's here—"

"No!" she interrupted me, her eyes on me and they were huge. "I just popped by... um..." She was faltering. It was going to have to be Roxie to the rescue.

Quickly I said, "Beth's here to buy that Dan Brown book. You know, the one about da Vinci?"

Hank looked down at me, likely wondering why I was sharing this absurd information.

"I told her we didn't have it. You wouldn't know where to get it, would you? She wants to read it, like, bad," I finished lamely.

God, I was such an idiot.

Hank looked at me, then at Beth, and cottoned onto the situation. If she was just looking for a book, I would hardly know her name or alert him to her presence.

His face softened and he moved away, taking his arm from around my shoulders.

"Beth," he murmured and my heart lurched for Hank, who obviously felt badly, but especially for Beth, who was humiliated.

"Maybe I'll try the Tattered Cover!" she announced gamely then looked at me. "Thanks for your help Roxie." She looked back at Hank. "Hank, great to see you. Maybe I'll see you around."

She moved to leave and I called out, "Wait!"

I stepped off my stool, bumping into Hank who was still close.

"Why don't you two go to lunch?" I suggested.

"What?" Beth asked, or kind of expelled in a breath filled with mortification.

"Sorry?" Hank asked, staring at me like I'd lost my mind.

I had an idea. It was a heartbreaking idea, but it was something.

She seemed sweet, she was pretty and she liked him. She liked him enough to come searching for him when she got back to Denver. She was normal and probably never had anyone shoot at her, nor ever would.

So she needed a snazzier wardrobe. Indy would help her out.

Maybe she didn't spread sweetened cream cheese on French toast, but I was relatively certain that Shamus would like her. Then again, Shamus seemed to like everyone.

I stepped away from Hank. "It's been busy, so I can't leave and anyway. Indy and Jet are bringing back food. You two go to lunch, catch up, you know… old friends and all that."

Hank was no longer staring at me like I'd lost my mind. He was staring at me like he wanted to strangle me.

I took another step away from Hank.

"I don't think—" Beth started.

"Can I talk to you a second?" Hank interrupted her and didn't wait for me to respond. He took my hand, nodded sharply to Beth, said, "Just a minute," and dragged me out from behind the counter and toward the bookshelves.

While being dragged, I caught a look at Uncle Tex who was shaking his head at me like I'd let down the side.

Hank dragged me past fiction, biography, crime, romance and straight to the open area that separated the front room from the back room (travel, health, social studies) and had a huge table on it with cartons of upturned vinyl wedged in them.

He stopped, turned and looked down at me.

I opened my mouth to speak but he said, "Don't say a fucking word."

I closed my mouth.

Hmm, seemed Hank was angry.

He took a deep breath through his nostrils, getting control.

Then he said, in a soft, dangerous voice, "Please tell me you didn't just try to fix me up with a woman I used to date."

"Hank—"

He didn't let me say anything. "I used to be patient. Now, I'm findin' it hard stoppin' myself from shakin' some goddamned sense into you."

"Hank—"

"Roxanne, I just experienced my *girlfriend* trying to fix me up with another woman."

"I'm not your girlfriend. I broke up with you."

He stepped closer. I stepped back. My bottom slammed into the table filled with vinyl. Hank filled the space I'd opened.

"That wasn't nice, doin' that to Beth," he said.

"Yes it was. You two could have hit it off. You'd asked her out before. I was doing her a favor," I defended myself.

"She and I went out twice. She was the friend of the girlfriend of a buddy of mine on the Force. If I remember, she was painfully shy, but sweet, and on her way to some job in New Mexico."

Shit.

Shit, shit, *shit*.

"I thought she was an ex-girlfriend," I told him.

"She never made it that far and wouldn't have. I was doin' a friend a favor, and even if it makes me sound like a bastard, I'll tell you I only did it knowin' she was soon gonna move to another state."

Oh shit, I thought.

"Damn," I muttered aloud, feeling like a total bitch. It must have taken all she had to walk into Fortnum's. I looked at Hank. "I'll go talk to her," I told him.

"No, you've done enough. I'll take her out to lunch and I'll pick you up from Tod's when you're done tonight. When we get home, we're gonna have a conversation and put this shit to rest, once and for all."

I didn't like the sound of that.

"Hank——" I started.

"I don't want you goin' to Tod's with anyone but Tex, Duke, Lee or one of his boys. Got me?"

His eyes were glittering angry, and I had the feeling he was barely keeping his temper in check.

I nodded.

The sleeping tiger had awoken and I was not about to prod him with a stick.

He stared at me angrily. I bit my lip.

Then I couldn't help myself. I hated that he was angry with me. I put my hand on his chest and leaned into him.

"I'm so sorry," I whispered.

"You can apologize later, after we've talked, when you're naked and in my bed."

Holy cow.

"Hank——"

He put a hand to my neck and tipped his head down to get in my face. "Roxanne, now's a good time to be quiet."

Shit.

He was still angry, and I felt like a total bitch.

I braced, getting ready for him to explode.

Then, to my complete surprise, his anger cleared. He gave me a light kiss and squeezed my neck affectionately.

"We'll talk later," he said quietly.

Then he was gone.

I stood there; it could have been minutes, it could have been hours. I just stood there, looking at the space where Hank had been, not quite able to process how easy it was to fight with him. Even when he was that angry, he could shift it and kiss me good-bye.

My phone rang.

I pulled it out of my back pocket, flipped it open and put it to my ear. "Hello?" I said, expecting just about anyone, Annette, Indy, Daisy, anyone.

I should have looked before I answered because it wasn't Annette, Indy, Daisy or anyone.

It was Billy.

"I saw you walkin' his fuckin' dog with him, sittin' in his goddamned lap in the car, kissin' him, you fucking *bitch*."

My breath left me and I stood stock-still.

"You're gonna learn, Roxie. You're gonna fucking *learn*."

Then he disconnected.

I kept the phone to my ear and stood frozen, continuing to stare into the space, unseeing, not breathing, scared stiff.

Billy was watching me.

"A little help!" Uncle Tex yelled from the front, jarring me out of my stupor.

I flipped the phone shut, shoved it into my pocket and shouted. "Coming!"

I'd think about it later. For now, I was protected, safe. The cameras were on me, even now. I was never alone. They'd find him before he could get to me. Vance was out there looking for Billy, and I knew Hank would keep me safe.

I realized what I'd just thought and closed my eyes.

Hank. I should tell him. I should tell Lee. I should tell someone.

I walked to the front and there were half a dozen customers at the coffee counter, two waiting to buy books.

"Girl, get the fuckin' lead out!" Uncle Tex boomed.

I decided I'd tell Uncle Tex later. I'd think about Hank and my conversation later. I'd kick myself for what I did to poor Beth later.

I walked to the book counter and rang up the books.

Chapter 22

The Good Lord Overwhelms Her on Occasion

"What do you think, Roxie?" Tod asked.

I looked up and noticed everyone was watching me, Indy, Ally, Daisy, Annette, Tod, Stevie and Jet. My mind had been elsewhere, mainly because I'd just lived the weirdest fucking day of my life.

Now, I was sitting, drinking a glass of sparkling wine in Tod and Stevie's living room (black carpeting, dove gray walls, mauve furniture, glass tables, sleek, feminine, stark white, human-sized sculptures here and there; it was totally gay and cool as shit). The Emergency Wedding Summit was in full swing.

Strewn everywhere were fabric swatches and ribbons of every color, wedding magazines from four different countries, examples of party favors, glossy brochures from wedding venues, information pamphlets for different bands and DJs and invitation samples. Lining the dining room table were seven (seven!) wedding cake tops ranging from the traditional bride and groom to a teddy bear bride and groom. *The* Wedding Planner Scrapbook was open on the glass coffee table, bursting with even more stuff than it seemed to carry the day before.

Discussion had been hot and heavy. Starting with wedding colors and veering crazily to wedding gowns, churches, bands, you name it. Indy had a definite idea of what she wanted, and every idea she had clashed violently with the one Tod had.

Throughout all of this Stevie calmly served hot and delicious hors d'oeuvres.

Also throughout all of this, I alternately wound myself up about the coming "conversation" with Hank and thoughts about my weird day.

Kristen Ashley

Earlier that afternoon, about half an hour after Hank left, Duke showed up and Indy and Jet arrived not much later with lunch. While we were eating, I told Uncle Tex about Billy's phone call.

"You've got to be fuckin' shittin' me!" he boomed, tuna sandwich residue flying from his mouth.

I dodged the bits of food and shook my head.

"Have you called Hank?" Jet asked, looking upset.

"Things were kinda busy," I answered.

"I'm callin' Hank. Give me your phone, woman," Uncle Tex demanded, holding out his big hand toward Indy.

Indy knew the drill with Tex and cell phones (as in, he had no clue). She took out her phone, flipped it open, scrolled to Hank's number and pressed the button before handing it to Uncle Tex.

I turned to Jet as Uncle Tex stormed away, taking his sandwich with him. "Hank and I had a talk last night."

Jet's upset melted immediately and she smiled at me. "That's good. Did you get everything straightened out?"

"Not exactly," I said. "Anyway, I just wanted to tell you that I mentioned something about me being gray, and Hank got a little... angry."

Jet blinked at me. "Pardon?" she asked.

"He said something about you two having a conversation and how whatever you two talked about in no way, or, I should say his exact words were..." I did a fake, deep voice. "'Roxie, hear this right fucking now, in no way does it transfer to you'."

Jet's mouth spread in a huge smile. "See! I told you he wouldn't think you were gray. Now you don't have anything to worry about."

Right.

I wished.

"What's this about gray?" Indy asked, looking between the two of us.

Before anyone could answer, Uncle Tex was back. "He wants to talk to you."

I closed my eyes for a second, wondering what Hank's mood would be after lunch with Beth. Then I took the phone.

"Hey," I said.

"You okay?" he asked, no anger in his tone, only concern.

I felt a little of my tension ebb away.

304

"Freaked out a little bit, but okay," I answered.

"I know it doesn't seem like it but this is good, Roxie. I'll call Lee and he'll tell Vance. We already know Flynn's been followin' you, but whatever he's doin', he's been careful. He's givin' Vance some trouble and Vance is a top-notch tracker. Now Flynn is getting desperate, angry and stupid and that's good. That means he'll make a mistake."

I nodded. That made sense, and even though Billy getting *more* desperate, angry and stupid was pretty fucking scary, getting him didn't sound good. It sounded *great*.

"Okay," I said into the phone.

"He has no idea the kind of protection you have. You're gonna be fine," Hank assured me.

"Okay," I repeated, believing him.

"Make sure you have someone with you when you go to Tod's," he went on.

"Whisky," I said quietly. "You told me that already."

"I know. I wanna make certain you got it."

Hank was *such* a good guy.

"I got it," I told him.

"I'll be at Tod's at nine to pick you up."

"Okay," I said, *again*.

"Later, Sunshine," and he disconnected.

I flipped the phone shut and handed it to Indy just as the bell over the door rang. We all turned to see who it was and my eyes widened at what I saw.

"Ohmigod!" Indy yelled. "Beth! I thought you were in New Mexico."

Shit.

Shit, shit, shit.

Indy hugged Beth and Beth said to her, "I moved back. I heard you finally hooked up with Lee."

"Yeah," Indy showed Beth her left hand, wiggling her fingers. "We're getting married."

"That's great!" Beth replied, smiling happily at Indy. Then her eyes slid to me and her face got pink. "Um, Roxie. Can we talk?"

Shit!

Shit, shit, shit!

Kristen Ashley

Indy, Jet, Duke and Uncle Tex all stared at me. Only Uncle Tex knew about my earlier idiotic blunder.

"Sure," I said to Beth.

We were all eating our sandwiches at the book counter. Beth and I walked over to a couch and sat down.

I turned to her and started quickly, "I'm sorry. It was stu—"

Her eyes were kind as she looked at me and she interrupted softly. "Don't be sorry. Hank told me about your... ordeal."

I gaped at her. "He did?"

"Yes. I'm so, so sorry you went through that. He told me, because of that, you're behaving erratically and you have trust issues." She patted my knee. "That's understandable."

Behaving erratically?

Trust issues?

Good God.

I was going to *kill* Hank.

Beth went on, "Anyway, what I wanted to talk to you about was... um..." she stopped, looking uncomfortable.

"Yeah?" I prompted, smiling at her even as I mentally planned Hank's untimely demise.

"You dress really cool," she blurted. "And I thought... maybe, if you don't mind, could you, maybe, um... take me shopping?"

I gaped at her again.

She went on in a rush, "I know, we barely know each other and it's like, really weird that I'd ask but—"

"I'd *love* that!" I cried excitedly, not thinking before the words flew out of my mouth.

Then I thought.

Oh shit.

What was I saying? I was leaving as soon as I could get my car. I didn't need to become Beth's personal shopper.

"That would be so cool!" she exclaimed while I had a mini-flip out. She hesitated a second before she hugged me. When she pulled away she said, "I try, but I can't really get it together. I'll try something new and end up looking like a freak. I just need a little fashion direction."

Damn.

I couldn't back out now.

And she was right. She definitely needed a little fashion direction.

"I can do that," I said on a smile.

"Thank you," she hugged me again. "Give me your phone, I'll program my number in it. Here's mine."

We traded phones. We traded numbers. She hugged me again. She talked to Indy, met Duke, Jet and Tex and then left, happy as a clam.

Well, at least I didn't feel like a bitch anymore.

That was good, right?

"What was that all about?" Indy called to me after Beth left.

"Roxie tried to set Hank up with that girl," Uncle Tex told her.

Indy, Jet and Duke stared at me like Uncle Tex told them I danced down the middle of Broadway wearing nothing but Mardi Gras beads and a smile.

"I thought *you* were his girlfriend," Duke said.

"I am and I'm not. I broke up with him," I replied.

Indy, Jet and Duke's stares intensified.

"Why would you do a fool thing like that?" Duke exploded, sounding a lot like Uncle Tex.

"Don't worry. He didn't really accept my breaking up with him. He still thinks we're together," I assured him.

Indy and Jet smiled at each other knowingly.

Good Grief.

I closed my eyes and rested my head on the back of the couch.

"Good fuckin' God. These fuckin' girls. I swear, they're gonna kill us all," Duke announced and I heard him stomp away, likely into the bookshelves.

I felt the couch move on either side of me.

I opened my eyes and turned my head one way then the other. Indy and Jet were there.

"You wanna talk?" Indy asked.

I closed my eyes again. "No."

"We're here," I heard Jet say.

They sat with me for a second in silent moral support then they both drifted away.

After closing, both Tex and Duke walked us to Tod and Stevie's house, leaving us when we were safe inside. Then they hightailed it home, making it clear that was as close as they wanted to get to The Emergency Wedding Summit.

Daisy and Annette were already there. Ally arrived ten minutes after we did.

Annette and Jason had spent part of the day getting over hangovers from the Lottie Strip Club Extravaganza and part of the day mountain biking again. Annette told me that Jason opted out of The Emergency Wedding Summit to watch a ballgame with Eddie at his house.

At that moment, I wished I was with them.

"Well?" Tod interrupted my thoughts. "You have style. You wear Jimmy Choo, Manolo and have a real pashmina. Your opinion *counts*. So, what do you think?" Tod asked, as if anyone who hadn't gone the way of five hundred dollar shoes didn't have the right to an opinion. He went on, giving an inch, "Okay, I'll grant that maybe chocolate isn't good for a wedding but we could pull off tangerine. I know we could." His stare moved from me and turned into a glare when it settled on Indy.

"Roxie? You okay?" Annette asked, her green eyes both sharp and kind as they looked at me.

Slowly, I put my champagne glass on the coffee table and stood.

"No," I said to Annette. "No, I don't think I'm okay."

Annette stood too, preparing. She'd known me a long time, she knew what was coming.

"Honey——" she started.

I turned from her to Tod. "Tod, you're sweet but it's Indy's wedding. The colors are pink and ivory, she's having a DJ, not a band, so they can play AC/DC or whatever the fuck she wants to hear. If she wants gerbera daisies, she's going to fucking well have them. And there will be no teddy bears *anywhere*. You of all people know India Savage is not a teddy bear person."

Tod blinked at me then said, "Okay, girlie. Sit down, let me get you more champagne."

"No," I continued. "I don't think I can sit down and I don't want any more champagne." I started pacing. "Oh... my.... God! Billy's out there, *watching* me. I was walking Shamus with Hank and he was *watching*. I was talking with

Hank in his 4Runner and he was *watching*. Hank kissed me and he was fucking *watching!*"

"Honey, come here," Annette said softly.

I ignored her. "I tried to fix Hank up with another woman today. What was I thinking? I cannot believe I did that! I humiliated Beth. It was bitchy. Even though I didn't mean to be bitchy, it was still bitchy. Hank was so angry with me. He was so angry it *hurt*. Then he wasn't angry anymore. Just like that, *poof!*" I flicked my hands out in front of me. "He had it under control and we were, like, normal again. What in *the hell* is that all about? Fighting is supposed to be out-of-control, ugly and brutal, where you say shit you can't take back and behave like idiots and someone, usually me, ends up in tears. I don't know how to fight like that, where you just say what you have to say and get over it. I mean, what the hell is that?"

I was now shouting.

"She gets like this sometimes. You just gotta roll with it," Annette explained to the room.

I continued to ignore her and ranted on, "Hank wants to have a conversation tonight. We had a conversation last night! I can't have another conversation! He'll say shit that freaks me out because he's, like, in my brain. We haven't even known each other for two weeks! How can he be *in my brain?* It's *unreal!*"

Everyone kept silent and watched me.

"Then he'll kiss me and I'll get dizzy and won't be able to think straight. This is too soon. It's too much, too soon. I need to think. I need to get my life together. I need to get... the fuck... out of here."

I started shaking and my nostrils started stinging and I knew it was coming. I couldn't have stopped it even if I tried.

I turned to Annette as the tears fell down my cheeks.

"Nettie," I whispered. "He's out there and he's *watching* me."

Then I couldn't see her anymore because she melted in my tears.

Arms closed around me and I heard Annette murmur in my ear. "Hush, sweetie. Hush now."

"He's watching me," I repeated. "He's watching me with Hank. I don't want his filthy eyes on Hank."

"Hush," Annette said.

I wrapped my arms around her and held on tight. She held me back and only moved to stroke my hair.

Kristen Ashley

After a while, I heard her say, "Can we use your bathroom?"

"I'll show you," Stevie said and his hands were light on me as they guided me up the stairs.

Annette and Stevie helped me clean up my face in the bathroom. I pulled myself together, holding Annette's hand as Stevie wiped my face with a warm, wet washcloth.

"Feel better?" he asked, smiling encouragingly.

"No," I told him, but I was trying to smile too.

He kissed my forehead. "You will," he said and then looked me in the eyes again. "It may seem like you won't, but you will. I promise."

I nodded, wanting to believe him, and with a hand squeeze from Annette, we walked to the upstairs landing and heard Ally say, "I'm gonna talk to Lee. The minute they find that asshole, I want my turn with him in the holding room."

"Ally," Indy said.

"Sugar, I'm talking to Marcus *to*-night," Daisy broke in. "He's gotta step his shit up. Ain't gonna be no holding room for Billy fucking Flynn, not if I have anything to say about it."

"Daisy," Indy said.

"No fucking way. I want a shot at him first. I'm gonna *kill* that motherfucker," Ally broke in.

"Ally," Indy said.

"No, *I'm* gonna kill him," Daisy declared.

"Oh for God's sake, no one's going to kill him!" Indy said, loudly this time.

Then Stevie, Annette and I jumped as we heard glass shatter.

After a second of loaded silence Indy said, now quietly, "Tod."

"Seen a lot of shit in my life." Tod's voice was vibrating with anger. "Lived in a closet for years, hiding who I was. My parents still don't know. Had friends die of AIDS, had other friends beaten up in parking lots and alleys for no other reason but because of who they are. Never has that been in my living room. Never have I seen a sweet, spirited being that fucking broken. No, I think *I'm* going to kill Billy fucking Flynn."

This announcement was met with silence from downstairs.

I swallowed and looked at Annette and Stevie.

Then I whispered, "Am I broken?"

310

Stevie's hand came to my arm. "You've been trying so hard to cope, girlie, that you haven't even realized you've been through hell. We've all been watching, we've all been worried. No one can be strong that long. It's good this is happening. Go with it. You need it."

"But," I began, "I'm not strong. I'm weak."

Stevie's brows drew together. "Why would you think that?"

"I cry all the time," I explained.

His hand went away from my arm and he waved it between us. "Oh, well. So does Tod and he's the strongest person I know. You would not even believe the shit he's been through in his life."

I blinked at him.

He linked his arm through mine. "That's for a different bottle of champagne. Let's get you an outfit for Daisy's party, hmm?"

He walked me down the stairs and I threw a glance up at Annette.

She stood at the landing staring down. When she caught my eye, she blew me a kiss.

Her eyes were filled with tears.

※※

We were all upstairs in the second bedroom, known as Burgundy's Room (Burgundy Rose was Tod's drag queen alter-ego), and we were all staring in disbelief at Annette.

Her hair was teased out to three times its volume (compliments of Daisy) and she was wearing a blood red, hoop-skirted formal with black marabou feathers drifting about the bodice.

"This is *phat*. I'm like, Scarlet-fucking-O'Hara," she announced, admiring herself in the mirrored closet door.

I looked to Jet. Jet was obviously struggling to keep her face noncommittal.

"Don't you think it's a bit much?" I asked.

"No... I... do... not," Annette replied. "It's the shit."

"I love it," Daisy declared. "It's you."

It was so not Annette that somehow, in some weird way, it worked.

The doorbell rang.

I looked at my watch. It was five after nine.

"Shit!" I yelled, jumping off the daybed. "That's Hank."

I was wearing a day-glo yellow, Lycra, strapless mini-dress. It wasn't what I was going to wear to Daisy's. That had been the first thing I tried on (picked out and then carefully packed in a garment bag by Stevie). The mini-dress was just one of the fifteen dresses I'd tried on for the hell of it.

"I have to get out of this dress." I was in a dither.

"I'll get the door," Stevie said.

Indy gave him a look. "I'll come with you."

I didn't have time to worry about their look. It was nigh on time for Hank and my "conversation" and I was not ready for it.

I pulled off the dress and hung it on a hanger. I put my clothes back on, handed out hugs, blew air kisses, apologized to Tod for not helping with clean up and ran down the stairs.

Hank, Stevie and Indy were not in the living room or the kitchen. I grabbed my bag and opened the front door to check if they were outside.

They were standing halfway down the front walk. Stevie was carrying my garment bag. Indy's arms were wrapped around her middle. Hank had one hand at his waist, the other at the back of his neck, rubbing there with his head tilted forward as he listened to Stevie saying something I couldn't hear.

"What's going on?" I asked, knowing exactly what was going on and walking to them.

Stevie's back was to me. He stopped talking and turned.

"Nothing, girlie. Get home," he said, leaning into me and he kissed my cheek.

I stared at him, not believing him for a second.

Indy gave me a hug. Stevie handed Hank the garment bag and Indy and Stevie walked into the house.

I looked to Hank. "What's going on?" I asked.

His arm went around my shoulders. "Nothin'. Let's go."

I planted my feet, stubborn to the last. "What did they say?"

Hank looked at me. I could see by the outside light that his eyes were soft but unsettled. "We'll talk in the 4Runner."

"Hank."

He pulled me into his side. "Please Roxie, get in the car. We're standin' exposed on the front walk."

I realized what he meant, nodded quickly and walked with him to the car. He opened the door for me and closed it when I got in. He threw the garment bag in the backseat, rounded the hood and got in beside me.

We didn't speak until we were on the road.

"Hank——" I started.

He cut in, "They told me you had a bad night. Just that. They're worried."

I looked out the side window. "I didn't have a bad night. I just had..." I struggled to find the word. Finally, I found it. "An episode. I'm fine."

He didn't say anything.

I turned to him.

"I'm *fine*," I repeated, maybe trying to convince myself.

He stopped at a stop sign, turned to me, lifted his hand and ran the backs of his fingers down my cheek. Then, without a word, he looked toward the road again and we were off.

I was so stunned by his loving touch, feeling the sensation of something knit together that had been torn apart in me, that I didn't say another word the rest of the way to Hank's.

I was staring out the side window again, lost in thought, when I felt the air in the cab of the 4Runner go funny.

I looked to Hank and I knew something was wrong.

"What?" I asked.

Hank drove right by his house and I watched it slide by. The outside light was on as well as the lights in the living room and kitchen.

"What?" I repeated.

"I didn't leave any lights on," he said. "Do you have Lee's number programmed in your phone?" He leaned forward to pull his own out of his back pocket.

I felt fear glide down my spine.

"I don't know," I answered.

"Sweetheart, get out your phone. I'll tell you the number."

With trembling hands I pulled out my phone. As I started to flip it open, it rang. I jumped, the phone went flying in the air and I fumbled it then caught it.

The display said, "Uncle Tex calling."

"What the..." I started to say.

Uncle Tex, to my knowledge, never used the cell phone I bought him and his cell was the only number of his I had programmed in my phone.

I flipped it open. "Hello?"

"Why'd you drive by? Saw you doin' it, fuckin hell," Uncle Tex replied.

I blinked in the dark cab. "Where are you?"

"Standin' in Hank's living room window. Jesus. What're you, goin' out for ice cream?"

I turned to Hank. He was driving and scrolling through his phone book at the same time.

"Uncle Tex is in your living room. He saw us drive by," I told Hank.

Hank glanced at me, flipped his phone shut and at the next crossroads, he swung a u-ie.

"We're coming back," I told Uncle Tex.

"See you in a minute," and Uncle Tex disconnected.

"What's Uncle Tex doing in your living room?" I asked Hank.

"Don't know. I gave him a key when you moved in, just in case. He obviously used it."

We skirted a block out of the way so Hank could park in front of his house. I got out of the SUV and met him on the sidewalk. We walked up together, Hank holding my hand.

He opened the door and dropped my hand, keeping me back at the door and went in first.

"Sweet Jesus." I heard my mother say from somewhere inside the house.

Holy fucking *cow.*

I pushed in beside Hank.

Shamus came lurching toward us, in full body wag. He head-butted Hank's thighs.

That was all I saw. I was staring at my mother and father, who were sitting on Hank's couch.

My Mom looked like an older version of me; tall, curvy. She'd gone a bit round and her hair was now dyed blonde. My Dad looked like a cuddly gnome; redheaded and blue-eyed. He was shorter than my mother (and me) by at least four inches and he sported a big beer belly.

Obviously, Uncle Tex had done as he'd threatened and called my Mom.

Shit.

"Sweet Jesus," my mother repeated, still staring at Hank and slowly coming up from the couch.

Dad was staring at me. "Roxie," he whispered and I watched as he also got up.

I took in his face wearing an expression I'd never seen before in my life. An expression that could only be described as "ravaged with worry".

"Dad," I whispered back.

Dad walked across the room, grabbed my upper arms and pulled me roughly to him.

After he hugged me he pushed me away, again with his hands at my arms, and stared at me. Although I knew the swelling on my face was long gone and the bruising was (almost) completely gone, the scabs where Billy cut me with his rings were healing, but still there.

"I'm going to fucking *kill* that motherfucker," Dad said.

I closed my eyes.

"Herb!" Mom snapped, and I opened them again. "Not in front of Roxie's young man."

Good God.

For the first time, Dad's eyes moved to Hank and he let me go.

"I'm Herb Logan, Roxie's Dad," he put his hand out toward Hank.

Hank took his hand and they shook. "Hank Nightingale."

"Sweet, sweet Jesus," Mom whispered, staring bright-eyed at Hank shaking hands with Dad.

Dad dropped Hank's hand and backed away.

"This is my wife, Trish. The Good Lord overwhelms her on occasion. I find it best to just ignore it," Dad advised Hank.

Hank smiled at Mom.

She stared at him a beat and then her eyes rolled back into her head.

"The Lord our Savior heard my prayers," she told the inside of her eyeballs.

"Mom!" I cried, sounding uppity.

Her eyes rolled back to normal and then she bugged them out at me. "What?" Mom asked, sounding just as uppity as me. "He's cute."

This was *not* happening. None of it. It was just *not* happening.

I turned to Hank. "You can kill me now. Just take out your gun and shoot me. It's okay. I give you permission."

Kristen Ashley

Hank looked like he was trying hard not to laugh. He pulled me to him with an arm around my neck.

"Sweet Jesus! Sweet, sweet Jesus!" Mom called to the Savior, caught up in the divine intervention that was Hank and me.

I narrowed my eyes at her. "Stop calling Jesus, Mom. Hank's gonna think you're weird," I snapped.

"She *is* weird," Dad said.

"I'm not weird," Mom returned.

"Trish, you're a fuckin' nut. Always were," Uncle Tex boomed, calling our attention to him for the first time, then he turned to Hank. "It runs on our side of the family."

That's when it hit me.

Mom and Uncle Tex in the same room. Mom and Uncle Tex in the same room after years and years of not talking to or seeing each other.

I looked between them. Then I looked again.

My eyes filled with tears.

"Mom," I muttered, staring at her.

Her eyes filled with tears too.

"I know," she muttered back.

I walked out from Hank's arm, hugged my Mom, then turned my head to Uncle Tex.

"Get over here," I ordered, my voice shaky with tears.

"Good fucking Lord. I wish Sweet Jesus would come and save me now," Uncle Tex said.

"Get over here!" I demanded.

He came over and his big arms went around us.

"Happy?" he asked over our heads as we repositioned ourselves to include him in the hug.

I looked up at him.

"Yeah," I whispered.

He was looking down at me and his eyes flickered. He waited a beat and then he kissed the top of my head. When he was done, he kissed the top of Mom's. She and I looked at each other and burst into fresh tears.

"Jesus fucking Christ," Tex groaned.

We ignored him.

316

We held on for a while then Dad said, "Okay, now that we've done the family reunion business, maybe we can talk about my daughter being kidnapped and stalked. I might want to know a little more about that."

I disengaged from Mom and Uncle Tex, wiping the tears from my face with my hand, and turned to Dad.

"Hank's handling it," I told him.

"Yeah. Tex told me." Dad didn't sound happy and he turned to Hank. "How 'bout we talk?"

"Dad," I butted in.

Dad interrupted me. "Tex tells me these are good people and they know what they're doin'. I believe him. But, Roxanne Giselle Logan, you got cuts on your face and fear in the back of your eyes and I'm your goddamned fuckin' father and I need to be *briefed* on this fuckin' *situation*. You got me?"

I'd heard that tone before so I kept my mouth shut and nodded.

"Herb. Your language." Mom had heard that tone before too, and she never kept her mouth shut.

Before Dad's head exploded, I suggested, "Why don't I make us some coffee?"

"I don't want no coffee. I want a fuckin' beer." He turned to Hank. "Is there a bar around here?"

Hank looked at me then to my father and said, his voice quiet, "There is, but there's also beer in the fridge."

Dad regarded Hank. "Son, we need to talk away from the women. I got things to say and Trish's ears can hear what's happenin' two doors down. You get what I'm sayin' to you?"

"What do you have to say that I can't hear, Herbert Logan?" Mom asked.

"I'm not leavin' Roxie." Hank ignored Mom, and how he said what he said stated quite clearly that he was not.

Dad watched Hank a beat and then I saw him smile.

Oh shit.

I thought I was in trouble: official, definite, certifiable trouble But I realized that *now* I was really in trouble.

Dad approved of Hank.

I knew he would, but I didn't know it'd make me feel all warm and squishy inside.

"I'll stay behind," Uncle Tex offered.

Dad nodded and turned to Hank. "That work for you?"

Hank didn't look happy, but he also nodded. Then his eyes came to rest on me.

I heard his non-verbalized request and walked to him.

His arms came around me.

"We'll be quick," he told me.

"Okay."

"Lock the door and don't open it to anyone," Hank said.

"Okay," I replied.

"The couch in the office pulls out into a bed. Your parents want to stay here, they're welcome," he went on.

That was *not* okay, but I said, "Okay," anyway.

He grinned at me and I got the impression he knew my thoughts. He kissed my forehead, let me go and nodded to my Dad.

Then they were gone.

"He's *cute*," Mom said to the closed door.

Shamus came and sat on my feet so I gave him an ear scratch.

"You're not spending the night here," I told my mother.

"Your father doesn't want you out of his sight," Mom told me.

"He just went to a bar with Hank," I pointed out.

"Well, you know what I mean," Mom returned.

"I'll get you a hotel," I offered.

"You are not getting us a hotel. We've got money. Don't fight it, it's a parent thing."

"Mom," I whined (yes, whined).

"Roxanne Giselle—"

"Trish, for fuck's sake, she's sleepin' with the guy. Get a fuckin' clue," Uncle Tex boomed.

I stared at Uncle Tex in horror.

Mom was totally unaffected.

"That's okay. I'm liberated," Mom announced. "I'll talk Herb into being liberated too. I don't think he'll care though. He likes Hank. I can tell."

Mom had never been "liberated" before. Billy and I had always slept in separate bedrooms when we visited, and my brother Gil and my sister Mimi also had the same arrangements with their girlfriends and boyfriends, and Gil had been living with his girlfriend for three years.

318

I looked at Uncle Tex. "Please make them stay with you."

"It's outta my hands," Uncle Tex said.

I sighed and gave in. I was too exhausted from my weird day and two bouts of crying fits to fight it.

"I like his house," Mom announced. "It's cozy, but it needs candles. And his dog is so cute!" Mom bent over and cooed at Shamus. Shamus sauntered over to her, smelled her outstretched hand and then gave her a sloppy, wet, doggie kiss on her cheek. "Ooo! He's sweet!"

I turned to Uncle Tex. "Will you shoot me?" I asked.

He put his big hand on top of my head and smiled.

Chapter 23

Get Over Here

When Hank and Dad walked into the living room after going out for a drink, Dad's face didn't look ravaged with worry anymore, which I thought was a good thing. Also, when Hank and Dad walked into the living room after going out for a drink, they were carrying Mom and Dad's luggage, which I thought was a very, very bad thing.

"Since we were out there, we got the bags from the rental car. And you women say men can't multitask," Dad declared, dumping the luggage in the living room.

"Oh dear Lord, he remembers one thing and he wants to be congratulated," Mom sighed and looked at me. "Men."

I wasn't in the mood for Mom and Dad's bickering. I was staring at the luggage.

"You aren't staying here," I declared.

Dad looked at me, confused. "Hank said we could."

I looked at Hank, then to Mom, then Dad, then Tex, and then I rolled my eyes.

I just didn't have it in me.

"Oh, all right," I gave in.

Mom and I got the sheets and extra pillows and made up the bed. Hank got beers from the fridge and we all talked. Uncle Tex left. I kissed Mom and Dad goodnight and they went to bed.

Nary a word was said about the sleeping arrangements.

Hank put an arm around my shoulders and walked me to his bedroom, hitting the lights as we walked through the rooms.

"I'm going to have to sleep on the couch," I told him once we'd made it to his bedroom. I got my nightie from under the pillow and started toward the bathroom while saying, "Do you have another blanket?"

"You aren't sleepin' on the couch," Hank told my back, as if that was that. Then he said, "I'll let Shamus out."

I turned around and saw him walk out of the room.

Well.

I did not think so.

I got ready for bed and was sitting on it, cross-legged, when he came back.

The minute he closed the door, I launched in. "Hank, if I'm not sleeping on the couch, then you're gonna have to sleep on the couch."

He lifted his arms, grabbed his sweater behind his back and pulled it over his head, dropping it on the floor. Then he sat on the bed to take off his boots. "I'm not sleepin' on the couch either."

He got up to take off his jeans, putting his gun, badge and phone on the nightstand.

I tried to ignore his (very nice) chest, but kind of failed because Hank had a super nice chest (and great abs too), and hissed. "Hank! My Mom and Dad are in the other room."

"So?"

"So my Dad's going to have a conniption if he thinks we're sleeping in the same bed under the same roof as him and Mom."

Hank, now naked (and looking *fine* by the way), got in bed.

"He's all right with it," Hank said with certainty.

I stared at him. "What? Did you two talk about it?"

His hand came out and he pulled me out of my sitting position. I toppled to my side and he yanked the covers out from under me and flicked them over me.

"No," he answered, looking down at me as I settled on my back.

"Then how do you know?"

"It's *my* roof," Hank responded.

"I don't understand."

Hank reached over me and turned out the light. Then he rolled me, tucked my back to his front and rested his hand on my thigh. "You wouldn't, it's a guy thing. You're just gonna have to trust me."

Shamus jumped up on the bed and walked around a bit. Then he settled with a doggie groan on his side, his back pressed into my front.

Oh well.

Whatever.

I was totally exhausted, way too comfy, and I had the human and canine Nightingale boys' warmth seeping into me front and back. I wasn't going to fight it.

I was about to fall asleep, mindlessly scratching the soft fur behind Shamus's ears, when Hank called, "Sunshine?"

"Yeah?" I mumbled, snuggling a bit deeper into him.

"I'm lettin' you go," he told me.

I thought it was weird that he'd announce this but it didn't matter, Shamus was fencing me in.

"That's okay. I'm good," I said. "Even if you do, I have nowhere to move. Shamus is plastered to the front of me and taking half the bed."

He was silent for a second and the air in the room started to feel close.

Then he said, "That's not what I mean."

I opened my eyes and looked, unseeing (for more reasons than one), into the darkness. "What do you mean?"

"When this is finished, I'll get your car back and you can go with Annette and Jason to Chicago."

I felt the muscles in my body tighten.

"Excuse me?" I whispered.

"I'm lettin' you go," he repeated.

I felt my lungs contract.

"Are you..." I hesitated, "breaking up with me?"

His hand moved up my thigh and wrapped around my waist. "You already did that, remember?"

I was *such* an idiot.

I felt my breath get shallow.

"Though, I need you to understand something," he continued.

I nodded my head on the pillow, but didn't say anything, *couldn't* say anything.

"I'm a cop. All I ever wanted was to be a cop. I protect people and keep them safe on a daily basis. Doin' it for someone I care about..." He stopped talking.

I stopped breathing.

He started talking again. "I understand why you didn't want me to be involved with this business with Flynn." He paused. "But you need to understand that I wouldn't have had it any other way."

I started breathing again, mainly because my body needed oxygen, and if I didn't, I would have died.

Not that dying would be a bad thing at that moment.

Kristen Ashley

I waited for him to say something else, like he didn't want to let me go, like he would have preferred if I didn't go.

But he didn't say anything else.

I let the silence stretch between us.

Then I asked, "Why?"

"Why what?"

"Why are you letting me go?"

His arm tightened. "A while ago, you said if you care about something, you have to set it free. If it comes back to you—"

"I remember," I whispered.

"I still think it's bullshit."

Even though I felt that thing that had knitted inside me was in danger of unraveling, I couldn't help but smile.

"So I go home to Chicago and you hope I'll come back to Denver?" I asked.

"No, you move on, I move on. If there's some way to move on together, that'd work for me. In the meantime, I'm not waitin' for you and I don't want you to feel obliged to come back to me."

My smile disappeared. My throat closed and Hank's face went into the back of my hair.

"You've been alone and felt trapped for a long time, Roxie. Soon, you'll be free of all this shit. You have good friends and a family that loves you. They'll see you through."

I didn't want them to see me through. I wanted Hank to see me through.

Good God.

I was going to start crying again. How many tears did a body make?

I knew this was good. I knew it was the right thing, but it felt very wrong.

"Last thing I want to do, last thing I ever wanted to do, was make you feel trapped," he murmured into my hair. "So, I'm lettin' you go."

That was when I knew.

I knew why his eyes looked unsettled after he'd talked to Stevie and Indy. I knew why his touch on my cheek was so poignant.

He thought he was making me feel trapped.

He wasn't letting me go because he wanted to, because I'd finally convinced him I wasn't good enough for him, because I was annoying and stubborn, because I was a nut or because my mother called out to Sweet Jesus.

He was letting me go so I could... finally... feel free.

324

Oh... my... *God.*

He was *such* a good guy.

The thing that I thought had started unraveling inside me tightened up.

Then steel bands slid across it and locked it into place.

"Whisky?" I called.

"Yeah?"

I took a deep breath.

Then I took a scary plunge.

"I think I've changed my mind," I said.

I felt his body grow tight.

"I think..." I whispered, "I don't want you to let me go."

I'd barely got out the "go" when Hank rolled me over, rolled on top of me and Shamus jerked and jumped off the bed as Hank kissed me.

He went straight into one of his make-me-dizzy, full-on tongue, brains scrambling, hands everywhere Hank Nightingale kisses.

One of my arms wrapped around him and my other hand slid into his hair. I pushed off with a foot and rolled him over, getting on top, laying kisses down on his neck and collarbone. I started down his chest when he yanked me up and rolled me back. He got on top of me again and kissed me, his hands sliding my nightie up to my waist and then beginning to pull my panties down.

It was then my phone rang.

We both stilled.

We listened to it ring until it stopped.

Hank's hands slid back up my hips, slow, not starting anything, waiting.

My phone rang again.

"Fuck," he muttered and shifted, moving to turn on the light.

Still under him, I twisted, grabbed my bag off the nightstand and snatched out my phone as the light came on.

It said, "Unknown Number".

I flipped it open. "Hello?"

"Were you fuckin' him?"

My body tensed.

Hank was mostly on top of me and looking down at me.

"Billy?" I said.

Instantly, Hank rolled away from me and knifed off the bed. I came up on my elbow and watched as he tagged his phone from the nightstand at the same time grabbing his jeans. Billy talked in my ear.

"Were you fuckin' him? Is he touchin' you now, you bitch?"

"Billy, where are you?" I was watching Hank. He'd hit a few buttons on the phone and it was tucked into his neck while he pulled on his jeans.

"Fuck you, Roxie. Fuck you and fuck *Detective* Hank Nightingale."

"You listening?" I heard Hank say into his phone.

"Is that him? What's he saying, the fuck," Billy snarled in my ear.

"Billy, you're in trouble. Desmond Harper's men are after you," I told him.

Hank looked at me, nodded and gave me an encouraging wink.

I felt relief flood through me. I was doing the right thing by keeping him talking.

"Harper's boys are behind bars," Billy replied.

"That was the other ones. He's sent more after you. Billy, you have to go. You have to get out of town. Harper wants his money back. He's going to find you."

"How do you know this shit? Goddammit! Did Detective Nightingale tell you?" Billy asked.

"Billy—"

"What else has he been tellin' you? Don't believe him, Roxie. Don't believe a thing out of that lyin' pig's mouth."

I sat up straight.

Um… I did not *think* so.

"Don't you call Hank a pig!" I snapped.

"Don't defend him to me, you whore."

Now, *this* was how I was used to fighting.

I threw the covers back and shot out of bed.

"Don't call me a whore!" I yelled.

"You left my bed two weeks ago, you bitch. Now you're fuckin' some cop. That's the goddamned definition of whore!"

"It was *my* bed, you idiot. You were my roommate and for some stupid reason, do *not* ask me why, I let you sleep there."

"You let… you *let* me sleep there? You were beggin' for it when I first met you."

"*I* was begging for it? You have a creative memory, Billy."

Even Billy, completely unhinged, couldn't fight that one.

"I wasn't your fuckin' roommate. You're my woman!"

"I haven't been your woman for three years, you moron!" I shouted.

"How you figure that?"

"Oh, I don't know," I got sarcastic. "Maybe it was when I put your shit in the hall and changed the locks. Or when I left you, like a *billion* times, writing you a note saying it was over. Or, maybe it was when I didn't let you put your filthy, stinking hands on me for the last eighteen months! That's how I figure it!" I shrieked.

While I was yelling, there was a knock on the door. Hank kept the phone in the crook of his neck, buttoned up his jeans and opened it. Mom and Dad stood there, Dad wearing his jammies, Mom tightly bundled in a robe. Hank stopped them from saying anything by lifting a hand and they stared at me, their faces worried.

"You don't want to leave me, Roxie. You know you don't, you always came back."

"I've been trying to leave you for three years, Billy. You've just been too fucking stupid to figure it out."

His voice changed, got quiet, went low. "Don't call me stupid."

"Billy, we're over. O... v... e... r."

"We're not over, Roxie."

"Yes we are."

He went silent.

I waited.

Then he said, "Fuck him, Roxie. Fuck him good tonight. Give him a piece of your fine ass he'll never forget. Go down on him, you're good at that. I re-member your mouth, so fuckin' sweet."

I swallowed and glanced at Hank. His face was like stone, his body com-pletely still, the fury coming off him like a physical thing and charging the air.

I realized then that Hank was listening. How he was, I didn't know, but he was listening.

Good God.

"Billy, you've got to—"

Billy cut me off, "'Cause tomorrow, you'll be with me. Tomorrow, he'll be lyin' in bed wondering where your sweet mouth is. And you and me... I'll make you forget him, Roxie. We'll be gone and you'll forget and it'll only be you and me."

"I'll never go with you," I said but I said it to nothing. He'd disconnected.

I flipped my phone shut, tossed it on the nightstand and looked at Hank.

Hank was staring at me but he talked into the phone. "You get him?" He paused. "Yeah. Keep me informed." He snapped his phone shut, threw his on the nightstand too and said, "He's in Colorado Springs."

I stood across the room from Hank and my parents, trembling and watching Hank, wondering what he was thinking. Wondering if now, after hearing what he heard, he'd not only let me go, but ask me to go.

"Colorado Springs?" Mom asked. "What's he doing there?"

"On the run. He knows Harper's boys are after him and he's not stayin' anywhere long," Hank told Mom then looked at me. "Vance is in C Springs, followed him down there. You kept him on the line long enough, they got a lock on his position. Vance is headin' there now."

I nodded

"Thank the Sweet Lord Jesus," Mom said.

"Atta girl, Roxie," Dad said.

I ignored Mom and Dad.

"Were you listening?" I asked Hank.

"Yeah. When I found out about the call this afternoon, I told Lee and the boys have been monitoring your phone. They put it on speaker. *You* okay?" Hank asked me.

"No," I said.

No, no, really just no. He'd heard it and he wasn't coming to me. I was standing across the room in nothing but a nightie, scared and trembling, and he made no move to me.

I knew this would happen. He didn't even want to be near me.

Hank looked angry. He looked so angry, he looked about ready to commit murder. He looked like he was expending every effort not to lose control. If he'd let go and started ripping the room apart I wouldn't have been surprised.

"Are you okay?" I asked Hank.

He didn't answer for a beat.

Then he spoke. "I'm gonna kill that motherfucker." His voice was so low, an edge sliced through it.

My head jerked at his words and I winced. I'd heard them many a time before but the way Hank said them made me believe him.

"Whisky—"

"Get over here," he ordered.

I blinked. "What?"

"Get over here," he repeated.

I stared at him. Then I skirted the bed and walked to him.

The minute I got within arm's reach, he snatched me to his body and his arms went around me so tight that for the first time in days my ribs hurt.

"Whisky, my ribs," I breathed.

His arms didn't loosen.

"He isn't gonna touch you," Hank said to the top of my head.

"Okay... um, Hank... my ribs."

"He isn't gonna get near you."

I realized what was happening.

He *had* been making every effort to stay in control. So much so, he'd been physically unable to move.

At my realization I melted into him, my arms went around him and I held tight too.

I leaned back in his arms and looked up at him. "Whisky, we're going to be all right."

He didn't say anything, but he let me go just a fraction. The tension started to ebb from his body and we stayed there, just hanging on.

"Welp! See you got this under control, son. We'll see you in the morning," Dad announced behind my back.

"Nightie night," Mom said.

The door closed.

Hank and I just held on.

Shamus sat down and leaned into our legs.

"I'm sorry you had to hear that," I said quietly.

"Lee plays by different rules than me," Hank replied, and I became confused at the sudden change of subject.

I leaned back and looked at him again. "Yes?"

"He recruits men who play by those rules."

I nodded, having no clue whatsoever what he was talking about but deciding things were sensitive enough. I should just go with it.

"They work for money. Their lines are blurred. Mostly they do right, but other times they do what they're paid to do and don't ask questions."

I put my hand to the side of his face and let it drift down to his jaw.

"Okay," I whispered.

"Sometimes they dispense justice. Their form, which isn't the same as mine. Sometimes Eddie and I play their game. Sometimes we use them to get what we need."

I thought it was good that he was so handsome, because when he got philosophical he made no sense at all.

"A while back, a man hit Indy," Hank told me. "Lee beat the shit out of him. He did it purposefully, methodically, leavin' a message. A man'll think twice before he touches Indy."

Oh shit.

I was beginning to see where he was going with this.

I pressed my body to his. "Whisky."

"Those boys don't take people to the holding room to hurt them. Interrogate them, yes, but as far as I know, no one has been held there and harmed on purpose."

"Maybe we should lie down," I suggested.

Hank ignored me.

"Vance was pretty pissed-off, the way he found you. Vance comes from a broken home. A violent one. His Dad set him out after the first time Vance stepped between him and Vance's Mom when his Dad was beatin' her. Vance was ten."

"Oh my God," I whispered, my mind filled with a ten year old boy trying to protect his Mom and being kicked out of the house for it. What did he do then? Was Vance ten years old and out on the street?

Good God.

It didn't bear thinking about, at least not now. I shoved it aside and focused on Hank.

It was like he hadn't heard me speak.

"Vance asked for a go with Flynn. Payback, instead of overtime, for his search for you. It would set a precedent, but the way Vance figured it, as a woman, you hadn't been given the opportunity to a fair fight. Flynn deserved the same treatment. Tex jumped on the bandwagon. Lee left it to me. I didn't agree. I was willin' to turn a blind eye, but didn't agree. Indy was about to lose a knee when Tex saved her. She'd been kidnapped and they were gonna shoot her to get her to talk. Lee felt obliged to Tex and they agreed to let Tex at Flynn, then Vance. Eddie and I stepped up the game to find Flynn before Lee in hopes that wouldn't happen."

I had stopped interrupting and let him be.

"I'm callin' my shot," he said, and I felt my heart spasm.

I sure as hell interrupted then. "You can't do that Hank. You're good. Your lines aren't blurred."

"I'm not askin' you, Sunshine. I'm tellin' you, I'm callin' my shot."

Holy cow.

"You can't do that for me," I protested.

"I can. I finally understand Lee. Anyone thinks of touchin' you, they think of speakin' to you that way, I want it known they should think again."

"Hank, someone finds out you could lose your badge."

"Then I'll work with Lee."

"Hank!"

"I'm only tellin' you so you'll understand. I'm not askin' for permission and I'm not lookin' for discussion."

Holy cow, cow, cow.

"Well, we are going to discuss it because I'm not going to permit it!" I snapped with a stomp of my foot. "You said earlier you never wanted to be anything but a cop. Now you're saying you're going to put that in jeopardy for me. And you think *I'm* nuts?"

His face changed. The stillness of anger went out of it, something else came over him, something I was a lot more familiar with.

He started walking me backwards to the bed. "So, you're staying?" he asked.

I shook my head like I was clearing it. "Excuse me?"

"Denver. You're staying?"

My eyes narrowed. "Do not even *think* of trying to change the subject, Hank Nightingale."

My legs hit the bed and I went down. He came down on top of me.

"Are you movin' to Denver?" Hank asked patiently.

Before I could answer, his lips went to my neck.

"We were talking about you putting your career on the line due to some macho idea of revenge," I reminded him.

"We're done talkin' about that. Now we're talkin' about you movin' to Denver."

His tongue touched the back of my ear.

My body did a quiver.

I jerked my head and neck away from him. "Hank, look at me. We need to finish talking about—"

His head came around and he kissed me. I forgot what we needed to finish talking about.

A little later, I'd gotten his jeans off him, managed to get my mouth on him (for a while; it must be said, Hank did like his control, not that I was complaining). He had his hand between my legs and his lips were against mine when he asked softly, "Are you movin' to Denver?"

Then his finger slid inside and his thumb did a swirl.

My neck arched.

"Yes," I breathed.

When I looked at him he was grinning at me.

Fucking Hank.

Chapter 24

Buttermilk

Hank's phone rang.

I opened my eyes and it was dark.

Hank was on his back. I was pressed to his side, my head on his shoulder, my thigh thrown over one of his. Half my leg had fallen between his and my hand was resting on his chest.

Shamus had his back pressed to mine.

I'd been fast asleep, my body relaxed, but it went tense instantly at the sound of the phone.

Hank grabbed it and flipped it open one-handed, not disturbing me, but his arm around my waist got tight.

"Yeah?" he said into the phone.

He listened. I waited.

"Tell me you're fucking joking," he growled, his voice vibrating with anger.

Shit.

Billy had gotten away.

I twisted my neck and pressed my forehead into his shoulder. My arm went around his waist and I held tight.

"Find him," Hank bit out and flipped the phone shut.

"Whisky," I whispered, and even I could hear my voice held a tremor of fear.

"He'll get him," Hank replied.

"Is Vance okay?" I asked.

"Flynn was gone when he got there. Trail's hot though. Vance is on it. Roxie, he'll get him."

I swallowed.

He tossed the phone onto the nightstand and both of his arms came around me.

"Relax, sweetheart. He's not gonna hurt you," Hank murmured.

Kristen Ashley

I nodded and forced the tension from my body. I was able to do this main-ly because I had help from Hank's hand stroking my back.

After a while, I fell asleep.

"He has no buttermilk."

My eyes slowly opened and I could see Hank's throat in the dawn's early light.

We were front-to-front, my thigh thrown over his hip, one of his arms resting lightly on my waist and mine was doing the same on his.

"Of course he doesn't have buttermilk. Who has buttermilk?"

I blinked.

Mom and Dad were in the kitchen and I could hear them talking as if they were in the bedroom.

Hank's house didn't have thin walls. It was just that my parents talked loudly.

"Well, if he doesn't have buttermilk, how'm I gonna make buttermilk pancakes?" Mom asked. "Sweet Jesus!" she cried. "He doesn't have flour either!" She said this as if it was a criminal offense.

"Of course he doesn't have flour! Does he look like a man who bakes?" Dad said in a loud(er) voice.

I looked up Hank's throat just as he tipped down his chin. His eyes were open.

Damn.

He was awake.

I closed my eyes and shoved my face into his neck.

"No, he doesn't look like a man who bakes, but Roxie's been here and she bakes," Mom returned.

"Yeah, like Roxie's been floatin' around makin' cookies while that sum a' bitch has been after her. Jesus, Trish."

I heard slamming cupboards.

"There's nothing in this house. Eggs. Bread. Milk. Lots of coffee and beer. I don't understand. He looks like a healthy boy. It's like he exists on coffee and beer. That can't be. What am I going to do?"

Good God.

334

My mother just called Hank a "healthy boy".

I shoved up closer to Hank's warm, solid body, mortification overtaking mine.

Hank's arm tightened.

"Make some fuckin' coffee," Dad answered as if that answer was obvious.

"Don't take that tone with me, Herbert Logan," Mom snapped.

"Don't tell me what tone to take, woman," Dad returned.

Mom ignored Dad's reply. "Go get some buttermilk. And bacon. And maple syrup." I heard a cupboard slam. "No, wait, I found some syrup," Mom said.

"Go where and get buttermilk?" Dad asked, his voice now incredulous.

"The grocery store," Mom answered like Dad was a dim bulb.

"Please, God, shut up," I whispered against Hank's neck.

Hank rolled me to my back and came with me, settling with him partially on top of me and partially up on an elbow. I opened my eyes and saw his were lazy and amused and his lips were twitching.

"What grocery store? We're in Denver. I have no idea where a grocery store is," Dad retorted.

"Well, drive around. Denver's a big city. There have to be hundreds of grocery stores. You'll run into one eventually," Mom replied.

I took in a deep breath and bit my lip.

Hank's eyes were smiling and his body started shaking.

I scowled at him and his lips spread into a grin.

"Let me get this straight," Dad clipped. "You want me to get in the car and drive around a city I've never been to in my fuckin' life to buy buttermilk?"

"Well, yeah," Mom said, as if that was a perfectly normal request.

"Fuck that. I'll find some fuckin' place that sells donuts," Dad told her and I heard movement in the other room as if Dad was preparing to leave.

"*Don't you dare buy donuts!*" Mom shrieked. "Hank's a cop. He'll think you're making some smart remark."

Hank's forehead dropped to mine and his body started shaking harder.

"This isn't funny," I whispered.

"You're wrong," he replied quietly, his voice trembling with laughter.

"People other than cops eat donuts, you know," we heard Dad return. "I'm not a cop and I eat donuts."

Kristen Ashley

"Buttermilk pancakes are Roxie's favorite breakfast. I want to make Roxie's favorite breakfast," Mom said.

"I'll get what I get," Dad responded, obviously not in the mood to discuss it anymore.

"You do that. I'll go get the dog. He'll probably want out and Hank and Roxie need to sleep in. They had a tough night."

Both Hank and my bodies got tense.

"Don't go near that damn room, Trish," Dad warned.

"I'm just getting the dog. I won't peek," Mom returned.

Hank lifted his forehead from mine.

"Please tell me your mother's not comin' in here," Hank said to me.

"Trish! Get back here!"

"Herb, relax."

Mom sounded closer. A lot closer.

My mother was coming in.

"We can hear you!" I shouted, in hopes of waylaying her.

Silence.

Hank and I were both naked and the sheet was around our waists. He pulled the sheet up to my chest just as Mom opened the door.

Good God.

Hank's head twisted to look over his shoulder. Other than that he didn't move, likely trying to shield me further with his body. I put my hands to his biceps, lifted up and peered over his shoulder.

Mom was standing in the doorway in her robe, her hand over her eyes.

"Mornin' kids. Don't mind me. Come here Shamus, come on boy." She made kissy noises, the whole time she kept her hand over her eyes.

Shamus lurched up, jumped off the bed and jogged out of the room, tail wagging.

As he wagged by Mom, she said, "Go back to sleep. I'm making pancakes but Herb's got to find buttermilk so it'll take a while. You have time for a snooze."

The whole time she talked, she kept her hand over eyes.

"Yeah, we heard," I told her. "Mom?"

"Yes, sweetie?" she lifted her head a bit, hand still on her eyes.

"Go away."

"Right, right. Going." She closed the door.

336

We heard movements, keys jingling, doors slamming. The whole time I lay on my back and watched Hank. His eyes were looking in the vicinity of my collarbone, his head slightly cocked, listening while a smile played about his mouth

When the noise died down, I said to him, "I'm sorry."

He dipped his head, rubbed his nose against mine and my belly melted.

"My parents are a little nutty," I went on.

He looked me in the eye. "Sunshine, first off, Tex is your uncle. And, no offense, I mean it as a compliment, but you're anything but normal. It isn't like I wasn't prepared."

"They're nice people," I explained, kind of desperately.

We'd just sorted things out. I'd taken a huge chance on us. I'd even promised to move to Denver. I didn't want everything to go balls-up in less than a day. I was hoping he wouldn't take what he just heard as an indication of his future life and run, hell bent for leather, to the next state and far away from me, my Mom and my Dad.

His hand came up and he trailed a finger down my hairline. He watched his finger, then his hand curled around my neck and his eyes came to mine.

"I know that," he said.

Obviously, he wasn't in fear of a nutty future life. Or maybe he was just resigned to it.

Either one worked for me.

I lifted up and touched my lips to his then settled on the pillows again.

After I'd done that, I noticed the amusement was out of his eyes. The lazy was still there, but there was also intensity.

"Any hope that your Mom went with your Dad to find buttermilk?" he asked, his eyes on my mouth.

I knew what he was asking and my melted belly did a funny, but pleasant, twist.

"She was in her robe," I pointed out.

His lips came to mine. "Yeah," he said against my lips and I could hear the regret.

I smiled against his mouth and watched, close up, as his eyes went languid.

"Kids!" Mom yelled from somewhere in the house.

Kristen Ashley

Hank pulled away a bit, shook his head and smiled. It was a good bet he hadn't been called a kid in a very long time.

"Yeah?" I yelled back.

"I'm taking Shamus for a walk. I got the key from the hook by the door and I'm locking you in. You two rest." Then we heard the door open and shut and she was gone.

Hank didn't hesitate. His arms came around me, he rolled me to the side and his face went to my neck.

It was clear we weren't going to "rest".

"How much time do you think we have?" he asked.

"Not long," I answered honestly. Mom wasn't exactly into exercise.

Hank's lips came up my jaw to my mouth.

"We'll be fast," he murmured there.

"No, Hank, I need to get up. Mom'll be back—"

He took my hand in his and pulled it between us, wrapping my fingers around him.

He was rock-hard.

My belly twist turned into a dip and I felt a spasm between my legs.

"We'll be fast," I said.

He grinned and then he kissed me.

We were sitting around the dining room table. I was wearing my nightie with Hank's plaid, flannel bathrobe wrapped tight around me. It'd been washed, like, a million times and it was huge, soft and snugly. It smelled like him, and the minute I put it on I decided I never wanted to take it off.

Dad was pointedly eating a donut, glaring at Mom and shunning her buttermilk pancakes.

He *had* found buttermilk, and I suspected this was not only because he usually gave into Mom (because he loved her), but also because he knew it was my favorite breakfast (and he loved me too).

Still, the donut was his way of not giving in completely.

In front of me, Mom set down a stack of two of her light and fluffy pancakes, smothered in butter and syrup, with two slices of bacon on the side.

She rounded the table carrying a plate and set it in front of Hank.

338

"There you go, Hank. Eat hearty," she said, patting him on the shoulder and returning Dad's glare.

I looked at Hank's plate. On it was an enormous stack of five pancakes and half a dozen rashers of bacon.

Hank stared at it for a second, not quite able to hide his surprise, before his eyes lifted to mine.

I gritted my teeth.

"Mom!" I snapped. "The entire offensive line of the Chicago Bears could not eat that much food."

Dad looked at Hank's plate then his eyes went to Mom.

"Jesus, Trish. You're gonna put the boy in a food coma. He's a cop, he needs to stay alert."

I looked to Dad. "Would you two quit calling Hank a boy? He's a grown man, for goodness sakes."

"He's your brother's age, Roxanne Giselle, therefore he's a boy to me," Dad returned in his Dad Voice.

I gave up and looked to Hank.

"You don't have to eat all that," I told him.

Mom sat down with her own plate and got all mother on Hank. "Yes you do. You need to keep your strength up."

I frowned at Mom. "He's not recovering from pneumonia. Trust me, he does *not* need any help keeping his strength up."

Dad burst out laughing.

Hank sat back in his chair and grinned at me.

"Don't be lippy," Mom said to me then turned to Hank. "She's always been lippy. Came out bawling and never shut up. I've spent thirty-one years of my life tearing my hair out because of her lip."

"Like mother, like daughter," Dad mumbled into his donut.

"What's that supposed to mean?" Mom snapped at Dad.

"Nothin'," Dad was still mumbling but his eyes slid to Hank and he rolled them.

"Do not roll your eyes at Hank, Herb. What's he going to think of us?" Mom clipped.

That's a good question, I thought.

"Figure the boy needs to know early what he's gettin' himself into," Dad told Mom then looked at Hank. "Take my advice, son. Run. Run for the hills."

Kristen Ashley

Mom's eyes bugged out and her fork clattered to her plate. "Do not tell him to run for the hills! Sweet Jesus!" she called to the ceiling and then looked at Hank. "We've been waiting a long time for Roxie to get herself a good man, a decent man. Thank the Good Sweet Lord you're sitting right here. She's a good girl, Roxie. She's a little wild, but not anything you can't tame, I'm sure of it," Mom declared with authority.

Hank pressed his lips together, likely so he wouldn't laugh out loud.

I noticed Hank's lip press, but only in a vague way because it was my turn to have my eyes bug out of my head.

"I don't need Hank to tame me! I don't need anyone to tame me. I'm not wild!" I snapped at Mom.

Dad let out a belly laugh.

"Not wild? Girl, you're too much," he said to me then turned to Hank. "You'd think there wasn't much trouble to find in a small town. Probably wasn't, but what trouble there was to find, Roxie found it, and if she couldn't find it she made her own."

"Dad!"

My father ignored me.

"Got good grades, which was a plain miracle considering she spent most her time beer-drinkin', joy-ridin', drag-racin' and toilet-paperin'." Dad looked back at me. "I don't even *want* to know what you were doin' on that golf course at midnight when the cops found you."

I put my elbow on the table and my head in my hand.

"This is not happening," I said to my pancakes.

"I told you to try out for the cheerleading squad, but did you listen to me? *No*," Mom put in, and I knew she was warming into her famous Cheerleading Squad Lecture that had been a constant in my life, even though I'd graduated from high school over a decade before.

When I looked up again, Mom was forking into her pancakes heatedly.

"The cheerleaders were good girls, never broke curfew, not once. I know because I was friends with their mothers. Had steady boyfriends. Wore cute, preppy clothes. Not Roxie. No. Curfew? What's that? Going to the mall, like, every weekend. Her closet had more clothes in it than mine! Always flouncing around in miniskirts. Nearly gave her father a heart attack every time she walked out of the house." She looked between Dad and me, fork lifted half-mast and glaring at us both. "The fights you two would have about those miniskirts.

340

And, Lord! Those tops! All cut up and falling off your shoulders so you could see your bra straps. Sweet Jesus. What the neighbors must have thought."

I looked at Hank, certain he was either going to run for the hills or tell us all to get the hell out.

Instead, his eyes were on me. They were lazy and sweet, and then he winked at me.

I felt something settle inside me, and where it settled, it grew warm.

Then I felt my face move. I didn't smile exactly, but I knew my face went soft and my lips turned up, and if my parents weren't there and the table wasn't between us I would have jumped him and torn his clothes off.

"Sweet Jesus," Mom whispered and the moment was lost. I looked to her and she was gazing between Hank and me, her face soft too, but her eyes were bright and happy.

My eyes slid to Dad and he was smiling at the last bite of his donut.

"Are we done telling Hank about my past as a juvenile delinquent?" I asked.

"Yep," Dad replied. He'd finished his donut and was wiping powdered sugar from his lips with his napkin.

"You weren't a juvenile delinquent. Just... spirited," Mom said. "Though..." she mumbled to her pancakes, "wish you'd have used that spirit to cheer on the football team."

I sighed, heavy and huge, and forked into my pancakes.

⌁

"Damn, Tex, this is fuckin' great!" Dad yelled really loudly, foam from his butterscotch latte coating his upper lip.

"Herb, keep your voice down," Mom stage-whispered.

We were in Fortnum's. I was sitting on the book counter and I noticed the Hot Pack, including Hank, Lee, Mace and Luke, all standing around the couches, had turned to look at my parents when my Dad shouted.

I looked over to Indy, who was behind the book counter, and Daisy, who was standing in front of it. Both of them were grinning at my Mom and Dad.

"I asked Hank to shoot me last night, but he wouldn't do it," I told them.

"Oh, sugar, chill. They're sweet," Daisy said.

"What do you say you call this? Lah-tay?" Dad, who was not one for fancy coffee drinks, asked, again loudly, calling our attention back to him. He still hadn't wiped the foam off his lip.

"Fuckin' A, Herb, you need to get to the big city more often," Uncle Tex suggested, handing a coffee to one of the two customers standing in front of the counter.

"Fuck that." Dad swiped at his mouth with the back of his hand when he caught Mom pointing to her own mouth, giving him a clue. Then he went on talking. "Ain't nothin' in the big towns I need. Anyway, I heard they started making these eye-talian coffee drinks in Miriam's Café." Dad looked over to Indy, Daisy and me. "They got frozen custard there too. That custard business pissed off the folks at Dairy Palace, which is right across the street. Ain't no cookie shake in the world better than frozen custard. I don't care if they double up the cookie crumbles, which was what they started to do."

"The Dairy Palace doubled up the cookie crumbles?" I asked, forgetting to be embarrassed by my father's behavior.

I loved cookie crumble shakes.

"Damn straight, Roxie," Dad told me. "You gotta come home. I know you like your cookie crumble shakes but you'll fuckin' flip over those turtle sundaes they make at Miriam's with the frozen custard. Swear to Christ, thought your mother would roll up and die after she got her first taste of one." Dad looked at Hank. "Roxie likes her ice cream," he informed Hank as if this was the key to future happiness with me.

"I'll remember that," Hank said.

His eyes came to me and I noticed his trying-hard-not-to-laugh look because it was now very familiar.

In fact, the Hot Pack were all now looking at me, all of them grinning. Except Luke, who was looking down at his boots, but I could tell his half-smile was in place.

I felt their grins in the form of goose bumps running along my skin and I said to the entire room, "Can we stop talking about ice cream?"

That was when Luke's head came up and his eyes sliced to me.

"I wanna hear more about ice cream," he said.

Damn.

The bell over the door rang.

"I'm not talking to you!" Jet snapped at Eddie as they both walked in.

At first I got worried, but then I saw Eddie's lips twitch.

"What now, Loopy Loo?" Tex boomed.

"I don't wanna talk about it," Jet answered, stomping to the book counter and slamming her purse into a drawer.

"What's going on?" Indy asked.

Jet glared at Eddie, who was entirely unaffected by the mental laser beams Jet was directing at his back. He walked up to the espresso counter as the last customer moved away.

"Everything. Lottie's so popular Smithie has to sell tickets. He's already given her a raise. She found a house, put in an offer and it was accepted. Mom's moving in with Trixie and the apartment has already been rented to someone else. I want to move in with Lottie but Lottie won't let me because she and Eddie had a *chat*."

Daisy and Indy nodded knowingly.

"What?" I asked.

"Eddie's kind of famous for his chats," Indy replied.

"Don't let Hank *chat* to you," Jet warned. "Chatting is bad. You end up agreeing to stuff you never would agree to normally after you've had a *chat*. And don't, under any circumstances, have a chat in bed. You could end up agreeing to anything during *those* chats." Jet's warning turned dire.

The light dawned.

"I think Hank calls them 'conversations'," I told her.

Her eyes got big and she nodded to me once, slowly, saying, "Unh-hunh."

"So what your sayin', sugar bunch, is that you are now officially moved in with Eddie," Daisy said.

"Yes. We've just beaten the world record for the fastest moving relationship in history," Jet replied.

Indy and Daisy smiled.

"No, I think I may get that one," I said.

Jet, Daisy and Indy looked to me.

"I'm moving to Denver," I announced.

Without hesitation, Daisy threw an arm up, punching the air. "Yee-ha!" she screamed.

Jet and Indy high-fived.

Everyone else looked over to us.

"Roxie's moving to Denver!" Indy yelled across the room to Lee.

Lee's eyes crinkled and cut to Hank.

Hank rocked back on his heels and he crossed his arms on his chest. I rolled my eyes at him, and when I was done with my eye roll his lips were turned up on the ends.

"You're moving to Denver?" Mom asked, staring at me.

Oh shit.

I hadn't told Mom and Dad yet.

"Um, yeah," I said.

Mom's face froze then she blinked.

"You can't move to Denver," she protested. "What're you gonna do at Christmas? Thanksgiving? Oh, Sweet Jesus. Easter! You know we always have a special honey-baked ham at Easter. You're the best with the Easter egg dyes, too. Mimi and Gil can't dye eggs like you. Who's gonna dye my eggs?"

"Mom, I'm thirty-one years old. We haven't dyed eggs in fifteen years," I reminded her.

She ignored me and went on, "And do they even have persimmons out here? How are you gonna make persimmon pudding? I can't *mail* them to you. You have to have them fresh or it doesn't taste right. You know that."

"Mom, I don't make persimmon pudding, you do."

"Well, I can't mail *that* to you either," she said and then whirled on Hank. "We get Christmas!" she told him, as if she was calling shotgun in the car.

"Trish, calm down," Dad ordered.

"I will *not* calm down. My baby girl is moving halfway across the country," Mom shot back.

"She's been moved away before," Dad pointed out.

"Yeah, but that was with Billy. We all knew he wouldn't work out. We're talking about Hank here. Look at him." She pointed to Hank. "She's never coming home. *Never*."

"She ain't movin' to the moon, Trish," Dad said.

"Might as well be." Mom turned back to me. "You hear even a hint that a blizzard's coming, Roxanne Giselle, you go straight to the store and buy toilet paper, you hear me? And make a pot of chili or stew. Don't get caught out. I don't want a phone call saying you starved to death, stuck in the house with no stew." Her eyes moved to Daisy. "I hear the blizzards are bad here. People die."

"That's usually old people, Mrs. Logan," Daisy explained. "And they normally freeze to death."

Daisy was trying to help but it was the *wrong* thing to say.

Mom's eyes got big, then her back went ramrod straight and she grabbed her purse from the espresso counter. "Right. We're going out to buy blankets. Hank had, like, one extra blanket. He needs blankets. And logs for that fire in the back room. We're getting blankets and logs. Come on, Herb."

Dad dug in. "Woman, I'm enjoyin' my lah-tay."

"*You want your daughter to freeze to death?*" Mom screeched.

Dad shook his head. Mom glared at him.

They settled into a staring contest.

I looked at the Hot Pack. "How many of you have a gun? Anyone? Someone shoot me!"

Then I realized that Luke was standing there and what I said was a little insensitive, considering he'd been shot in the belly a few months before.

"Um… sorry Luke," I finished, feeling like an idiot.

Luke crossed his arms on his broad chest and smiled at me, but didn't say a word, which I decided to take as indication that he bore no ill will.

Hank disengaged from the Hot Pack and walked to me. He walked right up between my legs, wrapped an arm around my waist and yanked me off the counter so I was standing full frontal with him. He tipped his head down to look at me.

"Your Mom can have Christmas," Hank said quietly.

"Thank you!" Mom shouted to Hank's back.

I shook my head. "You do not even know what you're saying. Do not give her Christmas. Christmas is Crazy Land in the Logan household and I think you've realized by now that that's saying a lot!"

"Roxanne Giselle Logan, do not tell tales out of school. So your father usually gets drunk and burns the turkey. It's Christmas!" Mom snapped.

"I do not get drunk! And I do not burn the turkey!" Dad yelled. "It's crispy. Everyone likes crispy turkey."

"No one *grills* a turkey, Herb. Standing outside in thirty degree temperatures with your Budweiser like it's the Fourth of July."

"Roxie likes my mesquite turkey. Don't you Roxie?" Dad called.

I closed my eyes, and when I opened them Hank's face was all I saw.

"Have you changed your mind yet?" I whispered.

Slowly, he shook his head.

"Give them time," I finished.

"Well? Roxie? You like my mesquite turkey, don't you?" Dad asked.

I put my forehead to Hank's chest for a second then lifted it away.

"Yeah Dad, I like your turkey."

It was true. I did. It was great turkey. The best.

The bell over the door went and I peered around Hank's shoulder to see Ally, Malcolm and Kitty Sue walking in.

My eyes widened, my body stilled and I stared at Hank who moved, placing an arm around my neck, holding me reassuringly tight against his side.

"Did you call them?" I asked Hank.

"Um... that would be me," Indy said from behind me.

Good God.

"Roxie's movin' to Denver," Daisy told Ally.

Ally's eyes got bright. "Righteous," she said.

Malcolm's gaze settled on me and his eyes crinkled.

"I'm so pleased," Kitty Sue smiled.

"Holy fuckin' shit," Tex boomed.

I looked at him, and his grin was so big it split his face.

"Don't look so damned happy," I snapped at him as he pounded out from behind the espresso counter.

"I heard your Dad was here," Malcolm said to me as he came close and kissed my cheek.

My eyes lost their scowl and I nodded to him with a weak smile.

"Right here," Uncle Tex said, pushing Mom and Dad forward.

"What's going on?" Mom asked.

"This is the rest of Hank's family. You already met Lee. This is his sister, Ally, and his mother and father, Kitty Sue and Malcolm," Uncle Tex did the introductions.

"Sweet Jesus!" Mom called. "Sweet, sweet Jesus. I'm so happy to meet you."

Mom went forward on a rush and gave Kitty Sue a big hug. To my shock, Kitty Sue didn't recoil and not only accepted the hug, but hugged Mom tight in return.

"I'm Herb. This is my wife, Trish," Dad said, thankfully going the shaking hands route with Malcolm.

"Good to meet you," Malcolm replied.

They dropped hands and Dad took Malcolm in. "Your boys been lookin' after my girl," Dad told him.

Malcolm nodded. "That's right."

For a few beats, Dad and Malcolm just looked at each other. Something passed between them, something I could feel. I felt the tears sting my eyes and I pressed deeper into Hank. Ally's gaze came to me and she winked. I smiled at her and felt the tears subside.

"Means I owe you a beer," Dad said quietly.

"I'd like that," Malcolm replied.

"I know. Let's have a party!" Ally announced.

I was beginning to realize Ally didn't need much of an excuse for a party.

"My party is tonight," Daisy pointed out.

"We'll have it Friday night," Ally said.

"Works for me," Indy put in.

"Me too," Jet said.

"You makin' those caramel chocolate brownies?" Uncle Tex asked Jet.

"What caramel chocolate brownies?" Dad asked.

Uncle Tex turned to Dad. "Loopy Loo's brownies beat the fuckin' shit out of your turtle custard sundaes any day."

"Them's big words, big man," Dad threw down the gauntlet.

"Fuckin' better believe it," Uncle Tex declared.

"You're on," Dad replied.

"I better make the brownies," Jet mumbled.

I noticed everyone had drifted over; Lee, Eddie and the rest of the Hot Pack.

"You boys have tuxedos?" Daisy asked.

All their eyes turned to her.

Even Daisy blinked under the force of the Hot Pack Stare.

"Okay," she gave in. "I'll let you all in with suits."

"Tuxedos?" Mom asked.

"Formal party, my house, tonight," Daisy announced. "Everyone's invited."

Mom gasped, then she uttered the immortal feminine words, "I don't have anything to wear."

"That's okay, Trish. I'll take you shopping," Kitty Sue offered, having missed most of the show and not having any idea what she was letting herself in for. I should probably have warned her, but there was no time. Mom was forging ahead.

"Herb, we better go now. We need to get you a suit. I hope we can find somewhere that does one day tailoring," she said to Kitty Sue, linking her arm through Kitty Sue's and leading her to the door. "We need to go somewhere to get logs and blankets. And we need to find a big grocery store. Maybe a Kmart, or better yet, a Target. They have ritzier stuff. Hank needs some stocking up."

"Logs?" Kitty Sue asked.

"I don't want Roxie freezing to death during one of your blizzards," Mom explained.

The bell over the door jingled as they walked out, Dad throwing an eye roll over his shoulder as he followed, carrying his latte.

Once they'd gone, Hank curled me so I was facing him and I looked up.

"I gotta go to work," he said.

I nodded.

"What time's Daisy's party?" he asked.

"Seven o'clock. Come with your belly empty, I'm havin' a secret buffet in the kitchen for VIPs," Daisy answered before walking away.

I put my arms around Hank as he watched Daisy walking away.

"The Rock Chicks have claimed you. You're stuck now," he noted, looking down at me.

"Funny, I was thinking that about you. Being stuck, I mean."

He rubbed his nose against mine, clearly not feeling stuck.

When his head moved away, I said, "I need to talk to Annette, tell her what's going on, and I need to call my clients. I don't think I'll lose any of them. I don't need to be in Chicago to do my work. After I got that award I recruited clients outside Chicago, in Des Moines and Cincinnati. They should be cool. I need—"

"Award?" Hank cut in.

I waved my hand between us. "Nothing, it was just some design award."

He grinned at me. The way he was grinning made me feel funny, all warm inside, like I'd done something great.

"Stop grinning at me, Whisky. It wasn't a big deal."

"Any award is a big deal."

"This one wasn't."

"Sorry, didn't you say you recruited two clients because of it?"

"Well, yeah."

"Then it was a big deal."

"Whisky—"

"Sunshine, quiet," he said and gave me a light kiss so I'd do as I was told. "I'll see you, and your folks, at my house at six thirty."

"Do you have a suit?"

"Yeah."

"Okay."

He gave me a squeeze and started to let go but I held on.

"You hear anything about Billy—" I began.

His eyes locked on mine and he interrupted me, "Yeah."

I sighed. "For a while there, I forgot about him."

Hank's arms tightened and his face dipped close. "Sweetheart, I promise, soon he'll be a memory."

I nodded because I believed him.

My body fitted itself close to his. Hank's head came down the rest of the way, this time not for a light kiss, but for a deeper one.

When I was dizzy, he let me go, and then he was gone.

Chapter 25

Mom Bombed

I was looking out the window of the black Explorer, processing my day and preparing for my night.

I was in Fortnum's when Luke walked in ten minutes ago, eyes on me and he said one word, "Home."

I guessed that meant he was my ride.

Annette and Jason had been spending the day casing the other head shops to check out the competition. I called to tell her Hank and I had sorted things out and I was moving to Denver. She was ecstatic. We'd been trailing each other for seven years, Indianapolis to Chicago and now to Denver.

"Bitch," she said. "With you and me in the 'hood, Denver isn't going to know what hit it!"

I thought it was more the other way around, but I didn't tell Annette that.

I'd also called all my clients and my landlord.

My clients were cool. They didn't care where I worked, just as long as I worked. My landlord was freaked out. The cops had called him about the break in and he thought my mutilated body was buried six feet deep in some woods somewhere. I calmed him down and convinced him I wasn't a voice from the grave. He wasn't too upset I was leaving, considering he'd never had a tenant who'd had their furniture torn apart and went missing for two weeks, presumed (by him) dead. Anyway, I was month-to-month and he was going to let me out of the lease at the end of November.

Simple as that.

In fact, everything seemed simple.

All that had to be done was find Billy.

No word from Hank, which I figured meant no good news. Also, there was no bad news, so I decided that no bad news was actually good news and I went with it.

"Babe," Luke called, pulling me from my thoughts.

I turned to him. "Yeah?"

His chin went up, pointing over my shoulder, and I realized we were parked in front of Hank's house. I looked toward the house, my hand going to the door handle, and I stopped dead.

"Good God," I whispered.

The air in the Explorer changed as Luke went into alert mode.

"What?" he asked.

"Look at the house," I breathed.

"What?" he repeated.

"Look at the house!" this time, I yelled.

I got out of the car, slammed my door and stood on the sidewalk staring at the house.

"Roxie," Luke, suddenly beside me, said, his fingers curling into the waistband of my cords. "Talk to me. What?"

"Pumpkins," I replied.

He looked at the house.

On the front stoop were two carved pumpkins. Also, resting against one side of the door, was a bunch of dried corn stalks bound together with more (these not carved) pumpkins and some gourds nestled at the bottom. On the other side was a decoration attached to the house made up of three painted wooden slats dangling from wire. The top slat was a witch flying in front of a quarter moon, the middle one said "Happy Halloween" and the bottom one was a black cat with its back arched.

I looked to Luke.

"Hank's house has been Mom Bombed," I told him.

Luke looked at me for a second then his eyes went to his boots.

He wasn't fast enough. I saw the half-grin.

"This is not funny. Hank's going to *freak*."

The door opened and Mom stood there. "Hey there, sweetie. Why are you standing on the sidewalk?" Her eyes went to Luke. "Luke, is it? Come in, I'll make you some cocoa."

"Oh my God," I whispered, horrified that my Mom offered hot cocoa to Badass, Super Cool Luke. I turned to Luke. "I've changed my mind. I don't want you to shoot me. I want you to shoot her."

His fingers came out of my waistband and pressed against my lower back, pushing me forward. The half-grin had gone full-fledged.

352

"I don't know why everyone thinks this is funny. This isn't funny," I grumbled on the way up the walk.

"It isn't funny because they're your parents," Luke explained. "To everyone else, it's just fuckin' funny."

We walked into the house and Shamus rushed me. He took in Luke, went into a skid and slammed into me, knocking me backwards into Luke's (very solid) body. Luke's hands came to my hips and normally I would have stepped away immediately, considering I was plastered against him, but I was too horrified by what I saw.

There were huge, empty, plastic shopping bags everywhere. Three new blankets and four fluffy pillows were stacked on the couch. The lamp Billy and I had broken had been replaced by another one, which now threw a soft glow on the room. In one corner, there was a four foot tall wrought iron candleholder with six, thick, green candles in the top, all lit and giving out the scent of bay. There were more candles in black holders on the coffee table, also lit. There were candles on the dining room table, ensconced in decorative corn husks and miniature gourds. On the corner of the bar, separating the dining area from the kitchen, sat an enormous Halloween bowl filled to almost overflowing with Halloween candy. I saw a new canister set for flour, sugar and coffee (I had no doubt all of them filled) against the back kitchen counter. Last, I could smell something cooking.

"What have you done to Hank's house?" I asked Mom.

"Just made it cozy. Kind of a thank you gift for letting us stay and for taking care of you," Mom answered and she looked to Luke. "You want cocoa?" she asked.

"No," he replied.

"Coffee?" Mom went on.

"No," he said.

"Tea?" she continued in dogged pursuit of being both a Mom and a good hostess, even though it wasn't her house. She was now sounding slightly surprised at the idea that Luke drank something as un-macho as tea (like he'd drink cocoa).

"No," Luke repeated.

"Oh, I know. A beer?" Mom kept going.

Luke shook his head.

I cut in, "Jeez, Mom. He doesn't want anything. Leave him alone."

Kristen Ashley

"Roxie, don't be rude," Mom told me. Then a buzzer went off. "I know what he'll want!" she shouted and she whirled, threw on a (new) oven mitt, opened the oven and took out a cookie tray. "Right here, hot and good. Fresh roasted pumpkin seeds. Come and get 'em."

I looked at Mom as she shook the seeds on the tray to Luke and me.

I ignored the seeds.

So did Luke.

"Where's Dad?" I asked.

"Negotiating with the log man. They say they don't do deliveries. Your father intends on getting those logs delivered. He brought me home and went back. He'll be here in time to get ready."

Dad thought he could negotiate anything with just a hint of good ole boy charm and a few off-color jokes. Most of the time, he wasn't wrong. I suspected the logs would be delivered tomorrow.

I threw off thoughts of logs.

Instead, I focused on getting ready. Getting ready sounded like a good idea. It meant escape, and escape was good.

"I'm going to take a shower," I announced and made to move away.

Luke's hand curled into my waistband again. He pulled me deeper into him and his mouth came to my ear.

"Leave me with her, I *will* shoot you," he whispered in my ear.

I looked over my shoulder at him and realized how close we were. His face was less than an inch from mine. I stepped forward and his hand dropped away.

Mom, undeterred by us ignoring her offering, tilted the seeds into a waiting bowl and walked them to the coffee table. Once she set down the bowl, she started to gather up bags.

"Luke, be a sweetheart and get rid of these," she said, shoving them into his arms and starting away before she realized he hadn't actually taken them.

I caught them before they fell to the floor and turned to Mom.

"Mom, I don't mean to alarm you, but Luke's here to protect me, so you have to leave him alone so he can do... whatever it is he does. What he doesn't do is clean up, drink cocoa or chitchat. Okay?"

Mom slowly turned and looked at Luke with rounded eyes before she nodded.

I twisted and said to Luke, "Come with me."

354

I shoved the bags in Mom's arms, gave her a peck on the cheek and walked by her, through the kitchen and into Hank's room.

Luke followed. So did Shamus.

I closed the door and turned to Luke.

"I'm going to take a shower. You're going to be good, try not to be sexy or freak me out or anything like that. I've got to concentrate. Preparing for a formal party is serious business. I don't need distractions."

His eyes went half-mast and his half-grin appeared.

"You're doing it!" I accused.

His eyebrows went up.

I shook my head. "Never mind."

Then I stomped to the shower.

<hr/>

Over an hour later, there was a knock on the bathroom door.

I'd had my shower, done my formal party makeup and was putting the finishing touches on my hair (loads of soft twists and up in a messy knot). I was wearing Hank's bathrobe. My dress, undies, jewelry, purse and shoes had been gathered and were all lying on the bed next to Luke (well, my undies were hidden under the dress, Luke didn't need to get any ideas).

Luke seemed to have no problem slipping into a Luke Zen Zone, lying stretched on Hank's bed, Shamus at his side, eyes closed, saying nothing but seeming totally alert.

I opened the door, expecting it to be Luke.

It wasn't Luke. It was Hank.

Shit.

Before he could open his mouth, I said, "I'm sorry about your house."

"Roxie—"

"I should have called to warn you but I'm running late getting ready."

"Roxie—"

"She's doing it to be nice, to say thank you for all you've done."

"Roxanne, let me—"

"She can be a little overpowering, I know, but I swear it isn't normally this bad. I think she's worried about me but doesn't want to say."

"Roxanne—"

Kristen Ashley

"We can move the stuff she bought to my new apartment when I find one and I'll get rid of the stuff at the front stoop the minute they leave."

His hands shot out and grabbed me at the waist. He yanked me to him and his mouth came down on mine.

He kissed me deep.

When he lifted his head I was dizzy and had forgotten my place in my jabbering apologetic explanation of Mom's craziness.

"What was that for?" I asked.

"To shut you up. You wouldn't stop talking."

"Oh."

I probably should have been angry but I wasn't. He was a good kisser and if I had to be shut up, that was a damn fine way to do it.

"I don't mind about the house, it looks nice," he told me.

"Okay."

"And I don't mind your parents. They're interesting and they care about you."

"Okay."

"And we'll talk about your apartment later."

I blinked. "What?"

He shifted me to the side and moved into the bathroom. "Are you done in the bathroom? I need to shower."

He bent over and pulled off a boot then twisted to throw it in the bedroom.

I watched it go, moving my body as the boot sailed by me. When I turned back, he did the same with the other boot.

"What about my apartment?" I asked.

"We'll talk about it later," he replied.

He started to pull off his sweater but I grabbed his arms and stopped him. He looked at me.

I felt something strange and unpleasant crawl along my skin.

"Don't you want me to move to Denver?" I asked quietly.

"Yeah, I want you to move to Denver."

I blinked at him again, confused. "Then, what about my apartment?" I repeated my question.

"Roxanne, we'll talk about it later."

It hit me.

356

"As in, we'll have a 'conversation'?" I asked, thinking about what Jet said earlier about Eddie's chats and the fact that she'd moved in with him, making them the fastest relationship in history.

Hank stared at me as if he was considering checking my forehead to see if I had a fever.

"Yes," he said slowly. "Two people talking is the same as two people having a conversation."

"Do you mean, a Hank Conversation? The kind with a capital 'H' and a capital 'C'?"

His brows drew together. "Have you been drinking?" he asked.

"No, I haven't been drinking!"

He sighed and straightened, giving me his full attention. "Maybe you should tell me what's on your mind."

I didn't actually have anything on my mind other than what was on his.

"Nothing's on my mind," I admitted. "Except, when we have this conversation, we aren't having it in bed."

After I made my declaration, he watched me for a beat then shook his head.

"Jesus, you're a nut," he muttered, pulling off his sweater.

"I'm not a nut!"

He tossed his sweater in the direction of his boots then his arm came around my waist and he pulled me to him again.

He bent his head to mine and with his lips twitching, he said, "I mean that in good way."

"How is calling someone a nut good?" I flashed.

"Sweetheart, are you done in the bathroom?" he asked patiently.

"Yes," I grumbled.

He kissed my forehead, let me go, walked in the bathroom and shut the door.

I turned, straightened his boots, folded his sweater and put it on the bed.

"Your Dad is a nut if anyone's a nut. He thinks my parents are interesting. Interesting! That's just plain crazy," I told Shamus who sat by the bed, staring at me and wagging his tail. "He hasn't called *them* nuts and they *are* nuts."

I put on my underwear, spritzed with Boucheron and carried on talking to Shamus.

Kristen Ashley

"As soon as Billy's caught, I'm taking you out to play Frisbee. If you don't know how, I'll teach you. I'm good with Frisbees. Gil and I used to play in the front yard all the time. We'll go and buy, like, ten of them just in case they get lost in trees or something. You and me will be Frisbee freaks. We'll enter competitions. They'll do documentaries about how good you are with Frisbees. You'll be the Frisbee Dog King."

I figured Shamus was in to the Frisbee gig as he got up on all fours and his body started shaking with his tail, his excitement was so great.

I leaned over him and gave him a full body doggie rub.

"I'd take you tomorrow, but Billy's still out there and I don't think Luke would like the whole Frisbee idea. He doesn't seem the Frisbee type," I told Shamus.

I heard a noise and turned my head to see Hank standing in the bathroom doorway, shoulder leaned against the jamb, belt undone, jeans mostly undone, socks gone, watching me.

"Frisbee Dog King?" Hank asked.

Oh shit.

Okay, so maybe I was a nut.

I straightened, looked to Hank and Shamus sat on my feet.

"Come here," Hank said softly.

"No," I told him. "I have a feeling you're going to ruin my hair."

"Come here," Hank repeated.

"No, Hank. It took me forever to do my hair."

"Sunshine…"

"Oh, all right."

I had to go to the other bathroom to fix my hair.

⊰⊱

Once I finished fixing my hair, I helped Dad tie his new bow tie to his new tux. This took me six tries. These six tries were interrupted by Mom slapping my hands away and trying to tie it six times herself. Then, I slapped her hands away and tied it on the second go of my second attempt.

"Don't know why I need to own a tux," Dad grumbled, pulling at his collar.

"Herb, we talked about this," Mom said.

"We didn't talk about it," Dad returned. "You just upped and bought it. I've worn a tux twice. To my senior prom, and you were my fuckin' date, and to our wedding, and you were my fuckin' date to that too. I'm fifty-eight years old, and counting today I've worn a tux three times in my life. I don't need to own one."

My Dad was as cheap as they come. He'd pinch the last drop of blood out of a penny (if a penny had blood). Unfortunately for him, my Mom spent money like it grew on trees. I knew that day shopping had been pure torture for him. The tux was just plain cruel.

"You have two daughters who, pray to the Sweet Lord Jesus, will get married one day. You'll need a tux for their weddings," Mom pointed out.

"Mimi says she's gettin' married in Vegas. I don't need a tux for that. I need a pair of shorts and a Hawaiian shirt and I've got, like, twelve of those."

Mom whirled on Dad aghast, and she exclaimed, "You are *not* wearing a Hawaiian shirt to Mimi's wedding. I don't care if it's in Vegas."

"I am," Dad said.

"You are *not*," Mom replied.

"Yes... I... am!" Dad repeated.

"Guys——" I tried to butt in (and failed).

"Well, Roxie isn't getting married in Vegas. Roxie's going to have a designer wedding. You'll need a tux for that," Mom told him.

This was true. I was going to wear Vera Wang and Manolo shoes. I was going to have shrimp cocktail (not those little, useless shrimps, but the meaty king prawn ones) and I was going to spend ten thousand dollars on flowers. There were going to be flowers *everywhere*. I told them about the flowers and shrimps when I was eight. They'd been saving ever since.

"The way she and Hank're going, Roxie'll be knocked up in a few months. It'll be a shotgun wedding and she'll have to get a dress from JC Penny."

Both Mom and I gasped.

"Dad!" I shouted just as Mom yelled, "Take that back, Herb!"

"Well, excuse me, but they practically jumped each other over the breakfast table. You were there, Trish, you saw it. Hell, she's livin' with the guy!" Dad defended himself to us both and then turned to me. "Not that I mind, Roxie. I like Hank. And it's your time. You ain't gettin' any younger, you hear what I'm sayin'? Anyway, Hank's a good-lookin' guy, you two'll make beautiful babies."

Good God.

"I am not getting a dress from JC Penny!" I snapped (priorities, of course). "And I'm not going to have a shotgun wedding! And I didn't practically jump Hank over the breakfast table!"

"Right," Dad said, just a hint of sarcasm in his voice (okay, a lot of sarcasm). "Jesus. I'd like a fuckin' grandchild before I'm slobberin' in my fuckin' Jell-O. Gil ain't ever gonna get married, he and Kristy don't *believe* in marriage, whatever the hell that means. Mimi goes through men like water. Roxie's finally caught herself a live one. Hank's a man's man. Roxie, the way I see it, you and Hank are my only hope," Dad told me.

How in *the hell* did we get on this subject?

I gave up.

"We're running late, I'm getting dressed," I announced, turning my back on them and flouncing out of the room.

I stopped dead when I reached the kitchen.

Hank was standing with his hips against the counter, palms on the countertop, an open beer in the fingers of one hand. His head was bent and he was looking at his feet. It was a pose of reflection. A pose that said he'd heard every word.

Mortification that he heard the ridiculous conversation was not why I stopped dead.

I stopped dead because Hank was wearing a suit. A dark gray suit with a midnight blue shirt, no tie, opened at the throat. His hair was damp and curling around his collar, a week or two past needing a cut. He looked good in a suit. He looked better than I'd ever seen him look. He looked so good, I couldn't even move.

His head came up and his eyes came to me, full-on grin in place, showing me he thought the conversation with my parents was amusing, not run-for-the-hills-scary-as-shit.

I put my hand to the counter to hold on and blurted, "God, you're handsome."

At my words, the grin left his face and something else came over it. There was no lazy in his eyes, they were just intense.

My legs went weak.

He stared at me for a few seconds then said softly, "You better get dressed."

I nodded, mentally shaking off my Hank Stupor and walked to the bedroom.

I got dressed quickly. We were already late.

The gown Tod loaned me was black satin. The skirt had a bias-cut, was full and had a beautiful drape. The dress was boat-necked, sleeveless and seemed elegant but plain... until you saw the back.

It was totally backless, all the way down past the small of my back, just barely, but not quite, to indecent level. Tod had explained he'd never worn it; hard for a drag queen to go backless, even though he tried. He'd bought it on a whim and tried everything he could think of to pull it off, but it never worked.

As far as I was concerned (and as far as Stevie, Tod, Jet, Indy, Annette, Ally and Daisy were concerned), it worked for me.

I put on a pair of black, strappy, high-heeled sandals, the diamond studs Billy got me and the diamond tennis bracelet Mom and Dad bought me as a bribe to graduate from Purdue in four years rather than the five I was heading for in my junior year. I didn't have a wrap or coat so I was just hoping Hank's 4Runner heated up quickly.

I grabbed my bag and ran to the kitchen.

"Ready, ready, I'm ready," I said, looking through my bag. "Shit! Not ready."

I'd forgotten my lipstick.

I whirled and ran back through the bedroom to the bathroom and pawed through my makeup, grabbed my lipstick and liner, shoved it in my bag, and on the way back through the bedroom collided with Hank.

The room was dark but I could see Hank from the light coming from the kitchen.

"Sorry, I'm ready now," I told him.

His hands were at my waist and they slid around my back. I felt them leave the satin and hit my skin and I shivered. His fingers trailed the edge of the material, just above my bottom.

"We're comin' home early," he said quietly.

"What? Why?"

He didn't explain, instead he said, "I'll arrange for someone to bring your parents home later." His fingers dipped into the material. "A lot later."

Holy cow.

"Okay," I agreed instantly.

I saw his shadowed grin.

"I take it you like the dress," I said.

361

"Yeah," he replied. "I like the dress."

I thought he was going to kiss me, a kiss that would necessitate me fixing my hair (again), but he moved to the side, one hand coming away and one hand sliding around my waist. We walked into the living room together.

Dad and Mom watched us.

"She's still wearin' the dress," Dad remarked somewhat bizarrely to Hank.

Hank didn't respond.

"I thought you went in there to tell her to change outta that dress," Dad went on.

"No," Hank replied.

"Herb——" Mom started, but Dad's eyes were bugging out of his head.

"She can't wear that dress! It's indecent. Her ass is hangin' out."

I looked behind me. I couldn't see my ass because Hank's arm was around me but I was pretty certain it wasn't hanging out.

I turned back to Dad. "My ass is not hanging out."

"It's almost hangin' out," Dad replied.

"Almost and hanging are two different things," I returned, beginning to get angry.

"Roxie——" Mom started again.

"Son, take my advice, you gotta get this girl in hand. You can't let her run around with her ass hangin' out. You allow it once, she'll do it again. Trust me. I know," Dad told Hank.

Good grief.

"My ass is *not* hanging out and Hank does *not* have to get me in hand," I flared.

Hank's arm tightened and he pulled me deeper into his side.

"Girl, you were almost the death of me runnin' around almost naked, your underwear showin'. I'm warnin' your boy here before you become the death of him," Dad flared back.

"Herb——" Mom said again.

"I didn't run around almost naked!" I snapped.

"That's not what Mrs. Montgomery said. Mrs. Montgomery said you looked loose," Dad snapped back.

Good God.

"Mrs. Montgomery also said that Ginny Lampard looked loose and she was president of the Youth Club at the Christian Church and wore button-down oxfords with a string tie every day of her life!" I shot back.

"Roxie——" Mom said.

"Herb, she isn't changin' her dress," Hank cut in, his deep voice low and not inviting argument.

Dad stared at him, agog.

"She looks beautiful. We're late. Let's go," Hank finished then moved us forward and opened the door, stepping away from me so we all could precede him.

Mom passed me, smiling.

Dad passed me, glaring.

I was trying hard not to do a cartwheel of joy.

Chapter 26
Daisy Doesn't Do Boring

"Holy cow."

I was standing outside Marcus and Daisy's house, understanding why it was called "The Castle". Mainly because it *was* a castle, complete with moat.

Mom stood beside me, staring at the house.

"Is Daisy wealthy?" Mom breathed.

"Her husband must have a real good job. What's he do?" Dad asked, standing beside Mom and staring up at a turret.

I looked at Dad, then I looked at Hank who had secured the car and was approaching us.

"Um..." I mumbled, not sure how much to share.

"Sales," Hank replied, stopping at my side.

"He must be a slick talker," Dad commented, clearly impressed.

I smiled at Hank, laughing under my breath. He grinned and took my hand.

"Sir. You can't park there." A valet was jogging up to us and staring at the 4Runner. Hank had parked beside two other cars, both of which I knew, Lee's Crossfire and Eddie's red Dodge Ram. They were the only cars that were parked near the house.

Hank flashed his badge to the valet.

The valet pursed his lips. "Go on in," he relented.

"It's good having a cop in the family," Mom said, *sotto voce*, to Dad as we walked across the bridge over the moat.

"Yeah, good parking anywhere. That's the reason it's good having a cop in the family. Jeez, Trish," Dad returned.

Hank squeezed my hand. I sighed, and for the first time in a long time, it was a happy sigh.

The front door was opened for us by a uniformed butler-type person and we walked down a long hall, the walls made of stone, a deep red, thick carpet runner down the middle. The hall was decorated in "Castle Chic" with sets of armor, torches and crossed swords.

Every once in a while, there was a table displaying a fabulously expensive necklace or set of earrings, a glossy brochure depicting a sunny vacation spot, a shiny crystal vase or a glass sculpture and all of them had a silent auction bid sheet next to them. A quick glance showed all of the bid sheets had bids. Some of the tables had elegantly dressed people standing around them. They all turned to watch us walk in. Most of them smiled at us, or I should say, most of the ladies smiled at Hank. Some of them just stared, wide-eyed and lustful.

At the end of a hall was a huge room with an enormous fireplace that had a roaring fire and more people standing around, drinking glasses of champagne. Uniformed waiters walked around with trays of champagne and hors d'oeuvres.

We barely made it into the room when I heard, "Yoo hoo!"

It was Tod and Stevie standing with Indy and Lee, Jet and Eddie and Carl and Ally. All the men were dressed like Hank, suits and open-necked shirts. They all looked heart-stoppingly, mouth-wateringly, unbelievably great. Indy had on a deep green, sheath dress with one shoulder bared. Jet was wearing a pale pink strapless number with a black ribbon at an empire waist. Ally was in a dark blue halter dress with a deep slit up the front and serious cleavage. Tod and Stevie were in tuxes.

Hugs, air-kisses and handshakes were exchanged. I introduced my folks to Tod and Stevie and Eddie stopped a waiter to get us glasses of champagne.

"Girlie, you look *gorgeous*. I'm giving you that dress. It was made for you," Tod said to me.

I laughed for the second time that night and I hadn't been there ten minutes.

"You can't give me this dress. It had to cost a fortune," I told Tod.

"Fortunes come, fortunes go. Gowns are forever and that gown was meant to be yours," Tod replied.

"Tod, the last time I wore a formal dress was to a frat party Christmas ball. Thank you but, I couldn't," I declined, I thought graciously.

"You can, you will, you won't give me any backtalk," Tod contradicted and then turned his eyes to Hank. "See she has somewhere to wear it," he ordered.

I looked to Indy for help, not only with the dress, but because I didn't know how Hank would take being ordered about by a gay man (or any man for that matter).

She was smiling huge.

"Don't fight Tod. You'll lose," she advised.

"Ha!" Tod barked. "You want to talk about your wedding colors again? Lee!" Tod turned to Lee. "How do you feel about tangerine and chocolate as wedding colors?"

"I thought we went over this—" Ally butted in.

"Shush, I'm not talking to you," Tod shushed Ally and his eyes cut back to Lee. "Lee?"

"Don't ask me, the wedding doesn't concern me. My job is to show up and I'll be sure to do that," Lee answered.

All the female and gay men's eyes grew round.

Eddie looked at his shoes. Carl grinned. Dad chuckled. Hank's arm slid around my waist but his head turned to the side. He was feigning avid interest in a banner with a crest that was attached to the wall.

All this meant Lee was very, very alone.

"I'm sorry?" Indy asked, turning to Lee.

"Do what you want. I don't care. I'll be responsible for the honeymoon," Lee told her.

"That's it? You *want* to have a tangerine and chocolate wedding?" Indy asked.

"I don't even know what that means," Lee returned, and when Indy opened her mouth to speak, Lee went on, his eyes crinkled at the corners. "And gorgeous, I don't want to know."

"I don't believe this," Indy hissed under her breath.

"Son, let me tell you something. Even if you don't care, pretend you do. Honestly, it's the best way to go," Dad, the voice of experience, decided to wade in. "She talks about toss pillows. You don't care about toss pillows. You don't even know what toss pillows are. *Pretend* that toss pillows are your highest priority in life."

Eddie chuckled under his breath. Carl did it straight out. Lee smiled at Dad. Hank was still memorizing the banner, but he was now biting his lower lip.

Mom turned to Dad, eyes narrowed and said, "Excuse me?"

"Trish, just last week we had a forty-five minute discussion about the curtains in the living room," Dad replied. "You think I give a shit about curtains? I care that there's beer in the fridge and the TV works. I don't care about curtains. I didn't hear a word you said about the curtains."

"You agreed to the curtains with the little trumpets on them! You said you loved the idea! I already ordered them. I thought it was all decided," Mom cried.

Dad looked back at Lee and nodded sagely.

Mom's face got red. "Are you saying you don't like the curtains with the trumpets?"

"I'm sayin' I don't care. Get whatever you want. I don't even *see* the curtains," Dad replied.

"Guys—" I tried to run interference.

"I just do not believe this," Mom groused. "I knew I should have gone with the curtains with the little horses and riders on them. The trumpet curtains are going to look silly. What are the neighbors going to think?"

"Mrs. Logan, for what it's worth, I think the neighbors are going to like the trumpet ones. The little horse and riders..." Stevie offered, wincing a bit and shaking his head.

"You sure?" Mom asked.

"I'm sure," Stevie assured her.

"Well then, thank you." Mom smiled at Stevie and took a sip of her champagne.

I turned into Hank's body, lifted on tiptoe and whispered in his ear. "You can come back into the room, crisis averted."

He looked down at me, eyes smiling.

Then he asked, "How much do you care about curtains?"

"Well..." I drew it out, because I cared about curtains, like, a lot. They set the tone for the whole room.

"Okay, let me rephrase that," Hank went on. "How much do you care that I don't care about curtains?"

I grinned at him. "Not much."

His smile hit his mouth. "We're set then."

"All my honey bunches of oats!" Daisy yelled behind my back.

I turned to see Daisy approaching, dragging Marcus with her. I blinked hard, so dazzling was her ensemble. She was head-to-toe rhinestones, sequins and beads. Her hair was held up in an enormous up-do, fashioned with tons of hair jewelry. She had sequins glued around her right eye, she was wearing a fortune in diamonds at her ears and throat, and her v-necked, ice blue, long-sleeved gown was entirely beaded, every inch of it. It had to weigh a ton.

More hugs, air-kisses and handshakes were exchanged as Daisy and Marcus joined our group. It was only slightly uncomfortable when Eddie and Marcus shook hands and only slightly freaky when Marcus looked intensely in my eyes, communicating something I didn't really get, before he kissed my cheek.

After we all settled into our huge huddle, Daisy leaned forward, waving us in.

All the women, Tod and Stevie leaned in. All the men started talking with Marcus.

"Do something!" Daisy hissed.

"About what?" Jet asked.

"About this party. It's a dud. Nothing's happening. People are just standin' around and talkin'. It's the most borin' party I've ever been to in my life. One of you has to do something." Daisy turned to Ally, "You're good at causing a stir. Start a fight. Do you have your stun gun?"

Again, I blinked at Daisy and this time not because I was dazzled.

Mom gasped.

"You're joking, right?" Ally asked.

"No, I'm not jokin'. What are they gonna say in the society pages? Daisy doesn't do boring. Daisy is not a dud. Daisy is all about excitement, comprende?"

"Daisy, I think it's a nice party," I offered.

Daisy turned to me, her eyes sharp as knives, "Nice? Nice?"

Yowza.

I backed up a step.

"Jumpin' Jehosafats. This is fuckin' *phat!*" We, and all the other guests, heard shouted from across the room.

We all turned to see Jason, wearing a rented tux, and Annette, wearing a pretty, sea green, scoop-necked dress with cap sleeves (obviously Stevie and/or Tod had intervened in the Scarlet O'Hara fiasco) standing across the room.

"Did you, like, move this place stone-for-stone from England or something?" Annette asked Daisy when she arrived at our huddle.

More hugs, handshakes and air-kisses were exchanged and a waiter brought champagne.

"No, Marcus built it for me, sugar. You look sweet," Daisy replied.

Annette smiled at her and then turned to the girlie group at large. "Get this!" Annette announced. "Smithie hired me to dance. He said I could dance to Bob Marley. He doesn't care, just as long as the customers get it."

I looked at Jason. He caught my glance and shook his head.

"Lottie and me are gonna work on my routines. I'll do Head during the day and be a stripper at night. How fuckin' phat is that?"

"She's kidding, right?" Hank murmured in my ear. I hadn't noticed he'd turned from the boy conversation to the girl one.

I ignored him, focused on helping Jason.

"Annette, maybe you should think about that," I suggested.

"Sweetie, Smithie loves you," Annette told me, shocking me with the news. "He said if I could get you to dance with me he'd give me a bonus."

"That's not gonna happen," Hank officially entered our conversation.

"Dude," Annette said. "She'd be *the shit* up there. I bet she'd give Lottie a run for her money."

"It's not gonna happen," Hank repeated, turning fully to Annette.

Annette ignored, or was oblivious to, Hank's warning posture.

"Dude. Seriously. Do you know how much Lottie gets paid?" she asked Hank.

"Don't see why she shouldn't strip, she's half naked right now," Dad put in.

"Herb," Mom said.

"I'm not half naked," I snapped at Dad.

"Your ass is hangin' out," Dad returned.

"Is it?" Annette asked, twisting to look at my back. "Let me see."

"My ass is not hanging out," I told Annette.

"Oh," Annette muttered, sounding disappointed.

We'd become the focus of attention of several partygoers who were standing close to our group.

"Maybe we should keep it down," I suggested.

"Oowee, free champagne!" We heard belted from across the room.

We all turned to see Shirleen standing there, afro huge with glitter sprayed in it. She looked gorgeous in a deep peach, square-necked gown, an orange, latticework, shimmering necklace adorning her throat from cleavage to chin.

She turned and nabbed a glass of champagne off the tray of a waiter gliding by her.

"Well, look at all of you," Shirleen announced when she arrived at our group. "Shee-it. It's like someone smacked you all with the beautiful stick. Ordinary people need not apply. God damn!"

"I want that necklace," I blurted. "It's gorgeous. But I want it in red. Where did you get it?"

Shirleen put her hand to her throat, her long fingernails were painted a pearlescent coral. "Leon bought it for me about two days before they shot his sorry ass. So not only did I get freedom from that stupid motherfucker, I got me a nice necklace as a keepsake. You can borrow it if you want."

I stared at her.

Mom stared at her.

Dad stared at her.

"Leon's my dead husband," Shirleen explained. "He's better off dead. He was a mean sonovabitch. Two days after they put him in the ground I redecorated the entire house then went on a cruise. Do you know how much food they serve on those cruises? Food everywhere, all the time. I even got me a piece of my own personal Isaac, you know, from *The Love Boat?* He was a cruise ship bartender and Jamaican. Don't remember his name, but he was nice to Shirleen, *real* nice. I gave him a tip he'll never forget." Then she laughed so hard, her entire body shook with it.

Mom, Dad and I just kept staring at her. Then Mom shuffled up close to Hank and I.

"Are you sure you want to move to Denver?" she whispered.

I looked at Hank.

He ran the tips of his fingers lightly along the edge of my dress at the small of my back.

A shiver went along my skin.

I nodded to Mom. "I'm sure."

She sighed. I noticed hers wasn't as happy as mine had been.

"Maybe we should mingle," Jet suggested, noticing that we had become the center of attention for the entire room.

"That's a good idea," Indy agreed.

"Where's this secret VIP buffet, that's what I wanna know. I'm starved," Dad asked loudly, causing some of the other guests' subtle stares to become a lot less subtle.

"Herb, keep your voice down," Mom whispered, also loudly.

Kristen Ashley

"I'll show you, Mr. Logan," Daisy offered, not in the least upset that her secret buffet was outed by my Dad. "Right this way."

Daisy, Mom and Dad peeled off and Marcus moved close to Hank and I while everyone wandered away.

"We need to talk," Marcus said to Hank.

It was clear by the look on his face and the tensing of Hank's body that Marcus wasn't proposing idle, party chitchat.

Hank nodded once. His hand drifted up my back to between my shoulder blades and he curled me to him, front-to-front. I tilted my head back and his face was as serious as Marcus's.

"I'll be a minute," he said.

I nodded.

"Keep Lee, Eddie or Carl in sight. Got me?"

I nodded again.

His hand went away from my back and he ran a finger down my jaw then he and Marcus were gone.

"I see you sorted some of your man troubles," Shirleen noted. She was standing beside me, but watching Marcus and Hank move through the big room.

I noticed Lee, Eddie and Carl watching Hank too. After Hank disappeared from sight, Lee's eyes cut to me, he said something to Indy and they moved away from the couple they were talking to and closer to me.

Indy caught my eye and smiled reassuringly.

I smiled back.

Then I realized something and it hit me so hard it had a total body impact.

"I think I'm in love with him," I said quietly to Shirleen.

"What, child? I couldn't hear you," Shirleen replied.

"I barely know him, but I think I'm in love with Hank," I repeated.

She turned fully to me and her eyes narrowed, mainly because I was beginning to freak out and I was certain it was showing.

"Calm down, girl. This is good. You should be happy. Hank Nightingale is a good man and he'll treat you right. I think you and I both know ain't a lot of men in the world like that. You got a shot at one, you hold on tight and you better fuckin' well rejoice," Shirleen advised, her voice serious to the point of being sharp.

"I think I'm in love with all of them," I said, ignoring her words and beginning to panic.

372

"All of who?" Shirleen asked.

"*Them.*" I threw my arm out. "Indy, Lee, Ally, Daisy, Eddie, Jet, Tod, Stevie… all of them," I answered.

Shirleen nodded. "Far as I can tell, there's a lot to love." Her eyes didn't leave me. "Why you lookin' like you been sentenced to life in prison?"

"Billy's out there, he's acting crazy. Or, I should say, crazier. There's no telling what he'll do. They might get hurt," I replied.

I'd felt it days before when Daisy got shot at when she was with me. But now it had intensified. It was something different, something more immediate, visceral. Something not to be borne.

"They know 'bout Billy?" Shirleen asked, cutting into my thoughts.

I nodded.

"All of 'em?" she went on.

I nodded again.

"Then they know what they're gettin' into," Shirleen declared decisively. "Trust Shirleen, child. Lotta folk would stand clear from a girl like you, leave you to go it alone, best as you could. And, I'm tellin' it to you straight, if this Billy is as much of a crazy motherfucker as he sounds and even as strong as you are, I'm guessin' the best you could do would fail. He'd end up hurtin' you or turnin' you and neither of those things are good." I felt my blood turn to ice and I stared at Shirleen. She kept talking. "These folk don't stand clear. Says a lot. Don't let it mess with your head. From what I hear of your people, you'll eventually have your chance to settle the score."

I couldn't say I liked the sound of that.

Shirleen's eyes had been clear and focused, but something drifted across them and her gaze left me. "I'm not ashamed to tell you, Shirleen has always had a soft spot for that boy," Shirleen murmured, almost as if I wasn't there.

She was staring at the place we last saw Hank and I could tell immediately that she'd slipped into another place. I felt something strange coming from her, something immensely sad, almost to the point of longing.

I stood stock-still as she continued, "He was a good kid, through and through. Good son to his parents, good brother, good friend to my nephew, Darius. Things changed, for me, for Darius. Hank never changed. He tried, harder 'n' hell, more even than Lee and Eddie, to pull Darius back, to save him…"

She stopped on a whoosh of air, as if she'd been sucker punched in the gut. I was confused, not knowing what she was talking about, but I had no chance to ask and I had the feeling she wouldn't have told me anyway.

Shirleen carried on, "I know where his head's at, so does Darius. We know where he stands. Even so... even so..." Her voice had dropped to a whisper, so low, it was almost like she was chanting. "Even so, I admire it. If I'd had me a boy of my own, I'd want him to be just like Hank."

I felt her words hit me somewhere private. Somewhere I didn't even know existed. Somewhere that was a place that only women like me had. Women like me, which was I suspected, women like Daisy. I was also guessing (correctly, even though I didn't know it at the time), women like Shirleen. Women who'd experienced bad things at the hands of men they'd opened their hearts to and women who hoped for something good to follow.

Daisy had found hers in Marcus. Even though he was who he was to the world, he was something else to her.

I'd found my good in Hank.

Shirleen, well, I didn't know about Shirleen, but I suspected she was no longer looking. Instead, her longing was the saving grace of a child, a child just like Hank.

Tears hit my eyes and my hand reached out, found hers and I held on tight. I could only guess that I was correct at what was causing her emotion. What I did know, it was there and she was letting me see it. I also knew, instinctively, this emotional display didn't happen often.

She squeezed my hand and then pulled hers away and downed her glass of champagne.

"I'm dry," she announced, breaking the mood and not even looking at me. "Where's that boy with the champagne?" she was looking around. "Hey! You!" she yelled then walked away from me to pounce on a waiter with a tray of champagne.

She didn't look back.

I didn't get a chance to process her words because I felt a touch on the skin at the small of my back. It was so light, there and then gone, it was almost like I imagined it. When I turned to see if it was real, I got an eye-full of a tanned throat coming out of a light gray shirt surrounded by a black suit.

I looked up.

Luke.

"Where's Hank?" he asked, deciding against any unnecessary pleasantries like "Hello".

He was scanning the crowd and looking unhappy. I'd never seen Luke look unhappy. Mostly, he just looked hot, or sometimes amused, which was just another form of hot. Now he looked plain old unhappy, which was also somehow hot.

"He's talking to Marcus." I replied then went on. "You look nice," and I moved a bit away from him, mainly because he did look nice. Really nice.

His arms were at his sides. When I moved away, his hand came out to curl around my waist and he pulled me back to him.

I figured this was part of his not-outside-touching-distance bodyguard gig and decided to reassure him, "It's okay, Luke. Hank's here somewhere and Lee's keeping an eye on me."

I heard a cell phone ring somewhere, but I ignored it because Luke looked down at me.

"You don't move away from me. We're findin' Hank. Now," he ordered.

Immediately at his words and his tone, I felt fear crawl along my skin.

"What's happening?" I asked.

Luke wasn't looking at me anymore. He was looking across the room. I followed his gaze and saw Lee, cell to his ear, his eyes on Luke. Lee's face was tight and he jerked his head towards the door. At the same time, he was repositioning Indy, moving her around to face one of the several doors leading out of the room. She looked up at Lee questioningly, but that's all I saw as Luke's fingers pressed into my waist insistently.

"Let's go," Luke said.

He started moving me toward the door. I noticed something happening; Eddie and Carl either both sensed imminent danger or had received non-verbal, badass-boys communiqués gliding through the air like radio waves. They were also on alert and on the move.

"What's happening?" I asked, not fighting it, but going with Luke. Fear was no longer crawling along my skin, but biting into me. Then, panic hitting me, I said, "We have to find Hank."

I no sooner said it when Hank and Marcus entered the room. Hank was striding with a purpose, his eyes locked on me, his face like stone. Marcus didn't look much different and was moving in the same way, his eyes scanning the room, likely looking for Daisy.

"Hank's here," I told Luke, beginning to pull away to go to Hank.

Luke yanked me to his side then stopped dead.

I took my eyes off Hank and turned to look at Luke. In mid-swing, my glance caught on something familiar. My head stopped and I stared.

Billy was standing in the doorway to the room.

His arm was raised.

In his hand was a gun and it was pointed at me.

Chapter 27
When My Life Began

I had to admit, Billy looked good.

The man-on-the-run thing was working for him. Faded jeans, his beat-up leather jacket hanging on him just right. His thick, blond hair was messy, his eyes were wild.

Other people had noticed Billy, but I didn't think they thought he looked good, mainly because they also noticed his gun.

I felt panic tear through the crowd. I heard small screams, felt people moving and caught Eddie and Carl's voices calling commands to the edging people.

All of this happened as if it was far, far away. Mostly, in those first few moments, it felt like just Billy and me in the room.

"Hand her over," Billy demanded, looking at me, still pointing the gun at me, but addressing Luke.

Luke's response was to shove me behind his back.

This meant Billy was aiming his gun at Luke.

"No!" I shouted, coming out of my frozen bout with terror.

At the same time, Billy screamed, "Goddammit, give her to me!"

"Don't even think about it," I heard and my eyes swung to the left.

I saw Lee had a gun trained on Billy.

"Fuck you!" Billy shouted, swinging his gun wildly, aiming at Lee.

I felt my stomach clench and my lungs squeeze, and visions of a tangerine and chocolate wedding faded into an even worse nightmare.

"Billy, no," I said, moving around Luke. "Don't, I'll go with you."

"Luke, get her out of here." This came from Hank, who was several feet behind Lee and moving forward.

He also had a gun, and it hit me, in a vague, slightly crazed (okay, maybe entirely crazed) way, how easily he handled it, just like he drove his 4Runner. Natural, like he was one with the gun. His right hand around the butt, finger on the trigger, the left hand cupping his gun hand. Both his arms were up, but cocked loose. His head was tilted slightly to the side and his gun and gaze were aimed at Billy.

Luke had already shifted in front of me, stepping back, forcing me to move with him. The crowd was still easing away. I noticed people exiting the room just as I saw Marcus, also carrying a gun, sliding along a back wall.

"Don't move!" Billy shouted. He hadn't noticed Marcus and he swung his gun back at Luke and me.

"Billy, don't. Please," I begged, peeking around Luke's body.

Luke kept moving back. He was unfazed by the gun as well as unarmed.

Billy didn't listen to me. He fired.

Luke's body jerked.

I screamed.

The gunshot caused pandemonium. My scream wasn't the only one. People were no longer cautiously moving, but now running everywhere, clearing the room.

Luke didn't go down. Instead, he shoved a hand in his jacket and pulled a gun out of a shoulder holster and trained it on Billy. I barely noticed because Billy was now pointing his gun at Hank.

Both Lee and Hank were side by side, maybe three, four feet between them. They'd both advanced while Billy had fired and were only six feet away from him.

Both brothers were in a faceoff with Billy.

This isn't happening, I thought with dread, and then I didn't think anymore. Instead, I moved quickly, thanking my many years of practice in high heels, because they came in handy. I came wide around Luke so he couldn't grab me and started toward Billy as fast as I dared.

"Luke, *get her out of here!*" Hank's voice cracked through the room.

"Billy, I'll come with you," I said, moving forward more quickly to avoid Luke, pulling at a strength I had no idea I possessed and ignoring Hank.

All I could think was that if I had anything to do with it, Billy wasn't going to shoot Hank or anyone. I didn't know if he'd hit Luke, but if he had, that was the end as far as I was concerned.

"Shoot him, Luke," Lee said.

"Roxie, get out of the way," Luke ordered from behind me. Then when I didn't do as he ordered he said to Lee, "I can't get a clean shot."

378

I made it to within arm's length of Billy and his hand came out and nabbed my arm, twisting me and pulling my back to him so hard I slammed into his body. His arm wrapped around my waist.

He was using me as a shield.

Hank's expression shifted, going from controlled rage to out-and-out fury.

Then Hank moved toward us.

Billy shook his gun at him.

Hank halted, but Lee moved forward.

"Stop fuckin' movin'!" Billy yelled at Lee and Lee halted.

"This isn't happening," I whispered my earlier thought aloud.

Someone was going to get hurt, probably already had been hurt. All I could think was that I had to stop it.

"We have to go," I said to Billy.

"I'm gonna kill him," Billy returned, still pointing his gun at Hank.

"No! Don't. Please, don't. Let's just go!" I cried.

"He tried to take what's mine. I'm gonna fuckin' *kill* him!" Billy yelled.

He was crazed, out-of-control and I was scared he'd do it.

I put my hand up to his arm, my fingers curling around his bicep just at the moment Billy fired again.

I didn't think, I just moved.

I twisted and shoved him with my entire body. He wasn't expecting it and we both teetered and then went down. Billy on his back, me landing on top of him. I tried to roll away. I wanted to check Hank, needed to do it, but Billy grabbed me and rolled us both. Coming up, he brought me with him and held me, my back to his front again, arm still round my waist.

He was breathing heavily now. I'd knocked the wind out of him but he was hanging on.

My eyes immediately went to where Hank was and he was still standing, much closer now, nearly on top of us. He, Lee and Luke had used the tussle to close in.

Hank's face was hard, a muscle moving in his jaw. He wasn't in control of the situation and I knew it was pissing him right the hell off.

All I felt was relief that he didn't seem to be bleeding.

Then everything happened at once.

Kristen Ashley

Billy whirled, taking me with him and pulling us several feet away from Hank, Luke and Lee. I saw, now, that Vance was moving down the hallway toward us, gun raised. Billy stopped pulling back and whirled again and I saw two more men, both wearing black suits, white shirts and thin black ties, both arriving from another doorway and closing in. I had no idea who they were, but they also had guns pointed at us.

Again Billy whirled and there were two more men I'd never seen before, coming from even another doorway. They were dressed a lot like Billy, except they looked cleaner and their eyes were not wild, but clear and purposeful. They also had guns pointed at us.

We were surrounded, with eight guns aimed in our direction and that didn't count Marcus, who I figured was somewhere in the room, although no one else was. And for that, I allowed myself a tiny prayer.

"Put down your gun, Flynn," Hank demanded.

Billy whirled again and we faced Hank.

"Fuck you," Billy retorted.

"*Put it down!*" Hank's voice was like a whiplash.

"Desmond wants to talk to you, Billy," one of the leather jacketed men said from behind us, ignoring Hank's order and all the other people in the room. Billy whirled us to face him and he kept talking, "Let go of the girl."

"Fuck you, and fuck Desmond too," Billy returned, shaking his gun at his new target.

"Would someone please shoot him?" Lee asked, his voice sounding impatient, like he wanted another glass of champagne and this was an annoying delay.

"Where? I got a clean shot at the back of his knee," Vance asked conversationally from behind us.

"Take it," Lee ordered casually and Billy whirled us around to face Vance.

"Billy, quit jerking me around. I'm getting dizzy," I complained stupidly, but in my defense, he was making me dizzy, and not in a good Hank-way.

"Now I got a clean shot," Luke shared. With our latest whirl, Luke was behind us.

"Just don't hit Roxie," Lee instructed.

Billy whirled us around to face Luke.

380

"Oh for goodness sakes!" I snapped, beginning to lose my fear as well as my temper. I'd never been held hostage, pre-abduction, so I had no idea they were playing with him, messing with his head.

"No one's shootin' him. Everyone stand down," Hank said.

I chanced a glance to my side and saw Lee's head turn to Hank.

"Stand... the fuck... down," Hank repeated, not taking his eyes, or gun, off Billy.

Billy moved us to face Hank, and Lee gave a nod to Vance and then to Luke. He dropped his gun arm and stepped back.

This was for show. I figured Lee was a faster draw than just about anyone. Don't ask me how I knew this. I just knew it like I knew that Wolford hosiery was the best, bar none.

I felt, rather than saw, Luke and Vance drop their weapons to their sides. I had no idea what the other men did. This should have changed the danger level in the room, but instead, with Hank facing off against Billy, it heightened so it was palpable.

"Let her go," Hank demanded and something about the way he said it made it sound like he was demanding more than just Billy taking his hands off me.

"She's mine," Billy returned, understanding Hank's demand and giving me a jerk to make his point.

"Let her go. Now. If you do, no harm will come to you. If you don't, I'll shoot you myself," Hank said.

It was clearly time for me to intervene. I didn't know, in such a situation, if Hank would get in trouble for shooting Billy, but I didn't want to find out. What I did know was that Billy was prepared to shoot Hank. He'd already tried it once and I wasn't about to let that happen again.

"Billy, let me go," I said quietly.

"No, Roxie. You and I are gonna walk out of here. We're gonna disappear," Billy replied.

"Billy, look around you. We're not going anywhere," I told him.

"You gotta learn, Roxie. It's you and me, just you and me. That's all it's ever been. That's all it's ever been for me. My life began when I met you," Billy said, and his voice was beginning to sound funny. It was not his slick talk. There was a thread going through it that made it tremble.

I closed my eyes, and when I opened them Hank was looking at me.

I kept my gaze on Hank, direct and steady, and said to Billy, "You know, he took me on a horse drawn carriage ride on our first date."

Billy's already tense body went solid as a rock.

"You promised me that, remember Billy? Said we'd go to New York City, have a carriage ride in Central Park. Do you remember?" I asked.

My voice was not cruel. It was soft with the sad memory of an unfulfilled promise.

"Don't, Roxie." Instead of sounding angry or crazy, Billy's voice sounded like a plea.

"He has a dog," I continued, still looking at Hank. Billy knew how much I liked dogs. "A Labrador," I went on. Billy also knew how much I liked Labradors. He'd never let us have a dog. We were on the move too much, and anyway, he didn't like dogs. In the last few years I didn't get one because I didn't want to bring a dog into my life with Billy. It wouldn't have been fair to the dog. I kept going, "You've seen him, when you were watching me. He's a sweet chocolate lab named Shamus. He sits on my feet and I'm going to teach him to play Frisbee."

"Roxie," Billy's voice was now an ache and I guessed I still felt enough for him to feel it slice through me. Nevertheless, I kept my eyes on Hank.

"He's got a good job, a nice house. He protects people for a living," I carried on and I felt Billy's tense body start to go slack behind me, as if my words were pulling all the energy out of him. His gun lowered a little and I knew I was getting somewhere.

"He has nice parents and his sister told me he did up the house himself. You ever fix anything Billy? You ever make anything that was going wrong go right?" Again, it wasn't an accusation, just a soft question.

"God, Roxie," Billy murmured, even lower, his voice shaking.

"I feel like I've been waiting," I said to Billy, looking at Hank. "Waiting for a long time, but I guess I know what you mean. My life began when I met him."

At my words, to my surprise, and likely everyone else's in the room, Billy just gave up.

His gun arm wrapped around my middle and he shoved his face in my neck.

"Roxie," he muttered there.

Hank started toward us slowly, not lowering his gun, not taking his eyes off me. They were not lazy, not in the slightest. They were hyper-alert and so intense I thought they might burn me.

"You want me to have that, don't you, Billy?" I asked quietly, my eyes on Hank.

"I want you with me," Billy said against my neck.

I took my eyes off Hank and turned to face Billy. He lifted his head at my turn and I put my hands to his cheeks. I looked at him and ran my thumbs down the stubble below his cheekbones. His blue eyes were filled with pain.

I wanted to care, but I didn't. If that made me a bad person, so be it.

"Billy, I don't want to hurt you, but I don't think I've ever been with you."

For the first time, I realized this was true. Billy was fun. He was freedom from the small town I grew up in. He was rebellion, which was something I'd been honing for a decade before I met him. He was also energy and adventure.

What he wasn't was a life force.

Not like Hank.

I put my forehead to Billy's.

"I'm so sorry," I whispered

And I was.

"You're the only good thing I have, the only good thing I ever had," Billy whispered back.

I didn't get a chance to reply. Hank was through.

I felt his strong arm wrap around my waist and, with a tug, he pulled me out of Billy's arms. We walked back several steps, clearing Billy, and then he swung me to the side. I collided with Lee and Lee pulled me back as I watched Billy try to lift his gun to Hank but Marcus was at Billy's side, his gun pressed to Billy's temple.

"Drop it," Marcus ordered.

Billy kept raising the gun, almost like he wanted Marcus to shoot him.

I held my breath. Lee kept moving us back.

Hank still had his weapon trained on Billy, as did Marcus, but Billy kept raising his gun.

"Drop it!" Marcus bit out.

Billy's hand twisted and I realized what he was going to do.

He was going to shoot himself.

Terror seized me and I screamed. "Hank, stop him!"

Kristen Ashley

A gunshot blasted through the room.

Everyone went still as we watched Billy's hand explode in a mist of red. He shrieked a hideous cry of pain as the gun fell free.

There was a nanosecond of silence.

Then Hank ordered, "Call the paramedics."

Hank moved toward Billy in my line of sight so I couldn't see.

I looked to Luke, thinking he shot Billy. Luke was shrugging off his jacket. Blood was running down his arm. The sight of it overwhelmed me. I sagged against Lee and he took my weight into his body at the same time he shoved his gun in a shoulder holster.

"Back off. Police." Eddie was there, gun raised, badge out. Danger was back in the room.

The two men who had to be from Chicago were approaching Hank, Marcus and Billy. They moved back when they caught sight of Eddie.

"Drop your weapons and against the wall," Eddie continued. Without hesitation their weapons fell to the ground and their hands went up.

The other two men in suits had disappeared, vanished, as if they'd never been there.

Billy was sitting on the floor, Hank hunched beside him, blocking my view.

"Get her out of here, Lee," Hank ordered, not turning to us as what appeared to be an army of uniformed officers, led by Carl, came into the room.

"Let's go, Roxie," Lee said into my ear and my body went stiff.

"Luke—" I started.

"He'll get taken care of, honey, let's go," Lee's voice was soft as he was pulling me back.

I started to struggle and Lee's arm went from gentle to no-nonsense. I gave up and allowed him to pull me out of the room.

⌖

I was sitting on a barstool in Daisy's kitchen, being mother henned by eight women and two gay men.

Kitty Sue and Malcolm had arrived late (thank God). Malcolm was somewhere with the men, Kitty Sue was with us.

384

There was so much food on the counter at my side it could have fed the Chicago Bears, Bulls and Cubs for a week. There were four uniformed officers helping themselves to the food.

When Lee guided me into the kitchen, I noticed Dad experiencing a fleeting relief, then he detonated, cursing and blinding. Lee went to him and carefully guided him out, but we heard him yelling all the way down the hall.

Jason followed them. His usual good-natured expression had again disappeared.

Detective Jimmy Marker had come and gone, taking my statement while he was there. The whole time I talked to him, Mom stood beside me holding my hand. Annette stood close behind me, taking the weight of my shoulders into her torso. At that time it was too fresh. I couldn't have held myself up without Annette, and like any best girlfriend would, she knew it.

Detective Marker told me Luke had a flesh wound in his arm. It was superficial and he'd be fine. He went on to tell me Billy was going to the hospital, under armed guard, but his hand looked bad. Finally, he told me that it was Vance who shot Billy.

"Boy's a good shot. So's Lee and so's Stark. Even though he used you as a shield, you were covered. If they'd fired, none of those boys would have hit you," Detective Marker said calmly, as if the whole time I had nothing to worry about.

"Stark?" I asked, confused.

"Luke. Last name's Stark. Known by that on the street, though Lee's boys call him Luke," Detective Marker explained.

"How do you know they're good shots?" I queried.

Detective Marker hesitated and shuffled a bit, realizing he shared too much and finally said, "Just do."

Now, with Detective Marker gone, the activity was beginning to die down and Ally was helping herself to some Brie and apple slices while Shirleen spread a wodge of pâté on some French bread.

"Well, sugar, you made certain sure I'm gonna get a doozy of a write up in the society pages," Daisy told me on a tinkling laugh, trying to lighten the mood.

"Damn straight, Daisy-girl. Never read the society pages but I sure as hell won't miss this one," Shirleen threw in.

Kristen Ashley

Annette's arm came around my chest and she kissed the top of my head. I leaned further into her, realizing, finally, that it was over.

Over.

Thank God.

I breathed another sigh. This wasn't a happy one. This one was relieved.

"I'm just glad he didn't tear her gown or get any blood on it. I don't know if blood washes out of satin and I don't want to know. That is a piece of laundry knowledge I'd be happy to go to my grave without. You girls are killer on my dresses, what with bar brawls and the like. I have to go shopping weekly to keep stocked up," Tod added.

"That's hardly the reason you go shopping, Tod," Stevie put in.

Tod turned to Stevie. "Excuse me, but Burgundy has to have choice. She never knows which way she's gonna go," Tod declared then turned to Shirleen. "By the way, is the offer open to me to borrow that necklace? It... is... *fine.*"

"Sho' 'nuff, sweet thang," Shirleen said.

I felt a bubble of hilarity start to rise in me, but caught Indy's eye and it disappeared. She and Jet were watching me like hawks and they didn't think any of this was funny.

"I'm okay," I mouthed to them.

Jet sucked in her lips. Indy looked about ready to hit the roof.

"Really," I said out loud.

Indy nodded her head with just a hint of a sad smile on her lips. I got the feeling that she wished she had it in her power to erase my whole history with Billy with a wave of her magic wand.

Jet simply said quietly, "Okay."

"What?" Mom asked, missing the byplay.

I leaned over a bit and rested the side of my head against my Mom.

"Nothing," I answered.

"Where on earth is Hank?" Kitty Sue asked, and she no sooner uttered the words then the air in the room charged and the Hot Boy Brigade (plus Dad) entered the room, led by Hank.

"Uh-oh," Ally muttered.

Annette's arm fell away and I straightened. I would have smiled at Hank, but one look at his face told me that was not the way to go.

386

"What's happening now?" I asked when he was a few feet from me. I was thinking Billy had gotten away again; visions of him bursting out of the back of the ambulance, still on the run and after me, filling my head.

Hank stopped right in front of me and I tilted my head back to look at him. His face was hard and angry.

Then he roared, "*What in the fuck did you think you were doin' out there?*"

Yes, Hank Nightingale, master of control, *roared*.

Hmm, seemed he was mad at me, not mad about the fact that Billy had escaped.

Well, at least that was good.

"Whisky—" I tried.

"Oh no," his voice instantly dipped low, dangerously low, "don't fucking 'Whisky' me. You walked right up to him!"

My relief that Billy was still under armed guard was short-lived and melted instantly into anger at Hank.

Excuse me but *I did not think so.*

I jumped off my barstool and got in Hank's face.

"He shot Luke!" I shouted.

"We had it covered," Hank shouted back.

"He tried to shoot *you!*" I yelled.

"We had it covered," Hank repeated.

"He pointed his gun at Lee!"

"We had it fuckin' *covered!*"

I put my hands to my hips. "I warned you, I wasn't going to let anything happen to any of you and I wasn't!" I was back to shouting.

"There were three of us and we knew Vance was closin' in and there was one of him. You made it impossible for us to take him down. What was in your head?" Hank was also back to shouting.

"He had a gun pointed at you. That's what was in my head."

"So... the fuck... what? It's happened before, it'll happen again. I can handle it. We had it under control."

Holy cow.

I shirked off thoughts of Hank having guns pointed at him and scowled.

"Hank Nightingale, don't you yell at me," I snapped.

"It wasn't smart, Roxie," Dad decided to throw down.

"Dad!" I turned to him.

Kristen Ashley

"It wasn't," Lee added, his voice sober and sharp.

My mouth dropped open and I stared at Lee.

"It sure the fuck wasn't," Eddie agreed, and he wasn't even there!

I opened and closed my mouth, words escaping me.

They were ganging up on me.

"Um… hate to butt in here, but, back the hell off," Ally put in, standing at the bar filled with food. She had a half-eaten apple slice held aloft and she looked cool as a cucumber.

"Ally, stay out of it," Carl ordered.

"Don't tell me to stay out of it," Ally flashed, dropping the apple slice and no longer looking cool as a cucumber.

"Everyone's fine, everyone's safe, it all worked out. Let's calm down," Annette offered, trying to play peacemaker.

"You don't know what happened in there. She fucking walked right up to him. There were nine guns in there, eight of them pointed at Roxie. She could have been caught in the crossfire," Jason threw in his lot.

Annette decided peacemaker wasn't a good fit for her and her eyes narrowed on Jason. "Well, what would you do? Hunh?"

"I wouldn't fucking walk up to him. Christ!" Jason shouted.

"Oowee, you white people know how to fight," Shirleen declared.

"Leave Roxie alone." Daisy barreled in, hands on hips. "She's had enough to deal with tonight."

"We're not done talkin' about this," Hank warned me, ignoring Daisy.

We were still toe-to-toe.

"We are *so* done talking about this," I announced, not backing off one bit.

"Hank, honey, maybe I should get you a beer," Kitty Sue tried to calm her son.

"He doesn't need a beer. He needs to talk some sense into Roxie," Malcolm stated.

Kitty Sue, who I didn't know too well, and always seemed quite even-tempered, went red in the face and turned to Malcolm.

"And exactly what sense is he gonna talk into her, Mal?" she demanded.

Malcolm turned to his wife. "The boys were handlin' it."

"Right. You know that and I know that, but in the heat of the moment she did what she had to do," Kitty Sue said.

"She nearly got herself killed," Malcolm shot back.

388

"Hardly. They wouldn't have let that happen. And I don't care if you don't like it, Malcolm Nightingale, but I rather like the idea of Roxie caring about my son so much. Not to mention having the gumption to put herself in harm's way for him. Just as long as harm didn't find its way."

"I like it too," Mom whispered, coming close to Hank and me, grabbing my hand and looking at me like she was proud of me.

I felt a rush of warmth spread through me, though not enough of a rush to make me less pissed-off. Still.

"Trish, you're a fuckin' nut. This is our daughter were talkin' about!" Dad exploded.

"Yeah, and seems to me *one* of us raised her right," Mom flashed back.

"Damn tootin'," Daisy said.

"Fuckin' A!" We all heard boomed from across the room. I looked beyond Hank and Mom and saw Uncle Tex was standing at the door. He was wearing jeans and a flannel shirt, and if it were possible, both his hair and his beard looked wilder than ever, like he'd been tearing at both of them. "How come I always miss all the action? God damn!"

Everyone stared at him.

"Well?" he boomed again. "What happened? You okay darlin' girl?" he asked me.

I nodded.

His eyes swung to Hank. "Nightingale?" he asked.

Hank moved to stand at my side. "Yeah." he said.

"Well, thank fuckin' God," Uncle Tex finished, completely oblivious to the charged air in the room. Then his gaze moved to the food. "Shee-it. Look at that food. Jesus Jones. What're we waitin' for? Let's get this party started. You got any hooch?" he asked Daisy.

"Champagne," Daisy replied, her lips turning up on the ends.

"Well, break it out, woman. None too happy I ain't gonna get my go with that jackass in the holding room, but whatever. Now, I reckon if there was an occasion to drink somethin' as stupid as champagne, this is fuckin' it." He looked to the room at large. "Am I right?"

Everyone kept staring at Tex. No one was quite ready to let go of the latest battle.

"Well? Am I right?" Tex boomed.

Finally, Indy spoke. "You're right, Tex. You are *so* right."

Kristen Ashley

"Marcus, sugar bunches of love, bring us some champagne," Daisy called to Marcus, but his head was already in their big, industrial-sized, stainless steel refrigerator. He turned, holding two bottles of champagne in one hand.

"I'll get the glasses," Jet offered, moving toward a cupboard.

Hank's arm went around my shoulders to wrap around my neck and I went stiff. I wasn't quite ready to stop being pissed-off at him.

His head dipped and his mouth was at my ear.

"We aren't done talkin' about this," he murmured there.

I twisted my head to look at him.

"Yes we are, Whisky. No more talking, no *conversations*. Officially, the minute that champagne touches my lips, Billy Flynn becomes a memory."

Hank stared me in the eyes; his eyes were working. I could tell he wasn't done being pissed either. Finally, he got it under control and his eyes cleared.

"You're off the hook, but only because this shit isn't ever gonna happen to you again."

I nodded in agreement, but felt like having the last word. "If it did, you have to know, I'd do the same thing. You aren't the only one who's allowed to protect someone you care about."

He went back to being pissed-off and clearly wasn't going to let me have the last word.

"Sunshine—"

"No, Hank. I don't want to hear it. Seriously. *Now*, we're done talking."

He watched me a beat, then two, and then his eyes changed again to a look I'd never seen on him before, and it was as far away from pissed-off as it could be.

Quietly, just for me to hear, he asked, "You really think your life began when you met me?"

My body jolted, and if his arm wasn't around my neck I would have backed away a step.

I wasn't ready for this. I'd said it in the moment and I'd meant it with everything I was, but I didn't want to discuss it.

Not now, maybe later.

A lot later.

"We're not talking about that either," I said to Hank.

He watched me again, a beat, then two, and then during the third, his arm tightened around my neck, curling me into him. On the fourth beat, I was

390

full frontal. On the fifth, his other arm wrapped around my waist and his face went into my neck. On the sixth, my arms wrapped around him tight and I pressed my forehead into his shoulder.

On the seventh, although it was right in the room, it seemed far away. A couple of champagne corks popped and a bunch of people both Hank and I cared about cheered.

Chapter 28
Normal

I saw Denver looming in front of me, and at the sight I had a little thrill that I knew was half fear, half excitement.

⌖

I'd been back in Chicago for three weeks, going out with friends to say farewell, arranging movers, packing, closing up the loft, meeting with clients, getting my ruined furniture towed away and dealing with the insurance company.

I'd gone down to Brownsburg for a weekend and dealt with the whole Gil and Mimi explosion when Mom, Dad and I told them all that had happened with Billy.

"I'm gonna fuckin' kill that motherfucker!" Gil shouted after I was done telling the story.

Good grief.

"No need, son. The man doesn't have a hand," Dad replied.

Gil's temper didn't seem assuaged.

My brother turned to me. "You wanna tell me why you didn't tell me all of this shit's been goin' on for the past however-many fuckin' years?"

"Um..." I mumbled.

The only answer I had to that was that Gil was six foot four and two hundred and thirty pounds of pure muscle, and if he knew he'd have snapped Billy like a twig.

Of course, in hindsight, maybe that wouldn't have been a bad thing.

Mom saved me. "All right, it's over. Roxie's fine. She's got a new man now, and Gil, you'll like him. Your dad likes him. I like him. Everyone likes him. So, let's move on. I made pecan pie. Who wants a piece of pecan pie?"

Mom's pie, over the years, had soothed many a foul temper.

We all moved to the kitchen and Mimi put her arm through mine.

"You sure you want to get into another relationship so soon after Billy?" she whispered to me.

I thought about it.

For about a second.

Then I nodded to her. "Yeah, I'm sure."

She looked dubious.

I showed her a photo on my phone that Ally took of Hank.

"Holy shit," Mimi breathed, staring at the photo.

"They're all like that in Denver," I told her.

"Holy shit," Mimi repeated.

I leaned into her ear and whispered a few other things Hank was like. Not the sexy, bedroom things, but the sweet, wonderful things.

"Holy shit," she said again.

"Mm-hmm," I replied.

Mimi gave me a hug.

Gil glared at me.

Whatever.

∗

Annette and Jason were still in Chicago, likely not moving out to Denver until the New Year.

They had more to do than me and they didn't have a hot boyfriend to get back to.

Half of Annette's staff were fighting to come out to Denver with her, half of them were fighting to become the new operating manager of what Annette was now calling "Head East". They also had to get things sorted for the new store in Denver, or "Head West".

Jet reported, during one of my many Rock Chick Phone Chats, that Smithie was not happy with the delay in getting his reggae-white-woman-stripper at a pole, but he was dealing.

Hank was the one that dubbed them the "Rock Chick Phone Chats". This was what he called them anytime I referred to something said in a chat I had with Jet, Indy, Ally or Daisy (for example, "Oh shit, you've been havin' another Rock Chick Phone Chat.").

I must admit, I referred to those chats a lot, mainly when I was losing ground and trying to make a point when Hank and I slipped into a Hank Conversation.

⇽╫⇾

I decided to take two days to drive out to Denver, doing the long haul the first day and stopping just over the Colorado border. I really should have powered through, but I didn't want to arrive and see Hank for the first time in three weeks red-eyed and skanky. I wanted a good night's sleep (didn't get it) and plenty of time to make myself look as good as I could (this kind of worked).

I had my now slightly longer hair in some nice waves and full-on makeup to hide the fact that I didn't get good sleep. I went the way of Colorado (it was apropos) and wore jeans, coffee brown, high-heeled boots and a grass green turtleneck sweater with huge cable knitting down the front. I finished this with my funky, super-long green, raspberry and cornflower-blue stripy scarf and knit cap because it was colder than Christmas outside.

I had another carload of stuff with me and I was moving into Uncle Tex's for the time being. I'd been surfing the 'net to find an apartment in Denver and I had two days filled with viewings ahead of me. What was left of my destroyed belongings were being picked up at the end of the week and I had to have somewhere to take them.

The staying-with-Uncle-Tex-gig and my own apartment had not gone down well with Hank. We'd had several "conversations" about my apartment. Hank saw no reason for me to have an apartment. He figured we were going to move in together eventually, why delay it? I dug my heels in. Not because I didn't want to move in with him, but mainly because I was stubborn and because I wanted to give him the chance to back out, just in case. Eventually, we compromised on a six-month lease (kind of; I got the distinct impression Hank wasn't exactly committed to the compromise, more like giving in so I'd shut up).

The backing out bit was the reason I was nervous. I didn't mind moving. I'd done it a lot, so I was a practiced hand. Hank and I had only had a week and a half of "normal" after Billy was caught, though normal had a weird definition in Denver, especially when it centered around Fortnum's. We'd spent the three weeks while I was in Chicago building our relationship over the phone. It was strange to feel something that seemed old and even steady in Denver was new over the phone.

Or, at least, it felt new to me.

Hank didn't act any differently.

⁂

After the big showdown at The Castle, we all partied in Daisy's kitchen until we'd made a sizeable dent in the food and an even more sizeable dent in the champagne stash.

Mom and Dad stayed the night with Uncle Tex in order to give Hank and I privacy. They'd roared off, all squashed into Tex's El Camino, while Hank and I stood watching. Hank had put his suit jacket over my shoulders to keep me warm.

When they were out of sight, I turned to Hank.

"It's over," I said, my voice dripping with happy relief.

Seriously, if I wasn't in a fancy satin dress, I would have done cartwheels.

His arms slid around me and he rubbed my nose with his. "Let's get you home."

I questioned him all the way to his house, finding out the two extra men in black suits were Marcus's boys. At Marcus's orders, they'd also been looking for Billy and reported to Marcus that there was the possibility that Billy had stopped following me and started to follow Annette and Jason. Once Annette and Jason pulled into the party, they'd seen Billy circle several times, and then, apparently, he found the courage to come in after them. He parked, exited his car and disappeared in the woods around The Castle.

Hank, Eddie and the Nightingale Investigation team had already decided that Billy had declared, during his phone conversation with me, that he was ready to make his move, and they weren't taking any chances. Therefore, Lee had assigned Luke to Roxie Detail as added protection.

Vance was on Billy's tail, as were Desmond Harper's boys, so they all knew he was at The Castle. Everyone was thinking Billy would never be crazy enough to approach the actual party. They thought he'd wait to catch Hank and I as we left.

Vance caught Luke on the way into the party, warning him Billy was there.

Coincidentally, at the same time, Marcus was telling Hank that Billy was on the property. They made plans to gather the women and get us to a safe place in the house and then go what Hank called hunting.

Billy walking in had been a surprise. Vance was hanging back and saw Billy slip in. That was when he called Lee.

The rest I knew, because I was there.

Desmond Harper's boys had been arrested.

Luke had stitches and had been released.

Hank had a phone call from Detective Marker right before we left Daisy's. Detective Marker reported that it was likely Billy would never use his right hand again. I had to admit, this made me sad, but in a weird, detached, anyone-losing-a-hand-was-sad kind of way.

"One more thing," I said, when we were in Hank's living room. We had given Shamus his greeting and Hank had taken his jacket from my shoulders and thrown it over the back of a dining table chair.

He turned to face me. "Yeah?"

"You need to tell me about Shirleen and her nephew Darius. She said some things tonight——"

His hand came out, wrapped around my neck and he pulled me to him. I put my hands to his chest and tilted my head back to look at him.

"Remember, I told you I knew good people who did bad things?"

I felt my stomach twist.

"Yes," I said.

"And remember when I told you Jet and I had a conversation about people we both knew, people Jet refers to as 'gray'?"

I remembered. He said they ran games, dealt drugs and likely murdered people.

I felt my stomach twist joined by a heart squeeze.

"No," I breathed.

"Yes," he replied.

I shook my head. I didn't want to believe that of Shirleen. I liked her.

"I'll tell you the whole story later," Hank promised, correctly assessing I'd had enough for one night. He wrapped an arm around me and moved me toward the bedroom.

"I don't think I want to know," I told him.

"Then I won't tell you the whole story later."

I nodded. That worked for me.

"Okay," I said.

We walked through the kitchen.

"Let's erase the night," Hank suggested when we neared the bedroom.

My stomach twist eased and my heart started beating again, much faster than its normal rate.

"Okay," I repeated.

⚊⚊

Friday, Hank spent the day at work sorting through my mess with Billy.

I spent Friday helping out at Fortnum's and alternately dancing attendance on, running interference with and reassuring my mental stability to Mom and Dad, Annette and Jason, Daisy and a variety of other people who dropped by.

Indy was going to have to hire someone else soon. The crowds were getting fierce, especially in the mornings, and we were all forced to pitch in to keep up with them.

Indy had the Bye-Bye Billy Party (the name was Ally's idea) at Fortnum's Friday evening, opening it for the private soiree because it was the only place that would fit us all in.

Even with short notice, and an almost shootout in the middle, word spread like wildfire that Indy and Ally were throwing a party. The party was well catered with everyone pitching in, most especially Kitty Sue and Eddie's Mom, a lady named Blanca. In fact, even though I'd never met them, Eddie's entire family came. In fact, everyone came such was the allure of an Indy/Ally party, bringing food and booze.

Uncle Tex and Dad had the Jet caramel layer squares faceoff and Dad had to back down and admit Jet's caramel-chocolate brownies were better than custard sundaes at Miriam's Café. After this happened, Mom called repeatedly to Sweet Jesus, swearing that Dad had never admitted to anything outside Brownsburg, Indiana being better and such an admission had to be divine intervention.

A couple of hours into the party, Vance walked in.

I noticed him immediately, not out of any heightened awareness gained through osmosis from the Hot Boy Brigade, but because the bell over the door went. I was standing with Indy, Ally, Jet, Annette and Daisy. Hank was across the room with Malcolm, Eddie and Lee.

I broke away from the Rock Chicks and approached Vance.

"Hey," I said when I made it to him.

"Hey, girl," he replied, his dark eyes doing a scan of my face.

I didn't know what to say, so I said, "I don't know what to say."

"Nothing to say," he told me.

Then I figured out what to say. "I'm sorry you had to do that."

"Had to do what?"

I sighed. "Spend days hunting down Billy then having to shoot him. I'm so sorry, Vance."

He watched me for a beat. "How much you got left?" he asked, what I thought, bizarrely.

"Of what?"

"Of whatever it is that's pulled you through this shit."

I shook my head, confused.

He got in my space. "Maybe you should know somethin' about me."

Oh no.

"What?" I asked, even though I didn't know if I wanted to know. Every time one of these boys shared, it freaked me out.

"I'm not sorry," Vance said.

"Excuse me?"

"That he's never gonna use that hand again. I'm not sorry. Not only that, but Roxie, I'm glad I got to do it. Fuckin' thrilled."

Holy cow.

I held my breath.

He got closer and said low, "Justice."

Holy, holy, cow, cow, cow.

I felt heat at my back, an arm came around my upper chest from behind and I was pulled into Hank's body.

Vance moved back, his eyes shifting to look over my shoulder.

"Hank," he said.

"Vance," Hank said from behind me.

Vance's shit-eating grin spread across his face as he took us in.

Then he said, "I'll let you two let life begin again, I'm gettin' a drink."

Good grief.

I closed my eyes and curled my fingers around Hank's forearm.

When I opened my eyes, Vance was still grinning at me.

Kristen Ashley

"I'm not going to hear the end of that, am I?" I asked.

"Nope," Vance answered.

He kept right on grinning.

I narrowed my eyes at him. "Don't you need a drink?" I asked, sounding uppity.

Vance started laughing.

Then he said, "Yep," and walked away.

After a few seconds I realized that Hank's body was moving and I was pretty certain it was with laughter.

"Don't you start, Whisky," I warned, looking out the window at the cars on Broadway, my back still pressed against him.

He kissed the back of my head.

"We'll talk about it later," Hank murmured.

"No, we won't. We're never going to talk about it. Never. Never, never, never," I announced.

Hank's arm tightened and I felt his breath at my cheek.

"Later," he promised.

Good God.

"Whatever," I muttered.

He let me go and walked away.

When I turned back to the Rock Chicks, they were all smiling.

Jeez.

⌦⌫

Some time later, Luke walked in.

He looked none the worse for wear. In fact, he looked just as good as ever.

"I'm sorry, I love Jason and all, but that man is fucking *hot,*" Annette declared, and luckily Jason was across the room talking to my Dad.

I disengaged from the Rock Chicks again and walked to Luke.

I didn't know what to say to him either, so, even though he was a badass and super cool, I just invaded his space, wrapped my arms around his waist, pressed my cheek to his chest and hugged him.

I know it was a girlie thing to do, but a bullet sliced through his flesh while he was protecting me. I had to do something.

After a few seconds, his arms came around me.

Not surprisingly, he didn't say anything.

Surprisingly, neither did I.

Then, quietly he said, "I know it hasn't been that long for you, but…"

When he hesitated, I said to his chest, "What?"

"Feel like having your life begin again?"

My body went stiff but my head tilted back to look at him.

"What?" I asked.

"Just checkin'. See, *my* life could begin again. I'm thinkin' about now," he replied.

I blinked at him.

"Are you fucking with me?" I whispered, my body still stiff.

He did his half-grin. "Yeah."

I pulled out of his arms.

"That isn't funny," I snapped.

"It's fuckin' hilarious," he told me.

I was in the middle of growling my frustration when Hank's arm went around my shoulders and he pulled me to his side.

"Luke," Hank said, his gaze was locked on Luke.

Luke's eyes cut to Hank. "Hank," Luke said back.

They just stared at each other.

This was making me supremely uncomfortable, so I decided to butt in to the badass, super cool, hot guy staring contest.

"Well, um… thanks for getting shot for me," I said to Luke, then wished someone would shoot *me*.

Luke watched me speak then his eyes went to Hank again.

"She's cute," Luke noted.

"I know," Hank replied.

"Oh for goodness sakes," I clipped.

"My favorite part from last night, outside of the 'my life began' speech, was when she told him he was makin' her dizzy," Luke shared, feeling verbose for once in his life.

"Didn't think it was funny at the time, but, in retrospect…" Hank to my shock agreed.

"The part about the dog and the Frisbee was a good touch too." Luke clearly felt in a talkative mood.

I'd had enough so I cut in. "Don't you need a drink?" I asked Luke pointedly.

Luke's half-grin went full-fledged. "Yeah," he said, but he didn't move.

"Well, why don't you go get one?" I snapped.

He reached out and touched my nose with his finger. Then he was gone.

I turned into Hank.

"I'm beginning to regret my actions last night," I told him.

"Finally," he said, sounding relieved and slightly arrogant.

I frowned at him. "Not because I did the wrong thing, but because...
never mind." I stopped and tried to pull away from Hank's arm, but it tightened
and I couldn't move.

"Sunshine?"

I looked up at Hank. "What?"

"You think they'd tease you if they thought you'd done something to regret?" Hank asked.

I thought about it.

"Probably not," I relented.

"You think they'd tease you if they thought you did the wrong thing?"
Hank asked.

I thought about that too. "I guess not."

He watched me for a beat then he shook his head. "Jesus, I can't believe
you hugged Luke Stark. Christ. They're probably laughin' themselves sick in the
control room."

Oh no.

I'd forgotten about the control room.

"Maybe we should leave before I do anything else embarrassing," I suggested.

"Feel like makin' any heartfelt speeches?" Hank asked.

I narrowed my eyes at him. "Absolutely not."

His other arm went around me and curled me full frontal into his body,
then his head dipped low.

"Maybe, from now on, those are best just between you and me."

"Hank Nightingale—" I started, but didn't finish because he kissed me
dizzy.

Saturday morning we were woken up by my mother yelling through the door to Hank's bedroom at the same time she was knocking.

"Kids! You awake?"

We weren't, or at least I wasn't.

"Yeah Mom," I called my lie.

"Tex is here. We're spending the day with him and Nancy. We're taking you out to dinner tonight. Malcolm and Kitty Sue are coming too. Meet you back here at six o'clock."

"'Kay," I shouted then I snuggled deeper into Hank's warm body, deciding to think about the scary get-to-know-the-parents dinner some other time (or never).

Shamus jerked to his feet when he heard the movement in the other room and he started walking around on the bed, or more to the point, on us, and tried to lick our faces.

Hank's arms went from around me to around Shamus and he wrestled him away, turning his back to me. Shamus didn't give much of a struggle as Hank got Shamus to his side and pulled the dog to his chest and started to rub his belly.

I got up on my elbow and watched for a few seconds then rolled away, snuggled into my pillow instead of Hank and closed my eyes to go back to sleep.

The bed moved with Hank and Shamus. Shamus obviously let loose, he started to walk on me and snuffle the covers around my body and face.

"What are you doin'?" Hank asked.

"Sleeping," I replied, even though it was obvious I was not.

"Get up Sunshine."

"No."

"Up," Hank demanded.

"No," I repeated.

"Sunshine…"

Shamus gave me a full face lick and I pulled the covers over my head. No sooner had I got them over my head when they were yanked off. The bed moved when Hank exited it then I exited it too, but against my will.

"Whisky!" I shouted, throwing my arms around his shoulders as he carried me into the bathroom.

"Time to shower."

"I want to sleep." It came out kind of whiney.

He set me down in the bathroom. His hands went to the hem of my nightie and started pulling up, but I caught his wrists and stopped him.

"Shower, breakfast and then we'll teach Shamus how to play Frisbee," Hank said.

My head shot up and I looked at him. "Really?" I asked.

He nodded.

I let go of his wrists, put my arms over my head and he pulled up my nightie.

Billy had confessed to beating me up, abducting me, shooting Luke and trying to shoot Hank. Assault, kidnapping and two counts of attempted homicide were kind of big crimes to commit. Hank told me he was going to go down for a long time. And that was just the time he was going to serve in Colorado.

It was Thursday, a week after the big event. Mom and Dad had left a few days earlier. I was going to leave for Chicago on Sunday.

Since our day teaching Shamus to play Frisbee (Shamus learned quickly, I knew he was a smart dog), Hank had been spending all of our time together showing me what normal was like.

I realized normal was good. In fact, normal was downright delicious.

I was curled up on the couch in Hank's TV room. It was evening, after I'd made Hank lasagna, after we ate it, after we did the dishes and after we settled in to watch a movie.

My phone rang, and as it was displayed on my cell as an unknown number, I flipped open my phone.

"Roxie," Billy said.

"Billy?" I asked, shock in my voice.

I was leaned up against Hank. Shamus was lying in his doggie bed in front of the TV.

Hank's body tensed when I said Billy's name and Shamus felt it from across the room using doggie radar. Shamus jerked from full-on his side to lying upright. Both human and canine Nightingale boys looked at me.

"Roxie, I'm—" Billy started.

I flipped the phone shut, opened it again and pressed the button until it went off. Then I threw it onto the coffee table.

Maybe I should have listened to him, though I didn't care. I wasn't in the mood and I figured it was likely I'd never be in the mood again.

"You need a new phone," Hank remarked, his body relaxing, his eyes moving back to the TV.

"You're right," I agreed.

His glance came back to me. "Sorry?" he asked.

"You're right," I repeated.

He did a slow blink. "Can you say that again?" he asked, his lips twitching. I gave him a look.

His body followed his eyes and he turned into me.

Then I said, "My phone has a Chicago number. Of course I need a new one. You don't want to be paying long distance charges every time you call my cell."

He ignored what I said. His body moved over mine, pressing me into the seat of the couch. His hands were sliding up my sides and I squirmed because it was ticklish.

"Hank, stop, we're missing the movie."

His arm went out and he nabbed the remote. He twisted, hit pause and the screen stilled.

Shamus settled back on his side with a groan, getting the all clear from his doggie radar as Hank threw the remote back onto the table.

"I was watching that," I protested to Hank when he came back to me.

"We'll finish it later," he replied, his mouth moving along my collarbone, his hands sliding back down my sides, and I squirmed again.

"Whisky, stop doing that. You're tickling me," I snapped, pushing at him.

His head came up and he looked at me. "What? This?" His hands went under my top and moved up my sides, even lighter.

I giggled, just a little, mainly because I couldn't help myself. I squirmed and kept pushing at him. He didn't budge.

Then I scowled. "Seriously, stop. I don't like being tickled."

"Seriously?" he asked, still watching me then he did it again.

"Dude! Stop!" I shouted and heaved. Heaving, I found, also didn't work. Hank was solid and strong, and although most of the time it was super good, there were times, like that one, when it was irritatingly bad.

I tried to grab his wrists. Instead, he grabbed mine, pulled them over my head, and after a brief tussle held them in one hand.

"Don't call me dude," he said, but he was grinning.

I frowned.

"Dude," I replied, just to be stubborn.

At my use of the word "dude" he used his free hand to torment me by tickling me again.

Half giggling, half squirming under him, some of the time shouting at him to stop, alternating with calling him dude just to be annoying, we eventually rolled off the couch.

I landed on top of him. My hands were freed; I sat up astride him and I started to search for ticklish spots on Hank. I found none, though he didn't let me try for very long, as in I was searching for about two seconds. This deteriorated into wrestling (because I was still trying), which degenerated to groping, which became far more serious and we ended up never seeing the end of the movie.

I didn't mind. It didn't seem like it was going to be a good movie anyway.

⌖

Early Sunday morning, I left for Chicago.

I'd packed a few suitcases to take back with me. Hank and Uncle Tex were going to move the rest of my stuff to Uncle Tex's while I was gone. Hank took my bags out to the car while I finished getting ready; at the same time I was eating a breakfast of Hank's scrambled eggs and toast.

I put my dishes in the dishwasher, grabbed my purse, shoving my lip balm into the easily accessible side pouch (because everyone knew, on a road trip, you needed easily accessible lip balm) and walked out the front door.

Hank was leaning against the side of the hood of my car, which he'd had returned from the impound the day after Billy was caught. He had his ankles and arms crossed and Shamus was sitting by his legs.

Hank was staring at his feet, looking both handsome and lost in thought.

I nearly tripped at the sight of him, but pulled myself together and walked forward.

His head came up and he watched me approach him.

When I got to within reaching distance, he uncrossed his arms and ankles, grabbed me and pulled me between his legs.

My arms went around his waist. I relaxed into him and I rested my cheek on his chest.

"You're stoppin' in Iowa?" he asked over my head.

"Yeah," I answered.

"You'll call me when you get a hotel." It wasn't so much a question as a demand. A worthless demand. We'd already had this conversation.

"Yeah," I said, feeling my nostrils beginning to sting.

"You're stayin' with Annette and Jason when you get there?" he asked, even though he knew that too.

Annette and Jason had left the day before my parents. I had no idea of the state of my loft, but I didn't want anything to do with it anymore. I didn't want anything to do with any aspect of my life that included memories of Billy, except to clean it up, pack it up and let it go.

"Yeah," I repeated.

His arms, already tight, got tighter.

"Jesus, Roxie," he muttered and his voice sounded hoarse.

My arms got tighter, too, and the tears started to fall down my cheeks.

"It's only a few weeks," I said into his chest, but you could hear the tears in my voice.

"Yeah," he murmured.

After a while, he demanded quietly, "Look at me, Sunshine."

I tilted my head back to look at him. The minute I did his came down and he kissed me.

I knew Hank's light kisses, necking kisses and make-me-dizzy kisses. This was a fourth kind of kiss, long, sweet and full of promise. It might have been the best of them all (okay, maybe not, but a close second).

His mouth came away from mine and he wiped the tears from my cheeks. Then he walked me to the driver's side, his arm hooked around my neck, mine around his waist. He gave me a light kiss. I got in and started the car, looked up at him, gave a weak smile and a stupid wave, then I drove away.

At the end of the block, I looked into the rearview mirror and he was standing in the same spot, eyes on my car, Shamus at his side.

I turned the car left toward University Boulevard.

When there was nothing but highway in front of me and Denver in my mirrors, I pulled out my cell, flipped it opened and said Hank's name into the phone.

It rang twice.

"You okay?" he asked in greeting.

"My life began when I met you," I told him.

There was a beat of silence.

Then I heard him say, "Sunshine—"

I flipped the phone closed, pushed it deep in my purse, but it rang once before I turned up Springsteen and I started singing with him to "She's the One".

Together, Bruce and I drowned out the sound of the ringing phone.

☙❧

Now, I was back.

It was nearly noon. I was on I-25 and well into Denver when I pulled out my phone, flipped it open and said Hank's name.

I was now beyond nervous. No longer excited, just totally scared to death.

For three weeks, Hank and I had talked almost daily. He'd missed calling me twice (I counted) because of work. Sometimes we could only talk for minutes. Three times (I counted) we talked over an hour.

"Jeez, Bitch! Starving people in Africa would get a new lease on life with the money you two spend on phone calls," Annette shouted each of the three times.

I ignored her.

Never did Hank give an indication he was going to back out.

Always he was just Hank.

Still.

In my car, Denver sliding by me, I listened to the phone ring and held my breath.

On the second ring, he answered.

"You in Denver?" he asked by way of greeting.

I let go of my breath. "Well, hello to you too," I answered, sounding up-pity.

"Sunshine, are you in Denver?" Hank repeated.

"You could say hello. It's the nice thing to do. What? Have you been taking Luke Etiquette Lessons while I've been gone?"

I was trying to cover my nerves.

A beat of silence and then, "Sweetheart, I'm gonna ask one more time..."

I bit my lip.

Then I said, "Yeah, Whisky, I'm in Denver. Exiting I-25 now."

"See you at our place." Then he disconnected.

I flipped my phone shut and my brows drew together.

Our place?

He must mean Fortnum's.

I pointed my car toward Fortnum's.

Chapter 29

Our Place

I walked into Fortnum's and everyone was there.

Everyone, that was, except Hank.

Lee, Mace, Vance, Eddie and Luke were relaxing on the couches with Jet sitting on the arm of the couch by Eddie. Ally was standing by Mace. Uncle Tex and Duke were behind the espresso counter. Jane was behind the book counter, Indy and Daisy sitting on top of it.

They all looked up at me when I walked in.

"Where's Hank?" I asked.

"Well, how the fuck are you too?" Uncle Tex boomed, coming out from behind the counter.

I grinned at him. I couldn't help it.

"Hey, Uncle Tex," I said.

He made it to me and his arms engulfed me so hard my breath went out of me in a poof. "Darlin' girl," he half boomed.

I smiled into his chest and gave him a hug back.

Then I gave hugs and cheek kisses to everyone else except Mace and Luke. I didn't know Mace all that well and I'd already had my lifetime quota of hugs from Luke.

Indy, Lee, Ally, Jet and Daisy stayed close while everyone else wandered away.

"Hank said he'd see me at our place. He should have been here before me," I told them.

The Rock Chicks looked at each other.

Lee got out his phone.

"Uh-oh," Ally said.

"Uh-oh what?" I asked.

"Uh-oh nothing," Ally muttered and bugged her eyes out and Indy.

I looked at Indy and my stomach did a scared to death curl.

"Uh-oh what?" I asked Indy.

"Um…" Indy mumbled.

Kristen Ashley

"Hank?" Lee said into the phone. "Yeah, Roxie's at Fortnum's." He paused then he said, "Right." Then he flipped his phone closed.

"Where is he?" I asked Lee.

"His house," Lee answered.

"What's he doing there?" I asked, my brows coming together.

"Waiting for you," Lee told me.

My brows came apart and I blinked. "I don't understand."

"He's comin' to Fortnum's," Lee went on.

I kept staring at him.

Daisy shoved forward, put her arm around my waist and started to move me to the espresso counter.

"Sugar, I'm guessin' your man didn't tell you, but some minds have changed while you've been gone."

Oh... my... God.

I halted and stood stock-still, staring down at her.

"What minds have changed?" I whispered.

"Well, Hank's..." She stopped and then started again, "He's not overly..." She paused, looking for the word. Then finding it, she spoke again, "*Fond* of you movin' in with Tex. See, he thinks—"

"Oh for fuck's sake. You're movin' in with Hank," Uncle Tex announced. "Silly, stupid girl nerves, movin' in with me then movin' into some apartment only to end up movin' in with Hank in a few months. You need to fuckin' *settle*, girl. Get over it and get over here. I'll make you a fuckin' latte."

I stared at Uncle Tex. "I'm not moving in with Hank," I said.

"You are," Uncle Tex returned.

Good God.

"Did you guys move my stuff to your place?" I asked.

"Hell no. Waste of time. I'll make you my new coffee. It's the shit. So damn popular, they're linin' up out the door for it in the morning," Uncle Tex answered.

I frowned at him. "I'm not moving in with Hank," I repeated, though I wanted to try his new latte.

"You are," Uncle Tex said.

"I'm not!" I yelled.

Daisy's arm went away from me and Jet came close.

412

"Maybe you should take it up with Hank," Jet suggested. "Have a *conversation.*" She smiled like what she said was funny.

Daisy smiled too, obviously agreeing.

I didn't think it was funny.

"Damn tootin' we're having a conversation. We're going to have the conversation to end all conversations," I declared, stomping up to the espresso counter.

Everyone grinned at everyone else.

I ignored all of them and Uncle Tex made me his latte with chocolate and burnt marshmallow syrup with a graham cracker on the side.

It was *lush.*

Five minutes later, Hank walked in.

I felt the air leave my lungs in a rush and decided immediately I was more than happy to move in with him.

I'd forgotten how handsome he was (well, I hadn't really, just that it hit me again and hit me hard).

He looked so good I felt my mouth go dry. He was wearing jeans, running shoes and the collar of a white t-shirt could be seen over his zipped up, collared, navy blue sweatshirt.

"Whisky," I said, or more like *rasped.*

He walked up to me, not saying a word; pulled my coffee out of my hand, put it on the counter, took my hand in his and dragged (yes, dragged) me toward the bookshelves.

I came out of my Hank Stupor and immediately decided I wasn't so happy to move in with him.

"Whisky!" I snapped.

He walked us through the front section, through the album section and into the back room.

A lone, male customer was perusing the travel books.

"Can you excuse us?" Hank asked the man.

The customer stared at him.

"I'm looking for a book on India," he said. "I'm going there on vaca—"

Hank turned to the travel section, pulled out five books at random and shoved them into the man's arms.

"Go," he ordered.

The man looked from Hank to me to Hank, shocked into near immobility.

"Hank—" I started, feeling sorry for the guy.

Hank leaned into the man.

The man caught the not-so-subtle hint and walked swiftly out of the room.

"I cannot believe you just did that!" I hissed to Hank.

Hank turned to me, backed me into the shelves, and, without further ado, he kissed me.

Long, deep, lots of tongue with his hands going up my sweater.

I went dizzy.

His mouth came away, but his forehead rested on mine. His hands kept roaming the skin of my back and he was looking into my eyes.

"Fuck, I missed you," he murmured.

Then he rubbed his nose against mine.

Okay, so I was back to deciding I'd move in with Hank.

"I missed you too," I whispered.

His hands stopped roaming and pressed me deeper into his body.

"Let's go home," he said softly.

I stilled.

"We need to talk about 'home'," I said.

"No talk. Tex and I decided."

I went rock-solid and changed my mind again about moving in with Hank.

"You and Uncle Tex decided?" I asked.

"Sunshine—"

"What about me?" I asked, taking my hands from around his neck and planting them on my hips while I pulled my head away from his.

Hank grinned.

I forgot how great his grin was (well, not really, but you know what I mean).

"Let's go home and I'll convince you," he suggested.

Good grief.

I had a feeling he could do that.

Stubborn to the last I replied, "We'll go to your place, get my stuff and go to Tex's."

Hank shook his head.

"Tex won't let you move in with him. We've talked, he agrees," Hank told me.

"Then I'll move in with Indy and Lee for a while."

Hank responded immediately, "Lee won't let you."

I knew that was true.

"Ally——" I started.

"She loses her Christmas present, she lets you move in with her."

"You give good Christmas presents?" I asked, curious for more than one reason.

"Concert tickets. Every year."

Damn.

Ally was out.

"Daisy," I tried.

His body started shaking with laughter, but this time he didn't bother to answer.

I narrowed my eyes at him. "Hank Nightingale…"

He pushed me back into the books, his mouth came to mine and he said softly, "Roxie, move in with me."

Good God.

My heart squeezed and my stomach melted.

I guessed he wasn't going to back out.

I thought about it (well, not really, but I pretended to think about it).

Then I sighed.

"Oh, all right," I gave in.

He kissed me again.

So, it wasn't the conversation to end all conversations.

Whatever.

We went back to the front of the store.

I decided to get it over with immediately.

"I'm moving in with Hank," I announced.

There was general merriment and a good deal of ribbing, mostly at my expense.

I scowled at everyone and nabbed my latte.

Kristen Ashley

"One for the road?" Uncle Tex asked, correctly assuming we weren't going to hang around.

"Yeah," Hank replied, wrapping an arm around my neck.

Uncle Tex started to make Hank a coffee and I stood, plastered against Hank's side, and felt the ugly scar on that secret, private place inside me that had been ripped apart and then mended. Well... it just disappeared.

Gone.

"A month," Duke said, interrupting my thoughts. Duke's arms were crossed on his big chest; his gravelly voice sounded almost (but not quite) happy. "A month of pure bliss. No bullets flying. No kidnappings. No dead bodies. No cars explodin'. No cat fights in Chinese restaurants. No shootouts at the Society Party OK Corral. No visits to the hospital. Absolute, fuckin' bliss."

He barely finished his last word when we heard a squeal of tires.

Everyone's gaze swung to look out the big plate glass window.

We saw a shiny, cherry-condition, red Camaro, circa 1983, braking, its tail flipping so that it was facing the wrong way on Broadway and it shuddered to a halt.

No sooner had it stopped then the driver's side door was thrown open and a woman got out.

She had gleaming, thick, black hair pulled back in a long ponytail. She was wearing a skintight black turtleneck, mushroom-colored cords and a kick-ass black belt.

She was stunning.

She walked to the front of the Camaro, her hand going to the back waistband of her cords and she whipped out a gun.

Hank tensed at my side and the room went utterly still except for a wicked undercurrent of energy.

She pulled the gun up in front of her and held it like Hank, natural, casual, in two hands, arms cocked, head slightly to the side.

The traffic was stopped at the red light on Broadway. She advanced, like a woman without a care in the world, down the middle of the wide, normally busy street toward a man who had alighted from a different car.

He too, had a gun pointed at her.

She halted.

They faced off.

"Jules!" he shouted.

416

At the call of what was likely her name, her arms moved slightly to the left and down. Without apparently aiming, she fired, twice.

And she took out the two front tires of his car.

"Holy crap," Indy breathed.

"Righteous," Ally whispered.

"Fuckin' Jules!" the man yelled and started running toward her.

She whipped around, ponytail flying, and ran back to her car, throwing the gun into the passenger seat. She got in and started reversing on a smoky squeal of tires, leaving the man in her dust.

All our heads followed her as the car twisted viciously around to face the right way again and she took off like a rocket.

The man with the gun turned toward Fortnum's, started running and kept going, right past Fortnum's down the side street.

"Stay here," Hank said to me, his hand was in his back pocket pulling out his phone. Then he moved to the door.

The place was a flurry of activity.

The Hot Boy Brigade was on the move. Out of Fortnum's they went, disbursing with barely a word to each other, instinctively knowing what they were doing.

I noticed it was Vance on his Harley who shot off in the direction of "Jules".

Indy turned to me and said on a grin, "Welcome home."

The Rock Chick ride continues
*with **Rock Chick Renegade***
the story of Vance and Jules

CPSIA information can be obtained
at www.ICGtesting.com
Printed in the USA
FSOW01n0744030616
21124FS